Any sexual abuse, no matter the form or degree, impacts the victim. Stevens portrays this beautifully in this exploration of a young woman's coming to terms with her past. And the parallel story of a woman grappling with workplace sexual harassment underscores the similarities in how society treats both types of victim.
Laura Davis, co-author of *The Courage to Heal*

For those among us who have experienced sexual abuse or harassment in our lives, the questions of fault, guilt and blame follow us even into dream. S.M. Stevens, in Horseshoes and Hand Grenades, confronts the issues and portrays both the abuse itself and the emotional trauma in its wake with understanding and authenticity. Astrid and Shelby are credible; their experiences ring true. Stevens's writing engages the reader in a series of situations that are honest, strongly and carefully drawn and painfully current. Her novel touches on what is most difficult in the lives of survivors of abuse while spotlighting the kindness and support of those who sustain them.
Susan Roney-O'Brien, author of *Legacy of the Last World* and *Bone Circle*

Reading this book, I felt kinship with the women, having had similar experiences. If this story gives just one woman the courage to speak out, or gives just one man a compassionate insight into how women cope with harassment but have the strength to maintain their lives (constructively and destructively), it will be a success.
S.D., Advance Reader Review

Horseshoes and Hand Grenades delivers a realistic portrait of women and their struggles. Surprisingly enough, Stevens manages to turn a hefty topic into an approachable one by way of a riveting read. As a woman who has endured workplace sexual assault, I particularly related to the authentic feelings of frustration, doubt, and trepidation that the characters in this novel experience. Every American should read this novel, as each character is someone you know. She is your mother, your sister, your daughter, your friend. She is your neighbor, your coworker, your aunt. She is you... In addition to being a page-turner, *Horseshoes and Hand Grenades* is a true-to-life tale of love, friendship, and betrayal.
Kimberly Coghlan, Coghlan Professional Writing Services

Horseshoes and Hand Grenades

S. M. STEVENS

Relax. Read. Repeat.

HORSESHOES AND HAND GRENADES
By S. M. Stevens
Published by TouchPoint Press
Brookland, AR 72417
www.touchpointpress.com

Copyright © 2019 S. M. Stevens
All rights reserved.

ISBN-10: 1-946920-71-1
ISBN-13: 978-1-946920-71-3

This is a work of fiction. Names, places, characters, and events are fictitious. Any similarities to actual events and persons, living or dead, are purely coincidental. Any trademarks, service marks, product names, or named features are assumed to be the property of their respective owners and are used only for reference. If any of these terms are used, no endorsement is implied. Except for review purposes, the reproduction of this book, in whole or part, electronically or mechanically, constitutes a copyright violation. Address permissions and review inquiries to media@touchpointpress.com.

Editor: Kimberly Coghlan
Cover Design: ColbieMyles, ColbieMyles.net
Cover Illustration: Natalie Simone, NatalieSimone97@gmail.com, Instagram: nootcreations

Visit the author's website at www.AuthorSMStevens.com

First Edition

Library of Congress Control Number:2019947023

Printed in the United States of America.

Almost only counts in horseshoes and hand grenades.

*Dedicated to victims of incest and harassment everywhere.
Regardless of the "severity" of the abuse,
your pain is real and you deserve to heal.*

Acknowledgements

Thanks to my early reviewers, especially Amy Tull Atwood, Gabby Boucher, Suzanna Roberts and Susan Roney-O'Brien. Thanks to Natalie Boucher for sliding the pieces of the puzzle into their proper places. Thanks to my family for their support of my writing follies. Most of all, love to my Craig, for encouraging and supporting my dreams.

I also want to acknowledge the team at TouchPoint Press and my editor Kim Coghlan, for making the story stronger with their comments and insights. And I must recognize Laura Davis and Ellen Bass, who wrote The Courage to Heal back in 1988, when public discussion of incest was still taboo, #MeToo and #TimesUp were decades away, and resources for victims were scarce. You are life savers.

PROLOGUE

My room is cold. I pull my yellow blankie up under my chin. I wish Tramp was here. Maybe I will fall asleep in time.

Footsteps come. They stop at the top of the stairs, by the big window I like because icicles fill it in the winter.

The footsteps start. They're here. Oh no. I shut my eyes and freeze. My door opens. He sighs. Sits on my bed, like last time. Don't look, he's not real. Don't touch my cheek, he's touching my cheek, or my neck, don't move. He's not here, he's not real. Go away. I can't talk. My mouth is gone. I'm gone. I'm not here. His hairy hand crawls down some other girl's front, making circles. He leans on her big and heavy and kisses her on the lips. That other girl is under his horrible fat body smelling his hard sour breath feeling his wet mushy lips. Don't move, I tell her. If you don't move, he'll go.

Where is everybody?

He gets up. I peek. He pulls at his saggy sweatpants, touches his short, brown hair with those hands. Don't. Breathe.

I'm in the bathroom. On the potty. Nothing comes out. I climb on the step stool and turn on the water. Water isn't enough. I put the bar of soap in my mouth like Mommy did when Julie and I touched our tongues together.

I look at my bed. Tramp, please come.

***

I was twenty-two when I let the memories in. They'd been fluttering around the edges of my brain since the chiropractor incident, like a bunch of random words straining to form a sentence.

I kept finding myself awake at midnight with my face tense and contorted, my eyes scrunched, and my mouth drawn up unnaturally. Frustrated, I decided to pay attention the next time the flutters tapped gently against the inside of my skull.

Once I gave them permission, they took shape.

And that was that. I went on with my life. It's not like what happened changed me or anything.

Part 1

Shelby

CHAPTER 1

My only pair of jeans with no rips at the knees. My favorite boots, brown suede—a splurge during a trip to New Jersey for a Bruce Springsteen concert junior year. Pale pink, scoop-necked shirt with lace trim because Tina insisted I go with sexy not funky.

I chewed my lip and stared at the jean jacket and maroon velvet blazer side by side on my bed. An early October chill had erased all traces of the Indian summer so a jacket was mandatory. But which one?

The doorbell rang, and I heard my roommate clamor over Jesse like a long-lost best friend.

"Tina, how are you," he replied. It was a statement, not a question, the word "are" dragged out. "Long time no see. Is Shelby here?"

I grabbed the maroon blazer and my pocketbook from the bed. And stopped.

Now that my blind date was here, my anticipation congealed into borderline nausea. I'd only been on one real date in the last four years. In college, I squeezed in flings and one-night stands during the good phases of my weight swings. What if Jesse flinched when he saw me? What if I flinched?

I walked downstairs, placing each foot in the middle of each step. In the living room, I raised my eyes to the couch, to Tina, and to Jesse.

No one flinched. Jesse was a miniature Richard Gere, with a slightly bigger nose and some acne scars. He had a few inches on me and a mass of black hair on the verge of forming big ringlets. He smiled. Tina was right. He had an awesome smile. I exhaled.

"Sorry about the tie. I didn't have a chance to change after work."

"Don't keep it on for me."

"Most excellent suggestion." He yanked off the tie, almost choking himself. "Well, ready to blow this pop stand?" I nodded. "Okay, later, Tina."

He led me to his car, an orangey-red hatchback. Not a car guy. But then, I wasn't a car girl.

"How long have you known Tina?" I asked, opening the car door. My foot caught in my pocketbook strap, and I tumbled into the car, banging my shin against the doorframe and wincing as Jesse got in. The radio blared, "These Dreams" when he started the engine. "Yuck, I hate that song," I said before he could answer my question. "Heart hasn't been the same since Roger Fisher and Steve Fossen left."

Jesse raised his thick eyebrows, grinned, and turned down the radio. "What was your question? Oh right, Tina. We met in grade school, but I don't really know her, if you know what I mean." I did know of course—Tina had told me, but it seemed like a safe first question. "But it was cool to run into her. And I'm glad I did." He stopped, as if afraid of talking too much.

"Mm-hmm," I managed. I could practically taste his musky cologne and feel his body heat in the car's close quarters.

"Hey, do you mind if we stop by my house before we go eat? I totally forgot something."

I shrugged. "Ah, sure, okay."

He rented a house with a friend five minutes away, a small, nineteen-fifties, boxy thing.

"Beware of the killer cat," he said, turning the key in the lock. "Do you like cats?" His tone suggested a lot rode on my answer.

"Yup, but I'm really a dog person. I mean, I love all animals, but dogs especially." I grimaced at his back. "And cats too, of course. I love cats." We stepped into a small living room. "Where is he?"

"See him under the table there? Thor, don't be rude. Come out and say hi."

"He's beautiful; ohmygod he's like a panther." I crouched down, arms at my sides. Thor was Maine coon cat size with a smooth, jet-black coat.

"He plays fetch. Check this out." He threw a crumpled ball of paper across the room, and Thor bombed after the prey, snatching it in his fangs and trotting back to Jesse. "Awesome, right? Who needs a dog?" He shoved the ball of paper into his coat pocket, and Thor disappeared.

"Me," I muttered as Jesse turned his back.

"I just have to grab a tape I'm giving back to a friend after dinner, but the basement's kind of messy so wait here, okay?"

I nodded and took inventory while he thumped downstairs. Ugly but new plaid couch, basic TV, a Harman Kardon stereo—that was a plus, and all surprisingly clean for two young guys. A definite step up from college apartments.

The restaurant—dark, crowded, and noisy—was also a step up from college because it didn't smell like stale beer or puke. The dim light blurred the pockmarks on Jesse's face, making him even cuter. After we ordered burgers and beers, I jumped into the awkward pause.

"So, Tina says you manage a restaurant in Brookline?"

He shook his head and furrowed his brows. "Noooo, I'm an assistant manager at a hardware store." His brown eyes watched me. "But it *is* in Brookline."

"Oh." The questions I'd thought up ahead of time were all about restaurants.

"It's called Handy Hardware. I know it's a dumb-ass name, but it's a totally big chain. It's just a way for me to make some money for now, anyway."

"That's good," I said, involuntarily glancing at a couple making out noisily at the next table.

"Tina said you work at some design firm?"

"I'm leaving that for a new job next week. Well, just an internship. At a public relations firm in Boston."

He stared blankly.

"PR is like selling things by persuading people to think or feel a certain way about a product," I explained.

"Like advertising?"

"Sort of, but more subtle."

"Oh. That sounds like a wicked cool job," he said, and took a big gulp from his mug. I touched my fingers to my upper lip. "Oops, thanks," he said, wiping a beer foam mustache from his lip.

"So, Tina says you're in a band?" Or maybe he used to want to be in a band. Or had a friend in a band once. Let's see how Tina messed this one up.

"Yeah, I am! With my roommate who plays bass. I play drums. We need a guitar player. And a set list. We're not ready to play out yet, but that's totally the plan. As soon as we start booking regular gigs, I'm going to quit the hardware store."

"Wow, that's, um, brave of you," I said, scratching my head. "Do you have a name yet?"

"No, got any ideas?"

"Hm. Maybe you could get the hardware store to sponsor you and you could be the Handy Hardware Band. Or the Handy Band," I joked.

He guffawed so loudly I cringed but recovered in time to smile as his laugh ended in a snort.

"Sorry, my friends tell me my laugh is annoying, but what can I say. It's the only one I've got." One side of his mouth curved up, and he shrugged.

"No, it's fine; I like it," I assured him, feeling like Clarisse telling Rudolph she liked his red nose in the classic Christmas TV show.

Music talk filled the rest of the date, trading stories about bands, songs, and concerts we liked. I managed to not say anything stupid, and we only had a few awkward lulls. Jesse would be my first drummer if this went well. I'd hooked up with guitarists and singers, but never a drummer. I'd never dated the assistant manager of a hardware store either, but the drummer part was cooler so I focused on that.

When we got back to Waltham Village, he walked me to the door of my apartment, resting his hand on the back of my jacket. "I like that you're casual and we can talk about music and stuff. The truth is, I wore my work clothes because I wasn't sure what you'd be wearing. When I saw you in jeans I thought, oh yeah, cool, this is good."

"What can I say, I'm a jeans and T-shirt kind of girl." I turned around to face him, my back to the door.

"Awesome. Me too. I mean, I'm a jeans and T-shirt kind of guy." He grinned, making his eyes adorably squinty.

"Hey, that's a good name for a band—The Jeans and T-Shirts. No, wait—Jeanie and the T-Shirts. Or—"

He interrupted my babbling, leaning in and kissing me quickly, his full lips soft and light.

I've always loved the first kiss. It was the best part of a new relationship. The waves of rolling warmth in the gut from the sheer physical contact. The tingles in the brain triggered by the body's sudden intimacy. All that anticipation, excitement, and promise. If the kiss sucked, all that promise crumbled into tiny pieces to be blown away by the next gust of wind. Some guys ruined the first kiss by using tongue, which was way too personal when your lips were getting to know each other.

Jesse kissed just right. I was sorry when it ended.

"Let's talk again. I mean, I'll totally call you." He turned to go.

Shelby

CHAPTER 2

Astrid's moving out day couldn't come fast enough. We'd met yesterday.

Anne, the office manager at public relations firm Campbell Lewis, had shown me to a tiny cubicle located right next to the kitchen. Believe it or not, the small kitchen was slightly bigger than my cubicle. Two desks were crammed into the cube, the far one occupied.

"This is your desk," Anne said, a little too proudly for the sub-par accommodations. "Astrid, I'd like to introduce our new intern and your new cube-mate. This is Shelby Stewart. She'll be working on Maggie's team." Anne turned to me. "We've been using one of the AE—I mean account executive—offices for storage, but we're turning it back into an office for Astrid, and then this will be your cube."

Astrid reached down to tug at her navy blue sling-back, exhaled dramatically, scooched her chair back until it hit the other chair—my chair—and unfolded her legs from underneath the desk, bumping them against the underside of the desk in the process.

She rose from her chair, turned around and stretched up to her full height, which was somewhere around model-tall in heels but probably more like a perfect five foot seven inches in reality. I vowed then and there to swap out my flat pumps for heels tomorrow. I didn't even like flat pumps.

Astrid's hair was straight and creamy blonde, streaked with honey and amber. It fell about six inches below her shoulders—just short of unprofessional.

Her light blue suit was ridiculously cute even though I wouldn't be caught dead in it. It tapered from substantial shoulder pads to a thin navy belt accentuating her tiny waist. Navy blue trim outlined the cuffs and pockets, and a power bow at the neck topped it off.

"Hi," she said, analyzing me with unimpressed crystal-blue eyes. She seemed ready to bolt past me, but either the lack of running room or a quick glance at Anne changed her mind. "Nice to meet you," she said, offering a slender, pearly-tipped hand.

"I'll leave you two to get acquainted," Anne said with a smile and what may have been a sympathetic look in my direction before turning and leaving me alone with this woman I immediately loathed and wanted to be at the same time.

Astrid sat back down at her desk and started writing on a pad of paper. The getting-acquainted period apparently over, I settled into the other desk, meaning I hung my coat over the back of the chair and studied the tax form Anne left me to fill out. I read all the fine print, probably making me the first person in the history of modern civilization to do that.

Ten excruciating minutes later, the phone on Astrid's desk beeped. "Yes, we have to share a phone," she said in a resigned voice without looking at me. She expertly pressed one of the dozen or so buttons on the phone and announced, "This is Astrid" into the speaker.

"Would you ask Shelby to come into my office? This is Maggie."

"Of course. Have a lovely day, Maggie. Bye." She pressed another button on the phone and turned back to her writing.

I walked through the office, peeking into the different spaces until I found Maggie at her desk, balancing a thick document in her hand as if debating its weight. She wore a simple black sweater dress, a necklace of chunky, multi-colored stones, and a massive, purple ring. The woman had jewelry and knew how to wear it.

Her trendy, short black hair made me wish for the hundredth time that I could pull off a short hairdo. You need a beautiful face for that, though. Other than one spur-of-the-moment close-cropped punk cut—a definite mistake—I kept my thick, light brown, not straight, not wavy hair long enough to distract from my boring brown eyes and the bony bump on the bridge of my nose.

"Your first project is straightforward," Maggie started in a professional but friendly voice. "I need you to write a press release about a client who's been promoted to vice president at his real estate development company, and to build a media list of newspapers and business and trade magazines to get the announcement. Here's a sample announcement you can refer to for the style."

"Okay." I started to leave but turned back. "You know I've never written a press release before, right?"

"That's okay. I've seen your writing samples. I know you can write."

Clutching the sheets of paper she'd handed me, I swung into the supply room for the media directories I needed to build my list, a stapler that seemed to be unclaimed, some staples, a tape dispenser—I'm not sure why, and three…make that four ballpoints since I lost pens on a regular basis.

After organizing my new supplies on the desk, I flipped through the media directories, quietly so as not to annoy the Amazon goddess. The fumes of discontent wafting my way from Astrid's desk made concentration tough, but eventually, my project absorbed me.

A few hours later, as my stomach started to growl, an adorable blonde guy poked his head in my cubby like an old friend. "New girl, want to get some lunch with us?" I jumped up, got tangled in my chair in the close quarters, and chased after him and a brunette woman as they strode down the hallway and out the office door.

"I'm Karen, I've been here a year. I'm in Jim's group like you, but I work under Harry, not Maggie. I used to work at a direct marketing company, but it wasn't really my thing," Karen said, tucking a strand of dark hair behind her ear while we waited for the elevator. "This is Michael."

"I've been here a year too, and hopefully I'm getting promoted soon," Michael said as the elevator doors opened.

We walked a few blocks up and down Boylston Street while Michael showed me the good take-out lunch places, odors of burgers and Chinese food drifting out of the opening and closing doors. On our budgets—they were both entry-level account coordinators—there would be no sit-down meals. As we walked, warmed by the surprisingly strong autumn sun, Michael and Karen ranted about the Red Sox losing a World Series game to the New York Mets because a fluke ball rolled right between Bill Buckner's legs. They took his error so personally that I resisted defending the poor guy.

After buying individual-sized pizzas, we headed back to the small conference room in the rear of the office, which soon filled with the yeasty smell of warm pizza dough. While we ate, I got a full rundown on who was who in the office and which clients were liked and which were difficult.

"What's Astrid's deal?" I asked, since they were so forthcoming.

Michael scratched his blonde head. "Don't really know her yet. She came from another agency and is supposed to be a hot-shit publicist."

"She's super intense, but seems nice, you know?" Karen contributed.

I finished eating, promised to go out with them soon for a drink after work, and re-entered cubicle world where Astrid was dumping a half-eaten salad into the trash bin. I struggled for something to say.

"That's a nice binder," I offered, eying the brown leather case on her desk. "Did you have it engraved with 'AE' for account executive?" I added, proud of myself for using the agency lingo.

She regarded me like a science project. "Yes," she said finally. "Before that, I had one with 'AC' on it for account coordinator, and when I get my next promotion, I'll get one with 'SAE' on it for senior account executive."

"Hmm," I said in response, which seemed to piss her off.

"No, of course I didn't get a *portfolio*," she said, emphasizing the correct name of the damn thing, "with my job title initials on it! Here's my card," she said, grabbing a business card from the silver holder on her desk and tossing it in my direction. "And it isn't engraved, it's embossed. I'm going to a meeting."

After she huffed out, I picked up the card from the floor. Astrid Ericsson. AE. Oh.

I spent the rest of the day learning how to use an uncooperative computer in the common area and staying out of Astrid's way.

Astrid

CHAPTER 3

"I can't believe it's come to this," I muttered as I prepared to wave the white flag and turn my back on all that is professional, dedicated, and chic.

Making sure none of the bustling Back Bay commuters were watching, I ducked into the alley off Dartmouth Street. It had taken weeks to find the perfect out-of-the-way place.

I walked in shadows to the best set of granite steps, also identified in a previous scouting trip, and wrinkled my nose. Fresh bird poop stared up at me. I would bring a handkerchief to sit on next time. No, something disposable. A handkerchief with bird shit on it was definitely not going into my gorgeous faux snakeskin briefcase. I reached into said briefcase, pulled out a few sheets of paper, and arranged them on the step.

I eased myself down onto the paper and extracted my black Ferragamo shoes—with three-inch heels and the most perfect little gold buckles—from my bag. Setting them down, I leaned over and eased off my outdoor running shoe. The Band-Aid on my heel was bloody but still in place. Gingerly, I slid on the Ferragamo and turned my foot this way and that in appreciation.

After repeating the operation on the other foot, I stood up, uneven on the cobblestones. Peeking out of the alley's end, I didn't see any co-workers or clients, so I pushed on into the early morning sunshine. *God, Francois would die if he knew I had worn "American shoes" with my houndstooth power suit. I bet no self-respecting Parisienne would be so weak as to wear sneakers, even if she never got a seat on the lurching subway.*

Walking back past the Copley MBTA station, I turned down Boylston to walk the block to Campbell Lewis, strategizing my day. I'd been there two weeks but hadn't even interacted with the partners yet. Maybe they're not taking me seriously. Maybe it was the blonde thing. I should get some fake glasses to seem older and more serious.

Approaching my cube a few minutes later, I heard that new intern rummaging around, so I stopped in the kitchen to grab a coffee. No need rubbing elbows more than necessary.

"The staff meeting is starting," Anne said, poking her head into the kitchen. "Let's go, everyone."

I took the three steps to my cube and stood in the doorway, juggling my coffee, briefcase, the embarrassing shoe bag, and my coat, which I'd tossed over my arm. What was taking Shelby so long? Didn't she hear the staff-meeting announcement?

"Oh, hi," Shelby said in an annoyingly submissive voice. "Time to go to the staff meeting, I guess." She stood there as if waiting for me to move out of her way.

"Mm-hmm." I squinted at her and looked pointedly at the side of the cube.

She blinked and stood there. God was she dense.

"Move!"

She jumped. "Oh, right, sorry. I'll get out of your way." She slid herself up against the cubicle wall. I almost laughed as she tucked in her chin and sucked in her stomach to let me pass. Brushing past her, I dropped everything but the coffee in my chair while she scurried out.

By the time I got to the conference room—thanks, Shelby—all the seats were taken, and even standing room was scarce. The partners, Terry Campbell and Jim Lewis, chatted in the corner of the room, exactly where the flip chart stood at last week's pitch to a new client in a three-hour meeting I had eyed covetously every time I walked by on my way to the ladies' room.

My boss, Brad, stood in between the agency's highest-ranking female, Maggie Hirsch, and one of Brad's other AEs, whose name I couldn't remember. I scurried over and wedged myself in between Brad and the other woman. My houndstooth suit complemented his charcoal gray suit perfectly.

"Sorry, it's a little tight today," I whispered to Brad.

"I like it tight. We must be up to almost forty people now," Brad said, scanning me from my recently touched up highlights to my heels, which he did every time he saw me, including at my job interview. I gave him my professional-with-a-tinge-of-sexy smile.

"Let's get started," Terry boomed, surprisingly loud for a man of relatively short stature. Maybe in his fifties, Terry seemed like the sort of guy you'd want for your uncle. His sly smile and the twinkle in his eye hinted he knew a few dirty jokes and wasn't afraid to share them.

"First, we have a promotion to announce. This person has been a huge asset to Campbell Lewis since joining us two years ago as an account supervisor. He's helped us double our events division and brought in clients like the New England Tennis Association and Barclay Concerts. You all know I'm talking about Brad. Let's congratulate him on a well-deserved promotion to vice president."

I looked up at Brad, who was about six feet tall, with sandy brown hair, and blue eyes reminiscent of a mountain pool. Looking right at me, he winked. The blood rushed to my head. He took a step forward and gave a few bows while thanking everyone like an entertainer from a stage.

"Next, I think you've all met her by now, but since the last staff meeting was cancelled, I want to officially introduce Astrid Ericsson, who is an account executive in our group," Terry continued. "She joins us after making a name for herself at one of our main competitors. Good job, Brad, for stealing her away."

I took a step forward and made a little curtsy, immediately regretting it as I saw a few women roll their eyes. Damn, I should have bowed. I gave the tiniest shrug, smiled confidently to undo the damage, and stepped back.

Jim whispered to Terry.

"And," Terry said, "we have a new intern—" He looked at Jim who looked at Maggie.

"Shelby Stewart," Maggie said.

"I give you Shelby Stewart, everyone," Terry thundered, making the intern's scared eyes pop out of her reddening face. God, where did she get that outfit and how many earrings was she wearing?

"Speech!" shouted Michael from across the room. The intern narrowed her eyes at him.

"Sure, let's have the new people say a few words," Jim encouraged.

Shelby looked like a perfect example of *How Not to Impress Your Co-Workers*. Slumping a bit, she inhaled deeply. "I'm really looking forward to learning a lot here. From all of you," she said in a small voice.

Time to show her how it's done, I thought when all eyes turned to me.

"I haven't been here long, but already I can tell what a first-class operation Campbell Lewis is." Terry and Jim nodded appreciatively in my direction. "I'm not speaking ill of the last agency I was at, but everything here is much more professional, from the people and the ethics to the office space. Although some of the cubes leave a bit to be desired." I paused to glance at Shelby while a few people laughed. "I've heard such amazing things about Terry and Jim being leaders in this industry. I can't wait to learn from them—and from everyone here. So I thank the partners and Brad for this opportunity, and I look forward to becoming a valued member of the team." Terry beamed, and Brad leaned into me slightly. Nailed it.

Anne rolled in a cart of pastries and juices while people broke up into small groups. Brad put his hand on my arm and gestured with his chin across the room at Terry, who was working his way over to me.

"Young lady, that was quite the speech. I never realized how spectacular I was," Terry joked.

"Really?" I asked, not skipping a beat. "Well then it's a good thing I'm here to tell you." I smiled my best smile—the one my mother said was my secret weapon.

"Oh-ho, she can bullshit with the best of them, Brad. You picked a winner. And you," he said, facing me, "have a great future in this business."

Astrid

CHAPTER 4

"Mom, what's with the hair? And why the Four Seasons?"

A hostess appeared to whisk my wet umbrella and lined trench coat away before I sat down.

"We," she said, rising from her seat in the restaurant of Boston's newest upscale hotel, "are celebrating."

I hugged her as she kissed me on the cheek. Her subtle scent of natural soap and jasmine perfume smelled like home.

"Sit down and I'll tell you everything," she said.

My mother was impeccably dressed as always, in her favorite tan tweed Chanel suit and ivory silk blouse. Forty-nine, independent since my father walked out fifteen years ago, and my idol, she taught me everything about making it in what was still a man's world, even in the mid-1980s.

"What are we celebrating?" I asked, picking up the heavy leather-bound menu without looking at it.

"My promotion. You are looking at the new Living Section editor for the *Portland Herald*."

I squealed with my mouth shut but still drew glances from a few nearby diners. "That's fantastic, I am so proud of you! When did it happen?"

"Last week. I wanted to come down and tell you in person." The waiter approached the table, a bottle of champagne in hand, a pristine white cloth over his arm. Another waiter deposited an ice bucket on a stand next to our table. "Ah, perfect timing. Thank you, Sidney."

Sidney proceeded to open the champagne and pour with a flourish.

"To my mother, the coolest person I know," I toasted as Sidney and friend melted into the background.

"To my daughter, the light of my life," Mom responded.

The champagne cooled and tickled going down.

"Of course, it's not quite as perfect as it sounds," she said, lowering her glass. "I really wanted Metro Editor, but I don't think Ralph is modern enough to put a woman in that job. He's a very old-school editor," she said as I drained my glass.

"Still, Mom, a section editor! But now tell me, why the red hair?" My mother's hair was blonde like mine. In earlier days, people often mistook us for sisters. Today, her hair was dyed shiny auburn, the dramatic tone making her skin too pale.

"My hair was getting so dull. Better fake and vibrant than authentic and dingy, I said to myself one morning. I think it might be too dark. But Bert likes it."

I raised my eyebrows.

She shrugged. "My new boyfriend." A girlish smile crept across her face.

"Mom!" I enthused. "You've never had a boyfriend!"

"Well, not that you knew about anyway," she said, looking at her menu. I let that comment pass. She looked up, still smiling that girlish smile, and shrugged again. "We've been dating for six weeks. I met him through work—"

"No! A workplace romance!" I was stunned. "But you said—"

"Let me finish. He owns one of the newspaper's major supply companies. He doesn't actually work at the paper."

My world righted itself.

"I want to hear about you. How is the PR firm?"

"Fine so far. My boss seems to like me. He asked me today to work on an important new project with him. The two of us are going to run the account. And I think I'm going to place my first story in the *Globe* soon."

Sidney was hovering, so we placed our lunch order—Caesar and Cobb salads so we could sample both.

"What kind of man is he?" Mom asked, as if there'd been no interruption.

"Well, he's very good-looking. It can be distracting sometimes." I scratched my ear self-consciously.

"Astrid! You're a grown woman. Keep your hormones in check."

I flinched. "You asked what he was like," I grumbled.

"I meant as a boss, not a potential boyfriend."

Best not to tell her about the flirting relationship Brad and I had developed, or how he increasingly found reasons to drop his hand on my shoulder or waist. Or that I fantasized about dating him and becoming the ultimate power couple, even though I had a boyfriend already and had been warned a million times about workplace romances by my mother.

"Remember, you have to keep your wits about you to succeed in the business world. Men are not potential husbands. They are stepping-stones on your path to success. Tread lightly but firmly to get what you want. And women—"

"I know, I know. Women are not friends; they're competition. You've told me this a hundred times," I said, my irritation at being criticized seeping through.

"So, how is your competition at this agency?" she asked.

"It won't be a problem. Half the people there are women, but only one is higher up than I am. She's actually a vice president. The rest are account executives like me or lower." My stomach growled as the odors of steak and potatoes floated over from the next table.

She fixed me with her steely blue eyes. "Okay," she said, breaking her gaze, "I know you'll be great. And how is your Frenchman? Is he supportive of your career?" she asked in that lilting tone that suggests the answer doesn't matter, when, in reality, it matters a lot.

"I guess. He thinks his high finance job is more important than my PR job, but other than that, Francois is wonderful, thank you. We just celebrated our six-month anniversary and he's making me dinner tonight."

She nodded. "I'd glad to hear you haven't had any more issues. Is he teaching you any French?"

"He's teaching me a lot about French kissing," I joked, watching for her reaction.

"Funny," she said drily, adjusting her napkin in her lap. "Are you being safe?"

I sighed. Mothers. I scanned the restaurant, noticing how the wall sconces shed streams of golden light down the dark paneled walls. "Yes, Mom, and you asked me that with my last boyfriend."

"I know, but you can't be too careful. Getting pregnant before you're ready could completely ruin your life," she said and pressed her lips together.

I fiddled with the cool stem of my champagne glass.

"And are you satisfying each other? It's so important to have a reciprocal agreement in the bedroom, you know."

I glanced around the restaurant, but no one seemed to be hearing our awkward conversation. "You know I love you, Mom, but I am not going to talk about this with you. Let's just say Francois and I are doing fine," I whispered.

"Good. One last piece of advice, and then I'll stop mothering. For today. I'm staying over tonight, and I want to have breakfast with you tomorrow. Oral sex should be the last thing you give up. The final frontier. Don't offer that too early. Then, when you do, he'll be extra appreciative."

Aargh. I would write an article someday: *The Ten Most Embarrassing Things to Discuss with Your Mother*.

I wanted to ask her if she withheld blowjobs from Bert. "I'm going to the restroom," I said instead, standing.

She was my mother, after all.

Shelby

CHAPTER 5

Tina had the first round waiting when I got to Daisy Buchanan's, a trendy basement bar on Newbury Street, a few blocks from the office.

The only other customers at five fifteen on a Monday were a couple of guys and a woman in power suits, inhaling martinis and talking over each other. One of them—a man with slicked-back hair and a pinky ring glinting against his cocktail glass—watched me take off my coat and climb onto the padded chrome stool at the bar-height table, making me even more self-conscious and clumsy than usual.

"Tina, I need help," I said motioning toward my standard black blazer and ten-dollar silk shirt. "Everyone in the office is super stylish. I can't keep wearing my two discount suits over and over, but you know I don't have any money."

She pushed a vodka gimlet toward me. "They can't expect you to dress great on what they're paying you. Don't worry about it."

She squirmed on her stool, yanking her mini skirt down to a decent level. Neither of us mentioned that good-old Dad supplemented Tina's entry-level salary in the events department of a nearby hotel.

"Maybe I could borrow a few things from you now and then?" She shrugged sure. Tina was four inches taller than I was, but I figured a blouse or two might fit. And she had way too many floral-patterned shirts for my taste, but some of the solids might work. "If I get hired for real, then we'll go on a shopping spree."

"Cheers to that," she said, her green eyes gleaming. "I am always up for a shopping adventure." She drained her glass. "You know, I feel like I never see you anymore. You spend so much time at Jesse's. That didn't take long. What's it been, like a month?" she asked, looking for the waitress.

"A little longer. And what can I say? I like hanging with him. It's totally bitchin' and he's like totally tubular," I said in a Valley Girl voice. "Even if he does laugh like a horse."

Tina cocked her head and squinted. "Do you actually like him?"

"Of course! He's really," I peered out the window, "comfortable."

"Ewwww, comfortable?" Tina repeated, pulling her curly black hair back off her shoulders and releasing it. "Is that the best you can come up with, my little unromantic friend? Is that your goal in life, a comfortable relationship? What about passion and excitement?"

"Take a chill pill, Tina. We have fun cooking dinner and watching videos. And playing with his awesome cat."

She rolled her eyes. "I know I fixed you guys up, but maybe you can do better."

I drew my eyebrows together.

"Seriously. You're the smartest person I know. Maybe Jesse isn't smart enough for you."

"Come on, Tina, look at me. It's not like I get my choice of guys like you do." The smarmy guy with the pinky ring stepped over and bowed before Tina.

"Excuse me, miss, you dropped your napkin," he said, straightening up and presenting her cocktail napkin.

Point proven.

Astrid

CHAPTER 6

"That wraps it up," Brad said, flipping the hefty three-ringed binder shut with a satisfied slap and sliding it away from him on the small round table in his office, where we sat side by side. "This is an excellent proposal. And we are an amazing team, Astrid Ericsson."

He leaned back in his chair and clasped his hands behind his perfect head.

I beamed triumphantly. "I know! Thank you so much for letting me work on this with you. It's like we think the same way, but even better together." I was gushing, but it was true. "We are definitely winning this project."

We basked in our mutual appreciation for a minute, and then I started to stand.

"Wait," Brad said, reaching out so his palm rested on my thigh. I quickly sat back down to alleviate the awkwardness of the situation, but he planted his hand more firmly. I felt the heat through my cream-colored wrap dress. "Let's talk for a minute. I like to get to know the people on my team. Do you like it here?"

"Of course, can't you tell?" I blushed. *An ounce of professionalism please, Astrid.* "I'm learning so much from you, and I hope you think I'm contributing."

"Oh, you are. Stick with me, and you'll go far. I'm sorry, by the way, that you're still sharing a cube. That office really needed a paint job. It'll be worth it in the end," he said, and he stroked my thigh. Confused, I turned my swivel chair to face him, backing up enough that his hand fell off my leg.

"Yeah, that's been," I paused as if searching for the right phrase, "a patience-building exercise, let's say." I smiled nobly.

"Well, you deserve better," he said. "Is your cube-mate annoying?"

My eyebrows rose slightly. "Of course. She's straight out of college; how could she not be?" He smirked. "But I actually felt bad for her the other day. She's following up on a press release, and of course, none of the reporters she reaches on the phone remember getting it, so she has to fax every single one a second time."

"Well, that's par for the course. We all had those shit jobs when we started out."

"I know. I thought about telling her my secret to save time, but…" I tilted my head.

"But, why share your hard-earned trade secrets with a mere intern—that's what you were going to say? Don't feel funny about that. I agree with you." He nudged his chair closer until our knees touched. "You can tell me though, right?" He leaned in. "I am your boss after all. I could demand that you tell me."

I laughed—entirely too girlishly.

"Come on, Astrid, what's your secret?" His eyes plumbed mine.

"Well, I just *pretend* to send the press release the first time around. I call the reporters, ask if they got it, and then send it for real when they ask me to. That way, they're waiting for it, and I save myself hours of work." I folded my hands in my lap.

"Genius," he said, taking my hand. I tried to glance over my shoulder at his office door. "Don't worry, it's shut," he said, tightening his grip.

"Brad, I—" He waited while I tried to process my conflicting thoughts—my attraction to him and my mother's stern advice about workplace dating. "I have a boyfriend," I said finally.

"And I have a girlfriend," he said, indifferently. He didn't let go of my hand, but he loosened his grip enough that I could pull back and stand. He watched me but didn't move.

"Thanks for this, this opportunity," I stuttered as I left.

Back in my oh-so-cozy cubicle, I sat at my desk staring into space for a minute. My fantasy romance with Brad, the real-life flirting, this very real pass, Francois, my career—they all bounced around my head in a jumble.

"Astrid, do you want a piece of cake? Karen brought some in." Shelby stood in the doorway holding a paper plate with a slice of yellow cake on it. "You can have this, and I can grab another one, if you want."

"No, thanks. I'm not hungry."

Feeling generous, I decided to drop a comment soon to let Shelby know my frustration about the cube situation was due to the close quarters, not her personally. Tomorrow maybe.

Shelby

CHAPTER 7

"Time for coffee," Astrid said as she stepped out of our cube into the kitchen, which was weird because she never announced her plans to me.

"Hi, Tom. Is that coffee fresh?" I heard her ask another one of the account executives.

"Yeah, it's only nine thirty, so I hope it's still fresh," Tom answered.

"Great." The cabinet opened, and a coffee mug clunked on the counter. "So how are you? Anything new and exciting?"

"No, just the same old stuff," he said, sounding surprised. He slurped his coffee. "How about you? Bet you can't wait to get into your new office."

"Yes, I can't wait," Astrid said, her voice sounding closer. "Can you believe I'm crammed into a cube with an intern? It's outrageous. I mean we're just crammed in there."

My stomach dropped. What a bitch. She knows I'm like ten feet away. I glared at my pad of paper, stabbed it a few times with my pen, and ignored her when she flounced in a minute later.

***

Later that morning, for the first time, I got to tell other people what to do. Maggie put me in charge of mailing two hundred invitations for a swanky reception we were organizing for our client, Gloucester Development Company. I felt funny overseeing a bunch of the real employees, including Michael and Karen, but Maggie said anytime we had a big fulfillment-type project, all junior staff pitched in.

We set up assembly-line style around the big conference room table: Rsvp cards, Rsvp envelopes, invitations, outer envelopes, and stamps. The ritzy nature of the reception meant we had to use real stamps—no metered postage for these babies, Maggie had explained. The outer envelopes had already been hand addressed by a professional calligrapher in flowing black ink.

"Who. Is. That." Karen stood behind me, peering over my shoulder through the glass wall into the reception area.

An unbelievably hot man studied the abstract painting on the wall. Black tousled hair, a face chiseled out of perfection and outlined with stubble. A classy suit that couldn't hide his awesome bod. For the first time, I found a man in a suit sexy.

"Please let him be a new client," I breathed.

"Please let him be *my* new client," Karen moaned.

"Figures," Michael said matter-of-factly, breaking the spell. We looked at him. "I think he's Astrid's," he said, surreptitiously pointing down the office hallway to the left of the conference room.

Astrid strode up—how she could stride in a straight skirt and three-inch heels I'd never understand—and kissed the mystery man on both cheeks. Taking him by the arm, she drew him back into the office. Karen opened the conference room door and watched them disappear.

"Back to work," I deadpanned, hoping I didn't sound like a factory foreman.

A few minutes later, Astrid and her boyfriend ambled by us.

"Let's get going. I have an important meeting after lunch," we heard him say. He seemed annoyed, but I wasn't positive because of his heavy French accent. Astrid seemed to hang back.

"Wait, let me introduce you to some more colleagues," she said, dragging him into our midst. All inserting, stuffing, and stamping stopped.

"Hey, everyone." Astrid smiled at us. I was still fuming from her comment in the kitchen, but I had to admit, when she smiled, the ice queen melted into the girl next door. "This is my boyfriend, Francois. Francois, this is—well, everyone." She leaned into him.

"Hello. I am very pleased to meet all of you," he said, although I noticed he didn't actually make eye contact with anyone. "And now if you will excuse us, we are going to lunch." He turned to leave, but Astrid, after seeming to scan the reception area, stood firm. Francois tapped his fingers against his leg.

"So, what are you guys doing here?" Astrid asked.

"We're mailing invitations." Michael piped up in the tone you might use with a child.

Astrid strolled around the large table, pausing at each station. "Nice stock," she murmured, fingering one of the Rsvp envelopes. When she completed her tour around the table, she sighed. "Well, okay, Francois, we can go."

"That was weird," Michael said as soon as she crossed the threshold into the reception area. The main door opened, and Brad and Terry walked in. Astrid turned to Francois and kissed him on the lips.

"You are the best," she said. "Oh, Terry, Brad, let me introduce you to my boyfriend. This is Francois. Francois, this is my boss Brad, and this is Terry." Hands were shaken all around. Astrid and Francois finally floated out of the office on a wave of sophisticated beauty.

"That. Was. Weirder," Karen said, watching the now empty reception area.

Shelby

CHAPTER 8

Call me sentimental and lame, but I loved going home for the holidays. When I walked through the lockless back door of the old farmhouse in the middle of nowhere, my brother Eric was talking to Mom, leaning against the woodblock table while she filled an apple pie on the kitchen counter. Eric always drove up to Newfield from New York City two days before Thanksgiving to avoid the nightmare traffic. I knew my other brother Kyle wasn't there yet. He always insisted on flying in from Florida on the holiday itself, making someone pick him up at Bradley Airport on one of the worst travel days of the year.

My mother stopped bustling long enough to give me a strong hug. Fifty-five and spry, with gray-sprinkled dark brown hair, she said she had decided to ignore aging altogether. It seemed to be working.

"When's the last time you brushed your hair?" she asked, smoothing my flyaways.

"You know it looks messy five minutes after I brush it," I said, batting her hand away.

"Well, looks like you need a haircut," she said, retreating to the counter and her pie. "I am very proud of you for getting that big job, you know."

"It's not a big job, Mom, but thanks," I said, rolling my eyes.

"Listen, Shelby," she said, popping the pie into the oven. I knew this voice. Something annoying was coming. "I've got a man for you to meet—the son of one of the teachers I work with. He's a lawyer in New York, and he's going to be in Boston soon. I told his mother you would meet him for coffee."

"Make that a whiskey, and maybe she'll go," Eric said, enjoying my red-faced discomfort at my mother's latest effort to control my life.

"A lawyer?" I wrinkled my nose.

"He'll love you. Just remember to brush your hair and maybe wear a little less makeup."

"Mom, no, I don't want you fixing me up." She looked hurt. "Thanks, though."

"But why not? What can it hurt?"

"A lawyer?" I asked again. "He probably sleeps in a suit and tie. Anyway, I'm—"

"Oh! Before Norman gets here, I wanted to tell you both—he's getting Coach of the Year from the state football association! But don't say anything yet—we're not supposed to know."

Eric and I rolled our eyes at each other.

"Speak of the devil, here he is," Mom said as my stepfather burst through the door, running a hand over his head as if his crew cut needed smoothing, stamping his feet even though there was no snow, and saying brrr even though it was in the thirties.

"Kyle will be here in a minute. He's looking for something in the barn," my burly stepfather answered Mom before she asked. Norman lumbered over and held out his arms. "Welcome home, Shelby."

Bracing myself, I let him hold me for two seconds before slipping away toward the living room. "Eric," I tossed over my shoulder, "let's go watch the football game."

Eric pushed past me and launched himself onto the floral-patterned couch, his long legs reaching to the end. I pulled his feet up and squirmed in underneath, putting his feet in my lap.

"Why do you like coming back here?" he asked, staring at the TV.

I looked at him blankly. "What are you talking about? You know I love family holidays." He pretended to watch the game. "Why? Don't you like coming home?"

"It makes Mom happy, so I do it, but this hasn't felt like home to me in a long time."

"Hm. I do miss Tramp. I wish they'd get another dog—"

"Hey, lowlifes, how the hell are you?" Kyle blew into the living room, his cheeks pink, and his soft brown hair dipping into his unfairly blue eyes. After handing out bottles of beer and hugs, he settled into the swivel chair.

"So, Shelby, making any money yet?"

"Fifty bucks a week, pretty amazing, right? But I'm hoping I'll get hired at the PR agency when my internship is over."

"Sweet. I know Eric's not making any money, but are you at least dating some hot Columbia freshmen, bro?"

"You're still a pig, Kyle. I prefer women my age, so I can have intelligent conversations with them. But the bigger the airhead the better is your motto, isn't it?"

"It's so good to be home," Kyle said with a smirk, putting his feet up on the hassock.

I snuck glances at my older brothers. Kyle, who taught high school chemistry in Florida, was the prettiest one in the Stewart family. Eric was more haunting with piercing eyes and a sharp jaw. He kept his dark, curly hair Jim Morrison length—a perk of still being a student. He was in his final year of a master's program for Spanish linguistics. Two years older than me, he seemed a hundred years wiser.

Sitting there watching the game, not talking, with the two people I loved most in the world, was why I came home. I'd tell Eric that later.

I heard Mom open and close the oven door. I inhaled to catch the scents of turkey and stuffing floating in from the kitchen. Something else mixed in with the food odors. The indescribable but distinct smell of my childhood living room. Something clicked in my brain.

Lying on the couch, watching TV. Norman is home from his teaching job at the high school, sneaking some peanut butter in the kitchen. Comes in, touches me. Eyes squeezed shut. Under my shirt. It tickles. Going so low. Please no lower. Touches my underwear. Stops.

I moved to the living room's other armchair, slept in the spare bedroom that night, and left at six the next morning.

***

It was moving weekend. Our lease was up in Waltham, and Tina and I wanted to be in the city. I couldn't afford the up-and-coming South End neighborhood like her, so we found separate apartments with older women looking for roommates—Tina in a classic brownstone and me in a modest house across the Tobin Bridge in Chelsea.

Sunday night, Jesse came over to check out my new place. "Totally gnarly," he drawled. "Cool furniture, bigger than the last place."

"Yeah, my roommate is like twenty-seven so she's got everything. All I need now is a dog to make my life perfect."

"I just wish it was closer," he said, plopping onto the slightly worn sofa and bouncing around a bit. "It took more than half an hour to get here. I totally liked the five-minute drive better."

"Me too, but this was the best thing I could afford, and at least it's closer to work for me."

"You can still stay with me on the weekends," Jesse said, pulling me down next to him.

"Yup, or you can stay here," I said as he leaned in to kiss me. I pulled back. "Not on the couch, okay?" He stared at me. "Come on," I said, "let's go christen my bedroom."

"Good idea, since we don't do so well on couches anyway."

I stopped. "What does that mean?"

"Just that most nights, we totally fall asleep on the couch at my house before, you know, doing anything."

"Well, that's what happens when we smoke pot and lie down. It's not my fault. It's simple biology."

"Yeah well, I'm just saying."

"Come on. But be warned, I still have boxes everywhere." I grabbed his hand and led him to the bedroom.

Astrid

CHAPTER 9

"Where's my smile, beautiful?" Sal asked as I passed the front desk at Dante's Gym.

I turned on my okay-you're-harmless smile for the patriarch of the family-owned health club five blocks from my apartment. Sal nodded his head of silvery hair, his eyes threatening to disappear into the folds of wrinkles on his tan face.

"And what demons are we exercising out today?" he asked, in what was a running joke between us after he saw me sprinting around the track soon after I joined the club a year before.

"Just run of the mill ones today, Sal," I said, stopping and shifting my exercise bag on my shoulder.

"Don't forget, my offer still stands. When you want to stop doing those baby weights, you let old Sal know. My grandson Tony is a great trainer. He'll fix you right up with some real weights."

I shook my head at him. "Like I've said a hundred times—I'm not trying to build muscle. I only want to tone. Even Tony says I'm doing it the right way." Hitching my bag up, I turned away. "Plus, my boyfriend doesn't want me all bulked up," I said over my shoulder as I headed toward the locker room.

Three hours later, exercised, showered, and primped, the scent of an undoubtedly fancy French sauce met me at the door of Francois's North End condo. The fire burned low, and the candles flickered high.

"I have a great boyfriend. Have I ever told you that?" I asked, slipping off my paradoxically down-filled yet stylish jacket.

"And I have a stunning girlfriend. Have I ever told you that?" Francois countered as he emerged from the small kitchen—insanely, enticingly sexy even though he wore a full-length apron over his linen shirt and pressed trousers. He hung my jacket on a hook by the door.

I stepped daintily out of my shoes and kissed him until he pulled away.

"Must check the sauce," he mumbled.

Two bottles of wine and one exquisite meal later, we cuddled on the dark leather couch in front of the flickering fireplace.

"Can I tell you about something that's been going on at work?" I asked, focusing my eyes on the orange, gold, and blue flames.

"Of course," he said, as if it were a stupid question.

"My boss has been flirting with me. More than flirting, really. He made a pass at me. I think he's getting the wrong idea about me."

"He's the one we met at the office, yes? The tall one named Brad?"

"That's right. I'm not sure what to do."

"Well, a little flirting never hurt anyone. It might even help you."

I sat up straight and faced him, the wine making me momentarily dizzy. "Are you serious? Francois, he made a pass at me," I said again.

"Astrid. I love you, but you are a flirt, and you know it. Perhaps you are sending signals you don't realize. Men will take any crumb from a beautiful woman and interpret it as a gourmet meal."

I squinted at him to hide the fact that maybe I brought this on myself—something I hadn't expected Francois to detect so astutely.

"Anyway, what does it matter? This job is just a diversion until you settle down with your rich husband someday, perhaps one with a bit of a French accent," he said. He wasn't joking.

"Francois, I've told you before," I said, furrowing my eyebrows, "I'm not going to be dependent on any man. I intend to have my own successful career."

He sighed and perused his manicured nails. "Fine, so if you want to keep working, but you don't want your boss to like you, then stop flirting. Remain professional at all times. Is that better?"

He pursed his lips and made an exaggerated frown. His pretend sympathy aggravated me.

"You could be more supportive. Or if you want to be all old-fashioned about it, you could defend me. He put his hand on my leg, Francois! He tried to compromise my honor. You should be going to, to, find him and punch him in the nose!" I said, my annoyance and the wine making me admittedly childish.

To my horror, he laughed. "You American women; you are so funny. I am not going to punch him in the nose." He embraced me, but I kept my arms at my side. "Come here, come here, *ma petite*. It's okay. Don't worry. It's not like you'll be working there forever." He tried to move my arms around his neck, but I stiffened. "Oops, I said it again. Look, why don't we forget this conversation ever happened?"

I wrenched free of his embrace. "I have a better idea. Let's forget this *night* ever happened. I think I should sleep at home tonight." I grabbed my shoes and jacket and put them on while waiting for the elevator. He didn't come after me.

The fresh air soothed my face as I stumbled down Hanover Street and grabbed a cab, not having the patience for the subway. On the ride home, I drafted an article in my head called How to Tell If Your Boyfriend Truly Supports Your Career.

The phone rang as I pulled off my coat at home.

"Astrid, I just wanted to see how you are." My mother's maternal sixth sense must have kicked in.

"Hi," I said, without much enthusiasm.

"What's wrong?"

"It's Francois. We had a stupid fight, and I walked out on him. I didn't mean to, but he made me so mad, and I left. Just like that."

"Tell me what happened," she said in a tone suggesting I'd screwed up, but maybe she could help me fix it.

I hesitated. "He can be so chauvinistic, like my career is always second to his. Like any issues I'm having at work don't even matter."

"Is that what you argued about?"

"Not exactly." I ran my finger back and forth along the marigold base unit of the phone hanging on the kitchen wall.

"Astrid, I can't help if you don't tell me."

I inhaled and exhaled. "He thinks I should flirt with my boss to get ahead."

"He suggested that out of the blue?" I could practically feel her probing gaze through the phone.

"No, not really. I was saying how my boss maybe misinterpreted some harmless flirting I was maybe doing—"

"Astrid Ericsson!" she interrupted. "How many times do I have to tell you? No workplace romances! And that means no flirting either. Honestly, you're too smart for this. Don't let a randy libido or poor judgement be your downfall. Please do not let me hear of this happening ever again. It stops now."

My cheeks burned, and my throat tightened as I nodded into the phone. "I know. I'm sorry, Mom."

"Who should be in charge of every work relationship?"

"I should, Mom."

"Who should *think* they're in charge of every work relationship?"

"The men and my boss if she's a woman."

"Okay then. Let this be the last time we have this conversation. I have to go now. I will speak with you soon."

I hung the receiver on the wall unit and leaned my forehead against the gold plastic, its smooth, cool touch doing nothing to slake my shame and misery.

Shelby

CHAPTER 10

"Wow, that's quite the operation," Terry said as I peeled off the leg warmers and stretch pants from under my skirt.

"You'd wear all this too if you had to stand *between* the commuter rail cars in the morning because there's no room in the cars. That winter wind blowing up your skirt can be pretty cold," I said, pleased at my quip, then wondering if I should have said that to the agency's partner.

Terry chuckled. "I'd say I'd like to be that winter wind, but I wouldn't want to be accused of harassment."

"Um, I think you did just say it, Terry," I said. If he could joke, so could I. "And it's okay. I have two older brothers." I took my layers into my cube, embarrassed by my last, non-sensical comment.

Maggie called me into her office two seconds later. "Sit down," she said in a voice that produced an instant lump of dread in my gut. On top of my hangover from too many beers last night, it was not a good feeling. While she settled into her seat, I sipped my coffee and focused on her stunning rectangular, white stone and silver ring.

"One of the brokers invited to Gloucester's winter reception said the Rsvp envelopes you sent with the invitations weren't stamped." She was so grave it was like I had scrawled dirty words across the invitations.

"We put stamps on the big envelopes, obviously. Are you saying the little Rsvp envelopes were supposed to be stamped too?"

"Yes, that's the proper etiquette. That's what the client expected."

"Wow, what a waste of money. Can't people buy their own stamps?" Quickly, I tried a more mature response. "I'm really sorry, Maggie, but I've never mailed a fancy invitation before, and I didn't know that was the rule."

"I should have made sure you knew, so it's partly my fault. And most people will call to rsvp anyway, instead of mailing the cards in, but I'll have to mention it to the client regardless."

The dread in my gut tightened into a knot. "You can blame it on the dopey intern, right?"

She half-smiled, and I realized passing the buck wasn't in Maggie Hirsch's nature.

"So, let's talk about something more positive," she said. "This is the last week of your internship, as you know."

"Mm-hmm." The dread twisted, unsure where to go or what to do.

"I've been very happy with your work and your dedication, and Jim likes what he's seen. We'd like you to stay on as an account coordinator."

"You mean, I'm being hired?" The edges of the dread dissolved.

She gave a short laugh. "Yes, it's a full-time job. You'll start to have contact with the clients, you'll get our standard starting salary, and you'll even have a business card."

A huge, unprofessional grin took over my face.

"Great. Now, there's one more thing we need to cover."

The dread rebounded at her tone, which was more like the "You screwed up the stamps" voice than the "We'd love to hire you" voice. I swigged more coffee.

***

I told Karen and Michael my good news over lunch in the small conference room. Astrid barged in right as I said, "So I'm a full-time employee now."

"Have you seen—" she started but stopped at my news. "Oh," she said, pursing her perfect lips. "Hey, Shelby, since you've been hired, can I offer you a piece of advice?"

Karen and Michael exchanged glances. I waited.

"Well, it's just that you'll want to appear professional now. So you should probably stop wearing lots of mismatched earrings, and maybe upgrade your wardrobe." She scanned my college clothes as I pulled a wave of hair forward over my ear.

"Okay, see ya, Astrid," Michael said as I stared. For once, Astrid took a cue from someone below her on the food chain and left.

"That bitch," Karen hissed. "Who is she to tell you what to do?"

"Don't listen to her," Michael said, patting my shoulder, his blonde head shaking. "You wear as many earrings as you want."

"Actually," I said slowly, "I hate to admit this, but Maggie said the same thing. She said the partners want me to dress more professionally."

The difference was that Maggie had seemed way more uncomfortable saying it than Astrid had.

Astrid

CHAPTER 11

"I know you've been avoiding me," Brad said, cornering me in his office and shutting the door, a few weeks after the thigh-stroking incident. His pinstriped suit jacket hung over the back of his desk chair, and his pale yellow tie was loosened.

"What? No, of course not—"

"Shhh, it's okay. But I know you have been. You never step into my office anymore. You stand in the doorway to talk to me. And we haven't been alone since then."

Alone with the door shut, I thought. Working so closely on the same accounts, I couldn't avoid him altogether, but I tried to make sure someone else was in earshot when I had to talk to him one-on-one. That way, he couldn't make another pass, and I couldn't be tempted.

"Look, I know this is confusing, me being your boss and all. So I'm going to cut to the chase."

I leaned against his closed door, my fight-or-flight instinct primed and ready to launch.

"I know you're attracted to me. And I am definitely attracted to you. We're two grown, intelligent people, who are allowed to enjoy each other—even if we're co-workers."

An involuntary image of me and Brad happily dating flitted across my mind, but I remained silent.

"So I have a proposition for you. You and I could have a thing." His eyebrows flicked up and down. "It doesn't need to be official, but we could be very good together, if you know what I mean."

"But," I said, confused, "you have a girlfriend. Are you saying you're breaking up with her?"

"Oh no, I can't do that. We've been together five years. You and me would be a separate thing."

"So wait." I squinted. "You want me to be something on the side? A little affair while you stay with your girlfriend?"

"That's right. We could have a lot of fun."

My brain's processing ability short-circuited.

"Think about it and let me know," he said, shooting me a smile and turning to shuffle some papers on his desk.

I started to leave but turned back to face him. I took a step forward. "I don't have to think about it. I have more pride than to be someone's little piece of action on the side. I'm offended that you even asked me. Is that all you think of me?"

He stopped shuffling. "Astrid, I have nothing but respect for you," he said, humoring me. He straightened up to his full six feet. "But remember—I always get what I want, one way or another. It's one of my more endearing qualities."

Dumbfounded, I stumbled to the ladies' room to breathe. I wished I had a girlfriend to talk to. I couldn't talk to my mother. She'd think I'd failed somehow, letting it get to this. I definitely could not talk to Francois. He'd probably make fun of me. We hadn't discussed Brad since the night we argued, but I knew he didn't understand the tightrope I was balancing on.

I clutched the bathroom countertop and leaned forward, barely seeing my reflection over the row of sinks. We were heading into a four-day weekend for Christmas, and then I was taking a week of vacation at home in Maine. Maybe by the time I got back, Brad would have forgotten his offer, and we'd be back to normal.

Shelby

CHAPTER 12

"Damn, it's cold," I said, my words muffled by the hair and scarf whipped into my face by the wind. Tina pulled a lock of dark curly hair from her mouth and rushed ahead of me to the door of Joe's Bar & Grille on Newbury.

"Aah," we said together as the wall of warmth in the bar started thawing our frozen faces.

"I'm so not looking forward to Christmas," Tina said, after we amazingly scored a table and got our drinks.

"Yeah, I'm not really either," I said, surprising myself. "Why aren't you?" I asked, licking salt off the rim of my margarita and taking a soul-reviving gulp.

"Well, there's my mother, and then there's my mother." She breathed out heavily, playing with the plastic straw in her strawberry daiquiri.

"Okay, so I'm guessing it's something to do with your mother?"

"She's a drunk, Shelby," she said stabbing at the strawberry in her glass with the straw. "A raving, raging alcoholic. Always has been, always will be. Holidays at home are torture."

I put my drink down and crossed my arms on the table. I'd known Tina almost two years and we'd been roommates for one, so I knew something was up with her mother, but I didn't know it was this bad.

"What exactly happens?" I asked.

"Sometimes it's okay, but eventually she has too much, and it goes downhill from there. We don't even go out to restaurants with my parents anymore because the last time she caused a scene. But hey, at Thanksgiving, she only passed out at the dining room table once."

"Is that normal?"

"Only in my house."

"I mean, does she pass out a lot?"

"That's her go-to-move. Been doing it since I was a girl. I'd bring a friend home after school and find her asleep on the kitchen floor. One time, her dress was up around her waist. I almost died." She sucked on her daiquiri. "And I never brought a friend home again."

"What does your father do?"

"Nothing. He and my sister pretend it's not even happening. But I can't take it sometimes."

We sat for a minute, Tina twisting a long black curl around her finger. Tears welled in her almond-shaped green eyes. I inhaled deeply to send courage to my brain.

"Ti, I do understand what it's like to be let down by your parents." Uncertainty tingled in my chest, but her sad eyes encouraged me on. Just say it. "When I was little, my stepfather molested me."

Her eyes opened wide, and she leaned toward me. "Oh my God, Shel, has anyone shot him yet?" Her violent reaction triggered pleasure somewhere in the back of my brain.

"No, he's still around, living in my old house, with my mother, teaching high school, coaching teenagers, and being revered as a fine upstanding citizen."

"She's still married to him? She lives with him? That's disgusting."

"I guess it is." We took long swigs from our drinks. I moved the menu around on the table. "But she might not even know. You're the first person I've told."

"Ever? Ohmygod. You've been holding this inside? Shel, you have to talk to someone. I saw a therapist for a while, you know. My sister thought it was stupid, but it really helped me. So are you going to say something to him? Or your mother?"

"I don't know. It wouldn't change anything. Every family has their secrets, right? It's probably easier to just forget about it."

"Hm," she said, watching me. "Well, I think you should think about telling your mother. It's not good to hold this stuff in. And you can always talk to me about it. Anytime." She raised her glass but stopped mid-air. "It really pisses me off when you think about it. Parents are supposed to take care of us. Instead, I was making my own breakfast in second grade, and you had a predator under the same roof." She took a deep breath.

"I guess you're right. I mean, isn't that the main job description? Love us unconditionally and feed us? And protect us from the monsters under the bed?"

Tina snorted. "Except in our case, they *are* the monsters."

***

Being home in Newfield for Christmas was harder than I expected. Swatting down the questions swarming my brain since my talk with Tina was harder than I expected too.

I'd toyed with using a snowstorm as an excuse for bailing, but it's hard for a born-and-bred New Englander to use a few inches of snow as an excuse for anything.

On the other hand, it was Christmas, so it was easy to fill up the time at bars and parties getting drunk and high with my brothers and friends. And avoiding my parents. So essentially, it was just like high school.

Except that when everyone was asleep, I snuck out of my bedroom to sleep in the spare room again.

Thankfully, New Year's Eve was not a Stewart family holiday. So Jesse and I took a road trip to Albany to visit friends of his, filling the travel time with lively games of Name That Tune.

When we checked into the motel he'd booked and started to change into fresh clothes, I wrapped my arms around his naked waist and snuggled into his neck. His chest, muscular and broad from drumming, drew me like a magnet. I kissed his neck and worked my way down.

Jesse groaned before stepping back. "Totally remember that for later, okay? My friends are waiting for us."

I turned away so he wouldn't see my embarrassed face and reached in my bag for my partying outfit.

We barhopped our way down Lark Street's cobblestones, peeking in the restaurant and music store windows, collecting friends along the way. A few appetizers, a bunch of tequila shots, and way too many pitchers of Genesee Cream Ale later, midnight came. When the lead singer of the house band started the countdown, Jesse was at the bar refilling pitchers. I watched him plow through the people jumping up and down in time to the countdown. With two seconds to go, he plopped the pitchers on a table, grabbed my hand, and yanked me up against him. "Happy New Year," he said, his lips tickling my ear. "I love you."

We kissed while midnight pandemonium surrounded us. I wound my fingers through his dark curls, and we kept kissing until an elbow from a spastic reveler broke us apart.

I pulled him back and put my mouth to his ear. "Jesse, I love you too." My heart lurched as I said the words. His beautiful Richard Gere face beamed, and his muscular drummer arms pulled me in tightly.

When the bar closed, I wanted to go to the motel and fool around, but Jesse wanted to hit one more party. An hour later, I ran out of small talk, and my throat was hoarse from too many bong hits. By the time we left, around three thirty, my eyes were rolling around in their sockets.

Jesse practically carried me into the motel room, where I crumpled onto the bed. "Don't fall asleep!" he warned me over his shoulder as he headed for the bathroom.

"Ahwont," I mumbled, before passing out.

The next morning, I woke with the world's worst hangover, my heart pounding like it was pushing sludge through my veins. Tiptoeing past Jesse into the bathroom, I brushed my teeth, once for last night and once for this morning. My mouth still tasted like the bottom of a garbage can so I brushed my tongue, but that made me gag and almost vomit. "I am definitely giving up coffee," I moaned to myself. Having a squishy stomach from a hangover was bad enough, but I knew with this nausea, coffee wouldn't stay down. That meant a throbbing caffeine-withdrawal headache on top of the hangover headache. Too much pain. I vowed to give up my three cup a day habit immediately.

Jesse wasn't impressed when I shared my New Year's resolution. We dressed and checked out without talking. Driving home on the highway though our hangover haze, I watched mile after mile of the Thruway and then the Pike get sucked up under the car. Paths of dingy snow in the middle of each lane wiggled like dirty ribbons against the black pavement. The heavy gray sky promised snow.

I leaned my head against the window and kicked myself for falling asleep last night. I couldn't think of a way to bring back our midnight euphoria.

We fell back into our regular pattern the next few weeks, Jesse staying at my Chelsea apartment once a week, and me staying at his house in Waltham some weekends. His band was finally together, so sometimes I skipped the weekends so they could practice non-stop.

Late one Friday night, I got to his house after he was in bed. I climbed in and snuggled up to his warm, sleepy body, but immediately stiffened. I swore he smelled a touch like perfume and sex. I sniffed his black hair and strong neck until he pushed me away and told me to stop.

"What are you doing?" he asked.

"Nothing." I looked away to hide my watering eyes.

When Jesse fell asleep, I went downstairs to find Thor. As usual, he was sleeping on the couch. As usual, he let me pet him for exactly ninety seconds before slipping away under the couch where I couldn't reach him.

Astrid

CHAPTER 13

After a week of simply spectacular skiing with Mom and some friends, I felt I could face anything, including Brad, when I returned to work. I didn't see him all morning but practically ran into him as I came out of the ladies' room mid-afternoon.

"Whoa, steady there," he joked, then stopped short. "Astrid. You're back."

His long-lashed eyes studied me. His subtly spicy cologne wormed its way into my senses. How could I possibly still be attracted to this man who had propositioned me so inappropriately?

He stepped close, backing me up against the wall of the hallway. "So listen," he said in a low voice, "I gather you don't want an official fling, but how about an unofficial one? A one-night stand, maybe?" He leaned in. "Mm, you smell good." He nuzzled my neck.

The men's room door squeaked open. Brad backed up and blew past me.

"Don't forget, I need that report by the end of the day. Don't let me down," he said, over his shoulder.

"Hi Astrid," Tom said, patting his hair as he left the bathroom. My cheeks burned. Tom didn't seem to have noticed anything. I exhaled and walked back to the office with him.

After that, Brad regularly found ways to torment me for rebuffing him.

At an important meeting for the tennis tournament, which was only a few months away, he had the audacity to play footsie with me under the client's conference room table. I stumbled through my presentation, panicked that someone would notice, and equally panicked that I would mess up this important career-advancement opportunity.

Increasingly, he'd run his hand along my spine when our colleagues were around, and I couldn't react. A possessive, intimate gesture, not a casual, light, "Here, you go first," touch. I sensed people starting to whisper behind my back.

But my work never suffered. I was forced to dedicate energy to plotting my moves around the office, but it didn't cut into the quality work I produced. As an account executive at Boston's leading PR firm, I was on fire. Brad needed me, and I delivered.

Then Kristy came.

Tall and gorgeous like Brad, they looked stunning together, even though her big black hair was permed within an inch of its life. To my sheer and utter horror, he assigned her to my biggest account, the tennis tournament.

"This event has to be managed perfectly. Not a single thing can go wrong," Brad explained at our team meeting. "So while we all know Astrid is very capable, I'm bringing in another account executive to help out."

That was also the day he stopped making innuendoes and playing footsie. He went out of his way to praise Kristy, to take Kristy to meetings, to do who-knows-what with Kristy. When he stroked her back in front of me, I cringed, for her—and for my flagging career.

***

"Valentine's Day is in a few weeks. What shall we do to celebrate our love, *ma petite*?" Francois could pull off the corniest comments sometimes, thanks to the delectable French accent.

"Every day with you is Valentine's Day, my love." I laughed at my idiotic inability to match his sincerity, but he didn't seem to notice.

"Careful," he said, steering me around a puddle as we exited the Italian restaurant. I felt the pressure of his hand on my back through my heavy winter coat.

"It's such a short walk. Should we stroll or get a cab?" I asked, as we walked away from Faneuil Hall.

"A cab, of course," he said as if I were a child. His sharp whistle attracted a cabbie immediately, so I dropped my waving arm.

Cuddling in the back of the cab, Francois kissed the top of my head. "When we get home, I will rub your feet and make you a cup of chamomile tea," he said.

I scoffed. "I don't need to be taken care of like a baby."

He withdrew his arm from around my shoulders. "I am trying to be nice. Why do you act like this?"

"I'm sorry. I don't know what's wrong with me. I am just so tired of people manipulating me and telling me what to do and not letting me do what I'm good at."

Francois turned to stare at me. "I've never seen you like this, *ma petite.*" He frowned. "Is it, perhaps, that time of the month?"

Suddenly I wanted out of that cab. And out of his arms. "No, that's ridiculous; it is not that time of the month, Francois! I just, I just need some space. I think—"

I froze for a second.

"I think we should take a break. Just for a while," I said.

He glared but said nothing.

"Here we are," the taxi driver said through the Plexiglas divider. "Home sweet home," he snickered.

"Astrid, are you sure about this? If you don't come in, I will not be happy."

I swallowed. "Just a break. Maybe only a few days."

Francois got out of the cab, handed a bill to the driver, and said, "Take her home to Brighton."

I cried during the dark ride home. I hadn't planned this. But I felt increasingly cornered at work, and I needed space and time to think, and to make sure Brad didn't derail my advancement. Maybe now I could even get to the gym for a long, overdue run, which always helped me de-stress and think clearly. I stopped crying. Asking for a break was a good idea.

***

Sal welcomed me back like family. He leaned his broom against the wall of the entry area and held out his arms. "Astrid, you're back! We missed you." I let him give me a quick hug. "What brings you back? What demons are you exercising out today?"

"Boyfriend demons, Sal. Vicious boyfriend ones." I rubbed my forehead.

"Is that why you're not smiling? Come on, a looker like you should smile more. Make the world a better place." He flashed his gap-toothed smile as if to prove the world needed more grins.

I grimaced. He raised his eyebrows.

"Sorry, that's all I've got today."

Shelby

CHAPTER 14

Long-distance phone bills petrified my mother, so any call from her was a big deal.

"I have some bad news to tell you, but I thought you'd want to know," she began. "Remember Adam Miller from Newfield?"

"Of course I remember him," I said, rolling my eyes and twirling the phone cord in the kitchen of my apartment.

"Well, I wasn't sure! Most people I give you news about you say you don't remember."

"Yeah, but Adam was in my class, Mom. He was part of the crowd I used to hang with at the abandoned racetrack. Or maybe you didn't know about that…"

"Hm. And I guess there are some things a mother would rather not know."

"Anyway, what's the news? Adam's not dead, is he?"

"No, but he was arrested for raping a girl. Someone from Petersburg. Isn't that horrible? A criminal, right here in our midst. The whole town is talking about it."

Criminal in our midst, I thought. Great name for a band. "Wow. He was always a little creepy, I guess," I said

"I also wanted to tell you that the state football association's awards dinner is next weekend. Can you come? You know, for Norman's Coach of the Year presentation?"

I shuddered. "I don't think I can make it. I have plans with friends next weekend."

"Are you sure? It would mean a lot to him if you were there. Kyle's coming up all the way from Florida."

"Really? What about Eric?"

"He hasn't told me yet. I'd like it if you were there."

I groaned. "Please don't pressure me on this, Mom." I looked at the phone and took a deep breath. "I really don't like being around Norman."

"What on Earth are you talking about? You've been around him your whole life." I was silent. "Shelby, what are you talking about?"

I couldn't stop now. "There's something I need to tell you. I'm not really sure how to say it. But if I were you, I think I'd want to know." She waited. "Norman used to come into my bedroom and…and do stuff to me. So Adam's not the only criminal in town." I exhaled.

She was quiet so long, I wondered if she'd passed out.

"What do you mean, 'do stuff'?" she asked, her voice strained.

"Well, it wasn't rape or anything, but he would kiss me and touch me. In places he shouldn't." My knees felt weak. I sat down.

"He's always been affectionate with you kids, I guess," she offered.

"This wasn't affection, Mom. It was…wrong. And gross."

"How dare you?" she asked, making my head snap up. "How can you do this after everything he's done for this family? He married me, a woman with only a teacher's salary and three kids to raise. He's treated you and your brothers like his own children. It's because of Norman that we were able to stay in this house, the house you love so much that you got mad when I talked about selling it a few years ago, I may remind you."

Bile rose in my throat. Childish fear and shame consumed me like I was six again. "I have to go," I said, wondering if she heard the tears in my voice over her indignation. "Bye."

I pressed the disconnect button on the handset and stared at it until my sobs overtook me. I put my head on the table and heaved until the phone blared at me, forcing me to stand up and put the receiver on its cradle.

***

I'd opened the door of the little refrigerated compartment where the memories were stored. Out in the open, they began to seep and reek. This was real now.

I cried all night and dragged myself to work in the morning. I considered calling in sick but didn't want to be alone with my thoughts. I pushed those thoughts away most of the day, until Karen innocently asked me how I was in the ladies' room. My face contorted, and just like that, I was weeping again. She hugged me, making me cry harder.

"What's wrong, Shel? You can tell me," she soothed.

I gasped for air between sobs. "I can't talk about it here. Maybe over a drink sometime," I said, knowing that would never happen. I couldn't bring this situation into my job.

"What's going on?" Astrid asked, barging into the restroom. I stepped away from Karen and turned to the sink, turning on the water to wash my hands. "Everything alright?"

"It's fine," Karen said, positioning herself between Astrid and me. "Shelby got some bad news is all."

I peeked in the mirror to see Astrid studying me, runny mascara and all.

"Oh. That's too bad," she said, and entered a stall.

***

Tina convinced me to reach out to my mother again now that I'd told her. I knew I couldn't leave this hanging. I needed to get my shit together. I drove home to Newfield that same night.

Walking up to the door of the big, white farmhouse, I felt like I was having an out-of-body experience. My childhood haven had ghosts, and they were out in the open now.

"It's okay," Mom said when I walked in. "Norman is visiting with Bob for a few hours, like I said on the phone." She ushered me into the den, like it wasn't even my house.

"So. What do we do now?" I asked after we sat down, Mom on the couch, me on a chair facing her.

"I've obviously been thinking about this nonstop, Shelby. I think we should just forget about it, for the good of the family. Can you do that? So much time has passed since you say it happened. Why make a bigger deal of it than we need to?"

A flicker of anger smoldered in my chest. "Did you even talk to him? Did you tell him you know?"

"I told him what you said. And he said he *did* used to go into your room to tuck you in. I do remember him doing that sometimes while I did the dishes. He was trying to help me out. Maybe you misinterpreted what happened." Her eyes were red, but her voice was firm.

"It was more than that," I said, emphasizing each word. "He kissed me. He touched me, in places he shouldn't," I said, distaste sour in my mouth.

"Are you absolutely sure? You were so young." I knew what answer she wanted.

"Yes. I'm sure."

She stared at me. "So now what?" she asked. A muscle near her eye twitched.

"I guess I just live my life. But please stop expecting me to adore Norman like everyone else does." She blinked. "I don't know what *you* do." She blinked again. "What *are* you going to do now?"

"I don't know. He's been my husband for more than sixteen years. I can't simply throw that away."

My smoldering anger ignited. I stood up. "And I've been your daughter for twenty-two years! Are you going to throw that away?" The tears started.

"What are you saying? You'll always be my daughter." She stood and reached out her arms.

"But I don't think I can respect you if you stay with him. The man who abused your own child."

She slapped me.

I froze.

"Don't ever say you don't respect me. I raised you. I put a roof over your head. *Norman* and I put a roof over your head. We put food in your mouth."

I didn't hear the rest because I was fleeing to the car. I backed out of the curved driveway on autopilot, blinded by tears. Jerking the car into gear, I wiped my eyes with my sleeve and drove as fast as I could back to the Mass Pike and home.

Astrid

CHAPTER 15

Everything progressed in line with my plan. Since putting things on hold with Francois, I was logging more billable hours than ever, which even Terry noticed. But it seemed like the more Terry liked me, the less Brad did. The day Brad blamed me in a department meeting for the agency losing a big author account was the day I broke. Something had to change. I couldn't let this man single-handedly ruin my career. I would play the game better.

"So Brad," I said, leaning against his office doorjamb and smiling my you're-special smile even though it pained me. "When is the big brainstorm for the pitch to the golf league?"

He glanced up from his desk, and his face warmed a touch at my smile. "It doesn't matter. You're not coming," he said, the warmth gone as fast as it came.

"What? Are you kidding?" Every cell of blood in my body plunged to my feet. My hands felt numb. "Who's going to be there?"

"Let's see," he said, tapping his pen against the desktop. "Me, Terry, Jim, Maggie, Kristy, Tom, plus Maggie wants to bring Michael and Shelby because she says they have good ideas, and they need the experience."

"How can you exclude me? I work on all the sports accounts."

"But Astrid," he said as if I were a troublesome child, "the group is so big already. You know Terry has this stupid rule about limiting the number of people in a brainstorm. And you did just screw up the Phyllis Martingale book tour. I guess you couldn't get along with her either."

"She was difficult and a prima donna. No one could make that woman happy!" I inhaled deeply and stepped into his office. "You have to have me there Brad; it would look weird if you didn't. I'll say something to Terry if you keep me out. And why does Shelby get to go? I don't think she's up to it. She was bawling in the bathroom yesterday. She's kind of a mess." I swallowed hard. "I'll work harder at getting along with everyone. I promise."

He studied me for a minute. "Okay, relax, you can come, but you have to make it up to me later. I'll talk to Maggie and nix Shelby. And, because I'm such a good guy, I'll give you a career tip. Be sure to impress Maggie in the brainstorming session because starting next week you'll be working on her team under Jim. I was going to tell you soon."

"Oh," I said, at a loss for words. "Why?" I managed to squeak out.

"You're just not the type of team player I need in my group. I'm on the path to being a partner, and I need everyone to work for the greater good, not look out for themselves. You could have attached yourself to my rising star, Astrid, but you blew it."

"I can't believe you're doing this," I said. All the fun accounts were in Terry's group. Jim and Maggie focused on real estate and other dry business ventures.

"Consider yourself lucky. I wanted to fire you after the Martingale thing, but Terry and Maggie stuck up for you and said we should give you a second chance."

Back at my desk, fuming, relief mixed with my anger.

At least I was free of Brad.

Shelby

CHAPTER 16

My mother's reaction to the Norman news tormented me, especially at night when I turned and twisted instead of sleeping. Her rejection hurt more than the memory of what Norman did, making me wish I'd kept the truth to myself. Even though she drove me crazy with her critical comments and constant nudging to do this or that, she was always there for me. Until now.

The images of my mom as the person who bought me a new outfit for the first day of school every year, and taught me the birds and the bees, and helped me find and buy my first car, were being erased by new images—her not believing me, siding with Norman, slapping me.

I blocked my emotions during the day since I couldn't afford to be caught crying in the ladies' room again. After that one time, I swore people looked at me differently—even people who normally didn't pay any attention to me. Or maybe it was insomnia making me paranoid. Either way, Campbell Lewis wasn't a place you could slack off while you got your shit together.

To make myself feel better, I decided to buy Jesse something special for Valentine's Day. At lunchtime, I rode the T to Filene's Basement at Downtown Crossing and shelled out a hard-earned hundred dollars for a hefty gold watch with silver trim.

The next day, I knocked on his front door and went in without waiting for an answer. "Up here," he yelled from the bedroom. "Just got out of the shower."

"Angels Don't Cry" by the Psychedelic Furs played on the living room stereo. One of my favorite bands—a good sign.

I threw a ball of paper to Thor twice and walked up the stairs grinning, hiding the gift bag behind my back. When he finished pulling on his shirt, I gave him a kiss. "So—" I started, but he interrupted me.

"Shel," he said, taking my free hand. "We have to talk. This isn't working." I heard Thor pushing his food bowl across the kitchen floor. "It's not you. It's me," he added.

"What do you mean?" I choked, my hand sliding out of his. "It's better than ever, isn't it?"

"No, it's not. We're totally in a rut. We don't talk about anything new, we don't do anything new, and we don't even fool around anymore."

It was about sex. I should have known.

"I'm twenty-six now, Shelby, and I'm looking for something more. Maybe you can find someone better for you." I wondered if he was going to use every cliché in the book.

My eyes jumped around the room, settling with difficulty on Jesse again.

"It's not just about the sex," he continued. "I never feel close to you anymore."

"But I love fooling around with you, Jesse," I grasped, trying to keep up. "It's just that we're always so tired when we get home, and it's so relaxing being with you, and then you bring out that stupid pot, which always puts me to sleep."

The corner of his mouth twisted up in a weak smile. We stood there between the bed and the door fidgeting. As the reality that he was breaking up with me gelled in my muddled head, I remembered the watch.

"I got this for you. For Valentine's Day." I held out the gift bag.

He didn't take it. "You don't have to do this, Shel."

"No, I want to. For what we had."

He gingerly took the bag and extracted the watch. His face lit up momentarily. "It's totally cool. Really. But you should take it back, get your money back."

I knew he was right, but I couldn't do it. Tina's voice in my head said, *Take it back, you fool; use the money for some shopping therapy.* But some twisted need to make him take it burned inside me.

"You keep it," I insisted before turning and lurching from the room, down the stairs, and out the door, for the last time. I drove away half blinded by tears, already missing Thor, a headache banging away behind my eyes.

***

"Let me do your nails," Tina said, brandishing a bottle of pastel pink polish in one hand and cotton swabs in the other.

"No," I groaned from her hideous turquoise couch. "You know I hate nail polish. It's too much work. Two days after you put it on, it's all chipped and you have to do it again."

Tina frowned. "Toenails?"

I caved. "Maybe. Later, though. Drinks first."

I was at Tina's South End apartment for the post-breakup emergency Girls Night Out she insisted on, although it was technically a Girls Day In, since it was Sunday afternoon and we stayed in to spare me the humiliation of crying in public. Thankfully, her roommate was away for the weekend.

I stroked the couch while Tina mixed up a pitcher of sangria—a splash of summer in the dead of winter, she said.

"He wanted more sex. Can you believe it? It's always about sex in the end," I yelled into the kitchen.

"Men are animals. They suck. We hate them all," Tina said, walking into the room, ice cubes clanking against the sides of the pitcher. I frowned. "Too much?" she asked. She set the pitcher down beside the glasses on the coffee table. I started pouring.

"You know," she said, "I've heard men are hard-wired to want more sex than us, to keep the species alive and all. Maybe it's not their fault." I shook my head and inhaled sangria. "But for women, sex isn't just sex. It's about feeling close. That's why we call it making love."

I didn't want to rationalize male behavior. I wanted sympathy. "I'm having a shitty week. I didn't even tell you I got kicked out of an important meeting at work last week. I don't even know why, and now I'll never have a boyfriend again," I moaned.

"Relationships are not easy, my little heartbroken friend." She settled into the cushy chair with her drink.

"Relationships suck, you mean," I said, grabbing a tissue from the end table. "Maybe our timing was off."

"What the hell does that mean?" Tina asked.

"Think about it. Even if sex is different for men and women, we all want the same thing in the end, to be loved by someone. Jesse said he wanted someone he could feel closer to because he's getting older. So both people have to want the same thing, with the same person, at the same time. It's amazing relationships ever work at all." I pulled my legs up under me.

"Take Rhett Butler and Scarlett O'Hara," I continued. I had been replaying *Gone with the Wind* in my head since re-watching it a few weeks before. "He loved her, but she didn't love him because she thought she loved Ashley. In the end, she realizes she does love Rhett, but by then, he doesn't love her anymore. They could have been a great couple, but their timing was off."

"That, and the fact that she was a horrible, scheming, selfish witch," Tina said.

"But you get the point."

Tina shrugged. "So do you think you and Jesse could get back together if your timing matches up some day?"

I swirled my sangria for a few seconds and then drained the glass. "No. To be honest, it's not like I ever would have married him someday or anything." A few more tears leaked out. "But now I have to find a place to buy my own pot."

Tina rolled her eyes.

Astrid

CHAPTER 17

"Astrid, in my office now, and get Shelby," Maggie said, uncharacteristically sharp as she marched past my office.

I summoned Shelby, wondering why Maggie would need the two of us together. We didn't share any accounts.

"Amy's mother died, so Amy can't run tonight's reception at Franklin Plaza. Shelby, you take point on managing the event. You know the logistics inside and out. I know you did most of the legwork for Amy anyway. Astrid, I need you to be Shelby's wingman. Do whatever she says, and watch for things that might go wrong. This will be Shelby's first big event, and obviously, she didn't have advance warning. I need you to make sure the whole night is a success."

I glanced at Shelby who looked terrified. I fiddled my pen back and forth in my hand.

"With all due respect, Maggie, wouldn't it be better if *you* ran the event with Shelby as your backup?" I smiled encouragingly.

Maggie looked disappointed. She sighed. "No, it would not be better. This client is needy and new in town. I'll be holding his hand and making introductions all night long. That's my contribution to the evening's success."

"Okay. And can I ask one more question? Why me instead of one of the other account executives in the group? I'm still so new to real estate."

"Because you have more event experience than anyone else, and I believe you can put your pride aside and do what's needed to make this night work. Am I right?"

"Yes, of course! I won't let you down." I turned to Shelby who hadn't moved since we entered Maggie's office. "Let's go sit down, and you can run me through the briefing sheet and timeline for tonight. Give me the lay of the land."

Shelby left the office as if in a trance. I walked behind her, lamenting the dubious honor Maggie had bestowed upon me. At least Shelby was wearing a somewhat stylish new suit, maroon with dark brown stripes, so her clothes wouldn't embarrass us at the event.

Four hours later, we jumped in a cab to the Financial District to set up for the post-work reception—an unveiling of the office tower's newly renovated lobby.

"You look nervous," I said as the cab driver ran a yellow light on Boylston.

She stopped gulping the crisp spring air and closed the window. "No, I'm not nervous. I'm just jittery because I gave up coffee. It's weird, but I can still feel the caffeine in my system, especially when I'm working on something important." A likely story.

As we entered the two-story-high lobby of Franklin Plaza, our heeltaps echoed around the empty space. "Wow, nice marble. How many kinds did they use?" I asked, scanning the apricot, honey, and cream-colored hues of the walls and floor.

"Six, plus some gold leaf," Shelby said, pulling materials out of her bag.

I knew better than to cross Maggie so I followed instructions and let Shelby deal with the caterer, the jazz quartet, and the building staff. At first, she politely asked for help when needed. "Astrid, do you think you could ask the maintenance guy for another extension cord?" By four thirty, she barked out orders like a five-star general. "Astrid, stop that, and help me move this first." I was impressed.

I don't think she took a breath until the first guests arrived.

"Relax; you did it," I said. "Everything is under control. Now it's up to the caterer and the musicians. We just watch to make sure everyone's having a good time and trouble-shoot any little things that come up."

Shelby's shoulders dropped about three inches.

"Nice shirt, by the way. New?"

She blushed, I don't know why. "Borrowed it from a friend," she said.

Before long, the ornate lobby pulsed with Franklin Plaza tenants and workers from nearby office buildings. My feet ached. I'd have worn lower heels if I'd known I'd be running an event. I looked longingly at the champagne flutes drifting by on the waiters' trays, cursing the Campbell Lewis prohibition on drinking and eating at client events.

"It's getting a little tight in here," I commented, noticing the waiters were having a tough time working through the crowd to replenish the food

Horseshoes and *Hand Grenades*

tables. I hoped we weren't breaking the building fire code with this many people in the lobby.

A waiter crossed in front of me, a massive silver bowl held as high as he could reach above the bobbing heads.

"What is wrong with people?" Shelby asked as two women grabbed at the silver bowl as the waiter passed, forcing him to lower it while they extracted a few shrimp. The bowl teetered as the waiter lifted it again and pressed on. "Should we do something?"

"What can we do? Tell people to have some goddamn manners?" I shook my head.

Amazingly, more people clutched at the bowl. The waiter's arm gave way, and the bowl of shrimp tumbled through the air. People backed up and watched the enormous bowl land on the marble floor with a resounding clang. I grabbed Shelby's arm and pushed my way to the accident scene.

"Eek!" a woman yelled, "I'm soaked!"

I watched through the crowd as a woman in a suit and heels slipped on the icy water spreading across the floor, screaming on her way down.

"Shelby, you need to—" I stopped. She stared at me, eyes wide. I took a deep breath. "I've got this. You go find the janitor and tell him to come back with a mop, pronto." Thank goodness she turned to follow my instructions.

Two more people had slipped and fallen in the slithering puddle of shrimp by the time I reached the crime scene. The jazz quartet's song ended in a painful saxophone squeak when the musicians stopped to check out the chaos.

"Everyone back!" I commanded, motioning people back until a circle formed around the wet area of the floor. "This floor is extremely slippery. Do *not* come any closer until we get it cleaned up." The people closest to me backed up a little but didn't have much room to maneuver in the packed room. The giant puddle inched toward the feet of the closest people. Amazingly, people farther away from the accident site continued talking and making merry. Did they not notice the band had stopped playing? They hadn't heard my announcement.

I jogged over to the band. "I need that," I said, pointing to the singer's microphone. "Can I have your attention please?" I tapped the cordless mike, which gave that solid thud indicating it was on. Why was no one listening?

"Look out!" I heard, followed by a chorus of "ows" and "oohs" as another body presumably hit the floor.

I sprinted behind the reception desk, pushed some papers aside, hitched up my skirt, and planted one knee on the mahogany desktop. "Give me a hand please?" I asked the stunned attendant. He mutely watched me hoist my other knee up, then took my hand to steady me as I stood up on the desk, just a tad wobbly in my Gloria Vanderbilt heels. Heads started to turn. Being five-eight had its advantages.

"May I have your attention please?" I said into the mike. This time, the loud chatter quieted to a low rumble. "We've got some water and ice on the floor over here." I pointed to the spill. "It's very slippery so please keep back and give us some space so we can get it cleaned up." As if on cue, a janitor appeared with a mop and bucket. "It will only take a minute, and then don't worry—we'll have more shrimp coming right out!"

People laughed. I saw Maggie and her client at the side of the room. They didn't laugh, but at least the client smiled when Maggie put her hand on his arm and leaned in to say something to him.

"Jazz band, take it away," I said and scrambled down to the tune of "The Girl from Ipanema."

I found Shelby near the side entrance, leading a paramedic to the middle of the room.

"You said you had two injured?" the man asked.

"Another one fell after I called you. I'm not sure what the body count is now." He frowned at her morbid choice of words, but she didn't notice. She spotted me. "Oh, Astrid, do you think you could help me get the hurt people to the caterer's station so they can be looked at—just not in the middle of the party?"

Fifteen minutes later, Shelby and I leaned against the wall of the back room, watching the paramedics wrap ankles and hand out aspirin.

"That was fun," I said, giving her my it-will-all-be-okay smile.

She looked up. "Thank you so much, Astrid. You saved my ass." I raised my eyebrows. "Really, I mean it. Thank you."

I smiled. "You're welcome. And it wasn't so bad, was it? This doesn't even make the list of the *Ten Worst Event Management Mishaps in Boston's History*." Shelby smiled back. "You know what? We should go out for a drink sometime."

Shelby's eyebrows shot up to her hairline. Was it that surprising for me to extend an offer of friendship?

"Um, sure, that would be great," she said.

"Okay. Now, we wait for this to wrap up in thirty minutes," I said, checking my Calvin Klein watch. "Hopefully the animals will have eaten their fill by then."

"Man, I hope they didn't pull the shrimp out of the janitor's bucket like they pulled it out of the caterer's bowl!"

I laughed until my empty stomach ached.

Shelby

CHAPTER 18

Astrid made a beeline for me as I tried to massage the stiffness out of my borrowed mitt.

"Hey Shelby, are you excited to play?" she asked, her TV commercial-ready hair swinging into place as she landed in front of me. We hadn't gone out for drinks in the month since the great shrimp incident—she was probably having the same second thoughts as me. But at least she was friendlier at work, so I didn't have to avoid her.

"Nope, I hate softball. I suck at it. And couldn't the company have waited until winter was over before we held this little outing?" I zipped up my sweatshirt and shivered.

"Softball season officially began weeks ago," Michael said, throwing his arms around me from behind, lifting me off my feet and setting me back down, my tattered Converse All-Stars stirring a tiny dust cloud around my feet. Moving to my front, Michael plopped a blue baseball hat on my head. "So buck up sports fans, and let's play some ball." He trotted off, handing out hats as he moved around the field.

"Do you *really* suck at this?" Astrid asked. "For some reason, I figured you'd be good at sports."

"Nope, not really. In fact, not at all. Totally. Not good." I clamped my eyes shut against the horrible memories of various middle and high school tryouts—softball, basketball and, because I was a glutton for punishment, track—my weak attempts to keep up with my athletic brothers.

"Well, stick with me. I was an all-star," Astrid said.

My eyes popped open. "Really? Literally or figuratively?"

She wrinkled her nose. "Literally, of course. I wouldn't call myself a star to stroke my ego. I was on the league all-star team in high school."

"Okay. I'm sticking with you then. Maybe you can take my turn at bat," I said, following her to a green wooden dugout where Terry, Jim, and Brad huddled over a clipboard.

"That works," Terry said, straightening up. "Everyone gather round so I can tell you which team you're on," he shouted to the people scattered around the field, some warming up and others talking and laughing.

"Terry," I said, tugging on the partner's sleeve. "Can I be on Astrid's team?"

A loud laugh made me look up to see Brad staring at me. The sun disappeared behind a huge gray cloud, darkening his clear light eyes to a sexy deep blue.

"Everyone wants to be on Astrid's team, right Astrid? She's the golden girl of Campbell Lewis after all," he said, his gaze wandering to Astrid.

She ignored him, turning away while tossing a softball a foot in the air and catching it in her mitt without even looking.

Terry, consulting his clipboard, reeled off the names on his red team and Jim's blue team to a chorus of cheers and groans from my colleagues.

"What about Brad?" someone yelled.

"I'm not playing because I'm umping," Brad replied. "It's a dirty job, but someone's got to do it. Terry can handle the Reds without me. But my condolences to those of you on Jim's team," he said, looking right at me and Astrid. "I may be an impartial umpire, but I'm pretty sure you guys are going to get your asses kicked."

"That's right," Kristy said, stepping so close to Brad their arms brushed, a red hat perched on her black, spiral permed hair. "We are going to crush the Blues!"

"Maybe not. We have a ringer on our team," I challenged her, my mouth suddenly dry. Astrid's head shook in my peripheral vision but my mouth kept going. "Our golden girl's got a golden glove, and we're going to kick your team's butt."

"Them's fightin' words, Shelby, but I like your spunk," Brad said in a fake Southern twang. He and Kristy laughed as my face warmed against the cool breeze, unsure if they were laughing with me or at me.

"You worked for Brad for a while," I said, as Astrid and I walked to the blue team's dugout. "Is it just me or is he kind of a jerk? I can't always tell if he's being sarcastic or not."

"Shhh, someone might hear you," she warned. We sat at the far end of the bench, and she leaned in toward me. "But yes, I think he's a jerk. I can't believe no one else sees it."

"Well, it is hard seeing past his good looks. He's obviously the best-looking guy at the agency." I looked at Brad stretching by the backstop. "And that bod," I said, waiting for Astrid to agree.

But she just stared straight ahead at the field where Michael tapped the doughnut off a bat and strode to home plate.

"Batter up!" shouted Brad.

Michael got onto first base right away, but the next three people grounded out. I breathed a sigh of relief. I was at the end of the batting order, so maybe I wouldn't have to bat for a while.

I jogged to right field, which I had requested as the position where I would least embarrass myself. Jim struck out two batters—he wasn't that good a pitcher, but the batters on the Red team seemed to swing at anything. Either they were sucking up to the partner or they were as bad as I was. Karen, the third batter, hit a grounder to Tom at shortstop who zipped it to Astrid at first base. Astrid plucked the slightly high ball out of the air and landed elegantly on first base seconds before Karen crossed it.

As our team cheered, I jogged to the dugout thinking maybe I would survive the game after all.

Four innings later, right field had stayed blissfully quiet, but I'd struck out twice.

"Don't worry, Shelby," Astrid said when her next at-bat came. "I'll make up for it," she tossed over her shoulder as she headed toward the batter's box. She crouched stylishly over home plate and wiggled the top of her bat in the air. Right as Terry pitched the softball, Astrid's stance shifted, and she whiffed the bat in the air a full two seconds after the ball crossed the plate.

"Striiiiiike," Brad yelled.

After hitting a few foul balls and then striking out, Astrid stomped back to the dugout and slumped beside me.

"Hey, sports fans," I said, mimicking Michael, "you've got a lot to be proud of. Just gotta keep the ball in the lines next time."

"It was Brad," she seethed so only I heard. "Was he making fun of you when you batted? Is that why you struck out?"

"No, I struck out because I stink," I said. Realizing she was actually upset, I changed my tune. "He probably didn't think he needed to psyche me out. But don't worry about it. You know how guys are. They're always pulling that shit. If you had brothers, you'd understand," I said, nodding.

She shrugged and sat there frowning.

"How about if I accidentally hit him in the face with my bat next time I'm up? Let's see," I said, closing one eye and peering at the batter's box through a circle made by my thumb and forefinger. "Yup, when he scooches down, he's at just the right height for my bat to clock him. Everyone knows I don't know what I'm doing out there. It would be totally believable."

Astrid kept staring at the pitcher's mound, but she laughed, and her shoulders relaxed. Her laughter petered out as she turned to me. "You are joking, right? You know you can't hit him. Although that would be great fodder for an article called *Ten Easy Ways to Torpedo Your Career*."

I scoffed. "You know I can't hit anything when I try. Not even his big head."

An hour later, the game thankfully was called when lightning threatened in the distance, but not after Astrid smashed her way onto base every time after that, with a few singles and a triple. And when Jim complained he was too old and his shoulder hurt, she replaced him as pitcher and did an awesome job, striking out a bunch of batters and snagging two line drives.

"Well, see you later Astrid. That was fun," I said as I dropped my mitt into the huge canvas bag Michael held open.

"Wait," she said. "We haven't gone out for drinks yet. Want to get one now?"

I chewed my lip, wondering how to get out of this. Tina and I were meeting up, and Tina had only heard bad things from me about Astrid. She knew the basics of the shrimp affair, as we called it, but I hadn't mentioned things warming up between Astrid and me because I wasn't one hundred percent sure they would stay that way.

"Ohhh, I'm actually meeting a friend. Too bad. Maybe next time?"

"Next time what—next time we have a company outing? Like months or even a year from now?" She smirked like she was joking, but her tone was flat, and her eyes looked down.

Guilt tweaked my Grinch-like heart.

"Well okay, why don't you come too? But didn't you say you live near here? Why don't you go home and change and then meet us?"

Astrid's eyes ran up and down my old gray sweatshirt and baggy navy sweatpants, and a smile touched her lips. "I think I'm okay. Let's go!" she said, her voice back to normal.

She spun around on her designer sneakers, and I sighed to the back of her color-coordinated baseball shirt and track pants.

***

"So you're the famous Astrid. The Ice Qu—"

I glared at Tina. The three of us stood in the entry of a Brighton bar Tina said *The Boston Globe* rated up and coming. My attempt to telepathically warn Tina that Astrid was coming and that she was actually kind of nice had failed.

Astrid cocked her head at Tina. "The what? Go ahead. What do you call me?" Her shoulders twitched almost imperceptibly, but her face was impossible to read.

"Um, Astrid, Queen of the Icy Shrimp Bowl?" Tina asked, looking to me for validation.

Astrid raised an eyebrow at me. "Really? That's what you call me?"

"I told Tina how you saved my butt at the Franklin Plaza reception. So we thought it was a fitting title." As Astrid turned back to Tina, I grimaced at Tina.

"Hm," Astrid said. "Not a bad title, I guess. Are you going to get me a sash that says that?"

Tina laughed.

"Yeah, and a tiara made of oyster shells." she said, gently elbowing Astrid.

They laughed together. "Don't forget the scepter with a giant shrimp on top," I mumbled, turning away and moving toward an empty booth, fake laughing while actually grimacing to myself. Which made me laugh for real.

As we settled into the booth, them on one side and me on the other, the mingled odors of greasy chicken, onions, and beer called to me, and I knew I would spend some hard-earned cash on restaurant food before the night ended.

"So, Astrid," Tina jumped right in after we ordered drinks, "how old are you?"

"I'll be twenty-five in May."

"Really? I thought you were older than that," I said.

"No doubt because of my immense wisdom and highly professional demeanor," she said in a neutral tone.

Tina and I stared at each other.

"I'm kidding! Come on, you don't think my head is that big, do you?" Astrid exclaimed.

I hesitated. Tina's boot skimmed my shin under the table.

"No, of course we knew. That you were kidding, I mean. Right, Tina?"

"Of course." She looked at Astrid. "So, where are you from?" The waitress plunked our drinks on the table, causing Astrid's martini to dribble down the outside of the glass. Tina repeated her question while Astrid wiped up the spillage with a napkin from the booth's dispenser.

"I grew up in Maine."

"Huh. You look so cosmopolitan. You must have been the classiest person there. Or at least in your town."

I rolled my eyes at Tina's assumption, but Astrid took it in stride.

"Oh no, it wasn't like that. Other than being good at softball, I was just a regular kid like everyone else."

"Come on, you must have been prom queen, head cheerleader and all that," Tina persisted. "'Most Popular' in the yearbook?"

Astrid took a sudden interest in her drink, stirring it with the miniature plastic sword. She hoisted the sword to her mouth and pulled off the impaled olive with her lips, which she slowly chewed and swallowed.

"Well, my mother and I moved a few times, so I never really got integrated into one particular group of friends," she said.

"That's your whole family? Just you and your mother? No brothers or sisters or cousins or—"

"Not everyone has a huge extended Italian family like you, Tina," I pointed out.

"Yeah, it's just me and my mom against the world," Astrid said, taking a big gulp of her martini.

"But where did you grow up? You didn't say where in Maine."

"In a town I'm sure you've never heard of." She pushed the three-quarter-length sleeves of her baseball shirt up over her elbows, then tugged them back down again.

"Try me. I've been to Maine a bunch of times," Tina said.

I watched them talk, fascinated. I'd never seen Astrid uncomfortable before. She spoke in the same flat tone she'd used at the softball field. Tina wasn't picking up the signals.

Astrid sighed. "Like I said, it was a few towns—"

"Okay, that's a boring subject. Let's talk about men or something," I said, wadding up the straw wrapper from my vodka and soda and throwing it at Tina, who shrugged. Astrid took another sip of her drink.

"Are you guys dating anyone?" she asked us.

"Negative," I said. "At least not me. Tina goes through dates so fast it makes my head spin." I fake smiled at Tina, who threw my straw wrapper back at me. "How about you?" I asked Astrid.

She smiled. "I've been dating this guy Francois for almost a year. We have one of those on-again off-again romances, but things are good right now."

"What does he do for work?" Tina asked in a robotic tone that suggested it was the first of many questions on a long list. I sat back, enjoying someone else being on the receiving end of her inquisition for a change.

"He's an investment banker at a big firm on Congress Street."

Tina nodded approval. "Where does he live?"

"In a condo in the North End."

"His own? He doesn't rent it?"

"Correct," Astrid said, giving me a sidelong half-smile.

Tina raised her eyebrow and nodded.

"How old?"

"Twenty-eight."

"Personality?"

"Hey, let's play a game," I interrupted. "I used to do this in high school with my friend Annie. We'd rate the guys in our class on things like face, body, brains, personality—"

"Sense of humor," Tina contributed.

"Face, body," Astrid said, laughing.

"Income," Tina said.

"Okay, let's have a warm-up. Rate that guy in the red shirt and jeans at the bar," I suggested. "What do you give him for face?"

"Seven," said Tina.

"Six," said Astrid at the same time.

"And I'll go with six. Not really my type. Okay, what about his body?"

"Nine all the way. He's solid," Tina rated.

"Hmm, I'll go with a seven. He looks like he works out, but he's soft around the edges. See that little gut hanging over his belt?" Astrid said.

"He's way too beefy for me. I like my men slender but muscular," I said.

"Ick, that means wiry, and that just sounds grody to me. Wiry," Tina said, like the word itself was nasty. "I like my men big and strong, and preferably in a suit and tie."

"Ugh, no, I hate business suits—on men *and* women!" I cried. "Give me a tan, slender man in faded jeans any day. And with no shirt." I wiggled my eyebrows at them.

"There is absolutely no chance of you two ever falling for the same guy." Astrid laughed.

"Back to the guy at the bar—"

"We can't go any further because we don't know his personality. I suppose we could watch him and guess," Tina offered.

"No, let's do someone else. Astrid, want to rate Francois?"

"That's easy, ten on all counts," she said, so smugly that Tina and I made fake gagging noises and laughed at her. Astrid shrugged, nonplussed. "You can laugh, but if I think he's a ten, then that's all that matters."

"Okay, but let's break it down," I challenged her. "Face?"

"Ten." She pulled her wallet out of her pocketbook and a photo from the wallet. Smirking, she showed it to us.

"Wow," Tina said.

"I remember him, from the office that time! Definite ten," I confirmed.

"Okay, he's a ten for face. Body?"

"Also a ten. No wait, a nine. He's in amazing shape, but I wouldn't mind if he were an inch or two taller."

"A chink in the armor," I said suspiciously, like a private investigator. "Watch out for Tina now. She's going to start telling you he's not good enough for you."

"What are you talking about, Shel? He sounds awesome so far," Tina said, shaking her head at me. "Intelligence?" she asked Astrid.

"Again, a nine or ten. He's extremely smart. So smart, sometimes I feel inferior."

"Please. I doubt that," I said. "What about sense of humor?"

Astrid scrunched up her mouth. "I guess a six. He can be fun and loving, but sometimes we don't get each other's jokes. I think it's the French thing."

"He's actually from France?" Tina asked. "We need to add a category for exotic-ness or something."

"How about we just consider that bonus points?" I suggested. "Now, Astrid, what's your overall rating for Francois?"

She tucked his photo back into her wallet and took forever putting the wallet back into her pocketbook.

"If I'm being honest," she said in a lowered voice, leaning in, "a seven or maybe even a six."

"That math doesn't add up. How can he score so high on everything else but average that low?" I asked.

"It's hard to explain. I love being with him. But sometimes when I try to envision our future, with successful careers, maybe a family, I have a hard time seeing it. I always end up in an apron pulling a pie out of the oven while he comes home from work, loosens his tie, and asks me what's for dinner."

Tina and I cracked up but stopped when we looked at Astrid. Her sad eyes suggested she was totally serious. She sucked on her martini again.

"Leeettttt's talk about how great I was at the softball game," I said to fill the silence.

"Okay, was it fun? Who won?" I could tell Tina wasn't interested, but at least she took the hint to change the subject.

"I was abominable, and Astrid was amazing."

Astrid peeked up from the rim of her martini glass, her eyes smiling at me.

"Seriously, Tina, she's a softball star. I thought she'd look like a baby giraffe out there with those long legs and all," I joked, "but she was quite elegant," I added in a stiff British accent.

Astrid put down the drink. "Baby giraffe? Really?"

"Yeah, but then you surprised me. You run more like an antelope. Fast and graceful. A gazelle. A springbok even," I rambled. "A springbok in her Reeboks."

"You should have stopped at gazelle, Shel." Tina laughed. "What the hell is a springbok?"

"I'm pretty sure it's a species of gazelle."

"You must be some animal lover to know what a springbok is," Astrid said.

"Oh she is," Tina jumped in. "Just don't ask about her dog Tramp though. It's a very sensitive subject."

"Do tell, sounds fascinating," Astrid said, turning to Tina like they were conspiring against me.

Tina backtracked. "I shouldn't have said that. It really does upset Shelby. Forget it."

"No, it's okay," I said, squinting at Tina. I turned to Astrid. "Tramp was my dog growing up. We got him as a puppy when I was six. He was a yellow lab and the best dog ever," I intoned like the story bored me. "He was my best friend, sometimes my only friend, and I wanted to take him to college with me, but my mother wouldn't let me. And then in my junior year, he died. I didn't get to say good-bye or bury him or anything." My monotone wavered at the end, and I gulped from my glass.

"I'm sorry for bringing it up, Shelby," Tina said.

Thankfully, the waitress swung by with another round of drinks.

"Thought you ladies might like another round," she said to no one in particular.

"Her tip just went up," I mumbled.

"I'm glad you told me about Tramp," Astrid said, making my moist eyes widen and my heart cramp. "Because now I see that Shelby Stewart isn't as tough as everyone thinks. It's nice to know you're human." She smiled like she meant it.

I sat up straighter. "Me? Tough?" I gave a short, skeptical laugh.

"Okay, maybe not tough. But smart. And talented. That might be one reason I didn't like you at work for so long." I dropped my chin and peered up at her under raised eyebrows. She shrugged. "Hey, blame it on my mother. She always warned me that every woman at work is competition. And I saw early on that you'd be moving up the ladder quickly."

Warmth seeped through my gut at this bizarre compliment.

"Well," I said, raising my drink, "here's to dead workplace rivalries."

"*À votre santé*," Astrid said as we all clicked glasses.

Astrid

CHAPTER 19

I rolled my shoulders back and knocked on the door of the condo. I knew I couldn't completely control what happened next, but I had completely controlled the preparatory phase, and I was ready. I'd resorted to analyzing my relationship with Francois as a business challenge because looking at it emotionally never gave me clear guidance on what to do. So, building on Shelby's rating game, I thoroughly weighed the pros, cons, risks, and opportunities of staying with Francois and of breaking up with him. I concluded that the risk of him expecting me to be a happy housewife was high, and the opportunity for me to find someone better suited to me diminished with each day I remained with Francois.

"Why didn't you use your key, *ma cherie*?" Francois asked, swinging the door wide.

"Because it's your key now," I said, standing my ground as his eyebrows knit together.

He leaned against the doorjamb and cleared his throat. "Go on."

"You're a wonderful man, Francois, and I adore you in so many ways. But I don't think we want the same things out of life."

His eyes bored into me, making heat rise in my face. I looked away.

"So I am breaking up with you. I'm sorry." We stood in silence for twenty seconds. I rubbed my thumb along the key in my hand, so small and naked once detached from its partners on my key ring.

His voice when he finally spoke was tight but controlled. "That's it? No discussion? You're calling all the shots on this?"

I nodded and looked at him. A vein throbbed in his neck.

"I'm sorry," I repeated. "And this means I won't be able to go to the black-tie function at your company on Friday. I'm sorry it's such short notice."

He sniffed and tossed his head. "I am not concerned with that. There are plenty of fish in the sea, and I'm told I'm quite the catch."

"Yes, you are."

"Then why are you doing this?"

"I told you. I have a different vision of my life and career than you do. You'd only be disappointed if we stayed together."

"*Your* vision. I had a vision too, Astrid. In my vision, we lived happily ever after, based here in Boston, maybe a small mansion in the suburbs, holidays in France, you managing our household, which of course would include several beautiful children, maybe writing books on the side."

He looked at me, waiting for me to change my mind. I shook my head.

He sighed. "I loved you, Astrid, and you're throwing away something very special."

"I'm sure you'll meet someone else in no time. Probably before me," I said.

"I'm sure I will. But I hope I never see you with anyone else because that will be very hard for me."

I waited, but he said nothing else. "So."

"So," he echoed. I pressed the key into his palm and pulled my hand back quickly when the warmth of his touch threatened my resolve. I studied my handsome boyfriend for the last time. The tight lines of his steely mouth were betrayed by eyes soft and touched with pain.

"Good bye, Francois."

"Good bye, Astrid."

I turned away. As I stepped toward the elevator, his final "*Adieu, ma cherie,*" followed me like a whisper on the wind.

***

"How did it go?" Shelby asked as I sank into Tina's tacky turquoise couch a few hours later.

"According to plan. No muss, no fuss. I prepared more than I did for my college finals," I answered, pulling a scrunchy off my wrist and smoothing my hair into a high ponytail.

"Wow. I cannot believe how calm you are," Tina said. "I'm always a mess in a break-up. Shelby too."

Shelby nodded and shrugged.

"You know, I'd pictured so many variations on the scene in my head before I went over there, that the real thing was decidedly anti-climactic. I was sure he'd have some kind of emotional outburst, some hot-blooded European spurned-lover reaction or something, but no. He was as calm as I was. I'm sure he'll be over me in no time."

"Are you sure you're over him?" Shelby asked.

I nodded. "We've broken up so many times, and each time I went back, I had more doubts." I swallowed over an unexpected and unpleasant lump in my throat. "It was time." My cheeks tickled annoyingly. "Oh my God, it's really over." I gasped as a single tear trickled down my face. "Did I do the right thing?"

"The Ice Queen melteth," Shelby whispered to Tina.

I stared at Shelby as she fidgeted, looking anywhere except at me. Her discomfort amused me.

"Sorry, shouldn't have said that," she said to the ceiling.

I giggled. They looked at me blankly. I giggled again, emotion bubbling out of me like effervescence from a champagne bottle.

"Is she getting hysterical?" Shelby said to Tina, not bothering to whisper this time.

"I don't know. Astrid, are you getting hysterical?"

I swallowed a new giggle and swiped my cheeks with my hand. "No, I'm fine. I'm so happy you guys are my friends." A last tiny sob escaped from my treacherous throat.

"Oh, Astrid, we're glad too," Tina said, patting my hand.

"Sounds to me then like it's time to celebrate instead of commiserate!" Shelby said, picking up the wine bottle and corkscrew from the table.

"Okay then!" I agreed. "Because yes, I'm fine," I repeated. "I'm actually excited to date someone new. But now I really need to get to the gym and get in shape so I look perfect when I meet the next guy," I said while Shelby popped the cork and poured three glasses of red wine.

Shelby rolled her eyes. "Come on, Astrid, you know you look amazing. How much weight could you even lose before disappearing?"

"She's right," Tina said. "You don't need to lose a pound."

"You guys don't know," I countered. "You don't see me naked, or in a bathing suit."

"Oh my God," Shelby moaned in apparent frustration. "You have no idea what it's like to be fat."

I looked at Tina who scrunched up her mouth and looked away.

"And you do?" I asked Shelby.

"Shel," Tina said, leaning forward and peering into Shelby's eyes. "Is it time?" she said mock-seriously. "Is it time to initiate Astrid into the things-you-only-tell-your-best-friends club?" Shelby squinted at Tina. "Come on, I've already told her about my alcoholic mother. Time to reveal your deep dark secret," Tina said cajolingly.

"Tina," Shelby cautioned, still squinting.

"You know," Tina stage-whispered slowly to Shelby, "the fat phase."

My eyes opened wide. "What? You were fat? When? How?" I asked as Francois faded into the background of my mind. "Not that it's a big deal, and I'm sure it wasn't that bad," I added as Shelby's face registered mortification. "You don't have to talk about it, if you don't want to."

Tina looked at Shelby and tilted her head toward me in encouragement. Shelby sighed.

"Fine. Let's re-live my fat phase, if it will make you feel better." She squirmed in her seat and tugged at the waist of her jeans as if she were gaining weight just talking about it.

Tina and I re-settled in our seats and faced her like avid students.

"So I was about twenty pounds heavier, off and on, in college."

"Oh my God, and you're only what, five two?" I exclaimed.

"That's right. Thanks for driving the point home." She rubbed her forehead as she talked.

"But how did you lose it? You look so good now."

"I came up with two rules that work for me," Shelby said, warming up to the topic. "Maybe you should take notes, Astrid. You can write an article called *Two Easy and Effective Ways to Lose Weight*."

I nodded in approval of the idea, even though she was joking.

"First, I stopped dieting. Completely. I tried every diet over those few years, and I'd keep the weight off for a while, but it always came back. So instead, I would be really good for two or three days and then have a normal day. That way, I didn't pig out on my normal day. I just ate regular meals and even a dessert if I wanted to." Shelby finished her wine and held the glass out for Tina to refill.

"Now do tip number two," Tina encouraged as she poured.

"The second trick was to tell myself the chocolate-chip cookie I wanted today would still be there tomorrow, on my normal day, if I could wait a little longer. That got me through my cravings. Sometimes I didn't even care about the cookie the next day. I still use that technique today."

"Fascinating," I said, taking mental notes and seriously wondering if I could turn this into an article for a women's magazine.

"Yeah, great," Shelby deadpanned. "I'm glad you all get so much pleasure and enjoyment from my pain."

Tina stood and clapped her hands. "Okay, after that successful distraction, it's now time for our movie. Drink up, and let's go. The movie's at eight fifteen, and Shelby hates missing the beginning. Chop chop."

Part 2

Astrid

CHAPTER 20

"Get in, get in," Tina urged, picking Shelby and me up in front of Campbell Lewis at five o'clock on the third Friday in June. "I can't double-park for long; there's a cop right there."

We piled into her Chevy Citation—nicknamed the Situation because it broke down on a regular basis—and joined the hordes of city workers fleeing to Cape Cod, plugging along toward ocean breezes, warm sand and fresher air than the city could ever provide. The horrendous drive took ninety minutes longer than it should have, but I was young and single and headed for adventure on a beautiful island with my girlfriends, so I didn't care.

We settled into seats on the top deck of the Woods Hole/Martha's Vineyard ferry, determined to soak up as much of the unseasonably hot sun as possible.

"You guyyyys, are we going to try to get lucky this weekend?" Tina asked, like a child considering doing something naughty behind her mother's back.

"I think it's mandatory," Shelby said in her matter-of-fact way. "Astrid?"

"God knows we all need it! This drought has to end," I said. Shelby nodded in approval.

"Listen, I have to say something serious. We must use condoms," Tina said like a high school sex-ed teacher. Shelby and I giggled. "I mean it. Have you been following this AIDS thing? It's spreading to women now."

"Of course I've read about it," I said. "As long we don't sleep with gay men or drug addicts, we should be okay." Tina glared. "But okay, we'll make sure any guys we sleep with wear condoms. Right, Shel?" Shelby nodded.

"We're so crass. We sound like guys," Tina said, a tinge of pride in her voice.

"Oh no we don't," I countered. "We could never sound like guys. Men are truly a different species. It's hard to know what they really want, from life *and* from us. I should write a book called *What Men Could Tell Us to Make Us Better Girlfriends*."

"Hm. Or how about, *What Women Don't Know About Men and Never Thought to Ask?*" Shelby offered.

Tina attempted to join in. "*What Women Don't Know About Men but Really Want to Know?*"

"Not exactly catchy, Tina, but keep trying," I said, laughing with Shelby. "Try this one: *What Women Don't Even Know They Don't Know About Men.* No, wait—*What Women Don't Really Need to Know About Men, Even Though They Think They Should*—"

"—and *What They Need to Know but Don't Have A Clue They Need to Know, Never Mind How to Ask*," Shelby finished.

Our laughs drew disapproving looks from the people next to us, which made us laugh harder.

I sighed that end-of-a-good-laugh sigh. "Why do I feel like our IQs just dropped twenty points?"

"That's okay. We're at the beach. Who needs an IQ?" Shelby asked.

We checked into the quaint old hotel I'd booked for us in Oak Bluffs, which was my treat because I made more money than Shelby and Tina did. After showering and changing, which took twenty minutes longer than it should have because Tina insisted on de-frizzing her humidity-enhanced curls, we walked to the center of town.

I quickly realized I was overdressed in my navy mini-dress and flat silver sandals. Tina and Shelby wore more appropriate shorts with somewhat dressy tops, although Tina's looked like something a grandmother would wear. Luckily for her, the guys would be checking out her almond-shaped green eyes or her strong, tan legs.

The novelty and number of restaurants and stores on Circuit Avenue bombarded my senses. We stopped in the souvenir and clothing shops, bypassed the lure of the ice cream parlor and fudge shop with their inviting burnt sugar smells, and noted the locations of the bars and dance clubs for later. Other than the occasional screaming child with frazzled parent in tow, everyone we passed was smiling and content. The Vineyard was a happy place.

Horseshoes and *Hand Grenades*

At one point, I waited on the sidewalk while Tina and Shelby rifled through a T-shirt shop exactly the same as the last three we'd been in. By the time they came out, I was smiling like a Cheshire cat, and not alone.

"This is Big Bill, you guys. He's going to show us the best clubs," I said, motioning toward Bill who—with his close-cropped blonde hair, ruddy cheeks, and slight beer belly—looked like he belonged in a lumberyard not on the Vineyard. Bill was instantly, obviously besotted with Tina, so while they got acquainted, I leaned toward Shelby. "He's going to get us some coke," I whispered.

Shelby's eyes lit up. "You do coke?" she whispered back. "I thought you didn't do drugs."

"I don't like pot, because it makes my brain fuzzy—"

"Which is exactly why I like it," Shelby interrupted.

"—but cocaine makes me sharper. Francois and I did it a few times, and I liked it more than he did."

Tina grabbed my arm, pulling us back into her conversation. "You're not so big, Bill, what's up with the name?" Tina teased.

"People call me that because of my big personality." He winked. "Come on, this way," he said. "Let's go meet the guys." Shelby and I exchanged hopeful looks.

"This is Ralphie and Carney," Bill said, as we squeezed into a car a few blocks away.

Ralphie, despite the 1960s sitcom name, was an extremely hot, blonde surfer dude, out from California for the summer. Carney, born and bred on the island, was attractive in a long-haired, fuzzy sort of way. Not my type, but Shelby couldn't stop staring at him.

Bill cut up lines while Ralphie rolled a ten-dollar bill. They cracked jokes left and right, making us comfortable right away, other than the illegal drugs giving Tina the shivers when she glanced around for cops every five minutes.

"Hey," Shelby said to Carney, "did you ever think of starting a band? Because Carney and Ralphie would be a great name for a band."

Carney glanced at Shelby, his eyebrows drawn together, and turned his attention back to the line of coke in front of him.

"Vineyard Coke's not a bad name, either," she said, drumming her fingers on her leg.

I widened my eyes and shook my head at her, but she missed my signal to stop with the band names thing. When the last line had been snorted, Shel and I wiped the powder from our noses and followed our new guides to the Lampost. Between the coke and the island air, I felt decidedly giddy.

The club smelled fusty, suggesting the ocean breezes never made it up the hill from the harbor and into the second story room. But the smell of heat and mild sweat pulsating off the dance floor soon dispersed the fustiness, or maybe I got used to it. The DJ played all the newest hits, and Ralphie and I danced whenever we weren't lost in ninety-mile-per-hour conversation at the bar. When the club closed, we jumped in the available cars and drove "up island" to West Tisbury where Ralphie and Carney were throwing an impromptu party at the house they rented.

The house, a throwback to the sixties, was adorned with shag rugs and bad paneling on the walls. I half-expected to see a beaded curtain in the doorway. A wraparound deck surrounded the place, although the only view was of the woods enveloping the house. Unlike at the Lampost, the ocean air clearly had no problem permeating this building, where a salt-infused dampness seeped from the furniture.

A dozen or so people were swilling beer, making cocktails, smoking pot, or doing lines. I felt surprisingly at home in this somewhat seedy environment. I'm sure the alcohol and cocaine contributed to my lowered standard. But the people were refreshing. Unlike in the Boston bars, people here didn't care about status, so there were no awkward moments when you tried to gauge if your career position made you desirable or threatening to the person you were speaking with. Everyone was equal on the Vineyard.

After a few more lines, Ralphie invited me to his room. I felt positively decadent jumping into bed so quickly, but all rules of decorum melted away on the island. I left Shelby doing shots with Carney and strolled willingly into my summer of love.

Shelby

CHAPTER 21

I saw Astrid and Ralphie sneak into his bedroom, looking like Malibu Ken and Barbie with their blonde hair and golden tans.

The sun was coming up when Carney led me to his bedroom, me practically high-fiving myself behind his back. Everyone said Carney was a total sleaze, but he was so cute, I didn't care. Cheap sex with Carney seemed the perfect way to cap off my first night on the Vineyard.

An hour later, I heard someone yelling through the house. "Will's leaving for Oak Bluffs if anyone wants a ride." I groaned and rolled out from under Carney's heavy arm.

"I should probably go," I said.

Carney snored.

Someone was actually brewing coffee in the kitchen as Tina, Astrid, and I left.

"That smells so good," Tina said inhaling.

"All I can smell is stale beer, tequila, and marijuana roaches," I said, rubbing my throbbing forehead.

"Got a headache, Shel? You should. You were soooo tanked last night," Tina said. I stared at her in a daze and couldn't tell if she was impressed or appalled. Was her hair actually brushed? And was that fresh makeup? I shook my head, immediately regretting it because it aggravated my headache.

Will waited in the driveway next to a rusty van, jiggling his keys. I hadn't noticed him before—or maybe he was in that group I did lines with on the deck—I couldn't remember. He was about five-foot-nine, Italian-looking, straight but shaggy black hair reaching his collar, a shadow of stubble on his face, and an adorable lopsided smile. Jeans, sneakers, and a T-shirt completed his rumpled island look.

"Who's this?" I cried as a small yellow Lab jumped out of the van.

"This is Pilsener," Will said proudly.

Astrid made a face behind Will's back and grinned. She knew how much I hated it when people named their pets after alcohol. I mean, I loved dogs, and I loved alcohol, but how hard was it to be a bit more creative when naming a pet?

"He's so cute," I said, playing with Pilsener's ears and burying my face in his fur.

"Come on, in the back," Will demanded. I moved toward the van's rear door.

"Not you," he said, cocking his head. "The dog. You can sit in front with me, like a person."

"I knew that," I said as Tina and Astrid smirked at each other.

I rose above my hangover to bond with Will over dog talk during the short ride to town. He dropped us at the hotel and promised to pick us up in the morning to take us to the best beach ever.

"Wait, when did he say he was coming back?" Tina asked, her voice as fuzzy as my head.

"In the morning. Pay attention," I said, pressing on my temples.

"It's already morning, nitwits," Astrid said. "It's seven o'clock."

"Hmph," I said, trudging my sorry, detoxing ass up the stairs and falling on the bed.

Five hours later, the phone in the room rang. Will was in the lobby and, apparently, it was officially morning, Vineyard time.

As Will drove us along Seaview Avenue, the isthmus connecting Oak Bluffs and Edgartown, Astrid gloated.

"No commoners' State Beach for us," she said. "We're beaching it with the locals."

Will turned to me and chuckled.

South Beach was a fantasy come true. Four guys were pushing a big box onto the sand. A generator, Will said, to power a stereo and the blenders people brought to mix frozen drinks. Coolers and even a half-keg dotted the sand. Grills were lit for barbecuing, and small groups of people disappeared into massive man-made pits dug for wind-free sunbathing. There were even two couches—one a dull blue, the other some nasty shade of beige.

South Beach became a party house before my eyes. The only thing missing was the bathroom, but there were Port-A-Potties in the parking lot for that.

The crazy atmosphere, the loud music, and the grinding of blenders yanked me out of my sleepy haze by my armpits. We picked up where the party left off last night. For about an hour. Then I snuck off to the edges of the madness with Tina. We joined Astrid and Ralphie in one of the pits, and I crashed back into sleep just as my headache threatened to come back.

"Wake up, angels. Time to hit Rachel's."

I opened my eyes and blocked the sun with my hand. Big Bill stood peering down at us. Immediately, I wanted to cover myself, but then I remembered I was at my good weight. I even had a decent tan for someone with Scottish ancestry.

"Ralphie, let's go," Bill said, nudging his friend with his foot. Ralphie lay beside Astrid, whose skin had turned the color of a perfectly toasted marshmallow right before it catches fire. "Will's waiting for us in the parking lot."

"How do you guys keep up this pace every weekend?" Tina groaned to Bill as we left the beach with sticky eyes and salty skin.

"Wait, I know," I said. "Party all night and morning, sleep on the beach during the day, and start over again in the afternoon. Is that the formula, Bill?"

He belly laughed. "Sounds about right."

"Can we please get food?" Tina begged.

"Not yet," Ralphie chimed in. "First we stop at Rachel's for the island's best Mudslide."

So we dragged our Coppertone butts into the van. My thighs burned on the vinyl seat so hot it felt gooey. While we drove, I considered our mis-matched trio: tall Tina in a terrycloth cover-up and wide-brimmed hat, taller Astrid in gold sandals and a long gauzy shirt, and short me—as usual the most underdressed—in jean cut-offs and a tank top. Sometimes I didn't understand how we'd become such good friends.

At Rachel's, Sun God Ralphie and Sun Goddess Astrid dawdled in the parking lot to nuzzle and enter a sun-worshipping pact while the heat waved around them. The rest of us dove into the slightly cooler bar and ordered our first round. I groaned as the icy brown Mudslide wet my parched, salty lips and cooled my hot, tired throat. It lived up to the hype.

"So, Shelby, tell me about yourself," Will said, leaning on the bar next to me as Suzanne Vega's new single "Luka" played over the sound system.

"I live in Chelsea, and I work in Boston. That's it. Me in a nutshell." I downed some more Mudslide.

"Chelsea?" he said with his lopsided smile. "I live in Charlestown. We're practically neighbors."

"You're not an islander?" I asked, trying not to sound disappointed.

"Being an islander is more a state of mind than a geography thing," Will said.

"Oh, good, then maybe I'll qualify someday."

"And what do you do in Boston?"

"I work at a PR agency. We have a lot of real estate clients—boring, I know."

"No, it's not boring," he said.

"What do you do?" I asked, to change the subject.

"Well, I'm a builder, so I do some jobs here and around Charlestown. You know, whatever comes along. Here, let me order another round," he said, brushing my arm as he reached past me to get the bartender's attention. I didn't pull back.

***

July 5, 1987

Dear Shelby,

I tried calling you many times, but your roommate always says you're not there, so I am writing this letter. Typing on the word processor takes some getting used to, but at least you won't have to deal with my chicken scrawl.

Something exciting happened at work last week. A girl came running into my classroom screaming, "There's a fire in the bathroom." I went in, and flames were shooting up from a plastic wastebasket, which had a large hole burned in the bottom. Since it wouldn't fit in the sinks or the hoppers, I chucked it out the window. My colleagues have promised me a fireman's hat. Isn't that funny?

I wish you would come home. We missed you on the 4th of July, and Memorial Day before that. I've never gone this long without seeing you. I wanted to drive to Boston and see you, but Eric told me to give you space.

I don't sense that he knows about your charges against Norman, but he does love you very much, as I do.

I've thought about your last visit many times. All these months later, my hand still feels the touch of your cheek, and my ears still echo with my sharp words to you. I am so sorry about both, but even mothers have a limit to the emotional beating they can endure. I don't know why I reacted so violently when you said you didn't respect me. I will always respect you, and I feel in my heart that you will always respect me.

I talked to Norman again, and he remembered doing what you said. He said one night you seemed troubled, and he stroked your belly to help you relax, and that he kissed you goodnight on the lips, like family does sometimes. Maybe he shouldn't have done those things, but his intentions were good.

I hope you can see that, and I hope your job is going well.
Love,
Mom

***

I tossed the letter in my desk drawer at home, where I threw all the miscellaneous junk I thought I might need again someday, even though I usually never did. I stared at my desk for a minute, chewing my lip. Then I sat down and wrote a note back.

***

July 9, 1987
Mom,
It happened more than once, and it happened in more than one place.
I'm away every weekend this summer, but maybe I'll see you at Thanksgiving.
Love,
Shelby

Astrid

CHAPTER 22

"I can't believe it's over," Tina whined, but we didn't complain about her whining for once because we shared the sentiment. After spending virtually every weekend on the island for ten weeks, our glorious Vineyard summer had officially ended. Labor Day had come and gone.

The gloomy air of the grungy graffiti-covered Pour House where we slumped in our booth only intensified the contrast between the recent past and the much less glamorous present.

"Astrid, come on, we need a book or article title to memorialize this," Shelby said.

"I'm too depressed to think of one," I said, staring into my light beer.

"At least we can dry out now. I drank more beer this summer than in all four years of college," Tina said, grimacing at her Heineken.

"Dry out? Why would you want to do that? It's not like our lives are ending," Shelby said, draining her bottle and stealing Tina's unloved one. "Remember the first time we went, when we took Route 3 and then sat on the wrong side of the ferry? We were so stupid then." Shelby guzzled Tina's beer.

"And remember when we realized we could stay over Sunday night, take the earliest ferry out of Vineyard Haven on Monday, and still get to work on time? That was a genius idea, Shelby." I scooped up some salsa and sour cream with a tortilla chip.

"Now here we are, stuck in the city again every weekend. This sucks," Tina said. We sighed collectively.

I lost myself in a reverie of the island's pulsating sunshine, white sand beaches, endless house parties, and visits to up-island beaches like Lucy Vincent and Lambert's Cove that were off limits to regular tourists.

"Hey, remember that first weekend down when we said we'd all have cheap sex?" Tina asked, trying to perk up the conversation.

"Tina, you failed." Shelby laughed. "You didn't have nearly as much cheap sex as we did."

I laughed, almost inhaling a black olive.

"Wait a minute—I'm the only one who *didn't* fail. I had two one-night stands. You guys both ended up with summer-long flings," she pointed out. "So my sex was cheaper."

"Well, my fling has flung," I said, smiling wistfully. "I wonder if Ralphie is happy being back in California."

"Yet you never gave in to poor Big Bill," Shelby said to Tina. "He tried so hard to seduce you."

"Noooo," Tina drawled. "Not my type."

We snickered.

"Hey, whatever happened to that handsome model guy you were sucking face with at the Northern that night a few weeks ago?" Shelby asked.

"Don't you remember the next day, at the beach? His back was as hairy as a woolly mammoth," Tina said with a shiver.

Shelby's face was blank, and I knew she didn't remember.

"Shel, are you going to miss Will as much as Astrid's going to miss Ralphie?" Tina asked.

"Hey," I interrupted, "I've always wondered, Shelby. Were you sleeping with Will and Carney at the same time? In the beginning?" I flashed my not-judging-just-curious smile.

"No! I only slept with Carney once, and there was a full twenty-four hours between them." Shelby looked up, thinking. "Almost twenty-four hours."

"That was a good call," Tina said. "Carney's cute and all, but Will had a car."

"And was less likely to be carrying a sexually transmitted disease," I pointed out.

"Plus," said Shelby, "with him in Charlestown, my fling isn't over. It's like I've still got a piece of summer because I've got Will."

I exchanged worried glances with Tina.

"What are you talking about?" I asked, looking sideways at Shelby.

"You're still dating him?" Tina asked.

Shelby sipped her beer, eyeing us over the top of her bottle. "Why wouldn't I? He's a nice guy, and we have fun."

"He's good summer fling material, but a boyfriend?" I asked. "Does he have any money?"

"He usually pays when we go out, if that's what you mean."

"Usually? He should be paying *all* the time."

"In what old-fashioned novel, Astrid? Anyway, he has his own business so he does okay." Shelby started gathering the salt crystals scattered on the table into a pile.

"He has a business? What's it called?" I interrogated her. "I didn't see a company logo on the side of that van. Working for yourself and having your own company isn't the same thing."

"Don't be so picky, Astrid. It's not like I'm going to marry him or anything. Man, you sound like Tina."

"What's that supposed to mean?" Tina asked, her voice rising.

Shelby studied her beer. "Only that you're super picky. If it's not the hairy back, it's the nasal voice, or he likes sports too much." She took a big swig.

"Come on, the sports guy was insane. He slept in sheets with Red Sox, Celtics and Bruins logos on them for God's sake, like a little kid!"

We giggled. "What, no football team logo?" I asked.

"Does Boston even have a football team? But Shelby, back to Will. If I'm too picky, you're not picky enough."

Shelby squinted at us. "Ooh, it's 'Girlfriend in a Coma'," she cried as the song in the bar changed. "That's by The Smiths, for you musically uninitiated." She looked at the speaker attached to the wall above her.

"You could do soooooo much better than Will, no offense to him," Tina said, ignoring Shelby's attempt to change the subject.

"Please, I appreciate your confidence in me, Tina, but I'm no great catch. He's better looking than I am, for starters."

"Are you kidding?" I asked. "He has crooked teeth, and you'd think he would have a better body for a builder. And you *are* attractive; *you* just don't think so," I reprimanded.

"And Will's not as smart as you, even if you are an incredibly clueless airhead sometimes," Tina said.

"Like now," I added.

"Aaargh, would you guys just chill? I'm going to the bathroom." Shelby lurched out of her seat, tugged at the butt of her black jeans, reached back to grab her beer, and fled.

"She doesn't get it. She needs my not-yet-published piece on *How to Spot a Loser Even When You're Sleeping with Him*," I complained to Tina.

Shelby

CHAPTER 23

At least my friends couldn't rag on me about my career. That fall Maggie assigned me to an amazing new account—promoting the construction of a new city park where a decrepit old parking garage was being demolished. And, she promoted me to account executive, less than a year after being hired.

"I do want to mention that you have an even greater responsibility to this company now, and I suspect you've been burning the candle at both ends, am I right?"

I swallowed. "I guess," I mumbled.

"Just take it easy. You need to be focused and fresh at work. You're putting in a lot of hours here, so you can't go out every night like you're still in college. In other words, don't burn yourself out, okay?"

I nodded. Rubbing my finger back and forth along the textured plastic arm of the chair in her office, I inhaled sharply. "Back to the raise—thank you, first of all. But second, I know I'm not supposed to know this, but I happen to know Cindy makes more than that, and she's a new AE too, and I bill more hours than she does. So shouldn't I make at least what she makes?"

Maggie stared at me while I counted the seconds in my head.

"She has been here longer than you. But I'll take it up with the partners," she said when I got to seven. I left her office petrified.

The next day, she said the higher raise was approved. In a hushed voice, she confided she was thrilled I stood up for myself because she made the exact same point with Terry and Jim beforehand, but they resisted going higher. This time I left Maggie's office elated because it dawned on me that they wanted to keep me happy.

Will and I celebrated with a candle-lit dinner in his Charlestown apartment. He didn't have much work so we never ate out, but his cooking made up for it. Plus, I got to snuggle with his dog Pilsener when we stayed in.

His apartment was a crazy, three-level space with the bedroom, living room, and kitchen each on different floors, in a tall, slender, slightly crooked old house typical for that historic neighborhood. Will lived rent-free in exchange for renovating the landlady's half of the house.

Talking about my career growth with him felt awkward, but he was a good sport that night, even buying us champagne. And when my work friends insisted on celebratory drinks after work the next night, he agreed to meet us for one or two at a new club off of Boylston Street. My coworkers and I were tossing back our fifth tequila shots when he showed up. Three more shots and far too much PR talk for his liking later, he insisted it was time to go.

When I couldn't fold myself into the cab without his help, I realized he was right. Halfway to Charlestown, the cab was spinning, or I was, but either way it wasn't good, and it got worse when I gave a small burp. I started to open the cab door, but Will grabbed my arm and banged on the Plexiglas divider. "Pull over. I think my girlfriend's going to get sick."

The cab lurched to a stop. Will helped me open the door and tried to hold my hair back while I threw up into the street, but he couldn't quite reach my head. Pieces of my hair dangled in my line of fire. I wasn't so drunk that I couldn't be mortified.

At Will's apartment, I weaved toward the shower to wash the puke out of my hair.

"Put this on," he soothed afterward, helping me into a soft, floppy T-shirt and tucking me into his bed.

"Sorry, I'm not feeling very romantic tonight," I slurred. He smiled, shrugged, and went upstairs to watch TV with Pilsener. How could Tina and Astrid not see how great he is, I wondered before I passed out?

That weekend, I bailed on Will and stayed at my apartment. I hadn't been sleeping well and thought my own bed might help, but I couldn't get comfortable there either. I suffered from headaches a lot lately, even when I wasn't hungover. And my neck muscles were so tense, none of my pillows felt right. One was too high, the other too low. Finally, I started using a rolled-up towel under my neck instead of a pillow.

I couldn't even sleep in my favorite position—on my stomach, feet hanging off the end of the bed, torso pressing reassuringly into the mattress—because my tight neck muscles complained when I turned my head to the side.

Maybe Maggie was right and I should stop burning the candle at both ends.

Astrid

CHAPTER 24

"By the way, I hate men," I grumbled uncharacteristically, plopping down on Tina's turquoise couch. Shelby and Tina raised their eyebrows at each other and snickered.

"Care to explain?" Tina asked, pouring us Bloody Marys because Shelby said she'd rather have a headache and a buzz than just a headache.

I pulled my legs up under me. "There's a new project being built on my way to the T, and the last few times I've walked by it, the construction workers have whistled and made annoying noises at me."

"Oh, I hate that!" Shelby said with a shiver. "Why do they have to make us feel like a piece of meat? Remember that old television commercial when the woman gets whistled at and she just smiles and winks at them or something? In real life—"

"—it's nothing like that, I know!" I finished for her. "Once when I was a kid, my mother and I went by a construction site, and when they hooted at her, she thanked them and kept walking. She said to me, 'It's only a big deal if you make it one.' But I'm sorry, I can't be nonchalant about it. It makes me feel so, I don't know, violated? Maybe I'm super-sensitive because of what happened when I studied abroad."

"When did you study abroad? And where?" Tina asked, stirring her Bloody Mary with a celery stick.

"And what happened?" Shelby chimed in.

"Junior year of college. I went to the University of London and traveled in Europe on my breaks. Being young, blonde, and obviously a tourist I swear made me a target for every creepy Greek, Italian, and Spanish guy out there."

"Wow, you made the rounds. What happened?" Shelby asked.

"Let's see. I was groped near the ruins in Italy. Flashed on my way up to the Parthenon in Athens. Although, if I hadn't gotten lost and taken the wrong path, that might not have happened. And I was harassed at a hotel in Valencia."

"Whoa, maybe you should write a book on *How to Get Harassed at the Seven Wonders of the World*," Shelby said.

"I don't think you should joke," Tina said, wrapping a chunk of black hair around her finger. "That all sounds awful. What did you do, Astrid?"

"Mostly I kept my head down because if you made eye contact, they took that as encouragement. And I'd try to find other tourists my age to do stuff with, or even just to sit by when I was alone. But that wasn't the worst of it." I drank from my cocktail but couldn't smell it because my memory was inhaling diesel fumes in a dusty train station.

"In Venice, I had the stupid idea of spending the night in the train station instead of getting a hostel because I was taking a five o'clock train in the morning. Mistake number one. There was hardly anyone in the waiting room, only me and two men who kept staring at me. I didn't dare to move. At one point, a security guard came in and looked around, and I thought he might help me somehow, but he ogled me as badly as the other guys."

I scrunched my shoulders up and down to relax them.

"When it got light, I thought it would be safe to hit the bathroom. I really had to go by then. But the bathroom was down a long platform so that was mistake number two. One of the creepy guys from the waiting room catches up to me and jabbers at me in Italian. I try to ignore him, but he reaches down and grabs my leg. I was wearing a skirt—mistake number three. I walk faster but keep going—mistake number four. I run into the ladies' room and into a stall. When I turn around to lock it, he's standing there exposing himself."

"Wow, flashed twice in one trip. That's got to be some kind of record," Shelby said but without the usual bite to her sarcasm.

"Thank God he was gone when I went out a few minutes later."

We drained our drinks in silence, and Tina poured another round from the pitcher.

"Something like that happened to me once," Shelby said. Tina shot a surprised look at Shelby and nodded ever-so-slightly. "This wasn't nearly as bad, but I had a weird episode at the chiropractor's last year." Tina looked puzzled. "I hurt my back so my mother sent me to this chiropractor. When he was adjusting me, he leaned on me a few times and I swear I felt his thing against me. Maybe it wasn't actually a hard-on, I don't know."

"Ew, if you could feel it, it was hard!" Tina said. "Did you say anything?"

"I was too freaked out. I didn't go back, though."

"Wow, I'm so glad nothing like this has happened to me," Tina said. "No, wait—there was one time in high school, I stayed over at a friend's house—a bunch of us did—and I slept on the floor of the den. In the middle of the night, her older brother came in and laid down next to me, and then he put my hand on his you-know-what. And he said, 'Do something with it.'"

Shelby's eyes widened, and I stifled a laugh.

"That was *so* wrong, right?" Tina asked.

"Yeah, that was wrong, unless you're the teenage boy trying to get lucky." Shelby laughed.

"It's not really funny," I said. "It's still a man preying on a woman because she's alone or in a vulnerable situation."

"I guess you're right," Shelby admitted.

"Anyway, since we're on the subject of men behaving badly, I'll be right back and tell you my work story,"

I went to go pee and forgot Tina's bathroom door had to be pushed extra hard to stay shut, so I heard Tina talking to Shelby in a low voice.

"I thought you were going to tell her. Why didn't you tell her?"

"I totally trust her, but I don't want to mix this personal shit with my job. We still work together, and I don't want her feeling weird around me. And I don't want people at work knowing."

Hm. Any inclination to bare my soul to them about Brad's reign of harassment last year was sucked up into the bathroom ceiling fan.

Shelby

CHAPTER 25

On a crappy, raw, and rainy October day, Maggie and I toured a Faneuil Hall real estate project with a new client. As we walked, she kept glancing at me. I felt weird and squirmy all over, but I wasn't tired, sick, or even hungover, so I ignored the odd feelings until Maggie pulled me aside while the client spoke with the onsite manager.

"Do you feel okay? You don't look well."

"I feel really strange, to be honest."

"I think you should go home. Get some rest and see how you feel tomorrow."

I didn't wait for her to tell me twice.

At home, I washed my face, changed into sweats, and lay down in bed. As usual, I couldn't get comfortable. I ignored my low, dull headache but couldn't ignore my neck, which was tighter than ever, like being squeezed in a vise and stretched like a rubber band at the same time. I groaned and readjusted the towel I used under my neck since my pillow stopped working.

I dozed, only to wake—the clock said thirty minutes later—with my head in indescribable pain. Moving my head an inch sent waves of throbbing agony across my brain. This wasn't a garden-variety headache. It wasn't a sharp pain in an isolated spot like a sinus headache. It was a putrid nausea, distressing every cell in my brain, my skull, and whatever existed in between. I knew if I didn't get up, soon I wouldn't be able to move at all.

My roommate was home—she worked the late shift as a nurse—and she drove me to the hospital. I struggled to hold my head still during the ride, to avoid setting off the excruciating waves again.

After forty-five minutes of painful waiting, two rounds of questioning, and one spinal tap to rule out meningitis, the doctor told me in a pleasant voice that I was suffering from a migraine.

I gulped down some narcotic painkillers at the water fountain and called Will. While I waited for him, the medicine dulled the edge of the pain, like a stone banging against a softer stone, gradually shaving away its edges.

I crashed at Will's that night in a drug-induced haze.

I called Maggie the next day, struggling to speak normally through the painkillers.

"Take as much time off as you need, Shelby. Everything is fine here."

"Are you sure? What about the plan I was writing for Gloucester?"

"I've got it covered. It will be fun for me to write a plan again. You've been doing such a great job, I haven't done one in ages."

"All right. I'll take a few more days then. This medicine is pretty strong so I'm kind of out of it."

"One more thing. Hopefully you're not too out of it to process this. We just wrapped up the numbers for our last fiscal year, which just ended, and you were one of our top five billers."

"Billers?"

"You logged more billable hours than almost anyone in the company."

"Oh."

"The partners, Brad, and I are taking all five of you to dinner at the Ritz-Carlton to celebrate. And there will be bonus checks," she said, her excitement making a dent in my stupor. "We were planning on doing it this week, but we'll push it off two weeks since you're not feeling well."

"That's awesome, Maggie. Thanks. I need to go lie down now. I'll be better soon."

But the next few days weren't any better. If I skipped a dose, the migraine rebounded, so I kept popping pills like a junkie.

I stayed out of work for three weeks, an unheard of amount of time. More doctor visits and different medicines didn't cure my headaches, so I vegetated at Will's, where he sweetly kept me clean and fed.

In the third week, Campbell Lewis held its top-biller dinner as scheduled, and Maggie said to come if I felt up to it, even though I was technically out sick. So I fumbled my way into a work outfit complete with nylons and heels, and put on make-up with shaky hands. Will said I was too out of it to go, but I figured I was pretty good at working through headaches by now, so I could handle this.

He dropped me at the Ritz, and I stumbled to the room the company had reserved.

"Hi, everyone," I said, peering at the ring of faces at the table. I squinted, bringing Astrid, Maggie, Terry, Jim, Brad, Kristy, and Tom into focus.

Everyone stared at me, but no one said anything. Finally, Terry bellowed, "Shelby," and led me to a seat next to Astrid. "Do you want a drink?"

Astrid shook her head violently.

"No, even I know not to mix alcohol and narcotics," I said. *Shit*, I thought, *should I have said that?*

I ate a little of whatever they were serving and wiped my mouth with my napkin repeatedly because it felt moist a lot. I even managed to add a little to the conversation, but my mouth seemed to move in slow motion.

I was able to read the four digits on my bonus check, though. That cut through my haze just fine.

At the end of dinner, as people were putting on jackets, Astrid put her arm around me and told me I looked like shit. "I almost cried when I saw you," was actually how she put it. She took my bonus check for safekeeping, poured me into her car, and took me back to Will's.

A few days later, I weaned myself off the narcotics and re-joined society. Drug-free, I became aware of my muscles working and stretching. I noticed the coolness of the air against my skin. I appreciated the rise and fall of my breathing chest. Even my pee tingled as if alive again.

I went back to work, ready to make up for lost time.

Four nights later, I couldn't sleep.

"What is *wrong* with you?" Will complained as I twisted in bed again.

"My back is killing me. How could I have hurt it when I haven't even exercised in forever?" I answered.

I lay on my stomach to relieve the pulling of my lower right back muscle. By morning, it throbbed as if inflamed. I wanted to jump out of my skin.

"Let's get you to the doctor." Will moaned, bundling me into a coat and helping me to the van.

Diagnosis: Kidney infection caused by an untreated bladder infection.

Treatment: A prescription that dulled the pain so I was back to work quickly.

Two weeks later, at home in my apartment, I puked my guts out repeatedly and then entered the horrible dry heave stage. I could barely stand after five hours of convulsions. My roommate drove me to the clinic.

As the doctor examined me, I suddenly couldn't breathe. A huge weight pressed on my lungs, making me scrape for breath. My hands tingled, and my thumbs locked against my outstretched fingers. My hands cramped completely, bending inward at the wrists.

"I can't move my hands! What's happening?" I cried, gulping for air.

"It's okay, relax," the doctor said, not reassuringly. "You're just hyperventilating. Breathe," she intoned slowly.

"But, but, do I need a paper bag?" I gasped between sharp inhales. "An oxygen infusion?"

Oxygen infusion, an annoying voice in the back of my head said. *Good name for a band.*

She shook her head. "You need to regulate your breathing. Just slow down." She watched as I struggled for breath. "Get her a paper bag," she commanded the nurse, shaking her head.

Diagnosis: Dehydration due to a stomach virus.

Treatment: A round of IV fluids at the clinic and rest.

At least that happened on Saturday so I didn't miss any work.

I had to admit I was breaking down. Every available bacterium and virus found my body an easy target. Maggie showed more understanding than Will. "When are you going to kick this?" he asked repeatedly, less patient with each illness.

His apartment was feeling mighty cramped, so I moved back to my place, just in time to move again. In the midst of my medical madness, my lease ended. Tina and Astrid helped me move into a Victorian house complete with mahogany woodwork, massive fireplaces, and four roommates, in a suburb north of Boston.

It was farther from work than before, but the back yard was ringed with trees, which made me irrationally happy—maples and oaks along the back lot line and tall, slender evergreens along the sides. I walked through the line of deciduous trees once, to see how far they went, but I ended up in someone else's yard in about ten seconds. My woods were a suburban charade. Still, I liked looking at a row of trees instead of a row of buildings.

I functioned okay at work, but my headaches and neck tightness never completely went away. Astrid worried, but I kept assuring her that it was a phase and that I was fine. A neurologist prescribed something new—

Fiorinal, which I loved because it blasted my migraine away like a foghorn cutting through low-lying clouds. It was also a good name for a band.

One day, Maggie sat me down and asked if something—anything—was bothering me. She suggested my physical problems might be related to something emotional. She seemed so Buddha-like in her quiet caring and wisdom that I found myself telling her what my stepfather did to me and how my mother reacted when I told her about it.

"What are you doing to take care of yourself? To heal?" she probed.

I cocked my head. "What do you mean?" I truly wanted to know.

"Well, you need to talk to someone. It's not like the bookstore has many books on this subject. Maybe you should see a therapist. I highly recommend it, and it's covered by our health insurance. Talk to someone about the abuse, and see if it helps with your headaches."

I couldn't stand feeling like an inferior non-contributor at work. I had to get my life back. So I agreed to look into it.

That night, I told Will my headaches and illnesses might be tied to a childhood trauma I hadn't dealt with. He hugged me tightly when I explained and asked if anyone had killed Norman yet. I smiled.

***

Ten days later, I sat down with Shirley. She had a long, thin face and short, red hair, and eyebrows permanently drawn inward, in what she must have thought was a sympathetic position.

"Shelby," she said, sounding as if she pitied me, "tell me about your childhood fears."

"What do you mean? Bogeymen under the bed, monsters in the closet—that kind of thing?"

"Yes—phobias, nightmares. Anything that recurred, or even happened once, that you remember being frightened of."

I chewed on my lip. "Well, I used to have nightmares about the Big Bad Wolf from Little Red Riding Hood. I don't remember the actual dreams, but I remember being scared and making the mistake of telling my brothers."

"Why was that a mistake?"

"Because then they tormented me by taking these tall, brown plastic cups we had in the kitchen, and putting them over their noses and pretending to be the Big Bad Wolf." I smiled.

She seemed to be waiting for something, so I mulled over my words.

"Hah, that's pretty obvious, isn't it?" I concluded.

She waited some more.

"The Big Bad Wolf pretends to be a grandmother, who's sort of a parental figure. So instead of a wolf in sheep's clothing, you have a wolf in parent's clothing."

"The villain is in the form of someone who is supposed to protect Little Red Riding Hood, not harm her," Shirley contributed, peering at me. I squirmed.

"There was another fairy tale one," I offered, shifting in my chair.

She waited. Therapists did this a lot evidently.

"This wasn't a dream, but I always had this fear of a big goat under our front stairs going up to the second floor and the bedrooms. It was always dark and quiet there. There was like a closet under the stairs, with a little door. I used to run up the stairs when I had to go to bed because I was afraid of the goat hiding in that closet. Like the Three Billy Goats Gruff, only instead of a troll under the bridge being the bad guy, it was one of the goats."

She watched me. Did she want *me* to figure out the hidden meaning? I thought I was paying her to be the analyst. I pulled at a thread coming loose at the ripped knee of my jeans.

"What do you think that one means?" I broke down and asked her.

"The goat, who is supposed to be the hero, or at least the good guy, has become the bad guy in your childhood."

Awkward silence. Again. I inhaled and exhaled loudly to fill the void.

"What are you thinking about now?" Shirley asked in her pitying voice.

"I'm thinking that you can read something into anything." I looked directly at her. "Or maybe I should just stay away from fairy tales."

The rest of the session was characterized by painfully long silences while she waited for me to say something profound. She said "mm-hmm," a lot, and raised those damn eyebrows. By the end, all I could think was how much she reminded me of Carol Burnett, which made it hard to take her—and therapy—seriously.

***

I didn't tell Will about my therapy appointment since he was impatient for me to get "back to normal" as he called it. I did tell my girlfriends over drinks at Astrid's apartment that weekend. That meant telling Astrid about Norman, which, surprisingly, made me feel pretty good. Tina said she was proud of me. Astrid didn't say much because really, what could she have said?

The two of them went into the kitchen to open more wine—the first bottle having magically disappeared during my soul-baring—and I heard them whispering as the fridge and a drawer opened and shut.

"You don't have to talk behind my back," I yelled. "I may be seeing a shrink, but I'm not fragile!"

Their faces when they came back into the living room were ominous.

"What?" I looked from one to the other and got nothing. They were dressed weirdly alike in straight-leg jeans that I could never pull off thanks to my wide hips, and light sweaters—Tina's an ugly shade of brown and Astrid's soothing beige. Tina looked at Astrid until Astrid broke the silence.

"We weren't sure if we should tell you this, but we've decided we would want you to tell us, if it was the other way around."

My stomach gyrated like a pinpricked balloon.

Tina inhaled sharply. "The other night, when you didn't want to go out with us, we were at the Sail Loft, and we saw Will there." She looked at Astrid for support. "With another girl."

"Well, I know he has a few good friends who are women," I said like a question.

"They were making out, Shel," Astrid said. "Sorry."

Tears flowed before my brain finished processing the information. Tina handed the wineglasses to Astrid, sat beside me, and wrapped me in her arms.

"Oh my God, what am I, poison?" I asked when the sobs slowed to whimpers.

"Don't say that. It's him, not you." Tina gave the stock response.

"No, it's me. Don't you see? How long did this one last? Five months? What am I doing wrong?"

They patted me and said all the right things, which I didn't absorb because all I felt was the heaviness of another failed relationship stuck in my chest. We covered the standard men-suck-and-then-you-die refrain, and they assured me I would find someone even better than Will. I cried for hours at Astrid's, I cried on the drive home, and I cried back in my bedroom, listening to Carole King lament over and over again that "It's Too Late" and he's "So Far Away".

The next morning, I was fine. I tested myself to be sure. I conjured Will in my mind, and all I felt was apathy, no regret. *I must be getting used to being broken up with*, I thought.

To his credit, he called that night to say he needed a less complicated relationship. I told him not to worry about it. Maybe I wasn't over my family situation yet, but apparently getting over him would not be a problem.

Shelby

CHAPTER 26

I decided to try another therapist. Lauren worked out of an old house converted to medical offices in upscale Brookline, just west of Boston proper. She was about thirty, with shoulder-length, wavy brown hair, and kind eyes.

Her small office had a desk, two chairs, and a few crammed bookcases. She moved her chair from behind the desk to a few feet from me, separated only by the old, braided rug on the worn, wooden floor.

Picking up a pad of paper and a pencil from the desk behind her, she asked why I was there. "I was molested, not really sexually abused, by my stepfather when I was little, and I just want to make sure I've dealt with it." The words were getting easier to say now that I'd used them with Tina, Maggie, Shirley, and Astrid.

She launched into the basics: my job, my friends, my hobbies. Easy stuff. Midway through the hour, she asked if I was comfortable telling her exactly what happened. I told her everything I remembered, the bedroom episodes and the living room couch ones.

"Do you know how old you were at the time?"

"No, but I think I was around five or six when my mother married him."

"Do you remember how you felt when he was touching you?"

"I tried not to feel. I didn't like it at all. I sort of froze."

She jotted something down. "And what bothers you most about these memories?"

I looked at my hands in my lap and picked at a hangnail. "I guess what I don't really get is why I didn't scream or anything, or tell my mother."

She waited for me to finish shifting around in my chair. "Shelby, you are a strong, mature woman now. But then, you were a very small girl who trusted that the adults around you were doing the right thing, and that they knew better than you. Kids back then were taught not to question authority.

Children who are being abused do not feel they have the right to speak up, if the idea even enters their head. You are very normal."

My shoulders relaxed a little.

She cocked her head and crossed her legs. "Tell me about your family life growing up. Was there any violence or substance abuse in your house?"

My eyebrows shot up. "No, it was generally a happy house. My mother and stepfather are teachers. We didn't have a ton of money, but we had enough. We got to go skiing, and we had friends and did sports and things. I mean, my mother drove me crazy with her nitpicking and rules but that's normal, right?"

"Any siblings?"

"I have two older brothers, Kyle and Eric. I'm really close to them."

"Tell me a favorite childhood memory."

I studied the dull, white ceiling and thought. "This is a little thing, but one of my earliest memories is playing in the snow with my brothers. My boot got stuck in the snow, and I couldn't pull it out, so Kyle pulled it out for me. I don't know why I remember that.

"And I always feel good when I think of the times my brothers had heart-to-heart talks with me. That was more in high school. There was this one time—I was a freshman in high school—and my brothers' friends were starting to notice me. At least that's what Eric said. We were at a party with his summer football team, and he took me aside and said, 'Men are animals. We'll do whatever you let us do. Especially if we're drunk. So you can't be drunk. You have to be the smart one.'" I smiled with my eyes. "The funny thing was, my brother Kyle gave me almost the same speech later that same night."

"Hmm. Interesting." Oh no. I sensed a Shirley-style pause coming. But Lauren continued. "Shelby, do you see what those two stories have in common?"

I shook my head.

"In both stories, your brothers are protecting you. You didn't get that from your stepfather, or your mother, so you relished it when you got it from someone else."

Our time was up, so we confirmed next week's appointment, and I walked out of her office building into the cool air. The sun had set, rush hour was over, and a hush blanketed this normally busy Brookline street. I felt weird—kind of unsettled. So I guessed therapy was doing something. I would come back.

Astrid

CHAPTER 27

"One more announcement before we break for food," Terry said in his theatrical baritone at the weekly staff meeting. "And I have to warn you, today's food is healthy. Our beloved office manager wants to make us all healthier, so instead of pastries we get yogurt and fruit this time." People groaned, but I flashed Anne a supportive smile. "The final announcement is that Kristy is leaving. Her stay was far too short, but she and her fiancé are moving, as he's in the service and is being stationed in Germany."

My smile cracked. My stomach felt like I'd eaten a dozen pastries. Kristy was the buffer between me and Brad. No, I'm being absurd. He hadn't harassed me in months and probably could care less about me now.

But there he was, skirting the people at the table who ladled yogurt and fruit into bowls, and working his way toward me. I turned to leave, but he caught me by the arm.

"Astrid," he said as if I'd done something wrong. "Kristy's leaving us; can you believe it? The little witch must have known all along she'd only be here a few months," he snapped. "So I guess it's back to you and me, kid," he said with a wink. My head spun from his instantaneous mood changes.

I swallowed and recovered. "Not really, Brad, since we don't work together anymore." I tried to sound disappointed.

"Maybe we can fix that. I could have you transferred back into my group," he said with a smirk. I was speechless. "Just kidding," he said with a laugh that suggested he thoroughly enjoyed my obvious discomfort. "See you around." He jostled past me, practically knocking me off balance.

***

I wanted to tell Shelby about Brad, so I dragged her away from her desk to a small cafe around the corner for lunch.

"Do you think they're treating me funny?" Shelby asked, breaking into my thoughts about how to broach the subject. "Astrid, I said do you think people at work are treating me differently than they used to? Since I got sick, I mean."

"No, not at all. Maggie and Jim love you! Maggie's always praising your work. There was one time right after you came back from that horrible three weeks out, when I heard you weren't invited to a big brainstorming session because they wanted you to ease back into your work. But other than that, I haven't heard anything."

Shelby nodded and seemed reassured. As she bit into her baguette, I knew I had to confess something.

"So, speaking of not being invited to big meetings—don't be mad at me, but I have to tell you about something bad I did once, but it was back way before we became friends, so you can't hold it against me." Shelby stopped chewing but said nothing. "Remember that time you were crying in the bathroom, and then you were un-invited to the golf tournament new business session later that week?"

She nodded. I could practically see her putting two and two together in her head.

"I was the one who got you kicked out of the meeting." Shelby's eyes widened in horror and then squinted into tiny slits. "I'm so sorry, but I desperately needed to be in that meeting instead of you. It's hard to explain, but Brad was making my life miserable and I needed to, to do something, well I just had to be in that meeting is all," I trailed off.

Shelby sat there moving her mouth into funny shapes and looking anywhere but at me.

"I'm sorry, I really am! Please say something." I leaned toward her.

She finally faced me, her eyes still all squinty. "The night before that was when I told my mother about my stepfather abusing me. That's why I was upset." Her voice was scarily calm.

"Oh wow, that makes it even worse. I am such a terrible friend. Please say you forgive me." I didn't even have an I'm-so-sorry-I-sandbagged-my-best-friend smile to try. Which was fine because I didn't feel like smiling anyway.

Shelby shrugged with a half-smile. "I probably would have done the same thing to you if the situation were reversed."

I wrinkled my nose.

"Really. You were such a bitch then!" She grinned. "Astrid, it's okay. Everything was different then," she said with no trace of sarcasm. "I forgive you."

I relaxed and crossed my legs, hitting my knee on the underside of the table. "Good, because you know you're my best friend, right?"

"Don't get sappy on me. Time to change the subject." Practical Shelby was back. "How's it feel being a senior account executive? Which we still have to celebrate properly, by the way. You know the partners are totally grooming you for management, right?"

"Why are you so sure?" I sipped from my Diet Coke and smiled modestly, but it felt insincere because I knew Maggie had me on the fast track to senior management. I bit into my ham and cheese croissant.

"You're the only account exec with three account coordinators under her, and now you've even got your own intern."

I giggled. "Not that I'm doing such a good job managing him. He told me I'm intimidating. Can you believe that?"

Shelby took a bite of her sandwich, looked at me, and swallowed. "Astrid, you *are* intimidating. As hell."

"Oh. I didn't realize that." I folded the napkin in my lap.

"Did he just blurt that out of the blue?"

"No, we had to sit down and have a talk with Maggie because he wasn't delivering. Every morning we'd run through his tasks, and every night we'd look over what he got done, and it was hardly anything. It was so frustrating. Finally, Maggie intervened. Sat us both down and teased out of him that he was so freaked out by me he couldn't concentrate and get any work done."

"Geez, dragon lady, take a chill pill next time." Shelby laughed.

"Seriously, I don't know what I was doing wrong. I was just being me. But Maggie suggested I be a little softer and kinder with him."

Shelby's eyes widened in disbelief. "Man, I wasn't that sensitive when I was a lowly intern." We laughed again. "Hey, Kristy didn't last long, huh? Who do you think is going to be Brad's whore now?"

"Shelby!"

"What? Am I being too crass? Even I know they were doing it, and I'm clueless about office gossip. And she was engaged all along apparently." Shelby shook her head.

"But who knows what was actually going on? Maybe Brad pressured her into it or something," I said.

"Come on, she's an adult. I'm sure she could say no if she wanted to."

I stood and scooped up my half-eaten lunch. "Let's go back to work. I'm not very hungry."

Shelby

CHAPTER 28

My second therapy session was like getting hit by a truck. An entire sixty minutes dissecting me in horrifying detail. I liked PR because I got to make other people look good and not focus on me. All this introspection was awkward and couldn't possibly be healthy.

Lauren wanted to focus on how the sexual abuse—she insisted on calling it that—affected me. I couldn't come up with a thing. So she ran me through some of the ways people cope—drinking (lots), drugs (check), cutting themselves (one half-hearted attempt when I was really pissed off because I caught Norman following me and my friends around town), and eating (yes, lots, that's why I weighed twenty pounds more in college and had gained at least five pounds lately).

"So pretty much I can blame all my bad habits on my stepfather now? This is awesome!"

Lauren raised an eyebrow at my sarcasm but said nothing. "Let's talk about sex," she said casually

I noticed with envy how smooth Lauren's navy blue leather chair looked. The worn fabric seat of my old chair scratched against my nylons. I should wear a longer skirt next time.

"Do you and your boyfriend have an intimate relationship?" Lauren asked.

"Actually he broke up with me right before our first session. I don't know why I said we were still dating."

"I'm sorry to hear that." She tactfully looked down at her lap while I breathed in deeply and noticed her office smelled like old books and wooden floors—the same smell I loved in the attic in Newfield, where I used to escape for hours with a few apples and books of my own.

I broke the silent mourning period. "I think I want to play the field for a while anyway. I've had two kind of serious boyfriends in a row. I think I'll try just dating."

"But tell me about your boyfriends. What did you want from those relationships?"

"Oh," I exhaled. "I don't know. I never thought about it. I wasn't looking for them to break up with me; that's for sure. My friends were always telling me I was too good for them."

"Do you agree with them?"

"No, because I don't think you have to have a college degree or make a lot of money to be a worthwhile person. Maybe they weren't the smartest guys, but they were fun, and nice to me." Did I sound defensive?

"So they weren't your equals intellectually?"

I gave in. "I guess not. Is that bad?"

"It's neither good nor bad. But in general, people are attracted to those of similar intellectual capacity—it makes for a more balanced relationship. You might think about that."

I stuck a mental post-it on my brain, reminding me to have this conversation with myself later. Or I could ask Tina and Astrid. They'd definitely have opinions on the matter.

As Lauren started to rise, signaling the end of the session, I stayed put. "Can I ask you something? Why do you think I blocked it out for so long? Obviously not everyone does that, right?"

She leaned against her desk. "No, but many people do repress their memories of traumatic situations or events. It's your mind's way of protecting you from dangers you can't understand or process at that time. And many of these people experience spontaneous recovery of the memories later in life, sometimes triggered by a sight or smell, sometimes with no clear trigger."

"Hm. Maybe their minds are just ready to deal with it. Like your brain doesn't want to keep a secret anymore."

"That may very well be."

***

My sentimental longing for a family Thanksgiving decimated by Norman and my mother, I wanted to beg off the trip home but didn't know how. Plus, I wanted to see my brothers, so off to Newfield I went. My mother was ecstatic that I came home, but her clinginess gave me the creeps.

After Thanksgiving dinner, Eric and I escaped to go see *Casablanca* at our favorite hole-in-the-wall cinema in Petersburg. He parked the car and moved to get out, but I hesitated. Thick snowflakes sparkled in the winter night sky and wafted down, settling on the windshield.

"Can I tell you something important?"

He shut his door and turned toward me. "Of course." He tilted his chin down and looked up at me in that classic big brother way.

"Um, we have a little family secret I want to tell you about."

He waited. "Go ahead," he prompted when I didn't say anything else.

I choked up phrasing my next sentence in my head. Why couldn't I even think about this subject anymore without wanting to cry?

"Norman sexually abused me when I was a girl."

His whole body sunk into the seat. "I'm sorry."

"Aren't you surprised?" I flicked away a tear tickling my nose.

"You know I can't stand the guy," he said as if choosing his words carefully. "This is one more reason to hate him." His disgust turned to concern. "What should we do about it? Do you want me to beat him up or something?"

I giggled through my tears and exhaled with a heave. "No, I guess not, but thanks for offering." Tissue-less, I wiped my nose on my jacket sleeve. "Eric, I told Mom."

"And?"

"And she doesn't really believe me, and she's mad that I don't like him. Oh, and she slapped me when I said I wouldn't respect her if she stayed with him." I wiped my cheek with my hand.

He growled as if in pain. "Our family sucks. Well, those two anyway. So what do we do now?" Him saying "we" made my heart swell.

"What can we do? We can't change it, and no one including me really wants to talk about it. I guess we just carry on."

Eric nodded.

"And it's good that he teaches at the high school so he's not around young girls," Eric said, making me feel guilty because I hadn't even considered that Norman might molest one of his students.

"Eric, I'm thinking of not coming home for every holiday from now on. It's getting so hard to be around them."

Illogically, I cried harder at the thought of *not* coming home for the holidays. I felt perched on top of a wall separating my previously happy home life from my new reality. I could see my mother and Norman on one side, and Eric on the other. Kyle I wasn't so sure about. I ached for the days when we were all on the same side and it was simple, even if my mother nitpicked and Norman lurked annoyingly in the background.

"Shel, listen to me. You don't have to do anything you don't want to anymore. You get that, right? Maybe you and I can have our own holidays together from now on." He dug a tissue from his pocket and handed it to me.

"Yeah, that would be awesome!" I blew my nose and we sat for a minute. "What about Kyle? Do you think I should tell him?"

He hesitated. "I guess that's up to you. But don't forget he's a card-carrying member of the Norman-Lovers Club."

I laughed and somehow felt ten pounds lighter. I opened the car door.

"Shel, there's something—"

"Come on, we're missing the movie, and I know you've always wanted to see this," I said, getting out.

We missed the beginning of *Casablanca,* so when it ended, instead of driving home, we went back into the cinema and watched it again.

Astrid

CHAPTER 29

Tina thinks she's gonna find the perfect man
Six-foot-two and sexy, clever, rich and tan.
He'll know just when to love her, and when to back away
Of course he'll think she's wonderful and let her have her way.

Tina thinks she's gonna find some fairy tale romance,
Storybook sweethearts and erotic tango dance.
She saw it in a movie once but when the lights went up,
All she had was gum and popcorn stuck to her black pumps.

Tina get a real life, perfection isn't real.
Time to stop your whining, see what you really need.
Stop searching for the ultimate, give up on the charade,
'Cause almost counts in more you know than horseshoes and grenades.

Tina thinks she's gonna get a picture-perfect home,
Just like in House Beautiful and Metropolitan Home.
A mansion up in Manchester and summers on the isle,
Spitfire travels in between, it's heaven for a while.

But surprise, the silver's tarnished and you'll need some elbow grease,
To keep the kisses coming and the blanket on your feet.
So toss your daydreams to the wind, set standards of your own.
Perfection is a myth, that's why perfectionists live alone.

Tina get a real life, perfection isn't real.
Time to stop your whining, see what you really need.
Stop searching for the ultimate, give up on the charade,
'Cause almost counts in more you know than horseshoes and grenades.

"Is this a poem?" I asked Shelby, looking up from the lined sheet of yellow paper covered with her messy scribbles.

"Song lyrics. My therapist suggested writing poetry or songs to get my feelings out."

"Do you want to talk about it now? With me? To get some feelings out?"

She moved her head around as if stretching her neck. "Not really. That's what the therapist is for." I studied her face. She seemed fine. "So, what do you think of the song?"

I sat on the couch and combed my fingers through my hair, still wet from the shower Shelby interrupted when she showed up for our girls' afternoon early.

"Well, let me get this straight. Your therapist wanted you to dig into your feelings, and a song criticizing Tina is what you came up with?"

Shelby's mouth tightened. "She also told me I should think about what kind of guy is right for me, and that got me thinking about how none of us have found Mr. Right. And Tina never will if she doesn't stop being so picky."

"Well, I agree with you that Tina is picky, but maybe she's just holding out for that bolt of lightning to hit her. Love at first sight."

Shelby scoffed. "Yeah, right. That's a nice concept, but unrealistic. How can you love someone you don't even know yet?" She laughed.

"What's so funny?"

"I was remembering this guy Jimmy Kilcoyne, from freshman year in high school," she said. "A friend and I went to a dance at the boys' Catholic school in Petersburg. She introduced me and Jimmy, who was so gorgeous. Wait—first I need to say my hair was really light then from being at the beach a lot that summer. But still brown, you know?"

I circled my hand in the air, urging her to get to the point.

"So at the end of the dance, we're making out when the lights go up. He looks at me and goes, 'Oh, I thought you were blonde' in this totally disappointed voice."

"What does that have to do with anything?"

"Nothing, I'm just making sure you appreciate the advantages blondes have in this world. So anyway, Jimmy and I talked on the phone every few days, and after about two weeks, he's about to hang up when he says he loves me. I start laughing and say, 'How can you love me, you barely even know me?'"

"What did he do?"

"He said bye and never called back. And that ended that." She laughed again. "And I was boyfriend-less again, for pretty much the rest of high school."

"Wow, too honest for your own good, aren't you?" I said. "But, I still think love at first sight can happen. Maybe it's not absolutely perfect that first second, but it's close."

So it's 'like at first sight' or something."

"No, it's stronger than that. You feel a connection and think, this could be the one."

"That would be hormones talking. Infatuation. Not love."

"Aargh, you are so difficult, Shelby. Why can't you let me have my dream?"

"Sorry, I thought we were talking theoretically." She moved closer and peered at me like a bug under a microscope. "Did I miss something? Did you fall in love with someone when I wasn't paying attention?"

"No. But I think I might have met someone I *could* fall in love with. At second sight."

"What?" Shelby shrieked, all cynicism gone. "When? Who?"

An uncharacteristically self-conscious smile spread across my face. "I met him last night with Tina at Joe's—"

The door of the apartment banged opened. A shivering, red-cheeked Tina and a strong blast of cold air came in from the hallway.

"Are you telling her about the guys we met?" Tina asked, shedding her plaid peacoat, hat, and gloves. "Shelby, you should have come out with us last night; we found you a guy," she said in a sing-song voice.

"You know I don't do blind dates."

"It's not blind if we've seen him for you," I explained, rubbing my hair with a towel.

"They were all super nice. Their names are Johnny, Dave, and Wade," Tina said.

Shelby burst into laughter. "Johnny, Dave, and Wade? Sounds like a bad country band."

"Well, believe me; they don't look like a bad country band. They're all seriously good looking, and they work together in the Financial District," Tina said. She sunk onto the couch.

"Which one is mine?" Shelby asked.

"Johnny's mine, Dave is Astrid's, and you get Wade," said Tina as if dealing out playing cards.

"We're meeting them tonight," I jumped in, "at the new dance club in the Theatre District, and you are coming, I don't care what you have going on tomorrow."

"I do have this support group thing that my therapist wants me to try. Maybe I shouldn't be out partying the night before that," Shelby said, but I could tell she was in.

"Shelby Stewart passes up a night with a gorgeous guy and free drinks? I don't think so. And did I mention he's gorgeous?" I said.

"Okay, okay. What does he look like?"

"He's super good-looking," Tina said, "you'll like him—"

"Except for the porn star mustache," I interjected.

"It's not that baaaaad," Tina protested, laughing. "He's got black hair, and he's really tan—I guess he just got back from Mexico. He's in his late twenties and looks like he's in really good shape."

"That's good enough for me," Shelby said. "Let the playing of the field officially begin."

***

"I think I liked it better at Joe's last night," Dave yelled into my ear as the deejay blended one thumping song into another at the club.

"Why?" I yelled back.

He grabbed my hand and maneuvered us between the dancing throngs out to the brightly lit and substantially quieter entrance area.

"Because we could actually talk. Do you want to get out of here?"

I thought for a millisecond. "Yes, but let me tell my friends."

"Okay, tell mine while you're at it. I'll get our coats."

Fifteen minutes later, we sat in a blissfully quiet restaurant in Chinatown, the cigarette smoke from the club replaced by the smell of greasy wontons. I adjusted my black leather mini-skirt against the vinyl seat and crossed my long legs under the table, hitting my knee against a bolt or something in the process.

"Ow," I said, rubbing my knee.

"Small tables, huh?" While he finished squeezing his even longer legs into the confined space, I admired his boy-next-door good looks—well-built, light brown hair and dark brown eyes, and a sweet smile. But I knew from our talk at the bar last night he also had a sharp and sarcastic side.

"This is so much better than the club, though," I said, my ears still ringing a bit.

"Now I can get to know you. And ever since last night, all I can think about is how I *really* want to get to know you."

I flinched. What did he mean?

"Wait—I don't mean get you into bed this second, not that I'd complain about that, if you were offering. I mean come on Astrid, you must know how beautiful and sexy you are."

I smiled cautiously and tucked a strand of hair behind my ear.

"What I mean is that I loved talking with you last night, and I want to know you a lot better. Starting with our words," he said as if talking to a child, but it came across as self-deprecating not condescending.

"Okay, what do you want to know?" I asked.

"First, and most important, do you have a boyfriend?" I raised my eyebrows. "Just checking."

"No. Girlfriend?" I cocked my head at him.

"Of course not or I wouldn't be here. What are your hopes and dreams?"

I stroked my lip, thinking. Francois never asked about my hopes and dreams. "I'd like to run my own PR agency someday, working on accounts that make me happy and do good for the world. Of course, I realize I'd have to have accounts that pay the bills too."

He nodded. "And—I know this will sound premature—but my last girlfriend was totally against kids. I found out after two years with her. Do you want to get married and have a family some day?"

I thought of my mother and our close relationship. I thought of my father who skipped out on us when I was seven.

"I think so, yes, but it's going to have to be the perfect guy. One I know I can trust for eternity." I grimaced. "Did that sound like a Hallmark card?"

"I think it's a great sentiment. So you definitely want kids?"

"Yeah, I do. But after I build my career."

"Of course; you're only twenty-five right?"

"Right. And you're thirty, right?"

"Yep. So I guess neither of us was too drunk last night to remember some numbers!"

We stopped talking while the waitress distributed dim sum and spring rolls on the table. I admired his trendy but not trashy button-up shirt and wondered what he looked like without it.

"So what about those Red Sox?" he asked to fill the awkward pause.

"Not so fast," I said as the waitress walked away. "I have a few questions of my own, now that you've interrogated me." I pulled a piece of paper from my purse. "I invested a lot of time into my last boyfriend too, and I don't want to make the same mistakes again."

"You have a list?" He laughed, and his eyes twinkled. "That's awesome. What mistakes did you make last time?"

"I'm asking the questions here, counselor." He nodded contritely. "Tell me, how do you feel about a woman working?"

"Seriously? It's 1987. Of course, women *can* and *should* work. And have real careers too, not just something to pass the time until they get married. I would want my wife to have her own interests and goals."

"Do you think men and women are equal?"

"Didn't I pretty much just answer that?"

"Not quite."

"Okay. Yes, I think men and woman should be treated equally, even though that doesn't always happen of course. I have a very strong mother and two very strong sisters, and I want them to be treated the same as me when it comes to work and society in general."

"Okay, moving on." I consulted my list. "Would you be threatened if your girlfriend made more than you?"

"Unlikely to be an issue—no offense—but I've been working longer than you, and I'm in the corporate law department of the city's biggest financial services firm."

I frowned at him.

"But no, I think my ego could withstand that."

"Okay, you pass. That's enough for now," I said, folding the paper in half.

"Wait, what else is on that list?" he said, grabbing for the sheet of paper.

I yanked it away. "None of your business. Yet."

"Oh come on. Tell me. Handsome?"

I rolled my eyes. He made sad eyes at me.

"Okay, yes, handsome matters. And you get a big check in that box. But you knew that."

"Always nice to hear someone say it. Especially a gorgeous, intelligent woman like you. Is smart on your list?"

I nodded. "Check."

"Funny?"

"Check."

"Charming?"

"Don't push it. Time will tell on that one."

We laughed together. His deep, rolling laugh was just one of his charming qualities, but I kept that to myself. I picked up my chopsticks.

"Can I have two more questions?" Dave asked. I nodded, transferring a spring roll to my plate. "What do you do for fun?"

"Well, I hang with my friends, and I jog. Although the jogging is for stress relief as much as fun."

"Friends are good. Yours seem nice. And I jog. Will you go with me sometime?"

"Sure, but I have to warn you," I said. "I've been running out a *lot* of stress lately, so I'm pretty fast!" He smiled, unfazed. "What was your other question?"

He leaned across the table and gazed into my eyes. "When did you put that list together?" he asked in a low voice that made the mundane question sound sexy.

I smiled my I've-got-a-secret smile. "Last night. After I got home."

Shelby

CHAPTER 30

As promised, Wade was handsome. No idea what he saw in me. The night was a whirl of neon lights, fruity drinks, and sweaty bodies. The pumping house music made it impossible to talk much, but Wade and I managed to shout some get-to-know-you stuff into each other's ears on the dance floor, while we goofed off to the fast songs and swooned on the ballads. His body heat penetrated his shirt and mine when we slow danced.

When the club closed, we took a cab to the Blue Diner for greasy food and culinary foreplay. We both knew how the night would end. Everything until then was just for show.

I woke the next morning in a strange apartment wearing only Wade's white muscle shirt. Possibly sexy at two in the morning, but in the light of day, its deep armholes simply left me hanging out in a totally unattractive way. While I stealthily dressed, Wade woke, rolled over, and smiled. "Hey, are you leaving? Don't you want to have breakfast?"

Last night had been fun, except when my hands started tingling and cramping in that awkward hyperventilating way, but now, my one-night stand felt strangely unsatisfying. I didn't want to prolong it. We awkwardly kissed good-bye, and as I headed for the T, I realized the topic of phone numbers hadn't come up, which was fine.

I barely had time to get physically prepared for my first support group session by showering and eating. As for getting mentally prepared, I had no idea how to do that.

I swallowed a handful of ibuprofen on my way out, hoping to get rid of the nagging headache from the late night and combination of whiskey sours, vodka gimlets, and shots of schnapps.

***

Six women of various shapes, sizes, and colors squirmed in their chairs, waiting for Lauren to start the session. Make that five because one girl sat completely still, slumped in her chair with her legs splayed out, her eyelids so low, I wondered if she were asleep. Her skin-tight jeans were torn, a black leather vest stretched over an old T-shirt, and numerous bracelets wrapped her skeletal arms. Two inches of pale blonde hair on either side of her part interrupted an otherwise jet-black head of hair. With her head hanging over her chest, it looked like a skunk perched on her head.

Lauren's greeting jolted me out of my observation of the odd girl.

"Thank you for coming and putting your trust in this group, and in yourself, as you work to continue healing. You were all sexually abused as girls, so you have that in common, although you may not feel like you have anything else in common as you look around the room. For all of you, the fundamental bond of trust that every child should be able to count on was broken."

I snuck glances around the room while she talked. A beautiful woman with mahogany-colored skin focused on Lauren and nodded, like she was watching a favorite professor lecture or something. Everyone else wore blank expressions. When I closed my eyes, I could hear the subtle shuffling of chairs and bodies.

"As you know, healing yourself from those atrocities is not a fast process, but you have all come so far in the past few months or years, as the case may be. My hope is that, in this group, you will draw strength and insight from the women around you."

I scanned the dusty-smelling meeting room where we sat, located down the hallway from the small office Lauren used for individual sessions. Not much in it except our chairs and a pitcher of water and plastic cups on an old desk. Two of those six-foot-tall windows you find in old buildings dominated the far wall. One was filled with forlorn, leafless branches and the other with the facade of a brick building.

"My role is as a facilitator, to get the conversation started until you get to know each other a bit. So today, I'd like to go around the circle and have everyone introduce themselves and tell us why you're here."

I shuddered inside. This was scarier than delivering an oral book report in front of the elementary school class.

Lauren turned to an overweight, thirtyish woman with dirty blonde hair and pale skin, wearing baggy jeans and a flowered blouse. The woman looked like she wanted to hide under a rock. I could relate. She opened her mouth, but nothing came out. Lauren tilted her chin up, as if she could draw sound out of the woman with her movement. The woman swallowed, stared at her feet, then at a midpoint between the linoleum floor and the eyes of the women around her, and spoke.

"My name is Jenny. I slapped my daughter." She seemed horrified by her own voice, but then the words tumbled out. "I've always had a difficult relationship with my Emma. She was growing up too fast, and it made me mad." She glanced at Lauren for moral support. "Last year—Emma's twelve now—I slapped her. In the face. For nothing." Her eyes glistened. "And I knew I needed help. Because I love her, and I hurt her, and I didn't even know why. Lauren helped me realize I was conflicted watching Emma because she's the same age I was when my father started raping me." Her tears spilled over.

A petite, Hispanic-looking woman cried too. We were off to a rousing start, I thought, amazed at this shy woman baring her soul to complete strangers.

"Thank you, Jenny. Well done. Diana?"

The beautiful black woman leaned forward. "I am Diana. I am a survivor of sexual abuse, and I am anorexic. I was having fainting spells at work—I'm an attorney—and the partners convinced me if I didn't seek help, they would fire me." Her annoyed expression softened a hair. "Of course, I'm glad they did, as it's helped me sort out quite a few problems," she said gently, leaning back in her chair. "And I'm glad to be here with you today," she added as an afterthought. Through those varied emotions, she looked regal, like some kind of warrior princess.

"I was made to go too," a young woman spat out, drawing a skeptical look from Diana. "By my aunt. I love her and all, but I didn't want to do any of this therapy shit. She said I had to get help after I got kicked out of ROTC at college, or she was gonna kick me out of the house."

This stocky woman with a pageboy haircut framing her brown, slightly freckled face seemed a few years younger than me.

"It's okay if anyone else, like Charmaine, is ambivalent about being here. This is not an easy process. Thank you for being honest, Charmaine, and we're glad you're here. Next?"

"I'm Frances," said an angular woman with short, graying hair. She cleared her throat and inhaled. "I've had a tough time with relationships for years, I could never make them work. I don't know why. Five years ago, this perfect person named Jane fell into my life, and I've done everything in my power not to mess this one up. Two years ago, we started talking about having a ceremony to celebrate our relationship, since we can't actually get married. That got her thinking about the church—she's a lapsed Catholic, and she decided she wanted to return to the church. She wanted me to go too, but she knows I gave up on the church a long time ago. We fought about it, and she moved out." The memory twisted her face.

She leaned forward. "At that point, I had to admit I was pretty confused about religion, about relationships, about lots of things. So I made a deal with Jane. I said I would go to therapy instead of church. And she agreed," she said with a smile. "I didn't even know I had been sexually abused until I started seeing Lauren. Digging into my issues with religion uncovered a deeper issue, and while it hurts like hell to dig it out, it's cleansing at the same time." She appeared pleased with her description, scanned the circle of faces for reactions, and settled back into her chair.

Jesus, I had to follow that? Why couldn't I have gone after Charmaine? "Shelby, can you tell the group why you chose to come to therapy and address the sexual abuse in your past?" Lauren asked.

I looked at the ceiling for inspiration. Nothing.

"Well, I remembered some stuff from my childhood a while ago, and I thought I had dealt with it, but then I kept—I keep getting migraines, and my boss said maybe my body is trying to tell me something. So I came to Lauren to make sure I had dealt with what happened, and to try to get rid of my headaches." *Lame, that sounded so lame.*

Lauren gave me one of her probing looks, lifted her shoulders, and turned farther around the circle, to the tiny Hispanic woman.

"Hi everyone, I'm Rosie." She smiled warmly, her high ponytail bobbing in time to the rhythm of her accented speech. "I have finally accepted that my Uncle Jorge's sexual abuse of me was coming out in weird ways and hurting me and my family. I had some problems with drinking and drugs, but mostly my problem was shoplifting. I was caught twice when I was a teenager, but they dropped the charges both times." Her eyes rested on each of us in the circle for a second or two as she spoke, like she was inviting us into her life.

"Then I met Renaldo and we got married, and we have four kids who are the best." She gushed like she was on a talk show. "And then, a few years ago, I don't know why, I shoplifted for the first time in years." Gushing over. A slight chill entered her voice. "I got caught and got arrested, and then I had to talk to Renaldo. I owed him that, to tell him all the stuff he didn't know about me. I said I wanted help, and he supported me. And that's why I'm here."

The girl with the skunk on her head was next. This should be interesting. She hadn't moved since we came in. But now, she pulled her legs up until she sat almost straight before freezing again.

"Kelly," said Lauren in the softest voice I'd ever heard her use. "You're safe here. These women will not hurt you. Can you look at me?" she coached, waiting until Kelly lifted her head. Kelly's eyes were weary and her face ragged and blotched with acne. She might have been anywhere from eighteen to thirty-five years old. "Focus on me, Kelly. You've told me this before. Tell me what you said at that important session we had together, the first time you opened up to me."

"I need help." I flinched at her soft, girlish voice, so different from the aged face and tough body. "The state sent me to a psych ward the first time I tried to kill myself. I hated the doctors there. After the second time, I met Lauren. I like Lauren. She made me see that I really do want to live. But not like I've been living, on the streets. I want to live in a real house someday—"

She stopped abruptly and physically retreated back into herself.

"Well done, Kelly," said Lauren. After a respectful pause, she shifted to face the group. "Fantastic, everyone, thank you for sharing your personal stories with the group."

Lauren encouraged us to talk about our childhoods without going into the abuse. Evidently a trust-building exercise. I'm not sure it worked, though, because it brought out our differences more than anything. The beautiful black woman came across as a cold, rich snob. She grew up in Newton with the picture-perfect family, drawing dirty looks from the stocky ROTC one who had seven parents and stepparents—that had to be a record. The gray-haired one, who must have been more than forty, got edgy talking about her life disappointments: pregnant at fifteen, put the baby up for adoption, bounced from job to job, bounced from partner to partner, and so on.

By the end, a fair amount of resentment was flying around the room. This one had a successful career practically handed to her and didn't appreciate it. Those two had loving husbands and children but this one's fiancé walked out on her. The only ones not irritated were Kelly, who was too out of it to notice the tension shooting around the room, and the petite Hispanic one—Rosie I think—who annoyingly beamed at us like we were her favored children.

Lauren's chair scraped loudly across the linoleum floor, cutting through the souring mood.

"Okay, it's time to stop, but before you go, I have an assignment for you."

Charmaine, the ROTC one, groaned.

"Don't worry; it's an easy one. I have said you are not alone in your experiences. One in three women has been sexually abused." She let that sink in. "So look at the women you see when you're out and about this week, and think about the fact that one in three of them has been sexually abused. They may be far along in their healing, they may just be starting, or they may not be healing at all yet. They may not even remember the abuse. But you have sisters everywhere around the world who know what you're going through. So be strong. Good work, everyone, and I'll see you next week."

Astrid

CHAPTER 31

We wanted to know all about Shelby's support group experience when we cozied up in Tina's living room Sunday afternoon, steaming mugs of tea in hand, scattered snowflakes meandering down outside the windows. Tina still wore her fuzzy flowered PJs, Shel wore old sweatpants, and I wore my favorite purple velour tracksuit.

"It was unlike anything I've ever done. It was funny; it was intense; it was bizarre." Shelby blew on the hot tea and sipped. "I'm kind of intrigued by the women. They're all so different." She stared into her tea. "But they're all so much more messed up than me. I felt like a faker in a way," she said in a strained voice.

"Nooo, you shouldn't," Tina said.

A tear dribbled down Shelby's cheek. Tina leaped over to Shelby and embraced her awkwardly where she sat, in the overstuffed chair. "Are you okay? I bet it's hard right now."

"Yeah, I'm okay. I get so emotional lately, sometimes at the strangest times. The other day Maggie said something nice, and I almost started crying." She flicked the tear away.

"Hm," Tina and I said at the same time.

Since the subject appeared closed, I put my mug on the coffee table. My turn. "Can I tell you guys about something that's been going on at work with me?" I asked. Shelby's eyebrows knit together. "I know, you think you know everything that happens there, but you don't," I said, more harshly then I meant to.

"No, I don't know everything. I've told you, I'm the last one to hear the office gossip because I don't pay a lot of attention to that stuff. But I thought I knew all about *your* life at work," Shelby said.

"Well, I haven't told anyone this. Not even my mother." Their eyes were riveted on me. "Brad—he's my old boss and one of the top people at the agency," she said to Tina, "put the moves on me a while back."

"What do you mean exactly?" Tina asked.

"He said we should sleep together, and he was constantly making sexual innuendoes. It's been better since I went to Maggie's group and since Kristy came. But now that she's gone, it's starting again."

"Like what? Is he propositioning you?" Tina asked.

"Not really. But every time I have to be near him, he finds a reason to touch me somehow, and he's always grinning like he knows he's making me uncomfortable. And when we're in staff meetings, he'll stand next to me even though I try to avoid him and he leans into me and stuff. Anything to make me feel awkward."

"What a jerk," Tina said. "Can't you say something?"

"To whom? The place is run by men, the partners are men, and they love Brad—he's probably going to be a partner himself someday. Even if I said something, he would just deny it, and then I'm screwed. So I just try to avoid him. But it's kind of wearing me down."

I looked at Shelby, who hadn't said anything.

"What? I don't know what to say," she said in answer to my gaze. "It sucks that he's being irritating, but he's not actually *doing* anything. Maybe you're making too much of this. Maybe it will just go away if you ignore him."

Disappointment pressed the air out of my lungs. "I guess," I mumbled. Shouldn't Shelby of all people understand the mental anguish that comes with inappropriate, sexually charged behavior? She looked a touch guilty but still didn't offer any inkling of support.

"Okay, girls, we need a happier subject," Tina said, "and maybe wine. Astrid, how's it going with Dave?"

"Eh. Great. Not great. I don't know. I really like him, but I'm not sure I'm in the right frame of mind to get into a relationship right now." The slight catch in my voice surprised me.

"Shelby said once the timing has to be right for both people at the same time. Maybe you'll feel different later on," Tina soothed.

"Astrid," Shelby said in a sharp voice. "Since you're already annoyed with me, I might as well tell you I'm quitting Campbell Lewis."

I turned deliberately to face her. "You're what?" I said.

"I'm quitting. I'm giving Maggie my notice. I've been thinking about it for a while. Nothing's been the same since I got sick. They treat me with kid gloves, and I'm not getting the juicy projects I used to. I just think it's time for me to move on."

"Oh my God, Shel. Did you get another job?" Tina asked.

"No, but I don't care. I've got a little saved, and I'll figure something out."

"So you're ditching me. Alone with Brad. Thanks a lot." I didn't know why her leaving scared me, but it did.

"Don't be so dramatic, Astrid. You're not 'alone with Brad'," Shelby said, rolling her eyes. "You don't even work with him anymore."

"What about the Christmas party, huh? So you're ditching me for that too?" I squinted against the angry tears.

Shelby inhaled deeply. "I'm not ditching you, Astrid. We'll still be friends. But no, I won't be at the party. That would be weird." She stood up and left for the bathroom.

Shelby

CHAPTER 32

December 10, 1987
Dear Shelby,
I feel a bit silly writing this letter, but I know you're upset about Norman, and I want to make it up to you. I'll explain in a minute.
But first, we have decided to go to Europe for Christmas this year. It was clear at Thanksgiving you didn't want to spend time with us, which I am trying to accept. So, since I've always wanted to see Paris and Rome, off we go. I know it's short notice. I hope you can forgive me.
Anyway, I tried to make you the beneficiary of one of my retirement accounts, which has $13,000 in it. There was a glitch in the paperwork, so it still lists Norman, but I thought you should know my intention is for you to get that money, should my plane go down. (You know how I love airplanes!) And if our plane does crash but he survives, you can shoot him. (Maybe do it anyway?)
I hope you can enjoy Christmas. Maybe we can see each other in January, and I can show you the photos from the trip. I'd like that.
Love,
Mom

***

"That is just so weird," Tina said, putting the letter down. "She says you can shoot him but she's going on a trip with him. Does she believe you or not? And I like how then she talks as if everything is normal, and like you'd even care about seeing pictures of their vacation together."

"I know. I'm not even answering. It's too confusing to even try to figure out. So it goes with the other one, into the black hole," I said dropping the letter into my desk drawer.

***

I was staring out the meeting room window at the few dead leaves still clutching onto the branches when Diana spoke, her warrior persona from the first group therapy session nowhere in sight. "I went home," she said quietly. "It was my mother's birthday, so my two brothers, and my sister, and I all went to the house in Newton. It was a big party, and it was horrible." She looked up at us. "You see, I remembered a few years ago that my sister abused me when I was a little girl, and she was twelve. I knew she did things to me when our nanny fell asleep—well, passed out, technically. But I never knew why. And I didn't remember a lot of details."

Everyone sat absolutely still.

"I've never said anything to Grace. I didn't know how to. But we found ourselves alone at one point, and without planning, I blurted out, 'Why did you hate Nanny so much?' She looked at me strangely and said, 'I didn't need a nanny.' And then I experienced the most vivid flashback I've ever had. It was so real it made me nauseous." She breathed in as if sucking for air.

"Go ahead, Diana. It's okay," said Rosie.

"I remembered her putting toys—a doll, and a rattle-type thing—inside me and saying, 'I don't need a nanny. I'm too old, Dee-Dee, but I have to have one because you need one. And you need one because you're a bad girl.' And she shoved things inside me, and it hurt so bad. I begged her to stop, but she wouldn't." Her voice dropped to a whisper.

My God, how was she not bawling?

"So after the flashback, I said to my sister, 'Grace, why did you do it to me?'" Diana stopped cold.

"What did Grace say?" Jenny encouraged as if speaking to one of her kids.

"She said, 'I don't know what you're talking about.' And she walked out on me. Then I threw up, like I did when I was five, the time she made me bleed. She told my mother the blood on my clothes was from a cut on her hand, but she gave herself that cut with a toy knife, to cover up what happened."

I swallowed some vomit that burped into the back of my throat. The room was quiet until Lauren spoke. "Diana, that was a big step, confronting your sister."

Diana gave a weak snort. "Lot of good it did me. She's still running the show, like she always did. She told everyone at the party I was sick and that they should leave me alone for a while."

The pain in Diana's eyes made me want to help. How horrible to have a sibling abuse you. "Do you think somebody abused her too, to make her that way?" I offered. Frances stiffened beside me. "I mean, I know it doesn't change what she did, but maybe there's a reason she's like that. And maybe someday you'll find out what that reason is," I trailed off. The chill in the room told me I was going down like a torpedoed submarine.

Lauren came in to save the day. "Yes, understanding what made your abuser do what he or she did to you can be helpful, but it is *not* mandatory for your healing. Your abuser's problems are not yours. And does it excuse your abuser's actions if he or she was a victim too? I ask you this: have any of you turned around and abused someone?"

A few women shook their heads. I held back my tears.

"No, you did not inflict what you experienced on anyone else." Lauren's voice grew strident. "I also want to say that you can confront your abuser if you want to. You can even forgive your abuser if you want to. But you don't have to do either of these things. And you should only do them if they are helpful to you. Understanding your abuser is not your job. Healing your abuser is not your job. Healing yourself is."

My face burned with shame from my weak attempt at showing support. My chest ached with unreleased sobs.

Lauren turned to Kelly, thankfully drawing attention away from Diana's saga and my misery.

"Kelly, why don't you tell us about your childhood? You told me you thought you were ready."

"Okay," Kelly said, as if preparing to tell us what she needed at the grocery store. "I grew up in Roxbury. My mother is a junkie. I never had a father. One night when I was eleven, my mother passed out after she shot some smack. Her pusher—I didn't even know his name—started coming on to me while I was watching TV. I tried to fight him off, but he kept coming. My mother came to and walked in when he was raping me." Her voice trailed off. Her white striped head dropped, and her shoulders slumped.

"Did she—what did she do?" Jenny asked.

"She said, 'You're gonna have to pay for that,' and he said, 'Your next trip is on me,' and she said, 'Fine.'" I heard a clock ticking somewhere when Kelly paused; funny I'd never heard it before. "After that, she realized I was a way for her to get free drugs, and she started pimping me out to all the dealers in town," she continued in her monotone, her pale face stony. "She told me it was the best way I could help her, and show her I loved her."

We sat in shock. Kelly hadn't spoken since that one time in the first session, and now she'd blurted out this horror. Lauren ended the session and went over to speak with Kelly, who seemed to have slipped back inside herself.

After using the bathroom and putting on my coat, I found myself going down the stairs with Kelly.

"Um, can I just tell you that I think you're really brave?" I asked.

She stopped and looked at me so I stopped too. Her eyes, so vacant in the session, warmed up.

"You mean for coming here?" Her voice sounded stronger in the small stairwell.

"I guess, and for talking about what happened and for, everything." I wanted to say for not giving up but didn't want to raise the idea that she might give up. Again.

"Hm. Coming here is easy. No one here wants to hurt me. The hard part is in your head." She actually smiled, but pain flashed in her eyes.

We walked out of the building and separated.

I stopped at a deli and bought a take-out sandwich. But when I got home, it smelled funny, so I put it in the fridge and took a bowl of Ben & Jerry's and the new *Rolling Stone* up to bed instead. My eyes were itchy and heavy, my neck was tight, and my nagging headache had amped up again, threatening to mushroom into a full-fledged migraine. Hearing Diana's and Kelly's graphic stories confused me. My confusion spread into a grief that invaded my entire body. I turned up the stereo so my roommates wouldn't hear my sobs as the grief erupted.

Astrid

CHAPTER 33

Campbell Lewis rented out a function room at a Landsdowne Street rock club for its annual holiday party, the trendy setting a nod to the growing number of employees in our twenties. A band Shelby would have loved performed songs I'd never heard. I socialized as required, moving back and forth between the main stage area and our private space at the other end of the club.

Brad seemed particularly jocular, shaking hands and hugging people all around. Maybe he finally got his partner promotion. A few times, I caught him watching me, but the layout of the club made it easy to avoid him—much easier than in the office.

At work, in an effort to make him lose interest, I had started wearing my older, less attractive outfits. But it didn't reduce his innuendoes and leers. Maybe I *was* overreacting, but I couldn't help feeling something malicious about him. I kept flashing back to the proposition and him saying he always got what he wanted and trying to sabotage me by playing footsie at client meetings.

But tonight was a company party with lots of people in close proximity, so I'd let my guard down. I even dressed sexy, in a hot pink halter-top dress with matching stilettos. I smacked my magenta lips together and smiled at my reflection in the ladies' room mirror, popped my lipstick back into my purse, and pushed out the bathroom door into the club, running smack into Brad, as if my musings made him materialize in front of my very eyes.

"Astrid," Brad said, smiling evilly. "How nice to see you here," he cooed.

I tried to move around him, but he grabbed my arm. His breath reeked of gin, and his glazed eyes struggled to focus.

"Not so fast. Come here; I really need to talk to you." I hesitated. "It's about work, and I promise I'll be good."

He steered me off to the side of the main room. When I realized he was heading toward an unstaffed coat checkroom, I stopped and tried to move away. He tightened his grip and pulled me into the small room. I couldn't believe how strong he was.

He pushed me up against the counter and pinned me, his arms on either side of me, his hands resting on the counter. I felt my heart pulsing in my limbs. Frantically I looked back toward the club but saw no one.

"Astrid," he slurred, "we need to stop playing games and get down to business." He giggled, to my horror. "See, I told you I wanted to talk about business."

He shifted his weight and adjusted his hands.

Suddenly his mouth was hard on mine. I struggled, but he grabbed my arms, digging in with his fingers. I couldn't move. *It's just a kiss*, I said to myself. *It's just a kiss. Let him get it over with.*

He leaned in and ground his hips against me. His hard-on prodded. In my mouth, his tongue probed. He clutched my hand and forced it against his crotch.

"Oh man that feels good. Doesn't it?" he mumbled and kissed me again. I felt faint. "I always knew you wanted me too, even though you like playing hard to get."

How dare he say I wanted this? Angry adrenaline raced through my veins. When he let go of my hand and reached for his belt buckle, I twisted away from his other hand and jabbed my knee up into his groin as hard as I could, nearly losing my balance.

"Owww," he howled, doubling over as I bolted back into the main club. The band had finished, and the crowd was thinning out. I mixed in with the small groups of people starting to leave, my breath slowly returning to normal.

Safely on the subway to Brighton, I clutched my arms around my torso and wept. None of the drunk or tired passengers noticed me, even though I wore no jacket in the freezing cold.

I would have to be more vigilant. How did I get myself in that position? I shouldn't have had three cocktails. Brad was so trashed, he probably wouldn't even remember any of it.

I needed Shelby and Tina, but they'd already left for their Christmas break at Tina's home in Schenectedy. At least I'd be in Maine with my mother tomorrow.

At home, I showered in scalding water and passed out. I slept fitfully, Brad's looming face and the weight of his body against mine startling me awake throughout the night.

***

I slid into my Calvins, zipped and buttoned, and squatted a few times to stretch them out. I whisked the thin, protective paper cover off my favorite, classic white blouse, nodding at my decision to get my white shirts dry-cleaned.

In the bathroom, I flicked a coat of mascara onto my lashes and skimmed sheer gloss across my lips. Yes, that was enough make-up. After studying my reflection, I reached for a scrunchie and pulled my hair into a sleek, low ponytail.

Back in my bedroom, I put on simple pearl earrings. The reflection in my small bureau-top mirror said no, too pretentious. I swapped them for a simple pair of small gold hoops.

I bundled myself into my navy wool coat and warm but fashionable boots and marched out of my apartment to be assaulted by a blast of frigid morning air. I stood firm against the winter wind at first but shivered when it hit me how cold it must have been last night when I rode the subway home jacket-less.

Halfway to my destination, I stopped in the middle of the sidewalk and clamped my eyes shut to think. I couldn't barge in and demand justice. I'd be pegged as a bitch. But I couldn't act the fragile flower to gain sympathy. It wasn't in me. I'd go with neutral. Concerned but matter-of-fact. Seeking help but not a damsel in distress or a screeching shrew. I resumed my walk at a slightly more relaxed pace, in line with the few other early Saturday morning pedestrians keeping me company.

Ten blocks later, I squared my shoulders and, fighting a gust of wind for control of the door, heaved open the heavy entrance of the Boston Police Department's Brighton district station.

The entry area was surprisingly quiet and subdued, nothing like the high-tension chaos depicted on *Cagney & Lacey* or *Hill Street Blues*. A tall, skinny, blonde policeman standing behind a counter glanced at me and continued whatever he was doing, his arms moving back and forth like he was sorting or stamping papers. I approached the counter and cleared my throat, partly to get his attention and partly because my throat felt scratchy all of a sudden. Again, he glanced but said nothing.

"I'd like to report an attempted rape, please." I swallowed. The words felt awkward and foreign on my tongue.

He stood up straight and looked me in the eye.

"Okay, one minute," he said as the main door flew open, bringing with it cold air, a ruddy-faced policeman, and an extremely dirty, disheveled man with a long beard and a wacky grin that seemed out of place considering the circumstances.

"Taking him to the holding cell," the cop said to his skinny colleague.

"Hi, Sheldon," the disheveled man said as he and his attending policemen started across the room. "Aren't you glad to see me again?"

I turned back to Sheldon who gave a soft sigh and rolled his eyes. "Ralph, when you're done, take this lady's statement on an assault charge?"

"Ooh, I'll take her statement!" the derelict said from right behind me, making me jump. "Put her in the cell with me, and I'll find out everything you need to know."

I wheeled around to face him, inhaling a nauseating combination of whiskey and urine. The drunk reached for me, but the ruddy-faced policemen yanked the drunk's arm and pulled him through a closed door off to the side.

"Have a seat," Sheldon said. "Officer Bryant will be right back to take your statement."

I sat on a hard wooden bench at the side of the room, smoothing my hair and tapping my feet until Bryant returned five minutes later. He brushed right past me on his way to another closed door.

"Ralph!" Sheldon said. Ralph turned back to see his colleague point in my direction. Ralph sighed, looked at me for a few seconds, and nodded in a resigned greeting.

This entire preamble was not instilling confidence that my charges would be taken seriously.

"Come on; follow me," Ralph said, in a voice suggesting I stood between him and the end of his shift and a warm bed or something. Which, it turns out, *was* the case.

Ralph led me into a large room with about a dozen desks, half of them occupied by uniformed and plainclothes policemen. Plus one policewoman. Ralph was also scanning the room.

"Rodriguez," he said finally, beckoning me to follow him to a desk where an olive-skinned, mustachioed man lazed with his feet up on his desk, legs crossed, staring into space. His pointed boots and geometric-patterned shirt glistened as boldly as his slicked-backed hair.

"Detective Rodriguez," Bryant said when we reached the man's desk. "This lady wants to report an assault. Do me a favor and help her out, okay?"

Rodriguez continued staring into space for another fifteen seconds, then pulled his legs down and turned toward us.

"You know you're supposed to get the initial report before I get involved," Rodriguez said matter-of-factly.

"Come on, man. My shift ended half an hour ago. You know she's going to end up talking to you anyway."

Rodriguez smirked and brought his gaze to me where it stayed. His eyes softened a tad, and the tightness around his mouth relaxed. "Fine. Have a seat, Miss—?"

"Miss Ericsson, two s's," I said and then cleared my throat, which was tickling again. Hopefully I wasn't catching a cold after last night's chilly commute home. "First name, Astrid," I said before he could ask.

"Okay, Miss Ericsson, tell me what happened," he said, sliding a pre-printed form into his typewriter and adjusting the paper until it was just so.

I opened my mouth and closed it abruptly with a small exhalation. Where did I start? With last night? A year ago, when I rebuffed his proposition and he tried to get me fired? Or was the real beginning way back when we flirted in my job interview?

"Miss Ericsson," Rodriguez prompted. "Can you tell me what happened?"

I focused my eyes, bringing into clarity the messy pile of file folders on a nearby desk and a wire trash can half full of Styrofoam coffee cups. Blinking as my head twitched involuntarily, I swung my gaze to Rodriguez's small brown eyes.

"I'm not sure where to start. Can I break it down into the five W's?" I asked.

His eyebrows arched. "The five what?"

"You know, the five W's, like a journalist asks in an interview. Who, what, when, where and why. And sometimes how."

He gave a slight eye-roll and a small shrug. "Sure. Whatever floats your boat." He faced the typewriter.

I crossed my legs, but immediately uncrossed them so I wouldn't look too casual. I waited for his prompt.

"Go ahead," he said, looking away from his typewriter and glancing at me. "Tell me who your perpetrator was. You want to start with *who*, right?"

It took ten minutes to get through the basic details of last night, possibly longer than the assault itself.

"You said he didn't force you into the coatroom," Rodriguez said. "So you went willingly?"

I winced at the picture his words painted. "Not completely willingly. I've been avoiding him as much as possible for a while now. But he is a higher up at the company, and he said he wanted to discuss something work-related."

"And did he? Discuss something work-related?"

"No."

"Does anyone at your place of employment know that he's been—" he glanced at his sheet—"harassing you?"

"No," I said, cursing myself for keeping his behavior to myself. "Just a friend who used to work there."

He shook his head. "Okay, so you say once you got to the coatroom, he attacked you."

"It's not just what I say, Detective Rodriguez," I said, staring at the nameplate on his desk and willing my temper to stay even. "It's what happened."

He shrugged. "You say potato. I say po-tah-to."

I resisted the urge to squint at him and turn on my what-the-hell-are-you-talking-about-can-we-please-focus smile.

"Did anyone at all pass by while you were in there?"

I sighed, closed my eyes, and re-opened them. "I couldn't see much beyond his body—he's quite tall and was very close to me. I did look out toward the club a few times and didn't see a soul."

He stroked his thin mustache. "Tell me again how he got you into a compromising position."

"He pulled me into the room and—"

"Wait. Stop there for a second. You said this was a coatroom. It's winter. No one else was around at any time?"

"This one wasn't being used. It was empty. There's another coat check near the front of the club."

"Okay. Continue. He pulled you into the room and—"

"Then he pushed me back and pinned me against the counter. There wasn't much I could do."

Detective Rodriguez studied me, his gaze taking all of me in at once. It wasn't like the leers I was used to, but it was uncomfortable just the same, as if he were sizing up my character and my physique at the same time.

"You're pretty tall and look athletic. You couldn't just run away?"

My heart beat faster at his accusatory words and the flashing back to the moment of Brad's attack. "Believe me I would have if I could. And I did eventually, as I told you. But I couldn't at first. He's more than six feet tall and very muscular." My face heated up as if I'd confessed my early attraction to Brad. Rodriguez was scanning his sheet of paper in the typewriter.

"Did you at any time tell him to stop or say 'no'?"

"I don't remember. But he had to know I didn't like it. I didn't kiss him back or anything."

"Hmph. Drunk man in a dark club with a pretty woman. Being direct probably would have been a good idea."

Anger welled in my scratchy throat. "Are you going to keep questioning me about all the things you think I did wrong, or are you going to help me?" I hated the quiver in my voice, but then again, maybe it would elicit sympathy.

His eyes swung to my face, then back to his paper. He seemed to be re-reading the entire report, and at an excruciatingly slow pace. Finally, he turned toward me, leaned forward, and clasped his hands between his knees.

"Here's the thing, Miss Ericsson. It's your word against his. You have no witnesses. No injuries except a questionable bruise on your arm. There was no damage to the club to suggest a struggle. You'd been drinking—"

"But—" I interjected.

"—as I said, you'd been drinking," he said over my protest. "I know he was too. You said he was drunk. But this is about your credibility. And alcohol weakens our judgement-making ability. It's a known fact. To press charges and win, you have to be able to prove the lack of consent. You don't have any proof."

The room spun a little around me. "So you're saying there's nothing I can do? He just gets away with this? Who knows what he would have done if I hadn't kneed him in the, in his crotch!"

Rodriguez smiled with half his mouth and sat back in his chair. "I think I know exactly what would have happened. So it's good you got away. Be thankful for that, and let the rest go." My entire body deflated. "You can press charges if you want, but I don't think you'll be successful. I'm just telling you the truth."

"This is ridiculous. He almost raped me!" My throat felt tight as if my windpipe were closing up. "There's nothing I can do? Nothing at all? What about a jury? I'd be a very credible witness," I said, dimly aware that several tears had begun a slow journey down my face.

He studied my face again. "Just be glad you were able to stop him. If things had gone further and you had physical evidence, you could've had a case. But that would come with a very high price. For one thing, you'd get dragged through the mud if there was a full investigation and maybe a trial. It's a rough road no matter how much evidence you have." He leaned in again, resting his hands on his thighs.

"Miss Ericsson," he continued in a softer voice. "I'm not unsympathetic. Believe me. I have a teenage daughter, and I'd kill anyone who did this to her. But my hands are tied without any evidence or a witness. Spare yourself the pain and disappointment of pressing charges and move on with your life."

"Move on? Don't you see my life is different today than it was two days ago?" A small sob escaped from my chest, startling me.

"I understand this is hard. Do you have any friends you can talk to about it? Relatives maybe? That might help."

"Yeah. Maybe." I collected my coat and purse and stood up. I came for justice and got resistance, doubt, and suspicion. My chest ached as I held in more sobs.

"I do believe you, for what that's worth," Rodriguez said, as if he'd heard my thoughts.

I nodded, afraid to speak for fear I'd burst into tears. I turned and rushed out of the station, as sullied and out of control as I'd been in the coatroom the night before.

***

"Tough drive home?" my mother asked, one eyebrow lifted, as I carried my luggage into the kitchen. I dropped my suitcase and rubbed my wet eyelashes with the back of my hand.

"Mom!" I sobbed, flying into her arms.

She stiffened and pushed me back to look into my eyes. "What on Earth is going on, sweetie? Come in, sit down, and tell me everything."

She steered me to the living room couch and pressed on my shoulders until I sat, weeping quietly. She pulled a tissue from the end table and pressed it into my hand.

"Tell me," she encouraged, her voice firm and fearful at the same time.

I shuddered out another sob and leaned into her until she embraced me. "Mom, it was horrible. Everything is a mess."

She stroked my hair. "This isn't just a boy problem, is it? Something serious has happened. You tell me when you're ready. I'm here," she murmured.

A minute later, I separated from her. I wiped my eyes, leaving a broad swath of black mascara on the pale yellow tissue. "Brad at work tried to have his way with me."

Her sky blue eyes flashed. "Your old boss? That Brad? Did he try to kiss you?" She sounded almost optimistic, that it might have been only an attempted kiss.

"No, Mom." I shook my head. "We were at the company's holiday party, at a club, and he cornered me in a back room and tried to get me to touch him. And he kept leaning on me and sticking his tongue down my throat. It was awful."

"Oh my baby, I'm so sorry," Mom whispered, embracing me again. "You said 'tried'— so he stopped before anything—before anything really bad happened?"

I nodded into her shoulder. "I fought back and got away."

She sighed heavily, my chin rising and falling with her movement. "Thank God for that." She tensed, and I knew she was thinking about how to solve this problem for me. "We need to contact the police."

I shook my head into her shoulder, sat back, and looked her in the eye. "No, Mom, I tried that. They won't help."

Her eyes hardened. "Well, let's talk more about that later then. For now, at least you're here, and you're safe."

I twisted the tissue in my lap. "I'm sorry, Mom."

"Why? What are you sorry for?" she asked.

"Because it's my fault. I flirted with Brad even when you told me not to. I actually had a crush on him at first, and I thought he liked me too, but everything just went wrong so fast and now—and now this."

Mom cradled her forehead in her left palm, her left elbow braced on her right arm, which she held across her body, as she massaged her forehead and looked down for a minute. Sighing, she dropped her left hand onto her right arm, hugging herself. She looked at me, her eyes so like my own but everything else about her so much wiser and experienced.

"Astrid, let me try to explain something. The reasons I say workplace romances are dangerous is because they can blow up and leave you vulnerable. They can be frowned upon by management—in which case you know who's leaving the company—the woman, not the man. They can be distracting—who wants to look at their lover in the middle of an editorial team meeting? And if you break up, things can get very awkward."

She waited until I nodded in understanding.

"And the reason I say flirting with co-workers is bad is because it can lead to a romance, but even if it doesn't, it looks bad. It can be misinterpreted. It can rightly be considered unprofessional by anyone who sees it, including the person on the receiving end of the flirtation. If you're not really interested in the person, he could say you're leading him on—or using your wiles to get ahead. There are just so many reasons flirting is wrong. Enough said on that?"

She paused until I nodded again.

"But none of that has a goddamn thing to do with a man forcing himself upon you," her voice dropped into a hate-filled whisper. "And that's what you described. Maybe it didn't get that far, but it sounds like his intentions were clear."

I stared at her, wide-eyed. She clutched my hands as if both our lives depended on it.

"So, now, how do we keep you safe?"

I shook my muddled head slightly. "What do you mean? I can't quit."

"I know you can't. I'm sorry about that. I wish you could. But," she said, scanning the ceiling and returning her gaze to me, "I think I can get you some mace. You carry it in your pocketbook *always*, understand me?"

I nodded.

"Okay. And look for a new job if you want to, but don't leave this one until you find a new one."

"I know, don't worry about that."

"That's my girl. My brave girl."

She hugged me again, stroking my back.

"Astrid," she said into my hair, "do you think this is going to make you fearful with all men?"

"What do you mean? Not all men are like Brad."

"I know. But this guy Dave you're seeing. Will you feel unsafe with him?"

"No, he's not like that at all. But who knows if that will even last?" I asked, stating a fear, not a desire.

"Well," she said, sitting back again, "if you want it to work out, then I want it to work out."

"And if it doesn't, then on to the next one like you always say." I attempted a smile.

"When have I ever said that?" she asked, shock on her face.

"You always say men are stepping stones, you always—"

"Astrid Ericcson, men at *work* are a means to an end. In the rest of your life, they are people like you and me, and very important ones at that. For heaven's sake, have I really been that confusing in my advice?"

"But you never needed a man!"

"That was different. Do you think I wanted to be alone all those years? You were my priority, and taking care of us was more important than romance. But I don't want that for you! Oh, Astrid, I want nothing more than to see you happy, and being in a loving relationship may be one of the things that makes you happy."

"Oh," I said, wiping my leaky eyes again.

She hugged me again and stood up. "I think we need tea, yes?"

I nodded and followed her to the kitchen.

Shelby

CHAPTER 34

Christmas was surreal. After Mom and Norman decided to ditch us kids and high-tail it to Europe, Tina had insisted I go home with her to Schenectady for a few days. Kyle decided to stay in Florida with his new girlfriend's family, and Eric hunkered down in New York working on his thesis. Astrid of course was home with her mother in Maine.

Tina hoped having me as a guest would inspire her mother to stay on the wagon, or at least stand beside it instead of kicking off her shoes, hitching up her skirt, and running off on another alcohol-fueled adventure.

Mrs. Romano seemed normal to me when we sat down for lunch a few days before Christmas, if a little June Cleaver-ish with her conservative dress and swept-up hair. Tina's father was working, so Tina, her mother, and sister reminisced and gossiped about people and places I knew nothing about. But Tina and her mother addressed each other so politely, it actually felt like we had traveled back in time and were guest stars in an episode of *Leave It to Beaver*.

"And where did you say your parents are for the holiday, Shelby?" Mrs. Romano asked, drawing me out of my thoughts.

"France and Italy. My mother and stepfather. He's not my real father. They're fulfilling some lifelong dream or something," I said, fiddling with my fork.

"How wonderful! But I expect you'll miss your family. We'll do our best to be your surrogate family for the next week or so."

"Mom, I told you," Tina said. "We're not staying a whole week."

Mrs. Romano placed her napkin on the table, ignoring her daughter. "Now, who's ready for dessert?"

Later, as Tina and I perched on her childhood bed, my friend launched into a sarcastic tirade.

"Yes, Shelby, you simply must be part of our loving home this Christmas. We are the perfect American family. You'll love it here. I know you've got some demons in your past, but here in the Romano household, we invite our demons right up to the dinner table. Nothing to hide here. We put our addictions on full display, and because you're here, we're going to do an extra special show this year. That's all I'm going to say because I don't want to spoil the surprise for you."

She flopped back on her pillow and threw her arms wide with a huge sigh.

"She seemed sober to me. She didn't have a drink with lunch," I offered.

"That's because she was already half in the bag, probably sneaking wine in the kitchen all morning. I can tell by the look in her eye," Tina said flatly. "Don't let her fool you."

So began several painful days of tense family time. Tina and I escaped the house for walks when we could and hung with her friends Christmas Eve. I tried to distract her with my funniest and most embarrassing stories from high school and college. Moping was minimal.

But being away from Newfield for the first Christmas in my life killed my holiday spirit as much as being home killed Tina's. My heart harbored a small place dedicated to holidays in Newfield that echoed with emptiness, and I missed my brothers. On top of that, it was a green Christmas, which, in the northeast, really means a muddy, brown Christmas.

Tina's mother got sloshy a few times during my visit, but no kitchen-floor-in-her-underwear episodes. Tina's father barely interacted with us at all, other than relaying boring stories over the Christmas meal.

So I sighed in relief as deeply as Tina did when we piled into the Situation for the trip back to Massachusetts. We agreed we felt so much like fish out of water in our hometowns that we must have become true Bostonians when we weren't looking.

***

The day after New Year's, I started work as the public affairs manager at the Commonwealth Zoo in Boston's downtrodden Dorchester neighborhood. Terry Campbell had actually told me about the job opening when I said I'd love to work in the music industry or with animals somehow.

The zoo director, Mike Evans—a friendly, young and ambitious guy with big plans—balked when I asked for a few weeks off before starting—I wanted to get my migraines under control. But he had no problem with me leaving early for physical therapy appointments, something my doctor set up at my last headache visit.

Mike seemed in permanent overdrive because they were preparing to open the jewel in the newly renovated zoo's crown—an African rainforest exhibit featuring dozens of endangered species including western lowland gorillas. The cutting-edge exhibit represented the zoo's best hope for true revival. Mike hoped it would bring the general public, government officials, and donors back to the zoo, after years of neglect.

Zookeepers and curators—the animal people—had already moved a few animals into the three-acre rainforest exhibit. The educators worked like mad, researching and creating signage and displays, and the plant people struggled to learn about hundreds of recently planted tropical species in record time. My main job was developing, managing, and publicizing the grand opening planned for late spring.

My first day, nothing could ruin my high, not even Sunday's *Parade* magazine article rating us one of the country's ten worst zoos. Nowhere to go but up, I figured.

Mike wasn't kidding when he said I needed to jump right in. On Tuesday, we met with the advertising agency creating *pro bono* advertisements for the rainforest. As I walked into the conference room, which looked like a schoolroom with its plastic chairs and red-trimmed windows accenting the white walls, my stomach flip-flopped. How would I convince two executives from one of the city's big ad agencies that I had any clue what I was talking about? Astrid said her mom always said there's no point in starting a new job if you don't feel nervous when you start it. Okay, but I wished my palms would stop sweating.

Gary, one of the ad agency's partners, introduced his colleague Aaron as a hot young copywriter for the firm. I almost blushed at his words because I was thinking Aaron was hot too, but in a different way.

Handsome enough to be in commercials instead of writing them, he had black, slightly spiky hair and sky-blue eyes. But unlike most guys that good looking, he seemed totally down-to-earth, smiling easily and talking respectfully to all of us. I took a cue from Tina and snuck a glance at Aaron's left hand. *Oh well*, I thought after seeing the thin silver band on his ring finger. *I can still look.*

After running through our initial ideas for the grand opening, Gary had to leave, so Mike suggested I give Aaron a tour of the unopened exhibit.

I shared what I remembered from my first tour of the rainforest the day before.

"This is a potto," I said, pointing to a ball of brownish gray fur in a small, glass-fronted exhibit. "The curators and keepers are going crazy trying to get his lighting right. He's nocturnal, but we want his sleep cycle reversed so he'll be active during the day when visitors are here. So far it hasn't worked." I tilted my head at the sleeping animal to prove my point.

Aaron wasn't saying much, so I rambled on.

"I wish I had a whole team of people struggling to get my life right!"

He smiled and cocked his head at me.

"Those are duikers," I said as we moved toward another section. "The smallest antelope in the world. I think. And the big, reddish-brown ones with the white stripes are bongos. Amelia's my favorite, the one with the crossed horns. Her horns could actually be dangerous to her though because they might keep growing against each other and create too much pressure. Hopefully not. I think she's beautiful."

A large pink bird swooped over us, leaving a rush of air in its wake.

"Whoa, what was that?" Aaron asked.

"That was, um, a bird."

He laughed at me.

"Come on; I only started yesterday. It's amazing I know as many of the animals as I do. Birds and plants though—not my strong suit."

"How about that one? What species is that?" he joked as we rounded a corner to see a man in a khaki uniform inside an exhibit, separated from us by a glass half-wall.

The man, ruddy and brunette, extended a grimy hand, looked at it, and withdrew it.

"Hi, I'm Nathan, the new horticulturist."

"What are you doing?" I asked after introductions, pointing to the pile of tropical plant fronds next to him.

"Pruning."

"Oh." I scratched my head. "I have a black thumb. Why are you doing that? It looks like you're destroying plants that were just put in a while ago."

"You have to cut off the damaged parts so the rest of the plant can thrive."

I traded surprised glances with Aaron.

"Plant care 101," Nathan said, turning back to his work.

As Aaron and I wound further into the humid exhibit, I felt the subtle pressure of his eyes. I hated it when people watched me walk. The attention made me even more self-conscious than usual, and my legs jerky. But I didn't mind when I turned my back against the rail of an empty exhibit and found him standing closer than I expected, staring at me. His blue eyes—so light in the meeting room—seemed darker in the filtered light coming through the white canvas rooftop.

"So, what do you do when you're not promoting bongos and pottos, Shelby Stewart?" He lingered over my name like he was trying it on for size. I liked that. *Married*, I reminded myself.

"Well, I go out for drinks with my friends, see bands, and movies. I walk any dog I can find. Listen to music. The usual, I guess. How about you? Constant celebrity golf tournaments and other ad agency type activities?"

"Hardly," he laughed. "I'm only a copywriter, not a big deal like Gary. Plus I can't stand those agency events." He shrugged. "But, Gary wants me to start dealing with clients directly, so here I am."

"So I'm your guinea pig?" I didn't know why I liked this idea.

"In a way. So say good things about me, okay?" He was serious underneath his joking tone.

"What's it worth to you?" I was flirting with a married man. And my heart was doing that little I'm-talking-to-a-cute-guy dance. Damn.

"How about a free dinner sometime?"

Okay, I had to stop this. "Shouldn't you be spending your nights with your wife and kids?"

His eyes hardened, and I regretted my words. "This job comes with a lot of overtime and business dinners, so my wife is used to me working late." A bird flying overhead cried out shrilly, drawing his attention up. "So say yes," he said casually, still looking up while I admired his Adam's apple.

"Yes," I echoed, like a foolish schoolgirl.

***

I forgot about Aaron by the next morning because it was gorilla moving day.

Two adult and two juvenile African lowland gorillas were being relocated from the zoo's satellite facility, where they'd spent years in horrible, cramped concrete cells with glass fronts and painted plants on the walls.

Mike gathered fifteen of us together at five thirty in the morning under a dark sky. I checked the tape and batteries in the video camera for the hundredth time.

"We've been planning this for a year. Now it's time to get it done. Remember, this is going to be stressful and potentially dangerous for the gorillas—and for us. We have a limited window in which to anesthetize, examine, crate, transport, and un-crate the gorillas. Let's do our jobs."

No one cheered or high-fived. The group was solemn.

The vet aimed a dart gun at Balozi (good name for a band), the ten-year-old, silverback male, through a small glassless window in the exhibit wall.

I cringed at the eye-stinging, acrid smell suddenly in the air.

"Gorilla musk," one of the keepers explained to me in a whisper.

The vet's third dart hit its mark. Balozi looked at it, pulled it out of his shoulder, and tossed it back toward the little window. Many darts and at least an hour later, the 400-pound animal was unconscious.

As soon as he hit the floor, four people scrambled into the exhibit, hoisted Balozi onto a stretcher, and carried him to a steel table in a holding area, where the veterinary team went into a well-choreographed sequence of tests. The vet examined Balozi's eyes, ears, and mouth. An assistant measured the length and girth of his arms, legs and torso, while someone else recorded how much he'd grown. Balozi's teeth were cleaned and his heart and lungs checked. It reminded me of a pit stop in an Indy 500 race—but way more cool. The entire examination took fifteen minutes.

By eight thirty, the van with four primate passengers was driving south to Dorchester. From the satellite office, I called the morning radio deejays to confirm that the Gorilla Express was headed down Interstate 93, sandwiched by its police escort.

In my car on the way to Dorchester, the smells of antiseptic and gorilla musk wafting off my clothes, I surfed the Boston stations. The gorillas were being called monkeys, chimpanzees, and other inappropriate names by the deejays, newscasters, and traffic reporters. But thousands of people now knew about the gorillas and their new home. Some on-air personalities even talked about the endangered species propagation program at the zoo. Mission accomplished.

The gorillas would be kept in their new holding area behind the scenes for at least a week, for observation and acclimation. So the fun was over for now. But I couldn't stop grinning the rest of the day. Playing *National Geographic* photographer was the highlight of my career so far. No, make that my life.

Shelby

CHAPTER 35

"I'm from the zoo. Mike Evans asked me to pick up a package your vet left for him," I said to the freckly man at the animal shelter's desk.

"It's not here yet. Give me a minute. I'll go find it," he said, leaving the large room through a back door. I sat in one of the two empty, hair-covered padded chairs and waited, inhaling the smell of wet dogs and bleach cleaner.

Already I loved my job at the zoo. So many guys to choose from, for one thing, between animal care and grounds crews. My office had a real window that opened onto a grassy area. The peacocks hanging around the office door freaked me out though, with their incessant cries that sounded like *heellllllppppp*.

Also freaking me out was a talk I had with a keeper in the Children's Zoo.

"So you're the one who's going to save us?" she had asked, her eyes wide. "Bring the world back so we can stay open and keep our jobs and keep helping the animals?"

The enormity of my task scared me. But I also realized I was up for it. Maggie trained me well, and I knew how to publicize and promote and negotiate. What I didn't know, I would figure out.

A man's rising voice drew me back to the animal shelter. A wiry guy was talking passionately to a shelter employee two desks over. His short, Army-type jacket was an unusual brown—maybe burnt sienna, instead of the usual olive green. His sandy blonde hair curled in ringlets around his collar.

"Just do it; please don't drag it out!"

"We're almost done. I promise. Sign here and you can go," the woman behind the desk said.

He scribbled on her paper and bolted from the room. I'm pretty sure he was crying.

I widened my eyes at the shelter employee.

She gave a tired smile. "His girlfriend's making him give up the dog because he kept chewing her shoes and pocketbooks."

"Seriously? Why can't she keep them off the floor so he's not tempted? Hmph."

"I know," she said as the back door opened and the freckly guy came back in.

"Here you go," he said, handing me a hefty envelope.

On my way out, I peeked into the next room where yips and barks came from a row of kennels.

"Do you think I could visit with the dogs before I go?" I asked the man. "I'm having serious withdrawal." My mouth twisted as I waited for an answer.

"Sure, come on," he said, beckoning me into the adjacent room. "But don't touch that one; I can't have you suing us," he said, pointing to a shepherd with an "I bite" sign on his cage. I spent a few minutes with the other dogs, my heart expanding more for each one.

I got up from my knees and walked back into the main room just as the door banged open. It was the man in the Army jacket.

"Screw her," he said to the woman at the far desk who had helped him. "She can go. The dog stays. Now please get me my dog back."

The woman grabbed a set of keys from her desk, rushed past me toward him, and turned back so I could see her laughing over her shoulder. After they left, I laughed too.

***

Aaron persuaded me to meet him for dinner the very next night. I parked near the South End restaurant and drummed my fingers on the steering wheel. What was I doing? *Should I turn around and go home?* But home meant cold leftovers and being alone with my thoughts and my messy room. Aaron, on the other hand, represented a work-related meeting with an interesting, adorable guy. I got out of the car.

I struggled to act casual while looking into his eyes over the candle between us. It wasn't a romantic candle, just the standard kind in a small, glass container you see at so many restaurant tables. I had kept my expectations in check throughout dinner—this was nothing more than a meeting between colleagues—but now over Irish coffee, I kept slipping into his eyes, a dangerous place to go. Something in them—sadness maybe—made me want to dive in and have a swim around.

"I married Debbie right after college," he said, bringing me back to the conversation and nuking any chance I might mistake this for a real date. I grabbed at the waiter passing by like a lifeline, ordering another vodka gimlet since the Irish coffee clearly wasn't going to be enough.

"I really love her and our baby Alex. In the early days, everything was perfect. Having Alex changed everything." I sensed an invisible line drawn on the table between us, separating his real, adult, married life from my less mature and more carefree existence. "Don't get me wrong," he continued, "I adore him. But he was colicky for an entire year, so we were exhausted."

"Sorry, colicky?" I scratched my head.

"That's when a baby cries at the top of his lungs for a really long time, night after night, and you don't know why or how to make it better."

My face contorted. Aaron's world and mine separated a tad more. I greedily inhaled the rest of my Irish coffee.

"Then there was the baby weight she couldn't lose."

I cocked my head and stifled a yawn. I thought about stealing Aaron's Irish coffee since he wasn't drinking it, but the waiter placed my gimlet in front of me just in time.

"She's always been really thin, so it drives her crazy to be ten pounds heavier than normal. I still think she's beautiful, and I tell her that all the time. But here's the thing with women."

I perked up. *A lesson on women? From a man?*

"If they don't feel good about themselves, they don't enjoy sex." He stirred his coffee but still didn't drink it. "Or maybe it's the baby always tugging at her breasts that makes her feel not desirable." *Ew.* "I don't know." He sighed and put down the spoon.

Uh oh. Was I supposed to offer advice now?

I cleared my throat. "I think that if you really love each other, and if you always remember you can talk through your problems, you and Debbie will be just fine."

He smiled. "Thanks, Shelby; that's good advice."

I laughed. "I heard it on a radio talk show once."

We parted with a quick peck on the cheek like normal work colleagues and promised to talk about the grand opening the next day.

Astrid

CHAPTER 36

"And then I kneed him in the balls and took off," I finished, starting to shake even though my apartment heat was set at seventy-five degrees. The fleeting security I'd felt during the holiday break at home with my mother—which I'd extended past the New Year claiming I had strep—was long gone. For once, I wished my two roommates were around more, but their bartending and waitressing jobs plus partying kept them out most of the time.

"Oh my God, Astrid. That's attempted rape!" Tina said, grabbing my hand and pressing it awkwardly. "You should call the police!"

"I went to the police and talked to a detective. But he said it would be hard to press charges since there were no witnesses. We were both drinking, and I didn't have any physical injuries."

Shelby scoffed. "Guess they don't care about the mental injuries. Or the emotional ones." She grabbed my other hand. "I'm sorry I wasn't at the party to protect you."

"And we're sorry we weren't here in Boston when it happened," Tina added.

I sniffled. "Thanks, but it's not like you could have done anything. I don't know how I let myself get in that position, but once I did, he overpowered me. It was horrible. Anyway," I said, pulling my hands back to wipe my eyes, "I can't stand working near him anymore. I wish I could afford to quit."

"If I did it, you can do it. And can't your mother help you out if you leave?" Shelby asked.

"She doesn't have much money. She's still helping me pay off my student loans, so I can't ask her to cover my rent too if I quit and don't find something right away. No, I definitely have to find another job first."

"Wait, I'm confused. I thought you guys were rich," Shelby said.

"Rich?" I swallowed hard. "Hardly. After my father left, my mom and I lived out of our car and in shelters for three horrible years. That's why I kept changing schools—because it took us years to get settled. She dug us out of that hole and makes decent money now, but she still doesn't even own a house and says she'll have to work until she's seventy. Why would you think we were rich?"

"I don't know. The designer clothes. The perfect hair."

I shook my head. "My mother does my hair for me. And the clothes—well, can you say Loehmann's, Syms, Frugal Fannie's?" Shelby looked puzzled. I shook my head. "Tina, we so need to take Shelby shopping at the discount stores sometime soon."

"Sure, you know I never turn down a shopping trip. But can we get back to Brad. If you can't quit, what can you do?" Tina asked.

"I don't know. And I'm afraid he'll try again," I said, hating how scared and weak I sounded.

"He won't," Shelby said emphatically. "There won't be another Christmas party for a year, and you don't work directly with him anymore. You have plenty of time to figure this out." She nodded as if I'd agreed.

"You should see someone about this, Astrid. A therapist, I mean," Tina said.

"Maybe." I shifted. "Can we talk about something else please? Shel, are you going back to your group therapy thing now that your job search is over?"

Shelby shook her head. "No, it was lame and I really don't have time. The job is super busy and will be for months. I need to focus on that. No therapy, no family, no boyfriend. That's my plan until summer."

Tina stared at Shelby and said nothing, but I scoffed. "Shelby Stewart, still the queen of compartmentalization."

"What's that supposed to mean?" Shelby accused.

"Just that you're really good at putting things aside to deal with later. As long as you realize, you *do* have to deal with those things at some point." I shook my head and rolled my eyes.

"Okay, okay. Hey, I have something funny to tell you. I almost ended up with no car!" she said, smiling. "I went outside to go to work a few days ago, and my car was gone."

"What's the funny part?" Tina deadpanned.

"The cops found it a few blocks away. They took the stereo system but left the rest. No damage or anything. Not even a broken window. I guess Toyota Starlets aren't in very high demand. And they're easy to break into." Shelby laughed, but Tina wasn't amused.

"I told you not to move to that neighborhood. And I still can't believe you broke your lease at the other place."

Shelby groaned. "I had to! The commute to the zoo would have killed me. And guess what? Now I know how to start my car with a screwdriver! They popped the ignition and I won't have time to replace it for a while, but my roommate showed me how to do it."

I smiled weakly at Shelby beaming—so proud of her newly acquired delinquent skill, and Tina scowling—so appalled and concerned.

"Anyway, don't worry, Tina, the neighborhood is perfectly safe," Shelby said.

"Unless you're a car," I contributed. They smiled at me.

***

The next day, I dragged myself to the health club, feeling more like curling up in front of the TV than running laps.

"What demons are we exercising out today, Astrid?"

For some reason, Sal's standard line made me teary. "All of them I wish, but none of them I'm afraid."

"Hmph," he said. "So no smile—"

"No." I cut him off. "Let me just be myself today, please."

He nodded, pursing his lips.

Ten minutes into my jog, I settled into a comforting rhythm. Twenty minutes more, and exercise euphoria set in.

Feeling more like myself, I walked toward the weight machines, wiping my face with a towel. Pulling the towel away, I bumped into a towering man with a wide chest and dark brown skin. I stopped breathing and felt cold sweat on my hot skin.

"Oh, sorry," the man said, as startled as me. "I wasn't watching where I was going."

I swallowed.

"Hey, are you okay? I didn't scare you, did I? You're pale as a ghost."

I shook my head but couldn't speak. I rushed past him, probably leaving him thinking I was insane.

I sat on the bench at one of the workout stations, letting the quivers in my legs subside. When my breathing slowed, I began my upper body routine, starting with bicep curls. Scanning the room, I noticed a scrawny, pale guy to the left watching me. Across the room, a guy I would usually have thought attractive stared unashamedly at me. Our eyes catching, he smiled and winked. I frowned and looked down. I moved on to the lat pulldowns.

The attractive man moved closer, picking up a small barbell from a rack near my station. I saw from the corner of my eye that he continued throwing lengthy looks my way. I refused to engage.

When he put down the barbell and stepped in my direction, I grabbed my towel and left for the locker room.

Walking back through the workout room after showering and dressing, there was no sign of the flirting man. I noticed Sal's grandson Tony guiding a handsome blonde man through some bench presses. Tony's eyes flickered to the fit man's groin every time the barbells went up.

Tony caught me watching and smiled. "Hey, Astrid, how's it going?"

"Okay. Hey, Tony, I was wondering. Do you think you could show me how to work with heavier weights sometime? I'd like to build up some strength, and my little three-pounders aren't really doing anything."

"Sure thing, Astrid. Just let Gramps know when you're coming in, and he'll book us a time," he said, running his hand through his thick black hair and turning back to his client.

I headed for the exit, shivering when the frigid January air snuck in with a petite woman struggling with a bag almost as big as her.

"Bye, Sal," I said, making Sal look up from his newspaper.

"Bye, Astrid," he said, flipping the page. "You take care of yourself now."

Shelby

CHAPTER 37

Aaron showed up at my office at five-thirty to show me the latest ad concepts. Since our dinner, we had developed a friendly rapport, so I wasn't surprised when he asked if he could lose the jacket and tie.

"Go ahead. I won't tell Gary you're stepping out of your uniform," I said like his partner in crime.

After draping his tie and suit jacket over the chair, he undid the top two buttons of his dress shirt. I couldn't help but notice the soft indent at the base of his throat.

"Hey," he said when we finished reviewing the new materials, "how about we get some fresh air before I go? Then we can miss the end of the rush hour traffic."

"Okay. Come on, I'll show you the parts of the zoo you haven't seen yet." I grabbed my keys.

Most of the animals were in for the night, but we bundled up and strolled around talking until past seven. Everyone else was gone, I knew, except the night security guard and one zookeeper, both probably tucked away in their offices. As we walked, I sensed electricity building between us. He hadn't mentioned Debbie or the baby once.

Neither one of us suggested it, but we veered off the path toward the rainforest building instead of going back to my office. He gently touched my hand when we got inside, making my heart flip. When I didn't pull back, he laced his fingers through mine. I pushed away my contradictory thoughts and enjoyed the peace and promise of touching someone I cared about. The winding path with its nooks, crannies, and smells was familiar by now, but part of me felt like I was walking it for the first time.

When we got to the hippo theatre—a small auditorium off to the side, with double-wide carpeted steps where eventually people would sit and watch the pygmy hippopotamus swimming underwater—Aaron pulled me in. We hadn't spoken in a few minutes, and we didn't speak now. He guided me against the wall and brushed my hair back from my face. He stood so close, I smelled a touch of his sweat cutting through the dirt, dung, and watery smells of the tropical forest.

He leaned forward an inch and stopped. He stared in my eyes, but he wasn't seeing me or asking me a question. He was asking himself something. He leaned in the rest of the way and kissed me. After rounding the bases in record time, we tore off each other's clothes. His long and lean body softened around the middle. He was beautiful.

We lay still on the carpeted stairs for a minute afterward and laughed with our mouths closed. Without a word, we gathered our clothes, looking around to make sure we hadn't alerted the zookeeper on duty.

"I can't wait to tell my friends I did it in the hippo theatre. I mean—not that I would—don't worry, I won't say anything about you, of course."

He kissed me to stop my stammering. "It's okay; it's a first for me too."

"Having sex in the hippo theatre or having sex with someone besides your wife?" I asked without thinking.

He stared at me, fastened his belt buckle, and grabbed my hand. "Come on, let's go."

Back at the office building, we sat on the cement steps outside the back door, facing each other. I leaned against the red-painted railing. Our knees touched. Heat radiated between us even though our breath fogged in the cold air.

"Sorry about the comment back there. It's none of my business."

"It sort of is, now. The answer is that I have never cheated on Debbie before."

"And I have never slept with a married man before, so we're even."

"Not quite. I mean, I'm the married one here."

Like I needed reminding. "I think—even though that was fantastic and I really, really like you Aaron—that we probably shouldn't do this again. I don't want to get in the middle of you and your wife."

To my surprise, his eyes were wet. "I know you're right. But you have no idea what this meant to me, Shelby. I needed to feel close to someone. It wasn't just a physical thing for me. It's emotional too." The mood was getting heavy. "I mean look at me, I'm practically crying," he joked.

Too confused to analyze it, I picked up his hand and kissed it. "Let's just see what happens. Let's not plan anything."

"Agreed." He kissed me long and hard, the railing jabbing into my spine. I reluctantly pulled away before the hormones rushing through me took away my reason again.

***

Amazingly, I found a parking spot right on Charles Street near The Sevens pub the next night. Annoyingly, I found no Tina or Astrid inside waiting for me.

I bellied up to the only available spot at the room-length bar, ordered a Guinness, and turned to scan the crowd through the gloom of the dark room, looking for someone I dared to talk to and who might want to talk to me. Everyone was in couples or small groups except one scrawny guy in a double-breasted Army jacket—oh my God—it was the guy from the animal shelter. Embarrassed for some reason, I turned back to the bar.

Halfway through my beer, someone at my shoulder asked, "Is it still raining out?" It was him.

I turned to face him. "It was when I came in," I replied, glancing down at my rain-sprinkled, A-line skirt.

"Oh," he said, sidling into the small space at the bar between me and a boisterous group of thirty-something guys.

Nick, as it turned out, was taller than I thought from a distance, maybe five eight. He was waiting for late friends too and had recently moved back to New England after ten years in and near New York City—everywhere from Harlem to Bridgeport, Connecticut. The conversation stalled when I asked what he did for work.

"I'm in the entertainment business," he answered, as if annoyed.

"Can you narrow that down a bit?" I asked sarcastically.

"The music business," he said, still uncomfortable.

Whatever. I dropped it. "So, do you have any pets?" I asked innocently.

"Yeah, a mutt named Gibson. He's part German Shepherd, part Border Collie, and probably part five other things."

We were still talking animals when Nick suggested walking to Quincy Market for another drink. Tina and Astrid were obviously blowing me off, so I followed him out the door and up Beacon Street. He struggled to keep my umbrella over me in the night's wind, until I laughed and told him to give it up. The rain was light anyway.

As a car approached coming down the hill, he scurried around me to the street side of the sidewalk. *Weird*, I thought. A few feet on, we moved to the side of the narrow sidewalk to let a group of people by. When we started walking again, for kicks, I positioned myself on his right. Sure enough, he moved around me to the street side again.

I couldn't take the mystery. "What are you doing?"

"My father taught me to always walk on the outside of a woman. To protect her from any cars that drive by and splash in the puddles."

"Really. I thought men were supposed to walk on the *inside* to protect women from muggers in the alleys."

"I can't protect you from everything, Shelby," he said with a chuckle. "Which do you prefer?"

"This is fine, thanks." *Strange man*, I thought, although his offer of protection made me glow faintly inside.

We talked through another round of drinks at Frog Lane as I tried not to stare at his hazel eyes with their long curly lashes. I'd never met a man so easy to talk to, except Aaron. I turned down another drink, fuzzily aware I needed to take it easy. Alcohol was affecting me faster than usual lately for some reason, and I still had to drive home. So instead of another round, we ambled out into the moist but now rain-free air.

"I want to buy you something," he said impulsively, eying the array of Valentine's Day paraphernalia at the kiosks lining the way to the taxi rank.

"Why would you do that?" I asked.

"Because I had a good time tonight, and I want to buy you something."

Strange, I thought again. I would make him regret his bizarre gratitude. "Okay, buy me that." I pointed toward a giant rubber inflatable heart, about four feet across and tied to a long stick. "Be mine" in white letters sprawled across a pink and red checked background.

He didn't flinch, just paid for it, grabbed my hand, and towed me toward the first taxi in line. I slid to the far side of the cab. Nick got in and tried to pull the heart in after him. It wouldn't fit so he got out, pushed the heart in first, and tried to wiggle under it, but there wasn't room. We cracked up. "I give," he said, pulling the plug and squeezing out enough air so we all fit.

"Do you want a ride home?" I asked when we got back to my car on Charles Street.

I didn't want to say goodbye yet. He said yes, so I unlocked the Starlet, put the semi-deflated heart in the back seat, got in, and reached over to unlock his door. As he lowered himself into the passenger seat, I pulled the screwdriver from its resting place—in one of the screw holes where the radio used to sit—and quickly used it to start the car. Shit, too late to be embarrassed by that one. After two weeks of starting the car this way, I hadn't thought twice about it.

Nick grinned and said, "Nice" in a long, drawn-out, and complimentary way. "Do you always start your car that way?"

"Yeah, it comes in handy in places like Harlem. You should know that." He laughed.

I drove to the house in Somerville he shared with two other guys, where he asked me in for tea or coffee. I really wanted to meet Gibson, so I got out of the car but changed my mind. "No, I really should go. Work tomorrow and all."

"Tell me your phone number," he said. I did. "Okay, I'll call you."

I smirked. "You're not even going to write it down? That's a new level of..." I trailed off, not wanting to confirm how pathetic women are when it comes to men calling them back after first dates. And this wasn't even an official date.

He was talking over my words anyway. "I'll remember it. I remember everything."

I was considering whether to say something sarcastic or accept that he wasn't interested when he kissed me. My knees wobbled like jelly.

We made out madly for a few minutes. He tasted like brandy. I was still in the throes of kissing when he pulled away abruptly and led me to the car door. "I'll call you," he said.

On the drive home, the streets were nearly empty. Sleepily, I wound my way south, back through the city and into Roxbury. My bed called my name, softly, invitingly...

Horseshoes and Hand Grenades

BAM! I jolted awake. The car swerved toward the center of the road. Instinctively, I turned the wheel toward the right to straighten out. I came to a rest near the side of the road. *Shit, what did I just do?* I slowly pulled back into the road. Ker-thunk, ker-thunk, went the tires on the right side of the car. Two flat tires! I must have hit the curb. What an ass I was.

This wasn't a place to wait in the middle of the night for a tow truck, so I drove home. The Starlet limped the last ten blocks. I parked it on the street, patted it on the hood in apology, and went to bed.

The next morning, I called Mike and said, with a twinge of guilt, that I had car trouble and would be late. Three hours and two new tires later, I arrived at the zoo, ready to work my eight hours. Nick was the last thing on my mind, so my jaw dropped when I picked up the phone around one and heard his voice.

"I wanted to make sure you got home okay," he said.

Luckily he couldn't see my face breaking into a grin. "Sure, I made it home fine. How did you get this number?"

"I remembered where you worked, so I called information and got it. I didn't want to wait until tonight to call you at home."

"Oh. Thanks."

"So, do you want to go out sometime?" he asked.

We set a date for the next week. I hung up, smiling to myself and wondering if a date with one guy and sex with a married man qualified as playing the field.

Astrid

CHAPTER 38

"I thought you were meeting your girlfriends tonight," Dave said, opening the door to his small and outdated but no doubt pricey Commonwealth Avenue apartment.

"I called Shelby to cancel, but she'd already left work, so I left a message for Tina at her job. I didn't feel like schlepping up to Beacon Hill and hanging in a noisy, crowded bar."

"Then welcome to my quiet and not crowded abode," he said, standing back and sweeping his arm to usher me in.

"You look serious," he said as we sat on his sofa. "Wine?" he asked hopefully, noticing I kept my jacket on and my purse in my lap.

I shook my head. "No, thanks. I have to tell you something. I'm feeling kind of weird about dating right now." I brushed a stray hair back from my face. "It's not you at all."

He twisted his face in confusion or maybe annoyance at my use of that tired line.

"I have really, really loved spending time with you the past few weeks. But I've got a confusing situation going on at work and—oh, this isn't going to make any sense—I just don't think I should date anyone right now."

He took my hand gently. "Okay, but can you please tell me more about this situation?"

I heaved a sigh. "One of the higher ups at the agency, his name's Brad, accosted me at our holiday party, and he makes lewd comments to me at work all the time. I used to think nothing bad would come of it, but after the party, I know I have to figure this situation out before I start a relationship with anyone. I don't want him to taint the start of something good between us."

His eyes narrowed and his mouth drew into a firm line. "What do you mean by accosted?"

I fiddled with the strap of my purse. "He tried to force himself on me."

He stiffened. "You mean he tried to rape you. Jesus, Astrid, have you told the police?"

"Please, I've been down this road, and that won't help. I just needed to explain where my head is at." I looked up at him. Anger filled his beautiful brown eyes.

"I want to talk to him."

"You? But we barely know each other. It's not like I'm your long-time steady girlfriend or anything."

"I don't care if I met you yesterday. This is wrong, and someone needs to hold this guy accountable."

I stared at a vein beating in his neck. "I appreciate that, but I don't think that will change anything. I need to deal with this on my own."

"No, you don't, Astrid. If you won't let me help, there must be someone you can tell at work."

I scanned the room. "I could tell Maggie, my boss, I suppose. She's the same level as him too."

"Okay, start there." He tucked his hand under my chin and made me look at him. "Promise you'll do it. You can't keep working in that environment."

"I promise."

He scooched over on the sofa and wrapped me in a bear hug. His strong hands stroked my cashmere sweater. "You may not be in the mood for this question, but I have to ask you something important." He let go and faced me. I waited. "Astrid Ericsson, will you be my girlfriend? So we can get that straight?" His tone was serious under the joking facade. "Because I am not letting you go. We can take it as slow as you want. We can only see each other once a week or even just talk on the phone, if that's what you want. But please don't tell me we can't see each other at all."

I wavered. My plan seemed solid when I got there, but I couldn't remember why I thought I needed to break things off.

"I'll make you dinner and rub your feet," he cooed, reaching for my Ferragamo.

I melted. "You drive a hard bargain. Okay then."

"Okay I can call you my girlfriend?" He brightened like a little boy at Christmas.

"Okay you can rub my feet," I said, putting my foot in his lap and grinning.

Shelby

CHAPTER 39

The narrow stairs creaked as I climbed to the top floor of a light blue Dorchester three-decker house. I raised my fist, hesitated, took a deep breath, and knocked.

A five-foot-tall, portly woman opened the door, her huge chest heaving with her breath, her wide mouth frowning.

"Ms. Hemings? I'm Shelby Stewart from the zoo," I said, extending my hand.

She nodded twice, her gray bun flopping a bit, her bright eyes boring into me. "I know who you are. You're the only little white girl I'm expecting today."

I froze.

She chuckled. "Come in, come in. Sit down, and we'll have some tea." Her voice was higher than I expected given the formidable reputation as founder of several of Boston's prestigious Afro-American arts institutions, not to mention a member of the zoo's advisory board.

She ambled her seventy-something-year-old, considerably overweight body to the kitchen, refusing to let me help. I waited in the quaint, formal sitting room. Between the grandfather clock, the flowered chairs—was that what chintz looked like?—and the tea she brought in, steaming in an actual teapot, I felt like I had stepped back into the early nineteen hundreds.

I declined cream and sugar, sipped a few times, and waited for her to speak.

"So your director," she said, in a sing-song voice, "tells me you are organizing the opening events."

"Mm-hmm. Yes." I put down my teacup.

"I'll get right to the point. Why are you having hoity-toity fashion shows and pop music at the opening of an *African* rainforest exhibit?"

Despite the light tone of her voice, her gaze was direct and accusatory. I felt smaller than usual and tried to wriggle up taller in my cushioned chair.

I cleared my throat. "When I started the job, I inherited a few events that were already scheduled, like the children's fashion show. It seemed like a good idea."

"Let me ask you something, Miss Stewart." She sounded like my mother when she's about to criticize me. "Just because someone hands you something in a pretty package, do you think that makes it 'a good idea'?" I resisted the incredible urge to slump in my chair. "You have to think about what's inside that package, and make sure it's what you truly want, and what you truly need, and if it's what others truly want and need, before you simply accept it."

I wished I were still clinging to my teacup but didn't dare pick it up.

"And what have you added since then? Jugglers and folk music, from what I hear?"

"I thought more activities for kids made sense," I mumbled. "Maybe I can help make it better?" I asked.

"How pray tell is a white girl from the suburbs going to help?" The question was harshly rhetorical.

"I don't know what being white has to do with it," my mouth said on its own. I clutched my hands in my lap to still them. "I know I'm white, I know I'm young, and I know I'm not from the community. And I don't even know much about the zoo yet. But I want to do the right thing."

She shifted in her chair—a considerable effort—and stared at me. I managed to hold her gaze in what I hoped was a respectful manner.

"This community has been waiting for almost twenty years—twenty years—for something good to come out of this zoo. We have watched patiently as the state messed it up again and again, and then forgot about us, leaving us with nothing to look at but a mountain of dirt that you now know as the rainforest exhibit. Now, with the grand opening upon us, we want a celebration that recognizes our heritage and the theme of the exhibit. Does that give you some idea what 'the right thing' is?"

"Yes, Miss Hemings, it does. I don't claim to understand how people in the neighborhood feel, but it's obvious to me now that the opening of an African rainforest should have African entertainment."

"Mm-hmm," she nodded, pursing her lips. She seemed to be waiting.

"I will take charge of making sure more appropriate activities are scheduled."

Still nothing. I scanned the room, wondering how to start on my new mission.

"Do you—" I cleared my throat. "Would you be willing to help?"

A sliver of a smile worked its way onto her lined face. "Why yes, I am willing. Because I'm in a good mood today—and because my community has been waiting for this for decades—I will help you book some real African music, and African dance, and African food, and even an African fashion show to balance out that other atrocity," she said, waving her hand as if dispersing a bad odor.

I scratched my cheek. "With all due respect, food could be tough. We'll be lucky if our vendor is ready for hot dogs and popcorn, and we need special licenses for more food I think, but I'll find out." I squirmed in my seat with building excitement, my mind racing. "What should we do next? And when should we—"

"Shh," she directed. "I will be in touch next week to tell you what I've done."

She leaned forward and re-filled my teacup.

"Now, let me tell you about the people and history of Dorchester so you understand where you're working, Miss Stewart."

And Althea Hemings proceeded to regale me with spell-binding stories for forty-five minutes, until I was dismissed.

***

January 22, 1988

Dear Shelby,

You didn't answer my last letter, but you didn't tell me not to write either, so here I am.

The trip to Europe was wonderful. I'd really love to tell you all about it someday.

I decided to see a therapist who specializes in helping women who feel they have been wronged in this way, to try to understand how you feel and why you're acting the way you are. She told me I am a victim in this situation too and encouraged me to take care of myself.

Even Norman is a victim, believe it or not. I made him go to the therapist with me, and it turns out, there is a reason why the lines between familial and romantic love are blurry to him. He told the therapist that when he was a boy, his mother used to climb in bed with him, to "teach him about life." It made my stomach turn, but it explains why he kissed you on the lips in a way that made you uncomfortable.

Maybe if Norman had seen a therapist way back when, none of this would have happened.

I strongly recommend you seek out therapy. I would be happy to pay for it if you'll let me. Maybe with some help we can all move on from this.

I miss you and love you,
Mom

***

"Got another letter from my mother the other day," I told Astrid and Tina, the three of us crammed into Astrid's double bed, sitting up against the headboard. Our legs were in order: my short ones, Tina's long ones, and Astrid's longer ones.

"Is she still defending him? Did you burn it?" Tina asked with a bitterness she only showed when protecting a friend.

"I put it in the drawer with the other ones." I shrugged. "Do you have any aspirin, Astrid?"

"Yeah, one second," she said, climbing across me and Tina and scrambling out of the bed. "Tina, come help me."

I eyed them suspiciously, but squinting made my head hurt more, so I closed my eyes.

When they came back, they sat on the foot of the bed facing me, coffee mugs in hand. I swallowed the pills with the water Astrid gave me.

"What?" I said when they just watched me. "You're freaking me out. Say something."

"Shelby, we're worried about you," Astrid started. "Do you remember anything about last night?"

"Um, duh, we went to a house party in Allston, and had an awesome time. Right? I remember beer, some speed, and um, lots of beer. And then we all crashed here. Duh again." I wasn't going to admit I barely remembered anything from last night.

"You passed out on someone's front lawn," Astrid said, emphasizing each word. "Down the street from the party."

I closed my eyes and stretched my neck side to side to hide my horror. "And you know this how?"

"We hadn't seen you for a while and were getting worried," Tina said. "We were about to go looking for you when this teenage kid walks up to the party, practically holding you up so you wouldn't fall."

"Oops?" I said. "So I got a little drunk."

"He said he found you passed out in front of his house. His mother made him bring you back to the party. She figured that's where you came from."

"There's more," Astrid joined in. "Once we got you back, you started telling some of the guys at the party you had a new diaphragm and wanted to try it out." My jaw dropped. They tactfully studied their coffee mugs.

My head spun. My mouth was more than hangover dry.

"Are you sure? That's pretty sad," I said in a weak voice I barely recognized. I knew they wouldn't make this up.

"You don't remember any of this?" Tina asked.

I shook my head. "I don't really remember anything except the first few hours of the party. And waking up here."

"So you didn't pass out," Tina said. "You *blacked* out. That is so dangerous, Shel. You've got to stop partying so hard."

My damn tears started again. "I'm sorry, I'm sorry. You know I get drunk so fast these days. I didn't even drink that much. It must have been the speed. Speed always screws me up."

"Don't apologize. Just get better," Astrid demanded. "What if someone else found you instead of that boy? You could have been raped, or murdered, or—"

"I think she gets it," Tina interrupted, probably because my face was turning green.

"I need air," I said, clawing my way out of the bed.

***

Awkward conversation over, we left to get bagels and chive cream cheese to soak up some of the alcohol and acid in our stomachs.

"Let's stop in here first. I need a few things," Astrid said, detouring into a convenience store.

Tina and I lounged near the front while Astrid cruised the aisles.

"Almost done," she said, rounding the end of an aisle near us and heading into the next one, a carton of eggs and a quart of milk in her hands.

Tina and I twiddled our thumbs, pretending to be impatient. In reality, my hangover made me indifferent.

"What the hell?" came a man's voice from the next aisle, at the same time as a crash. We stepped over to look.

Astrid stood in the middle of a pile of broken eggs and splattered milk.

"Jesus, lady, what's wrong with you? All I did was reach past you for the ketchup!"

Tina pushed past the fuming man. "Take it easy, can't you see she's upset?" She took Astrid's arm. "Come on, let's go."

"What about the mess?" Astrid asked.

"It's okay. They'll clean it up. Come on, and careful of the puddle."

"I didn't see him coming. I was reading labels, and this arm came over me, and I jumped," Astrid explained as we walked to the bagel store, leaving the fuming man and the scrambled eggs behind.

"It's okay. I would have done the same thing," Tina soothed.

We got our bagels and cream cheese and headed back to Astrid's. On the way, we passed a park where bundled kids played as bundled parents watched.

"Do you guys mind if we sit here for a while and eat our bagels?" I asked.

While Tina pulled out bagels and napkins and Astrid opened the cream cheese container, I watched a little girl with an adorable smile and light brown hair pinned by two barrettes.

"How old do you think that kid is?"

Tina passed me a bagel, tightened the scarf around her neck, and studied the girl. "She's about the size of my niece, so maybe six?"

The girl wore a sunny yellow parka, purple flowered leggings, and white boots. She jumped on the wooden merry-go-round and twirled around, making me nervous she would slide off. She laughed and screeched with excitement, then jumped off to talk to a fluffy tri-colored puppy some guy was walking on a leash. After that, she drew in the dirt of the sandbox for a while, and later pouted when her mother told her not to hang upside down on the high part of the jungle gym. I was fascinated.

Astrid told Tina work was calm because Brad had been on vacation for two weeks. Her shaky voice and the convenience store incident made me doubtful about how calm her life really was. Tina bitched about her hairdresser for a while. I kept watching the girl.

When our hands got too cold to hold the last bits of our bagels, we went back to Astrid's.

Walking up the stairs, my chest felt tight, like I'd pulled a muscle—a weird hangover symptom maybe. As soon as Astrid opened the door, I lunged for the bathroom where I slammed the door, slammed the toilet lid down, and sat. My stomach was being wrung like a wet towel, but I didn't have that retching need to vomit.

She was so young, I thought, as my raspy breaths moved in time to the clenching of my stomach. *I was so young.* When I revisited the scenes with Norman in my mind, I pictured myself in an older body, maybe ten or eleven years old. Watching the six-year-old in the park made me realize how small and defenseless I was at that age. The thought of Norman or any man lying on top of that little girl made me wish I could throw up. I wanted the filth out of my system. Suddenly I hated Norman more than anything, and the hate pushed aside the sorrow that derailed me seconds before.

"Aaaargggghhh," I screamed. It relieved some of the pressure inside me, so I did it again.

Tina banged on the door. "Shelby, please tell me you're okay!"

I opened the door and stared at her. "I HATE HIM SO MUCH!" She pulled me into a hug as my anger reverted to sobs. "He's an asshole; he's an asshole," I repeated.

"Yes, he's an asshole," Tina confirmed.

When my breathing slowed and I could move, I dropped onto the living room couch. The smell of onion bagels wafted over from the bag on the coffee table. One of Astrid's roommates peeked into the living room, quickly looked away, and headed for the shower.

"It was the little girl, wasn't it?" Tina asked. I nodded. "I was six too, when my mother had her first really bad spell, at least that's the first one I remember." She sat down next to me. "I grew up knowing what I was dealing with. I didn't just remember it a while ago like you did."

I heaved a shuddering sigh that went all the way down to my toes.

"You know," Tina went on, "every Christmas, we'd take a family picture. I can look at ten years' worth of those pictures and tell you how drunk my mother was in every single one. My favorite pictures were from the good years. The year when I was six was a bad one. But I survived. And you're going to survive, Shel."

I wiped at my tears and looked up to see Astrid staring at us, horrified.

"I have to go make a phone call." She grabbed the phone from the kitchen wall and ducked into her bedroom, shutting the door on the phone cord.

"I bet you anything she's calling her mother," Tina said, "to tell her how much she loves her."

We smiled weakly in envy.

Shelby

CHAPTER 40

I will not guzzle my alcohol, I reminded myself as I drove up the Jamaicaway. I was nervous about meeting Nick for a drink, and I was still freaked out over my blackout at the Allston party. God, I hoped I could hold a decent conversation without being fully lubricated. Guess I was about to find out.

Maybe I should have stuck to Plan A, meeting Aaron at my house for a quickie after work, which we'd done a few times since that first night. Speaking of quickies, in addition to not getting drunk, I vowed to not fall into bed with Nick on the first date, either. I should take it slowly for once.

Rush hour traffic made me half an hour late and cranky. As I walked into the Newton Corner bar, static cling making my black and white striped skirt stick to me, I spotted Nick at the crowded bar.

"Traffic sucked. I am so ready for a drink," I said too loudly, making a few heads turn. Great opening line. Nick seemed a little too amused by my flustered state. He quickly got a beer from the bartender and led me to a table where he plopped down my beer but didn't sit down himself.

"Let me go say good-bye to my friends," he said, and headed back to the bar.

Embarrassment washed over me. I tapped my fingers against the beer bottle and avoided looking toward the bar. I vaguely recognized the song on the radio but couldn't remember the name. When Nick returned a minute later, my beer and my pride were both half gone.

I cleared my throat. "You know those people?"

"Mm-hmm. See the blonde girl? Hadley? I—" he coughed, "I used to date her."

"Really?" I said with an involuntary head twitch. "When did you break up?"

He looked at someone walking by the table. "A few days ago."

I swallowed a strange gurgle—half laugh, half sob—before it escaped my throat. "Oh. Does she know we're on a date?"

"She does now."

Thankfully, his friends including the extremely pretty ex-girlfriend left soon after that so I could focus on Nick.

His hazel eyes were green on the outside, brown on the inside. He wore faded jeans and a green and white striped, boat-necked jersey. It takes a strong man to pull off a boat-neck, I noted.

We talked about me, particularly my job, longer than I wanted to. He was super interested in the gorillas and the rainforest exhibit, and all my grand opening preparations.

"Did you know that if you stare at a male gorilla, he perceives that as a threat and might even throw feces at you? I saw Balozi do that once to one of the keepers."

"Seriously? You have got to take me to see the gorillas so I can say I've had every kind of shit thrown at me in my life."

We laughed giddily and then sighed.

"Enough about my job. You were a little evasive the other night about what you do for work. What exactly do you do in the entertainment business?"

"I played guitar in bands for years, touring locally and around the country." That fit. Long hair, funky clothes.

"Really? Any bands I would know?"

"I doubt it; it's been a while. You were probably in high school then," he rationalized.

"Still, though, playing guitar on a national tour is pretty impressive."

"It gets old fast. I hated being in a different city every night. I've travelled enough to last me a lifetime."

"So you're looking to settle down, at the ripe age of…"

"Twenty-nine." *Six years older than me.*

"But I thought every guy wanted to be a rock star, if only for the groupies."

"Believe me, that gets old too." I raised my eyebrows so he protested further. "I'm serious. I even used a stage name—Vic Tornado—so when girls came up to me after the show, I could pull out my license saying I was Nick Moreau and convince them I had no idea who Vic Tornado was."

I laughed. "Wait—you're not gay, are you?"

He scoffed. "No, I just don't need groupies to get dates."

"Okay, so groupies are for the weak or unresourceful. But if you're not playing now, what are you doing?"

"Different things. I still play and write, and I sell some songs now and then. Right now, I'm designing a high-end audio store right next door."

"Hmm," I said, tilting my head. "So your job is interesting but hardly top-secret. Why were you so cagey at The Sevens when I asked you about it?"

He sipped his beer. "I guess I lived in New York too long," he explained. "Everyone there is obsessed with who you know, and I got sick of it. The second you say you're in the music business, everyone wants to send you a demo tape."

Still sounded way cool to me, but I didn't want to appear uncool by saying so.

"At least it wasn't as dangerous as being a pro hockey player." He grinned and raised one eyebrow.

My eyebrows shot up. "You played professional hockey?"

"I played what's called juniors for a year. But I was getting creamed, so the coach stopped playing me. See, in high school, I was a dirty player but faster than everyone else, so I could get away from the bigger guys." I sensed where this was going. "In the pros, everyone was bigger than me, and just as fast. I didn't have a chance."

"So playing dirty turned out to be your downfall?"

"Not being six foot and two-hundred pounds was my downfall."

I chuckled. "So then what?"

"Then I went to Berklee to study music. But let's get back to you," he said before I could ask about the prestigious music college. "Tell me about your family."

"Erm, well my mother and stepfather—" I paused, hearing Astrid's voice: *"Don't go there. This is straight out of my not-yet-published book, 'Questions Men Ask on First Dates but Don't Really Want Answers to.'*

"Wait, I want to know more about the girl at the bar. So, messy break-up? Mutual understanding?"

"It wasn't a big deal. She'll be fine. Although I always feel bad for any woman returning to the dating pool."

"Yeah? Why?"

"Because I have four sisters, and I've seen what they've dragged home over the years. It's safe to say it's easier for men to find good women then the other way around. Hell, men can even find three or four good women at a time."

I ignored the implication of that. "So, it's harder for women basically because men suck?"

"Because ninety-five percent of all men are assholes. Only about five percent are truly good human beings that a woman would want to date."

I laughed, even though I wasn't sure he was joking. "That's a pretty dire statistic. Maybe you're close, but ninety-five percent? I've dated some really nice guys." Not that anyone ever said I was getting the cream of the crop, but I kept that thought to myself. Besides, with Nick, I thought my luck was improving.

He lowered his chin and looked up at me with a mock challenge. "Yeah, but would you want to marry any of them?"

I wrinkled my nose and refused to answer.

"Just being nice isn't enough," he continued. "Were they responsible, hard-working, loyal, trustworthy, not to mention reasonably intelligent and basically not sleaze balls? If they weren't, they're not in the five percent."

"So let me guess. You're in the five percent, right?"

"Naturally," he said, without a trace of sarcasm, although his eyes laughed. I was starting to agree with him.

***

I rushed to make Ramen noodles and carrot sticks before Aaron got to my apartment. Yet I still managed to overcook the noodles into a soggy paste, so I tossed them and dug leftover salad out of the fridge.

When Aaron still wasn't there at seven, I pulled a Dixie cup filled with ice out of the freezer. I peeled the top edge off the paper cup, braced myself, and jammed the ice against my neck, shivering at the solid chunk of cold.

Soon, the doorbell rang. I stifled a gasp at Aaron standing on my porch. He was the best-looking man I'd ever been with, and the bugs flitting around the porch light gave him an erratic halo. But based on the mixture of excitement and guilt on his face, he didn't feel like an angel.

He followed me into the kitchen, where I put the Dixie cup in the sink. "It's a physical therapy thing, for my migraines," I said, in answer to his inquiring look.

"Wait, don't put it away. Bring it," he said softly but firmly, any hint of angel replaced by a rip-roaring devil.

"Mm," I said. I grabbed the cup and led him upstairs.

***

The next day, Busu—an eight-year-old male gorilla, and Sabra—a six-year-old female, were going into the indoor exhibit for the first time, and I would get to play wildlife videographer again.

In his life cycle, Busu was the equivalent of a human teenager, and his personality showed it—mischievous, somewhat pushy, and not fully aware of his own strength. He had light silvery-gray fur, intelligent eyes, and a muscular body, slender when compared with the paunchy Balozi, who was a few years older and boasted the build to go with his dominant male status. When upright, Busu was about my height.

Other than the recent past spent in the holding area of the rainforest exhibit, Busu and Sabra had spent most of their lives in the suboptimal conditions at the satellite zoo.

The head zookeeper opened the grate between the holding pen and the small tunnel leading to the indoor exhibit, giving Busu and Sabra access to the huge space under the building's white dome. I waited, video camera in hand, on the public walkway. Staff and volunteer researchers waited at various observation areas. We all held our breath. A chorus of walkie-talkies hissed the zookeeper's announcement that Busu had entered the tunnel. Less than a minute later, he emerged into the exhibit. He scanned the realistic rocks forming the floor and walls of the exhibit, and stepped farther in. The researcher next to me scribbled furiously on her notepad.

Busu looked slowly up and all around, for a full minute. It hit me he had never seen anything eighty feet high before. His old world topped out at six feet. For that matter, he had never seen rock—not even fake rock, or birds overhead, or real plants. It was all new to him, and my throat swelled as I watched, my smile uncontrollable.

Sabra joined Busu, and they explored every inch of the exhibit, their tentativeness filling the air with the now familiar musk. I couldn't film it all because the exhibit was designed as five different spaces, not all visible from one spot, giving the gorillas safe places to be away from each other if needed.

They touched everything, their amazement possibly as monumental as ours. They nibbled at plants with thin, wide lips, and tested the rock for handholds with their leathery palms and long, dexterous fingers. The flutters and cries of birds darting overhead didn't faze them, as if some instinct had awoken, and they knew this co-existence was natural.

At one point, Sabra settled down beside a ten-foot-by-ten-foot glass panel designed to let visitors observe the gorillas up close, although it was clear to me the observations would be two-way. I lowered the video camera to the floor, squatted down, and reveled in the proximity to this gorgeous, wild beast. We were only ten inches apart. I peeked into her dark brown eyes; no whites showed under the jutting brow.

Sabra was shorter and rounder than Busu, with nearly black, plush fur and a shiny black chest. Her nose fascinated me, two oblong nostrils, almost connected, gently flaring. Her feet and hands were longer than a human's, but incredibly similar to ours beyond that. The same look and shape, the same joints and knuckles. *Anyone who doesn't believe our species are related should sit where I am,* I thought.

Something in the gorillas' pure beauty and vitality moved me. I flicked a rogue tear off my cheek, embarrassed. No coworkers noticed though.

Damn emotions.

Shelby

CHAPTER 41

"It's only eight thirty. Want to go for a drink somewhere?" Nick asked as we left the Back Bay restaurant, me trying to walk like a normal person, not an overly self-conscious, clumsy person.

I blurted out what I really wanted. "Should we go back to my house?"

Twenty awkward minutes later, I slid off my heels and took two beers into the living room. As soon as I sat, he took both beers and put them on the side table. He leaned toward me.

I barely remembered the alcohol-fueled kisses outside his house in Somerville the night I met him. At the end of our first date, he'd given me a quick kiss on the cheek before we got in our separate cars and went our separate ways. Tonight would be different.

My second real kiss with Nick lived up to my hopes. It wasn't the usual soft, tentative first kiss. It was a kiss with purpose. But he took his time. No teeth or tongue at first. His hands moved to the sides of my face. I savored the rush of blood traveling from my lips to my extremities.

"Let's go upstairs," I whispered, after a long, intense, uninterrupted kiss.

Hitting play on my tape deck and shoving three days' worth of clothes from the bed, I tumbled onto the comforter, pulling him with me. He launched himself to the side so he wouldn't land on top of me. My smile was smothered by his hard but gentle kiss. The Cure's *Staring at the Sea* album played, and we cracked up when the track switched to "Let's Go to Bed."

"I didn't plan that, I swear," I insisted, although I had thought about which cool band to have cued up in case we ended up back at my place.

Later, I stroked the soft, fuzzy blonde hair on his arms. Nick definitely wasn't scrawny like I thought at first. More like wiry with lean but strong muscles, the way I liked men. I started playing with the thick golden hair on his head.

"Did your grandmother ever complain that these curls belonged on a girl?"

His eyes crinkled. "My mother never let me grow it long enough to get curly. When I started touring, I grew it long, but it wasn't curly, I don't think. Maybe because it was bleached to death and chopped into a million different lengths."

"Ah, you cut it yourself?"

"Yeah, why not, I didn't really care what it looked like, as long as it was punk enough."

"Let me guess. You cut it without looking in the mirror, right? With rusty scissors? The Keith Richards thing."

"The technique may have been Keith, but the look was more Rod Stewart. At least that's what everyone told me." Now that he mentioned it, with his high cheekbones and square jaw, he did look a little like Rod Stewart.

"Rod Stewart, now there's a male slut for you."

"Being a male slut isn't all bad, you know. Let me show you."

In the middle of round two, I felt a huge surge in my chest, which I figured was caused by how much I was in like with Nick, until I licked my lips and tasted salt. Luckily he couldn't see my face. Still, I had to stop. I rolled over as the silent tears grew into soft sobs.

Nick shifted position and opened his eyes wide when he saw my face. He lay back and said nothing.

"This has never happened before," I whispered, more to myself than to him.

He stared at me so intently I had to look away. "Listen. I don't know what's wrong. If you want to talk about it, I'm here. If you want me to leave, I will. Or if you want me to stay here and hold you, I will."

I processed that while my breathing slowed. "How about you stay here but don't hold me?"

"Okay."

I lay still for a minute and found myself reaching for him. I snuggled under his arm, my head on his chest, breathing in his slightly spicy smell. I focused on his hand stroking my hair until I fell asleep.

***

"So, how was it?" Tina asked. I could practically feel her quivering through the phone.

"Tell us everything," Astrid commanded into the mouthpiece of the extension phone in Tina's apartment.

Nick had hugged and kissed me warmly before leaving that morning, but I was too embarrassed to do much more than mumble bye. After he left, I re-played last night's episode in my head, looking for answers, but found nothing. So I'd cranked up my stereo and started cleaning my bedroom instead.

"It was," I said from the kitchen, banging the phone cord against the wall, "interesting."

"Come on, give. What happened?" Tina implored.

"We ate dinner at Skipjacks, and then went back to my place."

"Shelby, my sleazy little friend."

"Thanks, Tina."

"Shh, let her talk," Astrid said. "Was it good?"

"It was great, but then, in the middle of…stuff, I started crying."

"You didn't! In the middle of doing it? Oh my God. *How to Kill a Relationship in One Easy Night.* Men are so egotistical, he probably thought he was either so good or so bad it made you cry," Astrid said. I blinked and shook my head.

"Astrid! Not helping!" I heard in stereo as Tina yelled through her apartment. "Shelby, I get it," Tina soothed. "Being in therapy can make you extra emotional. That's all it was. So what did he do?"

"He was totally cool about it. It bothered me more than it bothered him. I'm still freaked out."

"Wow, some difference from Will, who couldn't run the other way fast enough when things got weird, huh?" Astrid said. "Okay, what else? What does he look like?"

"He has this French Canadian hockey player look about him—something to do with the angles of his face. High cheekbones, shoulder-length curly hair. He has Robert Redford arms."

"Is that like Bette Davis eyes?" Tina asked.

I rolled my eyes at the phone receiver. "No. It's much better. His arms are hairy like Robert Redford's, all golden."

"As long as he doesn't have a hairy back. You don't want to be confusing him with those gorillas at work." Astrid was on a roll.

"Clean and smooth as a baby's bum. His back, that is."

Their laughter tinkled through the phone.

"Anyway, I have to go. I'm cleaning my room." Ten seconds later, I decided they hadn't heard me. "I'm going to—"

"We heard you," Tina said. "Okay, have fun. We'll talk to you soon."

***

March 6, 1988

Dear Shelby,

I realize you need space, but I want you to know your family is here for you, whenever you need us. You haven't answered me about the therapy, but I am enclosing a check that should cover a few sessions. Please give it a try.

Meanwhile, I am tormented daily by our severed relationship. Only a parent understands what it feels like to lose a child. I can only pray you are not lost to me forever. And I pray you never have to endure what I am enduring. I know you're not trying to be selfish, but I can't help but feel betrayed that you're withholding your love from me, who raised you for twenty-three years.

We are all trying to move on here. Norman is under consideration for a job as assistant principal at Petersburg Middle School. They really want him to coach the varsity boys' football and varsity girls' basketball teams, but there are no job openings at the high school. So by getting him into the middle school, he can coach the high school teams. That's the third biggest school system in the state!

We think of you daily.

Love,

Mom

***

"Leave me alone!" I yelled at the letter. "Why won't you just leave me alone?!"

I mashed the paper and the check into a ball and dropped them into my desk drawer.

Shelby

CHAPTER 42

Nick insisted on giving me a back rub so I sat on the floor of his living room, leaning against his legs as he sat on the couch. Gradually, my shoulders relaxed, and I closed my eyes, soaking in the blissful pain as he dug out sore spots. Moving to my neck, he rubbed for ten seconds and stopped.

"You know, there's something weird with your neck. There's a huge lump here," he said, pressing on the right side.

"I know." I shrank away. "It's a muscle spasm. That's one reason I get migraines."

"Hm. Does it feel good when I press on it like this?" He touched the spot gently.

"I can't even feel that."

He pressed harder. That hurt and triggered a sharp pain in my eyebrow, but it was good pain, like a release. "Aaah," I moaned, "stay there for a minute." Reaching my limit, I was about to say stop when the intense pain eased.

"It's going away," Nick said proudly. He continued massaging as I tried not to groan with pleasure. "So you said the muscle spasms are one reason you get migraines. What are the other reasons?"

A danger flag waved in the back of my brain. Better give the stock answer, not the truth.

"The doctors aren't sure, but chocolate, cheese, and red wine can all be triggers." My traitorous mouth kept going on its own. "And my stepfather sexually abused me when I was a girl. That probably has something to do with it." *Shit.* I froze, waiting for his reaction. His hands stopped.

He came around to the front of me, his hazel eyes fierce. "Is he dead yet? And if not, who's going to kill him?"

The intensity of the satisfaction rushing through my body shocked me. Why did it feel so good when my story caused murderous reactions?

Nick paced around the room as if releasing energy. I wanted to kiss him right then and there, but this didn't seem like the moment. Instead, I told him everything. About Norman and how the people in town think he's a hero, and about my mother still being with him.

"This is what was bothering you that night at your house, isn't it." It was a statement, not a question.

"Mm-hmm. How come you're not heading for the hills?" I tried to joke.

"I didn't run that night, and I'm not running now." I bit my lip. "Look, Shelby, it's not your fault he did this to you. You're the victim here. This just makes me want to keep you safe from someone like him ever hurting you again."

I inhaled and shivered at the same time, shaking tears loose of my eyelids. Nick sat beside me, pulled me toward him, and wrapped his arms around me, where we stayed for a few minutes. I had never felt so protected in my life.

***

March 15, 1988
Mom,
Please stop sending me letters for a while.
Here's a poem I wrote. Probably not very good but it's how I feel.
Shelby

The Family Tree

The family tree is dying
Time and elements slough off damaged bark
The roots lose their hold
Branches pull free
Leaves drop one by one

What is family anyway, the sum of all its parts?
Not all formulas add up before they're torn apart.

Treading the line between selfishness and self-help

S. M. STEVENS

I didn't set the line, I'm just trying to stay afloat
How I do it is up to me, just as your way is up to you.
What helps one hurts another.
The pain of choice never ends.

The family tree is dying
Time and elements slough off the damaged bark
The roots lose their hold
Branches pull free, leaves drop one by one
Seedlings may sprout elsewhere
To start a stronger family tree.

Shelby

CHAPTER 43

"We're not going to make it to the Orpheum for the concert, are we?" I asked, hoping Nick didn't hear the traces of my last migraine pill slurring my words.

"Nope, but I've seen Squeeze twice before," he said, kissing me again.

"I've always wanted to see them," I mumbled from the side of my mouth.

He pulled back. "Do you want to go?"

"No, this is better," I said, leading him to his bedroom, where a blast of heat hit me in the face. "Man, can't you turn the heat down?" I groaned.

"I like it this way. It's to make sure you wear as little as possible."

I happily obliged.

Afterward, we lay side by side, his left arm around me, his right hand making circles on my chest in a soothing, non-sexual way. The sensation couldn't have been more different than when Norman touched me in the same spot.

"Hey, want to watch a Smiths concert since we didn't make it to Squeeze?" Nick asked, jumping out of bed just as I started to doze off. "I got a new concert tape from my friend who runs a used record store. It's a bootleg so it's grainy, but the sound is pretty good."

"The Smiths? Hell yeah!" I threw off the sheet and jumped out of bed, putting on sweats and a T-shirt while Nick fiddled with the VCR in the living room.

"Okay, it's working. Come on," he yelled. "Do you want one?" he asked as I padded through the small linoleum-floored kitchen to the living room where he waited, holding out a bottle of beer.

I sighed. "I guess I better not. Don't want my migraine to come back."

"No problem. I'll drink it for you." He grinned.

We watched and listened, Gibson nestled in front of the couch between Nick's feet and mine. At the end, I realized it was the first concert tape I'd ever watched without someone gabbing in my ear, making me miss half the music.

"It's only ten, and I'm not tired," I said, wired by Johnny Marr's jangly guitars and Morrissey's humorously pathetic lyrics. "Let's do something else."

"Hmm. I know." He disappeared into the bedroom and returned holding something behind his back. "For our next adventure—" he bowed and twirled his free hand out like a magician, "I present, the cribbage board." He produced a wooden game board and caressed it like a game show model displaying a prize.

"Cribbage! I haven't played in years. So yes, bring it on," I said. He pulled a deck of cards out of his jeans' back pocket and sat facing the coffee table.

"No you don't," I said, shifting to sit cross-legged and sideways on the couch, facing him. "You have to turn this way so we can't see each other's cards," I admonished, moving the cribbage board and cards in between us on the couch.

"Hmph. I can see you're a worthy opponent," he grumbled, setting the pegs while I shuffled the cards.

"Cut for deal," I commanded.

"Prepare to be humiliated by the master," he said gleefully when his two beat my Jack for the cut.

"So this is going to be a competition of words as well as cards, eh?" I raised one eyebrow.

"Oh trust me, you won't have any words to describe the beating you're about to take." He dealt the cards and picked up his hand.

I scanned my cards and smothered a smile. "We'll see about that."

Forty minutes and too many insults to count later, I moved my peg into the final hole. I lifted my arms in the air and cheered, making Gibson whine with concern. "Ha ha, where's your tough talk now?"

He laughed and squinted evilly. "It's best out of three you know. Deal, sucker."

I sighed dramatically and scooped the cards into a pile. "Fine, if you want more punishment, two out of three it is. And then you'll change it to four out of five. I know your kind."

Mid-way through the second game, Nick got serious. "Shelby, are you really okay that we didn't go to Squeeze?" he asked, combing his fingers through his messy curls. "I didn't mean to ruin your night, but I get tired of being around people sometimes. In fact, I don't even like people at all. The consequence of living in a city too long."

"It's fine; this is fun. And if you don't like people, I guess I should be flattered you hang out with me."

"Well, it's the least I can do. I mean clearly you need someone to teach you the finer points of cribbage. Consider it charity."

I narrowed my eyes at him. "Well then, I guess I'll admit that I'm really not here for you at all. Gibson is my true love," I said, reaching down and stroking the dog's black head to hide my suddenly fiery cheeks.

***

In the morning, after a proper and thorough greeting, we spooned cozily. Suddenly the comforting safety I felt in his arms surged to a scary level. My heart skittered wildly, thumping against my ribs. My armpits started sweating. I lunged out of bed, grabbed his hockey shirt from the chair, and ran to the bathroom. I gulped for air and splashed cold water on my face. In the mirror, a scared, pale face stared back at me. *I can't do this*, I thought. *I can't get serious with someone now. Not even Nick.* I had to stick to my playing-the-field plan.

"Are you okay?" Nick asked when I walked back into the bedroom.

"Had to pee really bad, sorry about that." He patted the mattress, but I started to dress instead. "Listen, I won't be able to see you for a while." I focused on getting my feet through my pant legs without tripping. He waited. "We're extra busy at work now, and I'll have to start working weekends soon, and I don't really want anything serious right now anyway, and it seems like we're getting too serious really fast—"

"It's okay, Shelby, whatever you want." He climbed out of bed. "Call me when your grand opening is over." He handed me my shirt. "And don't take any shit from those gorillas."

***

"Lauren?" I said into the phone.

"Hi, Shelby, how are you doing?"

"Okay, I guess. Headaches aren't gone, but that's life I guess." I rolled my eyes at myself. "What's up?"

She drew a breath on the other end of the phone. "I thought you would want to know. Kelly committed suicide last night. Overdose."

I squeezed my eyes shut, remembering Kelly's slump and her skunk hair, her waiflike voice, and our short conversation in the stairwell. And I remembered her saying she wanted to live after all.

"Oh. Thanks for telling me," I said.

"Are you going to come back to group? We'd all like that."

I rubbed my neck with my free hand. "I don't know. Maybe. Work is still so busy." My voice caught. "But I'll think about it."

"Okay, please do. And you know you can call me anytime."

"Thanks. Bye."

***

An ice storm was forecast, so I had an excuse to stay in by myself that night. I couldn't stop wondering how desperate Kelly must have felt to end her life. But she hadn't showed us any emotion. Like she lived in a shell we couldn't break through, even though it still wasn't strong enough to protect her.

Saturday morning, I woke at seven to the sound of gunfire. I padded down the stairs to the back porch where the winter air wiped the sleep from my eyes. It took a minute, but I realized the pops and cracks weren't gunfire but tree limbs breaking under a thick, ponderous coating of ice. The trees were beautiful, though, the silvery-white of every branch and twig in crisp relief against the wet blackness of the tree trunks. It looked like a painter had white-washed the landscape, pigment sticking to the treetops and adding a milky coating to the pale blue sky and dull green grass.

A sharp gust of wind followed by a loud pop made me jump. I turned to see the top of an oak snap right off. The severed hunk jutted out at a precarious angle. It started to descend as if in slow motion but quickly gained speed, propelled by its own weight, until—fifteen feet about the ground—it jerked and stopped, swaying in mid-air. A strong strand of unbroken heartwood from the tree's core had refused to break, and it held the treetop suspended as if for dear life. I held my breath, watching it hover. When the strand could bear the weight no longer, the entire treetop—six feet of trunk, limbs and branches—slid down the side of the tree, ripping ice off the branches it passed on its way to the earth. When it hit the ground, a thousand tinkles of ice breaking off in jeweled clumps masked the thud.

The evergreens in the backyard bowed in surrender, knowing they didn't have a chance against the one-two punch of ice and wind. They curved forward onto the icy lawn, some of them slowly bouncing a few feet above the ground, trying to hold firm against the wind's wail and the weight of their icy jackets. Others touched their tips to the ground in supplication.

I watched and listened to the destructive symphony in awed despair for ten minutes before my tingling nose and fingers drove me back to bed. I curled up in a fetal position, seeking warmth. I pulled a pillow over my head to mute the carnage.

When I woke a few hours later, the backyard screamed devastation. The ice-coated branches were still breathtaking, but broken treetops scarred the landscape every ten or fifteen feet. The breaks were violent, with jagged edges outlining the exposed, pale orange insides of the trees. Weaker ones had toppled over completely. The young oak I saw break earlier still stood.

Our neighbor was cutting his bowed evergreen tops with a chain saw to lighten their loads. Each freed tree sprang up, shedding ice on the way.

The ice storm was the subject of national news reports for two days—and local reports for a week. An unfathomable number of trees were destroyed, roofs crushed, and tangles of power lines draped ominously across suburban and city streets. I knew the homes and power lines would be fixed in a matter of weeks, but I wondered how long it would take for the raw insides of the scarred trees to darken and heal, and blend into the landscape to be forgotten.

Part 3

Astrid

CHAPTER 44

"Maggie, can I talk to you about something personal after the meeting?" I asked, having finally worked up the nerve to confide in her. We were filing into the conference room for the staff meeting. Brad was nowhere in sight.

"Of course," she said, and walked to the front of the room. Brad brushed by me, glaring. When he joined Maggie and the partners, he continued glaring at me until Terry started speaking.

"Big news, everyone," Terry boomed, quieting the chatter. "I am pleased to announce that Brad Butler is now a partner of Campbell Lewis." Terry started a round of applause. I clapped stiffly.

Brad beamed and shook hands with the partners, then actually raised his hand like a politician waving to a crowd.

"Are you changing the name to Campbell Lewis Butler?" Michael yelled out.

"No," the normally reticent Jim Lewis said. "We expect to have other partners soon and can't add all of them to the company name," he said, glancing at Maggie.

"Not unless we want to sound like a law firm with six people in the name," Terry joked.

"There's more," Terry said, like a circus ringleader entertaining the crowd. "Brad has been named president of the Boston PR Association. This is a real feather in our cap, and we know he'll represent us well, and he'll do a bang-up job leading the association to new achievements. Let's hear it for Brad, everyone."

I tuned out the Brad lovefest. As I left the conference room a few minutes later, Brad caught up with me. "Astrid, I'd like to see you in my office please. Now," he said, loudly enough for people nearby to hear.

I shuffled behind him into his office, where he shut the door. I felt numb.

"So," he said, standing close enough that I smelled his coffee breath. "What do you think of me being named partner?"

I cleared my throat. "That's great, Brad. Congratulations." I looked away, but he moved back into my line of vision.

"You realize what this means, don't you? This means I'm your boss again. Now, I'm everyone's boss." He stretched up and straightened his already straight tie. "Ah, it's good to be on top. Which do you like better, Astrid, being on top or bottom?" He smirked.

I couldn't believe I ever found him attractive. I pressed my lips together.

"You know what else this means?" he asked, leaning toward me. "Now that I'm an owner of the company, in a way, I own you too." He raised his eyebrows. "What do you say to that?" he asked with childish mirth.

I tried to glare. "Are we done here?" I asked, hoping he didn't catch the slight tremble in my voice.

"Almost. I heard you ask Maggie for a meeting about something *personal*. Don't get any ideas about talking to her, or anyone, about the holiday party." I blinked and looked away while my heart took a little dive. "Did you think I was too drunk to remember that? Oh I remember it, Astrid," he said in a low but threatening voice. "But no one will believe you if you say anything. I'm untouchable now. So save yourself the trouble, and save your job while you're at it. I assumed you were smart enough to realize that." He took a step closer. "Don't say anything. Got it?"

I nodded. A bead of sweat trickled down between my breasts.

"Good. Now we're done. For now."

He stepped aside and watched me open the door and leave.

***

"I know I should start looking for a new job. I can't work near him anymore. I don't even want to go in on Monday. I'll call in sick."

"Easy, Astrid," Tina soothed for the third time since our emergency girls night started, ending my ramble. "It's going to be all right." She patted my shoulder.

"It's like I'm in the Twilight Zone. I love my clients and my boss and the work, and everything's great, but then he appears, and all my confidence goes up in flames. I feel schizophrenic. Like I'm living a bifurcated life."

"Ha, bifurcated life. Good name for a band," Shelby said. She put her feet up on the coffee table and tapped her toes together repeatedly.

"You'd think he would have found someone else to torture by now."

"What makes you think you're the only one? He's probably harassing all the pretty women at Campbell Lewis." Shelby sniffed and jerked her head up like she knew she was right.

"Shelby," Tina said sharply. "If you're not going to help with Astrid, why don't you get us some drinks?"

"Finally," Shelby said, "we've been here almost an hour. I'm parched." She jumped up and headed for the kitchen of Tina's apartment. When she got back with two open bottles of wine, she plopped down on the couch, splashing wine onto her shirt. She made a face. "Who wants red and who wants white?" she asked, picking up the red.

"Just pour anything," Tina said. "Why aren't you being more sympathetic? You of all people should understand what Astrid's going through, being preyed on by a man like this."

Shelby's eyes darkened for a second and then glassed over again. Her eyes narrowed. "I'm having a bad time lately too, you know. I missed two days of work last week with a stupid migraine, and my boss wasn't happy. We're behind schedule on the grand opening. Nick and I are over—"

"You ended that, Shelby! You can't complain about that one. And work problems are nothing compared to fearing for your safety," Tina said.

She made a dismissive noise. "Brad's full of talk, but he hasn't tried anything."

I stared at her, a squawk stuck in my throat.

"Not since the Christmas party, anyway. And don't look at me like that." She turned toward the window. "The problems of two people don't amount to a hill of beans in this crazy world," she muttered.

"What?!" Tina said. "What the hell are you talking about?"

Shelby faced Tina. "I said lots of people have way worse shit going on than us." She gazed out the window again. "Way worse," she repeated.

"Oh, so you don't think Astrid's problem matters?" Tina retorted.

"Not as much as some people's," Shelby said matter-of-factly.

"Then why were you just asking us to care about your work problems? Really, Shelby, you're starting to piss me off." Tina stiffened, her mouth in a tight line.

"Bite me, Tina. I'm leaving." Shelby clunked the bottle onto the coffee table, looked at it like it was the thing in the room she cared most about, stood up, got her coat, and left.

"Thanks, Tina," I said, rubbing my face.

"You were so quiet. Aren't you mad at how she's acting?"

"Of course I am. I'm just not Italian like you. Plus I'm a little depressed right now. I'll be mad later, I promise."

Shelby

CHAPTER 45

Back at my apartment, I sat in bed and downed a few whiskeys. Drunken sleep slipped over me.

Gasping ragged breaths, I clawed my way out of the blackness suffocating me. Squeezing my eyes shut and open, shut and open, I got my bearings. At home. In bed. My T-shirt damp with rank sweat. Every hair on my body prickling. My stomach clenching.

What the hell *was* that? It wasn't gone. A dark, heavy, unnameable fear overwhelmed me. Not a fuzzy nightmare but something potent, attacking every cell. This couldn't have come from inside me, could it? Was there someone in the room, or trying to get in? No, outside my fear-filled room, I heard two of my roommates talking downstairs. The noxious fear seeped into the corners of the room and curled back to find me again. I was too afraid to cry. If I fell back asleep, I would be right back in its clutches; I knew it. So I stared into the dark, helpless. I sat up in bed, my head pressed into the headboard seeking hard, real, safe contact. *Must stay awake. Must stay awake.* Like tentacles wrapping around me, squeezing my chest, poking into my eyes, now slithering through my hair, the terror pulled me back under. I shuddered, drowning. Struggled a mental battle against it. *Let me out, dammit!* Wrenched free of the black quicksand, chest heaving, breaths escaping my nose in loud puffs like a scared animal.

I got a sip of metallic-tasting water from the bathroom faucet and then paced my room. I would not fall asleep again. I couldn't. I turned on the light, threw a pile of clothes off the armchair, and read for two hours, falling into a light, dreamless, sitting-up sleep sometime after dawn.

***

No one seemed surprised when I showed up at group for the first time in weeks. Frances gave me a quiet "welcome back" with a touch on the arm.

"You all know about Kelly," Lauren started. "I thought she was going to make it, but sadly I was wrong. You can all decide if you want to have our regular session, or if you would rather do something different today."

"I am staying, and I am working," declared Charmaine, her chin jutting out. "I'm not gonna end up like that."

"None of us are going to," said Diana. "We owe it to Kelly to keep going, to get our lives back." The others nodded.

"Good," Lauren said, rolling her shoulders up and back. "Now I need to make sure you all understand something very important. What happened to you was not your fault. You were not an adult, and you were not equipped to deal with it. I mean, what should eleven-year-old girls be doing? They should be playing kickball and getting their first crushes, not being forced to have sex. What should eight-year-old girls be doing?" She looked at Rosie. "Playing house and doing somersaults." She looked at me. "And six-year-old girls should be feeling life with every fiber of their young bodies, not shutting themselves off." She looked around the room. "They should not be suffering what you suffered." Lauren's voice rose, pleading. "If there is any small part of you that continues to harbor guilt, if you think you are one iota responsible for your abuse, I'm begging you to let go of that guilt."

We were stunned. Lauren was always calm, never emotional. She didn't want another Kelly.

After a water break, Rosie wiggled in her seat until everyone else was seated.

"I have big news. I decided to tell my whole family about the abuse last night because we were all together. My mother was there, and her sister—that's my Aunt Concha—and my Aunt Eva—that's my Uncle Jorge's wife, and all my cousins—"

"Slow down, Rosie, we can't keep up with you. Uncle Jorge is your abuser, right?" Frances asked.

"Right, but he's been gone a few years, probably run out of town over some drug deal. He was my mother's brother. Eva is Jorge's wife. She stayed when he left. I don't know why. Okay?" Ignoring our confused looks, she continued. "So, I told them—all of them! The kids were playing outside—you know they don't care how cold it is—so I told the whole table of adults that Uncle Jorge, that bastard, raped me over and over when I was in third and fourth grade."

"Fantastic," Frances said. "I mean, that you told all of them," she added quickly.

"You go, girl!" Charmaine chipped in.

"Continue, Rosie," Lauren interrupted the comments of support. "How did people react?"

"My mother started swearing at me like a crazy person. She got right in my face, and I thought she was gonna hit me. But my Aunt Concha pulled her away and told her to cut it out. She said Jorge always was a piece of shit and she was ashamed that he was their brother. She hugged me and held me like a baby, saying over and over again she was sorry." The room filled with tears.

"What did Jorge's wife do?" Jenny asked.

"She was just kind of quiet like for a long time. Then she left without saying anything, but she gave me a hug first. That was all." She pursed her lips. "But that was enough, I guess."

"Rosie, it must have felt validating to receive emotional support from some of your family," Lauren said.

"But wait, I haven't told you the best part," Rosie said directly to Lauren. "The way I felt after—like I was high, and like I'd taken charge for the first time—that's the way I feel after I steal something and I get home and realize I didn't get caught. But this high was way better!"

I felt strangely satisfied for Rosie, as if she were my own sister. And a touch jealous of her natural high.

"And sorry, I'm not done," she went on. "I have to say one more thing. I want to confess that I lied in the beginning of this group when I said I hadn't shoplifted in years. I was still doing it sometimes. But now I'll never do it again because I found something better," she said with a wide smile.

"Hm," Lauren said. I could practically see the wheels spinning in her brain. "Rosie just shared a big secret with us. Would anyone else like to open up about something you've never told anyone else before?" She scanned our faces.

I shifted in my chair and scratched my nose.

"I will," Frances said. "I never even told Jane this because it's pretty weird. When I was a kid and all this stuff was going on, I made a confessional out of a big shipping box my father had got somewhere. My mother said I wasn't old enough to start real confession at the church, which made me mad. I was drawn to the church confessional because it had this warm wood and secret openings. It seemed like a really beautiful phone booth to me—and the best place to call God from." Her shoulders heaved with the memory. "So I made up my own version. I'd go in my box to make peace with God. My parents thought the box was a clubhouse or doll house, and sometimes I'd even take dolls in with me to fool them." She smiled weakly. "When they thought I was telling stories to my doll, I was actually praying," she whispered, then sat back signaling she was done.

"I've been faking orgasms with my husband for years," Jenny blurted out, flicking her blonde hair out of her face. "I have a hard time staying interested during sex, but he's so hurt when I don't enjoy it, so I started faking it. I can't remember the last time I had a real orgasm."

"Jenny, that is so understandable, that you have issues with sex," Diana reassured her. "If he doesn't get that, he's not good enough for you."

Lauren twitched a little at that comment.

"Maybe you could talk to him," Diana said. "It's so important to have an honest dialogue with your partner." She leaned into our circle of chairs. "My secret is that my fiancé didn't leave me because he couldn't handle the abuse, which I said in an earlier meeting. He left me because I'm a control freak. While he slept, I would compulsively neaten all the clothes in his dresser. Then I'd worry that he would notice, so before he woke up, I'd muss them back up again. He caught me doing that once, and after that, every OCD thing I did, even little things like making all the labels on the cans in the cabinet face the same way, they drove him crazy. Maybe if I had told him the truth, he would have understood me better. Maybe he wouldn't have left."

No one spoke for a minute of silent solidarity.

Then Charmaine shocked us all by confessing she had a crush on Jenny. She sounded proud when she dropped her bombshell but immediately looked shame-faced as reactions spread across the faces around the room. Lauren intervened.

"Charmaine, that was very brave of you to share that. Jenny, would you like to tell us how Charmaine's statement makes you feel?"

"Wow, Charmaine, I'm, I mean—" Jenny stammered. "I mean, it's flattering, so thanks I guess, but I'm not that way. You know—I like men, and I'm married."

"Oh, I know that. I'm not expecting anything. In fact, if you liked me back, I'd probably have to re-visit the whole thing. I was just saying it." Defiant Charmaine was back. "Although I could help you with that orgasm problem."

We broke out in somewhat nervous laughter. The room sighed as the laughter died off. I was next.

"I've never told anyone this story." I licked my lips. "I had this baby doll when I was a girl. Just a plain old doll with rubber hair sculpted into her rubber head. I remember beating her viciously when no one was looking. I was so mad at her—I don't know why—and I just spanked her naked body over and over." I shuddered. "Creepy, right?"

Lauren shook her head. "No, nothing you felt or said or did was creepy, Shelby."

"Can I say something else?" I asked, pushing my shoulders back. Lauren nodded.

"A while ago I was at a party, and I'd been drinking for hours, and someone gave me speed, which always messes me up, but I took some anyway. I was completely blitzed by ten o'clock, probably. That's the last thing I remember. My friends told me I passed out in a yard down the street, but I don't remember anything until waking up the next morning. I've never blacked out like that before. It freaked me out a little." I reached for my glass of water on the floor by my foot.

"That's not so embarrassing," Rosie said. "Lots of people drink too much and black out."

"I guess. But my friends said I was pestering guys at the party, saying I wanted to try out my new diaphragm with them." My cheeks burned. A few people stifled giggles. I looked at Frances, whose eyes were laughing, and my embarrassment faded away. I laughed out loud, and everyone joined in.

"That's okay, Shelby. I've been told I started doing a striptease at a party once, asking anyone and everyone to take me to bed. Evidently alcohol and sexual confusion don't mix," Frances said.

"Shit, you don't have to be abused to know that's true," Charmaine said, and everyone laughed some more.

When we calmed down, Lauren beamed at us like a proud parent. "Look at what you've done. You have all opened up and shared something with this group of women—your friends—that you've never told another living soul. What does that mean?"

"It means we know everyone here has done stuff as bad and as stupid as the rest of us," snorted Charmaine. A few more giggles escaped the group.

"What Charmaine is saying, not so eloquently," Diana chimed in, "is that we can trust each other. We *do* trust each other."

"And how fantastic is that," Lauren said. "You came into our first meeting nervous, maybe suspicious, and maybe scared. You were taught at an early age that interpersonal relationships were scary and not to be trusted. And yet here you are, having established bonds of trust with each other. Now you know you can build equally strong relationships with your loved ones and new friends you have yet to meet. So do it."

"Let's go forth and conquer," Diana said softly, not using her warrior voice.

I had a lot to think about that night. Good thing I broke up with Nick and was on the outs with my girlfriends. I needed physical and mental space to figure some stuff out.

***

"Kyle, it's Shelby," I said into the phone. "I need to tell you something, about me and about Norman. Mom and Eric know, and I want you to know."

"Okay," he drawled as if he didn't like the idea.

"Norman sexually abused me when I was a girl—" I stopped to let that sink in.

A weird grumbling noise came through the phone. "What exactly do you mean, Shel? Can you tell me exactly what happened?"

A twinge of uncertainty tweaked at my heart. "Well, okay, if you really want to know."

I told him everything in nauseating detail, right down to Norman's breath smelling like the peanut butter he'd snuck from the cabinet. By the end, silent tears streamed down my face.

"That's terrible, sis. Can I ask you something?" I gave silent assent. "Why didn't you say anything to make him stop?"

My hand gripped the phone.

"I was a kid, Kyle. Kids don't think they can speak up to adults." My voice cracked, so I paused for a deep breath. "We kind of expect them to tell us what's right and wrong."

"I guess you're right. But still, how do you feel now? It's been years, and obviously you have to get over this at some point."

Angry disbelief sucked the air from my lungs. I couldn't breathe for a few seconds.

"Get over it? Get over it?" I asked, my voice getting higher and my breath coming fast. "Kyle, maybe I can heal from this, maybe I can move on with my life, but I will never get over it because it's always going to be there. A shitty reality that I can't change."

"Okay, okay, I get it. You know I love you, right? And what he did was wrong, and it hurt you. But Norman's a good guy overall, Shel. Do you think you can ever be friends with him again?"

My hands started to tingle and cramp. "Fuck you, Kyle."

I hung up.

Shelby

CHAPTER 46

The next group therapy session was a heated talk about how people suck. They don't believe us—they do believe us, but want us to pretend it's not a big deal—they get impatient waiting for us to heal.

"It's amazing we ever manage to heal," Jenny said. "If we listened to everyone else, we'd never make any progress."

"I know, right? We have to find the strength in ourselves because no one else is going to find it for us," Rosie said, nodding over and over.

"Maybe with more support, it wouldn't take as long for us to face what actually happened, instead of burying it and minimizing it for years," Frances said, sending a shiver of recognition through my forehead. "For a long time I didn't even admit I'd been sexually abused because Father O'Grady never actually touched me. He just made me touch him, and he touched himself. I didn't know what to call that."

"Frances," I said, startled at my own voice. "Clearly, what he did was sexual, and clearly, it was abusive."

"It doesn't matter what actually happened," Rosie jumped in. "Any level of abuse is damaging."

"That's right," Diana said. "There's no such thing as a mild trauma. Once you cross that line into trauma, some damage is going to happen."

"What you guys all went through—my experience wasn't nearly as severe, but—" I stopped and gulped.

"But what, Shelby?" Lauren prodded.

"But it was still wrong. Like Diana says, a line was crossed. My childhood—my life—was affected." I started to cry. "Maybe I would be a different person if that hadn't happened. Maybe I'd be more confident, or outgoing. Or maybe I'd be the same, I don't know. And I'm tired of my family acting like it doesn't matter because it *does* matter. It *does* matter, it *does*…" I trailed off, unable to talk through my tears.

"About time," Rosie said in her warm voice. I glanced up in time to see Lauren shoot her a reprimanding look.

I retreated into my thoughts for the rest of the session. I had wondered a lot lately when the abuse would stop being the focus of my life. I wanted my old life back. I wanted to be ignorant about my past. I wanted bohemian weekends on the Vineyard, and I wanted to be able to have casual sex with complete strangers again.

But now, amidst all the irritation and confusion, I felt a small but substantial thing forming inside me. Maybe it was the seed of that high Rosie had talked about.

As we bundled up to leave, Lauren put a hand on my arm. Her eyes glistened. "Shelby, see you next week?"

I nodded, tears re-forming in my eyes. She smiled, squeezed my arm, and left.

***

Lying in bed that night, I had the strangest feeling I was back in Newfield as a girl. I sat on the back porch steps in the sun, which I did a lot then, rubbing my bare feet over the sand and small rocks that collected between the bottom step and the driveway. I sat there when I was little and everyone else went about their business inside. I sat there as a teenager, usually at ten in the morning when all self-respecting teenagers were still hours from waking.

I remembered a permeating melancholy with no nameable cause. As a girl, I was troubled by a general sense that time was speeding up so fast that soon I wouldn't be able to keep up. As a teenager, I attributed my malaise to a fruitless search for the meaning of life.

Maybe it was neither of those things.

Maybe those warm steps became a refuge after Norman started touching me. And maybe the melancholy was my soul shutting itself off from the world's pain and confusion.

Shelby

CHAPTER 47

Astrid took one look at me and let loose on Tina. "What is she doing here? You said it was just you and me." She froze in the door of Tina's apartment, clenching her fists a few times.

"Shelby has something to say to you. Come on in," Tina said calmly. "Please," she whined when Astrid hesitated.

I gave Astrid a weak smile. "You don't have to stay long if you don't want to, but please listen to me for a minute?"

Astrid exhaled dramatically. "Fine." She stomped in, shed her coat when Tina insisted, and leaned against the living room wall, arms crossed.

Tina sat in the comfy chair, but I stayed standing so I could look Astrid in the eye.

"I'm really, really, really sorry I was such a jerk to you. I was going through a lot of my own stuff—not that that's an excuse for treating you like that—and I'm sorry."

Astrid made a small movement forward.

"I'm not done," I said. "What you've been going through with Brad—it's wrong, and it *does* matter. I'm sorry I minimized it. I do that with a lot of things." My voice caught. "But not anymore," I declared, forcing a smile. "The first step in healing is admitting you have a problem, right?"

"Um, Shel," Tina interrupted, "I think that's for alcoholics and addicts. I think in your case, you're supposed to admit you're a victim and you're not to blame for any of it."

I rubbed my forehead with the palm of my hand. "I know that. I get a little confused sometimes." I re-focused. "Anyway, Astrid, if there's anything I can do to help with the Brad situation, I'm here for you."

She launched herself at me and hugged me, clinging as if I were a lifeline or something. "Thank you, Shelby, that's all I wanted to hear."

I hugged her back.

"And I'm glad you're feeling better," she said, sitting on the couch and patting the space next to her. I sat cross-legged on the end, facing her and Tina.

"So how horrible is it at work?" I asked, noticing that her highlights were barely visible and she wore baggy sweatpants and a ratty T-shirt adorned with an amateur image of the Rolling Stones' "December's Children" album cover.

"It's okay, I guess. It's mostly bearable because he's in meetings non-stop these days. But he always tries to stand or sit next to me at staff meetings. And anytime he passes me in the office, he winks or glares at me—I never know which it will be. It's like he's toying with me." She picked at a hangnail. "And when that happens, I find it hard to concentrate because everything he's said and done to me keeps playing back in my head. Especially the Christmas party and him saying he always gets what he wants. I'm trying so hard to focus at work, but I'm not as good at that as I used to be."

Tina and I exchanged a look.

"That doesn't exactly sound bearable," Tina said.

"There must be something we can do. Why can't you tell Maggie?" I asked.

She shook her head. "Even if she doesn't tell Jim and Terry who made the accusation, Brad will know it's me, and he'll get me fired. I'm sure of it."

"Then what about an anonymous letter to those guys telling them what Brad's doing?"

"No, they'll just ignore it if it's anonymous."

"Hm, I guess you're right. Then maybe it really is time for you to quit," I said. "Don't worry about getting a new job. You manage what—ten accounts now? And how many staff? If I can find a new job fast, you know you can too."

She shrugged, still fiddling with her nails. "It's not that simple. You know I can't risk being without a job even for a week."

"So look for a job now, while you're still there. That's how most of the world does it anyway," I said.

"It's not just that," she said, looking up at me. "I really love the agency overall, and I love working with Maggie—she's so much better than my boss at the other agency. I even like my clients more than I thought I would. I had this vision of me and Maggie eventually running the place when the old partners retire."

I scoffed. "Time to kiss that idea good-bye now that Brad's a partner. I'm sorry, Astrid, but you know I'm right."

"Astrid," Tina said in her firm but loving voice, "you've said all this before. It's not like you to be so wishy-washy. You know you can make a new vision somewhere else. Aren't there a ton of PR firms in Boston?" She looked at me, and I nodded. "You can be just as awesome at another place, one where you don't have to look over your shoulder all the time."

Astrid heaved a sigh. "It's not fair that I should have to leave and he gets to stay. But I'll think about it, okay? And if I really think I can't make Campbell Lewis work, then I'll look for another job." She re-crossed her legs as if signaling the topic closed. "Let's talk about something more upbeat."

"Okay. So how's Dave?" I asked.

She smiled the first genuine Astrid smile I'd seen in ages. "He's good."

"Whoa, are you blushing? Man, Astrid, what's going on with you two?"

"Nothing, we're just dating. But he's really great, and I've never felt this way about anyone before."

"Looks like at least one of us might get a fairy tale ending with the perfect man," I said to Tina wistfully.

Tina scoffed. "Before you can end up with the perfect man, Shel, you have to learn to recognize the perfect man."

I scowled at the unexpected attack. "That's good advice coming from the girl who ditched a guy because he didn't look good in jeans."

She shrugged. "I know, you and Astrid are right. I am too critical. But you're not critical enough. You keep picking guys who are beneath you. It's like you don't really want to find the perfect man."

I twitched as a bolt of revelation shot through me. "Maybe you're right. Maybe I don't want to," I said slowly, thinking. "I mean, maybe I didn't want to. To find the perfect man. Think about it. It's not like I had the best role models when it comes to marriage. So maybe," I drew out the words, catching them as they trickled from my brain, "maybe that's why I always dated guys who weren't good enough for me. Then there was no chance of commitment, no chance of getting married, and no chance of something horrible happening, to me or my kids if I had any."

"That makes sense," Astrid said. "You even used to say that about Jesse and Will. 'It's not like I'm going to marry him,' you'd say to us."

"It's so simple now that I think about it."

"Maybe that's why you sleep around, my little slutty friend," Tina said. "No offense," she added quickly.

I ignored the jab. "Definitely no chance of commitment with a one-night stand, that's for sure." A door into my psyche opened up. "That's why I wanted to be fat in college."

"What are you talking about?" Tina asked skeptically.

"If I was fat, no guys would be interested in me, so there was no risk. That was definitely my subconscious speaking, though, because on the surface, I was dying for dates." I scrunched my mouth to the side in thought.

"So being fat was like a protection?"

"I think so. First I was fat," I said, putting it all together. "I kicked that through sheer willpower. But then, I started sleeping around. And when I dated, it was always guys I knew I'd never get serious about. One protection after another."

No one spoke for a minute. My mind was piling my new insights into an orderly stack.

"See," Tina said finally. "You didn't need months of therapy; you just needed to talk to your friends." We all laughed.

"Oh, it feels so good to be with you guys!" I said. "I've never had close friends like you before." I looked at my hands in my lap and twisted my ring.

"Awww, well we're here for you, now that you're done being a jerk," Tina said.

"Can we please forget about my little phase?" I pressed my back against the couch, stretching the muscles. Astrid looked as exhausted as I felt. "Now that we've psycho-analyzed me to death, I have a burning question." I paused for dramatic effect.

"What?" Astrid asked.

"Where the hell did you get that T-shirt?"

"Yeah, out of a dumpster somewhere?" Tina asked.

Astrid frowned and wrapped her arms around her torso. "It was my mother's. She gave it to me."

"Oh, sorry." Tina gulped. "It's not really your style is all."

Astrid studied the Rolling Stones image on her chest. "You're right. Maybe it's time to retire it."

"No! I know someone who can give it a very good home," I said. When they turned to me, I pointed at my chest with both thumbs.

Astrid laughed. Tension broken.

Astrid

CHAPTER 48

I dug through my closet, pushing aside the browns and grays that had inched their way toward the center over the past months. Tina called me wishy-washy. More than anything my girlfriends had said the other day, that comment nagged at me. My mother taught me it was better to make a bad decision than to make no decision at all. Even though I still didn't know what to do about my job, I could at least start to dress like myself again.

After wrestling a classic-cut, sleeveless coral dress and multi-colored paisley blazer out of exile in the darkest recesses of my closet, I scanned the row of shoes on the closet floor. Had I really put my coral heels away, replaced by conservative brown and black footwear? I pulled up a chair so I could poke around through the boxes of seldom-worn shoes on the top shelf of my closet. Not finding the coral ones in the first few boxes, I tugged at a box almost out of reach. It teetered on the edge of the shelf and then plunged to the floor, the coral heels spilling out, along with a five-by-seven manila envelope.

I picked up the envelope, emptied out the somewhat-forgotten stash of mementos, and sifted absentmindedly through the cards, letters, and photos. I stopped at a picture taken by my mother the day I moved to Boston. "Astrid on the first day of the rest of her life," she had penned on the back. I stared at my image in the photo. Taking it to the mirror on my bureau, I held it up to compare. *How did I age so much in less than four years?* I looked almost...haggard. I frowned and turned away from the offensive reflection.

The last item in the envelope was a slim, homemade booklet with the title *Words of Motherly Advice* sprawled across the cover. Unbeknownst to me at the time, my mother had left this booklet on the desk in my dorm room after dropping me off at college freshman year. Wound up with the excitement of opportunity and a new beginning, I had only skimmed the pages when I saw the booklet later that night. *Be yourself, be strong, never walk alone at night*—nothing I hadn't heard already from my mother over the years.

Now, I turned the handful of pages and read each carefully, as if time spent reading my mother's flowery handwriting could somehow inject her strength into me.

I re-read the final page called "Master of Your Destiny" three times.

Life doesn't always go the way we plan. Don't lose sleep fretting over what you can't change. But do look for ways to change the things you can. And never accept a bad situation if there is one cell left in your body that can fight to make it better. Strong women don't let fate rule them. Strong women flow with the waves of fate, accepting what they can't change, but nudging, shifting, or downright blasting the things they can.

I pressed the booklet to my chest and closed my eyes.

A minute later, I tucked the booklet into my sleek black pocketbook and snapped the gold clasp shut with as much purpose and confidence as I could marshal. I finished dressing and strode out the door for work ten minutes early so I'd have time to pick up a *Boston Globe* on the way. I wouldn't have a chance to look at the Help Wanted section until tonight, but I couldn't risk all copies of the paper being sold by the time I got home later.

Shelby

CHAPTER 49

The letter rested beside me on the wooden bench as I lifted my bum, tugged my skirt down, and sat again.

I breathed deeply a few times and scanned the zoo grounds. The young spring grass seemed emboldened by the sun's warmth as it stretched toward the eggshell blue sky. Every few minutes, a new group of kids and parents approached the ticketing area to my right. I vowed to open the letter after fifteen more people came through the turnstile.

Twenty people later, my lunch break ticking away, I tore off the end of the envelope and pulled out a folded piece of newsprint and a sheet of yellow lined paper, which I unfolded and read.

***

Hi Sis, how are you? I know we haven't talked in a while. I'm not sure if you're mad at me after our last phone call. But I hope not, so I'm writing to say hi. I would have called, but I wanted to send you this article from the sports page of the Petersburg newspaper.

Mom sent me this. It's about Norman, who I guess isn't high on your list these days, but your friend Annie from high school is interviewed in it. I thought you might want to see what she says. I told Mom to mail it to you, but she says she's giving you space.

You know I want you to be happy, but I hope when you're ready, we can all be a family again. Last Christmas was weird, even though I had a good time with Jamie's family. She's awesome, by the way. I think she might be the one. I can't wait for you to meet her.

Love,
Kyle

P.S. Mom is pretty upset you won't see her or talk to her. She's a victim in this, you know. As a victim yourself, you must get that.

***

I tucked the letter and envelope under my leg and unfolded the newsprint.

Petersburg Covets Coach Humbertson

Norman Humbertson, one of two finalists for the Petersburg Middle School assistant principal job, is aware he was proposed for the role due to his coaching skills as much as his long career as an educator, and he's not apologizing for that.

"The superintendent and the middle school principal created the job description. If they think I'm a good candidate for the job, who am I to question that?" Humbertson said in a recent phone interview.

A history teacher and head football coach at Newfield High School for eight years, and coach of the girls' varsity basketball team for five years, Humbertson has an enviable track record when it comes to athletics.

In 1987, he was named Coach of the Year by the Massachusetts Football Association in recognition of his success building the Newfield program from a second-rate venture at best to the school's most popular sport. Much of that popularity comes from the team's success in recent years, including two state championships and making it to the district tournament five years in a row.

He hasn't had as much time to build the girls' basketball program, but has still made his mark. The girls went to the state tournament the past two years, although they were knocked out in the early rounds.

Humbertson's former athletes sing his praises.

"Coach Humbertson is awesome. He taught me so much about the game and got my skills up to a new level. I feel so lucky to have had him as my coach," said Jimmy Anderson, who played varsity football under Humbertson from 1984 to 1986 and now plays on the University of Massachusetts team.

"One reason Mr. Humbertson is such a good coach is he gets right in there and shows us how to do things. He doesn't just yell at us from the sidelines. He comes onto the court and shows us how to block and rebound," said Annie Irish, who played forward on Humbertson's varsity basketball team for the 1980 and 1981 seasons.

Asked about rumors that Peterborough Middle School Principal Hal Riley wants Humbertson to start a summer basketball program for middle school boys, Humbertson is diplomatic.

"Let's not get ahead of ourselves. I don't even officially have the job yet. But if I do get it, and Principal Riley wants a summer youth program, I'm all for it. Helping young kids learn and love the game is rewarding, and I'd be honored to do it."

***

The ham and cheese sandwich I'd wolfed at my desk before coming outside balled up like a fist in my stomach. I rubbed my suddenly throbbing temples and inhaled sharply, realizing I'd been holding my breath.

Annie didn't know about Norman. I couldn't be mad at her even though her praise of Norman made me want to punch something. I squinted at the article in my lap as if the heat of my stare could make it spontaneously combust.

"Ow!" I yelped as a skateboard rammed into my shin.

"Sorry!" yelled a redheaded teenager as he sprinted toward me. "Accident, I swear!"

I pinned the skateboard under my foot and glared at him as he neared me.

"Whoa, I didn't think there was even a slope there. It got away from me. I'm really sorry." He hung his head, but not before I took in his scrubbed cheeks and embarrassed gaze. He was younger than I thought. Maybe ten or eleven.

"Timmy, get over here," a woman commanded from the entry area.

"Can I have my skateboard back, please?" he asked in a hushed voice.

"Yeah. Here you go." I nudged the board to him with my foot. "Have fun."

He grinned, revealing a missing canine tooth, grabbed his skateboard, and ran back to his mother.

"Enjoy the zoo!" I shouted.

How old was he, I wondered? I sucked at guessing kids' ages. I blamed it on being the youngest in my family. Was he in fifth grade? Middle school? I scanned the families strolling toward the Plains exhibit and Adventure Area, wondering about the ages and grades of the girls especially—something I'd started doing since working at the zoo. The younger girls showed no signs of self-consciousness, skipping and running, the journey to the next exhibit almost as fun as actually viewing the animals in the exhibit. The older ones whispered with their friends, elbowed each other occasionally, and giggled constantly at things I couldn't hear or see. What did they worry about when they were alone? Getting their first bras? Their periods? Zits? When their father or uncle or sister would violate their private places again? Lauren said one in three women was a victim of sexual abuse. Was one in three of these girls a victim? Did she live with the torture of that every day? Did she blame herself? How was it changing her life?

I had no answers and no power to help them. I shivered and left the bench to return to my desk, where I could at least help my colleagues do something good for the endangered species in our care.

Astrid

CHAPTER 50

"Maggie, there's no easy way to say this." I looked directly at my mentor, seated across from me in her office. "I'm giving my two-weeks' notice. I found another job."

"You're what?" she asked, eyes wide.

I repeated the repugnant words.

She stared at me while her desk clock ticked the seconds away. "I'm very sorry to hear that. Where are you going?"

"Jodie King & Company."

She nodded. "Promotion?"

I shook my head. "No. I'll still be a senior account executive. But it does come with a nice raise, and Jodie says if all goes well, I could be an account supervisor within six months or a year."

"You could be account supervisor here in less time than that. Are you open to counteroffer?"

My waistband cut into my abdomen and my chest was tight. "I'm sorry, no. It was just—it's just time for me to go. To try something new."

Maggie picked up a pen from her desk and tapped it against her leg. "Well, I can't pretend I'm not disappointed. I had big plans for you, Astrid. Can I ask why you decided to change? Did Jodie come after you?"

Guilt forced my gaze away from her steady brown eyes. "No. I saw their want ad."

Maggie said nothing. I looked back at her.

"Maggie, I need to tell you how incredibly lucky I feel to have worked with you so closely. You've been an incredible teacher, and I respect you and your work and your ethic so very much. And we have great clients who have provided me wonderful opportunities."

She stopped tapping her pen. "But?"

"But, I didn't feel I had a choice. This was something I had to do, not that I wanted to do."

"Hm." She shifted in her chair. "Astrid, is there something you're not telling me? If you were so happy with me and your clients, were you having a problem with something else here? Or someone? An interpersonal issue maybe?"

I flinched and wondered if she'd noticed. Her brow furrowed. "If there's anything you can tell me, you would be doing me—and the agency—a favor. If someone is making you uncomfortable, please tell me."

I bit my lip but caught myself. Quickly I smooshed my lips together as if smoothing my lipstick to cover my nervous movement. "Theoretically, if someone were making me uncomfortable, what action would even be taken?"

She blinked twice. "I guess the partners would discuss how to discipline or possibly fire that individual, if there was solid evidence of the egregious behavior."

I nodded. The partners would decide. Of course. And evidence would be required.

"Theoretically, I wouldn't want to make an accusation that couldn't be backed up and cause trouble for Campbell Lewis or you."

Maggie sighed. "So your mind is made up. You're leaving us."

"I'm doing what I think is best for me."

She nodded again and stood, holding out her hand. "I'm sorry it didn't work out," she said quietly.

I stood up and grasped her warm hand. "Thank you again, Maggie, for everything. And you know I'll do my best to help transfer my accounts over the next two weeks."

"That's fine, Astrid." She let go of my hand. I turned to leave. "And Astrid, something tells me our paths will cross again."

I gave my genuinely wistful smile. "I would like that."

Shelby

CHAPTER 51

"To Astrid's new job," Tina declared from Astrid's bed where the three of us sat cross-legged in a circle, wineglasses in hand.

"To new beginnings," Astrid replied. She sounded like she meant it. Her face had its wholesome girl-next-door aura back. She'd booked an appointment to have her hair foiled and presented me with the Stones T-shirt when I came in that night.

"And to no more Brad Butler!" I cheered. "Did he squeeze in any final obnoxious comments before you left?"

"Eh," Astrid shrugged. "He pretty much ignored me. It's like his hold on me is loosening link by link, and I can sense freedom around the corner." She laughed with me and Tina at her melodrama. "I feel better about this decision every day."

"Totally tubular, dude," I said with a Valley Girl lilt, making us crack up again. "Now let's toast to your long weekend away with Dave. Are you excited?"

"Of course." Astrid giggled.

"Just don't pull a Tina and decide a few hours into the trip that it was a bad idea. Tell us again about your fun bus ride home that time, Tina."

Tina ignored me and raised her glass. "To life being somewhat normal again." She and Astrid raised their glasses. They waited for me.

I rested my wineglass on my thigh. "About that. I've been thinking. I don't feel normal yet."

"I said *somewhat* normal, Shel—you've never been completely normal," Tina deadpanned, drawing a high five from Astrid.

I frowned. Tina backtracked.

"You're serious. Oh. But you said your headaches are a lot better, and you're fine with group therapy ending. You haven't had any more blackouts. So what's up?"

I waited. Saying it to my best friends would make it real. "There's something I need to do," I said finally. "I have to confront my stepfather."

"Are you sure you want to do that?" Tina asked.

"I don't want to do it. I *have* to do it. I need him to admit what he did and for my mother to believe me."

My friends nodded.

"And I figure if no one else is going to stick up for me, I have to stick up for myself."

"Okay, then you should do it," Astrid agreed. "But don't say you're on your own because you're not. We'll stick up for you. You know that. And your brother Eric is on your side."

"And your therapy friends," Tina added.

"I know, you're right," I acknowledged, encouraged by their support but also suddenly exhausted. I put my wineglass on the bedside table and curled up on the bed, soothed by their quiet conversation.

***

"This is the nicest thing anyone's ever done for me," I said to Astrid, whose focus was on the Mass Pike westbound.

"I know; you've said that three times."

"I can't believe your new boss is letting you take two days off so soon."

"I said it was a family emergency. What else could she say?" Her eyes left the road and settled on me. "Now stop stalling and work on your notes."

"You're such a taskmaster," I grumbled.

"You know how important preparation is. You don't want to leave anything unsaid. You've got one shot at this. Now, get to work."

I sighed heavily. "If you're trying to make me less nervous, it's not working." I reached for the radio.

"Ah!" she reprimanded, stopping my hand with hers.

Sighing again, I studied the blank sheet of paper in my lap. Closing my eyes, I wondered what I was doing. The only thing I knew was that it was not humanly possible to prepare for a sit-down with my mother and stepfather to discuss his sexual abuse of me.

But thirty minutes later, that's what I was doing. Sitting in my childhood living room, trying not to smell Norman's aftershave and mild BO. Mom's face had more lines than I remembered. Norman had lost weight, and his crewcut had gray mixed in with the brown. My mouth was as dry as if I'd smoked an entire joint by myself.

"Your friend seems lovely," Mom said, glancing toward the door of the den, where Astrid waited.

"She's one of the two best friends I've ever had," I said, my throat catching. I swallowed hard and faced my stepfather. "We need to talk about what happened when I was a girl. What you did to me, Norman," I said, choking out his name.

"I know," he said, his beefy face reddening—and what seemed like sincerity in his eyes. "I need to tell you that I am so sorry if I ever hurt you, Shelby. I never meant to. What I did was wrong. I was sick, but I've been getting help, and I hope you can forgive me. I wish I could take it back."

I stared, unseeing. "You've been getting help?"

My mother put her hand on my arm. "Remember I wrote in my letter that we were going to therapy?" I pulled my arm away. "That's when Norman told me about his mother climbing into bed with him—"

Thankfully she stopped describing that image.

"So you admit you sexually abused me?" I said directly to Norman.

"That's strong language, Shelby," Mom said.

I turned to face her. "But that's what it was, Mom. Sexual abuse," I said, emphasizing each syllable.

"Shelby," Norman said, "I know I kissed you on the lips, and I shouldn't have, even though we are family. And I may have leaned on you when I was hugging you good-night."

I squashed a gag, my insides trembling.

"You used to kiss me like we were lovers," I said. "You French kissed me. You got on top of me. I was just a little girl!" I shuddered, and a sob burst from my chest. Norman looked sideways at my mother. "And you touched me, you—" my face twisted—"you caressed me, all over my front."

"I may have gotten carried away once, but I'm sorry, like I said," he said, shifting in the chair.

"It wasn't once! Aargh, you are such an asshole! I know it was more than once. I remember it happening in my bedroom—*and* on the couch. How many times was it, Norman? Huh? How many months did it go on for? Thankfully I can't remember. But because of you, I blocked all out kinds of things in my life, good and bad. Because of you, I forget things, and I don't even notice life going on around me, and I sabotage my own relationships and—" The sobs wracking my body made me stop. I rested my head in my hands.

"I'm truly sorry if you think I'm responsible for those things," Norman said, sounding like he thought he was noble or something.

My mother's legs appeared in front of me. I looked up. She glared at Norman.

"You said it was only once, and it was only a kiss. You lied to me!"

He blanched and shrunk into the couch for a second, but immediately, his swagger was back. "I know, I know, I haven't been honest," he said, like he was acknowledging that he forgot to take out the garbage again. "It's hard for me to admit what I've done, and I'll just say again, I'm sorry, and I would take it all back if I could."

My mother's stone face melted a touch.

"Please don't be mad at me, Phyllis. I was sick. I'll keep going to therapy. I promise."

She took his hand.

I stood up, legs shaking, stomach roiling.

"You both make me sick. I'm done here. But one other thing," I said, my voice a bit stronger. "You can't take that assistant principal job."

"What on Earth do you mean, Shelby?" Mom asked.

"I mean he shouldn't be around young girls. I don't know his exact taste, but he can't be near sixth grade girls. Who knows what would happen?" My fist clenched and unclenched on its own.

"But Shelby, everyone loves Norman. What would people think if he withdrew from consideration?"

"She'll tell them," Norman said. He turned toward me. "That's what you're saying, isn't it?" His voice had a new edge to it.

"Oh no, you can't! You can't tell anyone about this!" Mom pleaded. "Please Shelby, don't do this to us," she ended with a whimper.

"If you withdraw from the running, I won't tell," I seethed, my stomach heaving. "But my conscience won't let me watch you get a job working with girls and risk you doing to them what you did to me."

They stared at me, then each other, then me again.

I needed fresh air as if my life depended on it. "It's your choice," I said, bolting from the old farmhouse on rubbery legs. "Astrid, let's go," I yelled through the den door on my way past.

I collapsed into the car, Astrid right behind me.

As Astrid started the engine, Mom ran to my window. I rolled it down. "Okay, you win, you win. Norman will find a reason to say he can't take the job."

I nodded.

"That's what you want, right?" she asked.

I nodded again.

"So you don't need to say anything to anybody."

I nodded, silently begging her to let me go.

She didn't move, so I turned to Astrid, who backed the car up. I don't know if Mom watched us go because I was transfixed by the endless tears dripping into my lap.

When we were free of the driveway, Astrid patted my leg. "You were amazing," she whispered. "I kind of listened through the door as much as I could."

I gasped. My chest hurt. "She said I won. Did you hear her say that? Funny I don't feel like I won anything." I slumped down, leaned my head against the car door, and closed my eyes as Astrid drove to the hotel.

***

"Can't we listen to music instead?" I asked, squirting toothpaste onto my toothbrush in the hotel bathroom the next morning. "My brain isn't ready for news yet."

"I paid for this hotel so we could have some decompression time. But we're still PR professionals. We have to know what's going on in the world," Astrid said from the other room, turning up the TV.

I rolled my eyes at my reflection and brushed violently as if I could scrape away the taint of yesterday's confrontation. It didn't work.

"Shelby, come quick," Astrid said in a tone that pulled me out of the bathroom mid-brushing. She stared at the TV.

"Norman Humbertson's nomination for the job continues to upset some local citizens, who say his appointment would be all about athletics, and not at all about academics," a stocky blonde reporter said, standing in front of Petersburg High School.

Cut to a visibly upset mother. "Carl Whitmore is so clearly the better candidate. I can't even believe this is a debate. This is a *school*. That means they should focus on teaching, not winning games."

Back to the reporter.

"The School Committee has scheduled a special meeting at three today, where they are expected to vote on the assistant principal position. Even that has opponents upset, as they say holding such an important meeting during the workday is an attempt to keep them out. For Channel 8, this is—"

Astrid turned the TV off.

I stared at the gray screen.

"Shel," Astrid said. I turned to her. "You're drooling," she said, touching her chin.

I ran into the bathroom and spat.

Astrid

CHAPTER 52

"Wow, what a circus," Shelby said, wide-eyed at the substantial crowd filing into Petersburg High. A few protestors chanted on the sidewalk, pumping signs in the air that read "Academics First" and "Don't Hire Humbertson" and injecting a level of excitement into the event that I hadn't anticipated.

"Come on," I said, taking her arm. "I'm here for you. If things get ugly, I'll be your spokesperson, okay?"

"Mm-hmm," she said, but I wasn't sure she really heard me.

"The meeting's been moved to the gym," a man announced, sweeping his arm away from a small theatre and deeper into the building. "Move along, everyone."

We followed the flow of people into a wooden-floored, cinder block-walled, sweaty-smelling gymnasium. Two sections of chairs divided the room, a microphone on a stand at the front of each section. Underneath the far basketball hoop, three men and two women sat at a long table, desktop microphones in front of them.

"This is good," Shelby said, stopping me from going further into the gym. We grabbed seats midway into the left section of chairs. She slumped down and rested her chin on her chest.

"Are you okay? You don't have a migraine, do you?" I hoped she hadn't taken a pill. She needed to be at the top of her game.

"No. I had a regular headache earlier, but I took aspirin, and it's gone."

The thumping of a finger on a microphone quieted the room. "Let's get started," said the woman in the middle of the long table, all business in a sharp suit, her auburn hair in a tight bun, and frown lines I could see from way back here. A name plaque in front of her read Chmn. Sally Holladay.

"This special meeting of the school committee has been called to allow for public comment on the selection of a new middle school assistant principal. Normally these appointments aren't so newsworthy," she said drily, nodding at the blonde reporter from the morning newscast and a cameraman, off to the side of the room. "But we understand people have concerns. Now is your chance to voice them before the committee votes on the appointment. But we *will* make a decision today. This process has dragged on much longer than necessary. I'd like to have the position filled before the end of this school year."

She cleared her throat. The other committee members shuffled papers or peered into space looking bored.

Shelby hunched in her seat. She might not have even noticed Norman and her mother come in at the last minute and sit beside an older couple near the front of the room. Norman and the gray-haired gentleman shook hands. That must be Whitmore.

"Those who would like to speak, please approach the microphone and state your name. You have two minutes, maximum, so everyone can have a say." Holladay raised her eyebrows as she scanned the large crowd, probably doing the math and realizing it would be a very long meeting if everyone did in fact have a say.

The first speaker, a swarthy man in his forties, jumped right into the controversy. "Let's cut to the chase," he said. "There's nothing wrong with hiring an experienced educator who also happens to be one of the best coaches in the state. Petersburg is a big city. We deserve a great sports program."

A tall thin woman at the other mike spoke out of turn, drawing a glare from the committee chair who nonetheless let the woman speak.

"You're just saying that because you want your son's football team to win State this year."

"Does that make me bad?" He raised his palms and shrugged, scanning the room. A few "yeahs" of support trickled around the room.

"But Norman Humbertson doesn't know anything about school administration! He's got no experience, except as a teacher. Carl Whitmore, on the other hand, is a seasoned professional who could help our kids get a great education."

And so it went, with thirty minutes of a sometimes-heated debate. Parents of high school athletes wanted Humbertson. Parents of middle school students wanted Whitmore. The cast of characters at the mikes rotated, but the script stayed the same. This was more painful than a community development meeting in Boston, I mused, peering at my nails. I'd stopped peering at Shelby because she hadn't moved the whole meeting, except to switch the cross of her legs a few times.

Finally, no one else waited in line at the mikes.

"Do you think Whitmore's got it?" Shelby asked, her eyebrows raised in hope.

"Have you been listening?" I whispered. "A toss up at best." Her eyebrows dropped and drew in. "Are you going to say something?"

She nodded but didn't move.

"Anyone else?" Chairwoman Holladay asked from the front of the room.

I stood up. "Yes, one more." I grabbed Shelby's elbow and eased her up. Her arm trembled. "You've got this." She blinked like a newborn fawn. "Really, Shel. You're going to be the heroine of my book called *The Bravest People I Know*." I squeezed her elbow and nudged her into the aisle.

"Please move along, miss," the chairwoman said.

The fawn analogy carried over to her awkward gait as she approached the mike. Standing there, tilting the mike down to her level, she seemed tinier than usual, like she'd been squeezed into a skin two sizes too small. She wore a simple, well-cut, pale-yellow blouse and tailored black trousers I'd insisted she buy after we agreed to stay for this meeting.

She cleared her throat. People stirred all around me. Norman and Phyllis watched, stone-faced.

"Norman Humbertson shouldn't get this job."

"State your name please."

"Shelby Stewart. I'm his stepdaughter."

The crowd buzzed. Shelby flinched from the sound.

I willed determination into Shelby with my eyes. Her shoulders went back a touch.

"He molested me when I was little. He shouldn't be around young girls," she said with more force.

Exclamations exploded around the room. A committee member knocked over his desktop mike, sending a grating screech through the PA system. Shelby flinched repeatedly as if invisible barbs pierced her clothes.

"And *that's* who you want educating our children!" screamed a young brunette woman, jumping up from her seat.

"Whoa, what happened to innocent until proven guilty?" yelled the swarthy man who spoke first when the meeting started.

"Quiet, please, quiet," demanded Holladay. "That's a serious accusation, Miss Stewart." To my surprise, she turned to Norman. "Would you like to address it, Mr. Humbertson?"

Phyllis turned white. Norman's face turned a deep red. He eased himself up and observed the crowd, his gaze finally settling squarely on Holladay.

"I unequivocally reject the accusation. I have never had anything but the best interests of my students, my athletes, and my family at heart." He sat down.

"She was a kid. She's probably mis-remembering it," a man yelled, launching another ripple of mutterings across the gym.

"She's a plant!" someone else roared.

"Order, please!" Holladay fumed into the mike. She turned toward Shelby. "I'm sure Miss Stewart is not making this charge for fun. But, Miss Stewart, as you have seen tonight, there are a lot of people who would say anything to get their way right now. We have his view—and yours. Is there anyone who can corroborate this?"

Shelby swallowed. "Um, my therapist knows all about it," she said as if asking a question.

Comments volleyed around me.

"She's seeing a shrink!"

"There goes her credibility," said a more sympathetic voice.

"She's crazy."

"Don't listen to her."

"Why is she saying something now? It's a set-up!"

The crowd was turning against her.

I stood up. "I can vouch for her," I said in my most commanding voice, flashing my I-know-this-situation-is-crazy-but-hear-me-out smile. "She told me all about his abuse of her."

"That's still hearsay," said a voice from the right side of the gym. The buzz built up again, punctuated by the gym door clanging open.

"There's no proof. It's still his word against hers." Swarthy guy again. I did not like this man. "And she was a child. No one knows what truly happened."

"I do. I saw it," said a voice from the back of the room.

A slender man with piercing eyes and shoulder-length swirling dark brown hair strode down the aisle between the two sections of chairs. A hum of whispers followed him to the front of the gym. I peeked at Shelby's mom, who had turned ashen. Shelby herself was pale, but a smile touched the corner of her mouth.

"Approach the mike, young man," chairwoman Holladay said.

He grabbed the mike stand opposite Shelby and looked at his little sister. His face said *I'm sorry I never said anything*. At least that's how I would write it. I sat down.

"State your name."

"Eric Stewart. Shelby Stewart's brother, and Norman Humbertson's stepson." He grimaced at the last word. You could hear the proverbial pin drop. "When we were kids, some nights, I would notice Shelby's bedroom door was shut, which was strange because she always left it open so the dog could go in and out."

He flashed a quick smile at Shelby and turned to face the committee.

"One time I got up to go to the bathroom, and Norman was leaving Shelby's room. I tried to go past him into her room, but he grabbed me by the arm and said, 'Don't worry; everything's fine. I was just teaching Shelby some things about life. That's a parent's job, you know, to teach their kids. This is just something I do to help out your mother. But don't say anything to her. This is a man thing.'"

He cleared his throat. I held my breath.

After a pause, he continued. "Then, he said, 'But your mother would be sad if she knew how much Shelby likes these lessons. You don't want your mother to be sad, do you...'" His voice died away as if he'd recounted enough.

Murmurs rippled through the audience. "Ew," said a female voice behind me.

"And you never said anything?" the original father said in a biting voice.

"He's not on trial here," the woman behind me yelled.

"It's okay. I'll answer that." Eric's intense, almost black eyes moved methodically around the room. "I'm guessing all of you have kids—or you wouldn't be here." A few people nodded. "If your six-year-old daughter, or son, was molested by an adult, and your slightly older child saw something and was told not to say anything by that adult, would you be mad at your children for being too afraid and confused to say anything?"

People all around the gym squirmed. The murmurs stilled to silence. The chairwoman covered her mike and consulted with the committee members nearest her. She uncovered her mike and spoke into it crisply.

"We're going to move into closed session now to take this to a vote. Thank you all for voicing your opinions. It's up to the school committee now." She stood. When nobody moved, she leaned back into the mike. "That's it. Good night," she said.

Eric rushed to Shelby and enveloped her. She bawled into his arm. The TV cameraman made a beeline for them, the blonde reporter close behind.

"Excuse me, excuse me," I urged, pushing through the departing crowd. I parked myself between the camera and Shelby. "Turn that off, please. A little privacy." I put my hand in front of the lens.

"Maybe a statement later," the reporter demanded.

"Sure," I said, having no idea if Shelby would want to talk to them. Anything to get them to leave us alone. I steered Shelby out of the gym. Her arm trembled under my grasp. "Over here," I said, tugging her away from the camera and toward a locker-lined hallway behind the gym. Eric stayed with us. Everyone else headed in the other direction toward the exit.

Safely in our corridor, brother and sister embraced again, both of them crying. I stepped away and leaned against a locker, facing the other direction.

"I'm so sorry. I'm so sorry," Eric muttered. "I did try to tell you that night at *Casablanca*, but you stopped me, and I used that as an excuse to chicken out. I'm so sorry," he said, snuffling.

Shelby's crying jag concluded with a shuddering exhalation. I shifted so I could see them. She let go of Eric.

"Stop apologizing. You made up for it tonight." She wiped her eyes with her sleeve. "You were kind of awesome, actually, riding in like a shining knight at the last minute."

"You messed up the metaphor a bit, but thanks," he said, grinning. She hit him in the arm, then leaned against the row of lockers.

"Eric, have you talked to Kyle at all?" Shelby asked.

"Yeah, once," he said, opening a random locker and peeking inside. "He told me you told him. He doesn't get it. But he'll come around, I think. Give him time." He shut the locker with a clang.

Shelby's face drooped.

"So, was Mom in there?" Eric asked, changing the subject although it seemed like going from bad to worse to me. "I didn't see her."

"I don't know. I didn't dare to look around. It was all I could do to keep standing."

"She was there," I said, "off to the side up front, with Norman."

Eric looked at me for the first time.

"This is Astrid, my awesome friend who helped me through the last two days," Shelby said, pulling me closer to them. "This is my brother Eric."

Eric and I rolled our eyes in sync.

"Yeah, I think she knows that." Eric laughed.

"Still, it's nice to meet you in person," I said with a friendly smile.

"In person? What does that mean?" Shelby asked, blinking.

"Why do you think I came tonight?" Eric asked. "Astrid called me this morning and told me about the meeting."

Shelby shook her head as if jostling thoughts into place.

"I got his number from your datebook," I explained. "When you were in the shower. Thought you might need some moral support."

"Shelby's lucky to have you in her corner," Eric said.

"No, she's lucky to have *you* in her corner," I said.

"Well, better late than never I guess," he said, pulling Shelby back against him so he could wrap his arms around her again.

"Let's get out of here," Shelby said, ducking out from her brother's arms.

"Don't you want to wait and see what happens?" I asked.

She scratched her head. "I can't change it at this point. We'll find out when we find out."

Eric and I made mini-shrugs at each other and followed her into the main hallway.

Outside the school's front doors, the TV reporter interviewed a parent who talked as much with her hands as her mouth. Seeing us, the reporter left the parent mid-sentence. The cameraman dropped the unit off his shoulder and lugged it over to us.

"I've got this," I said, sheltering Shelby for the second time that night.

"What do you have to say about Humbertson losing? Do you feel responsible for Whitmore getting the job instead of your stepfather?" She thrust the mike in Shelby's face.

My heart flipped for Shelby. *Justice.*

"I'll speak on behalf of Miss Stewart," I said, hooking the mike with my hand and directing it toward me. From the corner of my eye, I saw Shelby and Eric step back. "And Mr. Stewart."

"Who are you?" the reporter asked impatiently.

"Astrid Ericsson. Friend of the family."

"Okay, fine, what comment do you have?" she asked, accepting she wasn't going to get anything from Shelby or Eric directly.

I straightened the collar of my coat and gathered my thoughts. "Shelby's only concern has been the safety and welfare of the girls who might come into contact with her stepfather. Speaking up tonight was not something she wanted to do—but something she had to do. Now if you'll give us some privacy, we'd like to be on our way."

"What about him?" she asked, pointing her mike toward Eric.

Eric shook his head at me.

"Ditto," I said into the microphone.

Threading through the twenty or so people still gathered in front of the school, we were interrupted again, this time by a woman about my age, who ignored me when I tried to slow her down.

"Shelby, it's me, Lisa Thompson from Newfield. I was the grade above you," she said, breathless as if she'd swum her way to us.

"I remember. Hi," Shelby said. She still seemed extra small.

"I just have to say, you rocked in there!" A smile teased Shelby's lips. "But I'm not surprised at what you said. He was my basketball coach, and he always had a hard-on at practice. You could see it through his sweatpants." The smile evaporated. "Anyway, I wanted to say I think it's great you stood up to him. Bye."

"That was not an image she needed to share," I said as Lisa left us. "Let's go." I moved toward the parking lot. Realizing I was alone, I turned back to see Eric and Shelby frozen on the sidewalk. Shelby's mother stood in front of them, crying.

"I'm sorry. I'm so sorry. I realize now everything you said was true. I'm so sorry I didn't know, and I didn't stop it. Please forgive me." She reminded me of a deer caught in headlights.

Phyllis watched Shelby. Eric watched Shelby. Shelby watched the ground.

"Mom, I know this has been hard on you. You're a victim too," Shelby said.

Phyllis hugged her daughter and then her son violently. "So we're okay?" she asked Shelby.

"Are you staying with him?" Eric interjected.

She turned to Eric. "Don't ask me that. It's not that simple. It's—"

"No!" Shelby said. "We are *not* okay. I need to *not* see you or talk to you for a while. And no letters either. I'm not punishing you. I just need time to deal with this and figure out what kind of relationship I can have with you. But I can't visit you and pretend everything is okay because it's not, and I would be a hypocrite if I acted like it didn't matter." She stepped back from her mother. "I'm sorry."

Shelby turned and walked robotically toward me. Her mother lurched after her.

"Let her go, Mom," Eric said firmly. "We're leaving now."

We made it to the car without being accosted again. All three of us leaned back against the car and inhaled the crisp, early spring night air.

"I guess I should hit the road," Eric said finally. "Long drive back home."

"Yeah, us too," said Shelby.

They hugged again. "Love you, sis."

"Love you too. See you soon?" she asked.

"Mandatory. We need to work on our new Stewart holiday traditions."

Shelby and I got in my car. I studied her until she caught me.

"You going to drive or what?" she asked.

I smiled contentedly. She was back in her own skin.

Shelby

CHAPTER 53

Work could not have been more intense as we entered the homestretch of grand opening preparations. We worked twelve-hour days, six or seven days a week. I didn't even have time to fool around with Aaron, which would have been a welcome diversion.

On a warm Friday night, we hosted the first opening event, a black-tie gala for donors and potential donors. I quadruple-checked every detail on my briefing sheet and racked my brain for anything that could go wrong but hadn't been considered yet. Event planning was easy, I'd told my handful of volunteers: you just had to think of everything. Before it happened.

The animals cooperated even though it was past bedtime for all of them except the nocturnal potto, whose lighting still wasn't adjusted right. Donations from mucky-mucks who normally never entered the inner city flooded in.

Saturday, butterflies flitted around my stomach all morning before the public opening. We had one shot to get this right and improve the zoo's reputation. Within an hour of opening the gates, people trickled in. By noon, a stream of visitors of all ages, colors, and incomes flowed in steadily. By two o'clock, a line stretched from the admission booths to the road.

I raced between animal encounters in the children's petting area at one end of the zoo and the rainforest itself at the other, where docents described the dangers of habitat destruction to people who just wanted to ooh and aah over the gorillas, the antelope, three species of monkeys, and seventy other types of fauna.

The main stage, in the middle of the zoo grounds, hosted the bands, including the folk singer I booked early on and a reggae band I'd booked for my own pleasure even though I barely got to hear them play. But the bulk of the music was African. I didn't even know the genre names because Althea hadn't enlightened me—she just said "book these people"—but the sounds coming from the stage were alternately uplifting, spiritual, thrumming and intense. I glimpsed stringed instruments I'd never seen before and more types of percussion instrument than I knew existed, although I recognized congas, bongos, and the hourglass-shaped talking drums.

A smaller stage featured a fashion show of traditional African garb, several buildings showed off African art, and the education center had African-inspired crafts for kids, like weaving mats out of strips of cloth.

Occasional rides in one of the golf carts and use of a walkie-talkie minimized some of my running around, but there was still a lot of ground to cover. By one o'clock, I had sweated my body weight and was fueled on adrenaline alone.

On one of my sprints across the zoo grounds, I almost bumped into Althea Hemings.

"Miss Hemings," I sputtered. "How are you? What do you think?" I asked, pointing toward a row of food vendors offering traditional African dishes.

"Mm-hmm," was all she said, but her lips twitched before she put her hand on the arm of her companion and shuffled on her way.

When two Boston TV crews showed up, I left volunteers in charge of the stage activities and coordinated interviews with Mike and the curators. The reporters ate it all up, even when a police horse in the background of the shot dropped "road apples" on the walkway.

Sunday was a replay of Saturday but with even higher attendance. When we closed the gates Sunday night, Mike threw us a party in the rainforest.

"Thirty-six-thousand people visited the zoo this weekend," he said to cheers from the staff. "That's more than *all* of last year. And we signed up—what was it Shelby?"

"We signed up ninety-seven new members! And, all the press coverage I've seen so far is positive, and the guy from the *Herald* said a reporter from *Parade* was floating around somewhere, but I don't know for sure."

We cheered again, drank heavily, ate lightly, and reveled in the enormity of our exhausting accomplishment. Aaron and his boss came to the party for a while. I'd barely talked to him lately except to coordinate the final promotional materials. At the party, he gave me a few suggestive looks, and we stifled laughs when a group of us walked by the hippo theatre, but I didn't see how we could sneak away anywhere. Plus, I wanted to celebrate with my colleagues.

***

Monday morning, the Grand Opening over, I lay in bed replaying the confrontation with my mother and Norman and the blur that was the school committee meeting. I had no idea what came next in my relationship with my mother or Kyle. But I was in the best possible place given the situation, I realized, just as my pager interrupted me.

I jumped out of bed and called Mike.

"I need you at the satellite facility, stat. One of the wallabies escaped."

A tiny shot of adrenaline worked its way through my veins as I dressed quickly and drove the Starlet to a suburb north of Boston. Our male wallaby, Matari, escaped from his exhibit overnight, Mike had said. A relative of the kangaroo but much smaller—not even three feet tall and roughly forty pounds—wallabies were stellar jumpers. Matari apparently leaped out of his exhibit, even though it was supposed to be high enough to prevent that. He then headed for the hills.

"He left his three female companions to go walkabout," I said out loud in the car in a dismal Australian accent.

At the zoo, I joined the staff gathered in front of the wallaby exhibit. Mike paced in front of us. Large nets and a few rolled canvas sheets were piled up at the edge of the group.

"He's not a danger to people, so our main concern is his safety. We can't have him injuring himself or being bitten by a wild animal, possibly a rabid one. This is the first escape from a Massachusetts zoo in as long as anyone can remember. Let's make sure it's a short one.

"Shelby, be prepared for calls from the press. The office knows to send all calls to you and you only."

I nodded sharply, my muddled morning-mind finally in full-throttle crisis mode. "Do you want me in the office or helping in the woods?" I asked.

"For now, with us. It should take a few hours for the media to catch up to this."

About twenty of us spread out in the nearby woods, where the keepers suspected Matari had gone. Half of us stationed ourselves in a randomly chosen spot with a fifty-foot-long net while the others fanned out, hoping to flush the wallaby from his hiding spot. We laughed at ourselves, some in business casual attire, some in zoo uniforms, and all looking pretty clueless as we spread out through the brush, catching the net in the branches as we moved.

The walkie-talkie on the hip of the keeper next to me crackled. Matari had been spotted, and he was jumping our way. Seconds later, we saw him. Unfortunately, he saw us too and quickly turned and bounded away in the other direction.

This game went on for hours, to no avail.

By noon, the press was all over the story, so I spent my afternoon conducting interviews with the TV and radio stations and local newspapers. A reporter from Boston's biggest radio station showed up at the zoo, as did some gung-ho junior state representative in a safari hat, thinking he might make a name for himself by catching Matari single-handedly. Mike tactfully informed him of the unlikelihood of that happening and sent the enthusiastic legislator on his way.

By dinnertime, the public was calling in regular sightings of the wallaby. All turned out to be misinformed, leading us to dogs, raccoons, and even one possum dead on the side of the road.

Tuesday was a repeat of Monday. Wednesday, Mike called us all together first thing. He stood next to a topographical map taped to a flip chart on an easel.

"We've confirmed that Matari has traveled as far as the Middlesex Fells Reservation. Numerous credible witnesses placed him there, and Joe," he nodded at the mammal curator, "found wallaby scat in this area late yesterday," he said, pointing to a red circle on the map.

"But the reservation's miles away," one of the keepers exclaimed. "And it covers like five towns!"

"Yep, Middlesex Fells is thousands of acres of rocky, steep, and heavily wooded terrain." He let that sink in. "Needless to say, the net approach is not going to work."

"Do we have a plan?" I asked, wondering how much of a field day the press would have with this latest development.

"Joe and his team worked all night, considering our options. We look at it like this. Matari has everything he needs to survive in the reservation for months. It's warm enough now, and he's got plenty of plants to eat and water to drink. The one thing he won't find is a female wallaby."

A few people tittered. I held back a laugh. Did I say field day? The press was going to love this story. I shivered in anticipation.

"So are we taking one of the females out to him?" I asked.

"No. We are setting three humane traps in the areas where he's been spotted. In those traps, we're putting hay soaked with the urine of the females."

I wrinkled my nose.

"That's it. Let's hope his libido brings him home," Mike said seriously.

Three days later, Matari sat in one of the cages, trapped by the promise of female companionship. He made the front page of both Boston daily papers and an inside page of the *New York Times*.

Sitting at my desk flipping through the press articles a few days later, I laughed at the preposterousness of human relations. Once we'd thought like a wallaby, we figured out how to get Matari home. Animals kept life simple. People made it complicated.

***

"That's so sweeeeet," Tina cooed when I told her and Astrid about Matari's homecoming at our next girls' night.

"It's not romantic," I scoffed. "It's biology."

She shook her head. "Shelby, my cynical little friend. Will you ever change?" She fake sighed.

"Do you think you'll ever see Nick again?" Astrid asked, getting all serious on me.

"I doubt it. I think I blew that one." I couldn't tell them the very thought of Nick—the most fascinating man I'd ever known—scared me. I'd thought back to my last date with him a hundred times, wishing I'd handled it differently. But I was a different person then.

"I could fix you up with one of Dave's friends," Astrid offered. "I think Wade's still single."

"Eh, you know how I feel about men in suits."

"You have *got* to get over that, Shelby!" Tina admonished.

I ignored her. "Besides, I do have a sort of boyfriend I've never told you guys about."

They both glared at me rather than being happy for me.

"And why haven't you said anything before?" Tina asked.

"He's married?" I asked as if I weren't sure.

Tina's jaw dropped.

"Obviously we don't need to tell you this is a bad idea," Astrid said.

"Bad idea? Shelby, you have to stop that this instance!" Tina cried.

"Easy, easy, Tina; it's not like I'm the married one." Her dagger eyes were getting to me. "Okay, I've been thinking of ending it anyway. I hardly even see him these days." The truth was, I felt like I was cheating on Nick when I was with Aaron, stupid as that sounded. "Fine. Consider it ended."

Astrid

CHAPTER 54

Julia Salvatore, executive director of the Boston Public Relations Association, resumed her spot at the podium in the Copley Plaza's banquet room. Straightening the lapels of her tailored burgundy blazer, she leaned into the mike.

"By the way, in case you didn't know, this is one of Boston's oldest hotels. You can sense the tradition as you walk through the hallways or dine here in this sumptuous room." She gestured toward the opulent decor, which included gold-painted chairs, crystal chandeliers, and the room's literal crowning glory—a mural on the ceiling depicting a blue sky dotted with light, gauzy clouds. "That history and tradition is one reason we chose this venue for our annual meeting and awards dinner, where we carry on our tradition of collaboration to advance the discipline of public relations, and our tradition of recognizing the year's finest work and practitioners."

As she spoke, Salvatore methodically scanned the room, her dark eyes inviting three hundred other sets of eyes into her conversation as if speaking to each of them personally. Her sleek, shoulder-length black hair shouted individuality and disdain for the big-hair trend. The features of her olive-toned face were delicate, but her voice commanded the room.

I scanned the room too, for probably the tenth time. Every time my gaze landed on someone I knew from Campbell Lewis or the agency I worked at before, my core of natural confidence strengthened. I felt as much a part of this crowd as they looked. Our table sat seven other people, three from my new agency and four from another. My new boss Jodie had sung my praises when introducing me to them, and all—the men and the women—had treated me as an equal throughout the conversation at the table, which grew louder and more animated with each course. *This is my element*, I thought.

I looked again at Brad, seated at the head table with the other association officers. President or not, he didn't seem like top dog tonight.

In fact, Julia Salvatore was clearly running the show. Brad looked as handsome and arrogant as always but—and maybe it was the light—his hair seemed to be thinning.

The Brad chapter of my life felt increasingly far behind me. He was merely one fish in this very big pool, which had room for both of us, especially now that I'd created some space by leaving Campbell Lewis for Jodie King & Company.

"The awards we've already presented tonight, like Campaign of the Year and Agency of the Year, also have a long tradition," Salvatore was saying from the podium. "Our final award, however, is only three years old. Our industry needs new blood to stay vital and current. So while we rightfully acknowledge the masters of our trade and the best of the work our industry produces, we also want to encourage new voices and to nurture the potential of our younger colleagues. That's why we created the Rising Star Award.

"Before I announce this year's Rising Star, I'd like to tell you how the winner is selected, as the process differs from that used for the other awards. Those, as you know, are voted on by all of you. Because the nominees for Rising Star are not as well known, the four officers of the association and I review the nominations and select the winner."

She paused to glance at Brad and the vice president to her left, and the treasurer and secretary to her right.

"This year's award, by near unanimous vote, goes to a woman who, ironically, has only been at her job a few weeks."

I inhaled sharply. Is this why Jodie invited me to come tonight and sit with her and her senior staff? *No, I'm sure a lot of people in this room are new to their jobs*, I rationalized. Still, I smoothed my hair and adjusted the shoulder pads of my sleek black blazer, chosen to add the requisite corporate touch to my silky red dress.

"She was in fact nominated by her previous boss. Soon after that nomination was made, the employee quit to take a new job. Nothing wrong with that. We've all changed jobs a few times in our careers, right?" A titter rippled across the room. "I offered to remove this candidate from the running, but her old boss said no, and her new boss agreed." She smiled at the room.

"Now to be nominated for Rising Star, you must have fewer than five years in the business, and you must excel in the three areas we define as critical skills for making it in the PR industry. First, it almost goes without saying that the person must be a strong practitioner in all facets of public relations—verbal communication, writing, strategy, publicity, event management, and so on. The winner of our award excels in all these areas. For example, she pitched feature articles to national business magazines on the trend known as the Graying of America, in an attempt to secure visibility for her client, a travel agency specializing in tours for seniors. Not only did she place a story in *Fortune* magazine, but in *Forbes* as well. Had she earned placement in *BusinessWeek,* she would have scored a hat trick, but two out of three is still enviable, wouldn't you say?"

Heads nodded around the room. I focused on my chest moving up and down with my breath, willing it to stay steady because now I knew Julia Salvatore was talking about me. I fought to keep a premature grin off my face.

"She also came up with the idea of a story on women making it in the real estate and construction industries, which was covered by our regional business journal as well as national real estate and engineering trade press.

"Our second requirement is that the winner possesses strong management potential. That pretty much explains itself. You can't rise to the top of this field if you can't manage the team under you. Our winner has successfully managed numerous account coordinators and interns in her short career."

People at the tables around me fidgeted, probably bored with her long preamble. I, on the other hand, hung on every word.

"Our third criterion is harder to define. The Rising Star will have that something extra, that special ability to come up with the creative answer that eludes others, or the insight to spot a problem, identify a strong solution, and make that solution a reality. This year's winner—wait, did I mention that after this woman changed jobs a few weeks ago, her new boss weighed in on her nomination? Well, she did, and she added to the nomination this person's idea to provide pro bono PR to the new Rape & Incest Community Hotline. As you may have heard, this new non-profit organization recently opened its doors and its phone lines in the South End."

She paused to take a breath. I turned to look at Jodie, who smiled and nodded.

"Now, without further ado, I would like to present the 1988 Rising Star Award to Astrid Ericsson, formerly of Campbell Lewis and now with Jodie King & Company."

Seize the moment, I told myself. I placed my napkin on the table in front of me, pushed back my chair, and rose to my full height as the audience clapped. The applause escorted me between the tables and to the stage, where Salvatore stepped away from the podium, shook my hand, and handed me a small plaque. Sadly, award winners didn't get to speak at the microphone, but I stood tall and beamed a smile with no precedent.

"Look over there," Salvatore directed, turning to the right as the association's hired photographer snapped away from the end of the stage, while the executive director and I continued to grip each other's hands, me holding the plaque to my chest with my other hand.

"Wait here," she whispered before returning to the podium. I stepped back and waited.

"That concludes our program. Thank you all so much for coming to our annual meeting. I'd like to ask all the award winners to gather up here so we can take some group photos. Everyone else, the bar in this room is closed, but the main hotel bar is still open if you're interested. Please enjoy the rest of your evening, be safe, and thank you again for coming."

I accepted congratulations and handshakes from the other award winners as they crowded up onto the stage.

"Form a line, please. Let's look like we know what we're doing," Salvatore joked as people jostled each other into a crooked line. I settled in between two men from the agency that won Campaign of the Year. "The taller ones—you know who you are—move to the middle so we have a cleaner line," the executive director instructed.

The man on my right nudged me. "Come on, that's us." I followed him toward the center of the group where Salvatore was guiding people into place. She firmly pushed me in between my new companion and Brad. As president and one of the taller people on the stage, he owned the middle spot. I prepared to acknowledge his presence, but he was engaged in conversation with the woman on his other side.

"Now please squeeze together," Salvatore said.

I held my breath, wondering if I'd have the courage to say something if Brad's hand stroked my back or lingered on my derriere. But all I felt was a light brush as his arm reached behind me. My companion on the right, though, used his hand to pull me slightly closer to him.

"Okay, we're all set," Salvatore announced after ten minutes of photographing the group and various subsets.

By then, most of the crowd had dispersed—gone home or to the bar, I presumed. After a visit to the ladies' room, I found my way to the bar at the edge of the hotel's marble-clad lobby, where my Jodie King & Company colleagues welcomed me with a small cheer.

"Way to go, Astrid," said Brian, Jodie's right-hand man, extending a glass of champagne. "We thought a celebratory toast was in order, so we got you this." The four of us raised and clinked our glasses. Champagne never tasted so fulfilling.

"Hey, Jodie," Terry Campbell boomed, inserting himself into our group. "Congratulations on your good taste in employees. You've got a winner here," he said, clapping a hand on my shoulder.

"No hiring her back, Terry; she's mine now," Jodie said with a grin.

"All's fair in love, war, and work, so I make no promises," Terry joked back. He turned to me. "You should ask for a raise, Astrid. You've just boosted Jodie's standing in the industry considerably."

Jodie narrowed her eyes at him. "Okay, Terry, you can go now," she said, but the Campbell Lewis partner was already moving toward a different group of people, waving to them as he approached.

"We do need to make hay with this," Jodie said. "It's good visibility for us. If the association doesn't publicize Rising Star, we'll be sure to send out a press release. But for now, I'm saying goodnight. I want to get home before my son goes to bed."

Before I could say good-bye, a new well-wisher interrupted. "Joe Miller," a dark-haired man my age said. "Nice to meet you, Astrid. And congratulations on your award. Boy, you can write your own ticket now!"

"Really, every agency in town is going to be after you," said another smiling young man, who seemed to be friends with the first one. "Enjoy it while you can. You've got one year until the next Rising Star is named."

He mock frowned. "But Joe, this poor woman's glass is empty. What can we get you, Astrid?"

"I'd love a vodka and soda, thanks," I said, flashing my you're-cute-but-don't-get-any-ideas smile and flicking my hair back over my shoulder.

Congratulations, introductions, and handshakes consumed me at that point. Midway into my second cocktail, the crowd of young men around me parted as if Moses had appeared. Brad Butler stepped up close to me, effectively cutting off the others nearby, so I had no choice but to acknowledge him.

"Congratulations, Astrid, well deserved." He held out a hand, which I eyed for a second before extending my own, which he gave a quick, professional shake and let go.

"Thanks, Brad. I appreciate it. To be honest, I figured you probably voted against me." My brazenness felt justified.

"Well, I never divulge how I vote on anything, but it's irrelevant now, don't you think? You won. That's all that matters." He drank heavily from his glass, the distinct smell of juniper berries wafting toward me. "What do you say we let bygones be bygones? After all, it's clear we're both going to be in this business for a long time. Let's start over." He smiled, and I remembered how charming he could be, thinning hair or not.

I gave my best conciliatory smile, relieved and reassured by the olive branch he proffered. "I'd like that. I'd—"

"Great!" he interrupted, "because I've got a business proposition for you. As president of the association, I need to raise our profile. No one's done much to promote this group in Boston business circles since the group was founded. We need to generate more excitement around the association, and we need to attract more young blood to the industry. What better way to do that than to pitch some stories on you, Astrid Ericsson, Boston's new rising star?"

He smiled encouragingly, and I wondered if he even remembered his comment to me once that I could have attached myself to *his* rising star if I had been more accommodating. Still, he seemed sincere, and a profile or two in local media would be great PR for me.

"Don't say yes or no, yet. But as president, I could really use a win like this. Let's have a quick brainstorm on the possibilities to make sure we can be successful." He consulted his wristwatch. "It's almost nine. How about we meet in my room in twenty minutes or so after we finish schmoozing with everyone else?"

My Brad radar fired up, but I knew I was in control. I didn't have to say yes to him. "Your room? And tonight? Why not in your office tomorrow?"

He shook his head as if I were a silly child. "Don't be so paranoid, Astrid. The room is a business suite that the association's been using all day. And Julia's going to be there too, right Julia?" He reached out and clutched a woman to his right by the arm, interrupting her conversation with a silver-haired man and pulling her into our twosome. It was the association's executive director. "But I forget my manners. Let me introduce you two properly. Julia Salvatore, Astrid Ericsson. Astrid Ericsson, Julia Salvatore."

"Very nice to meet you again, Ms. Salvatore," I said, shifting my cold glass into my left hand, wiping my right hand against my jacket and extending it.

"Please, call me Julia, and it's good to meet you officially," she said, taking my hand.

"Julia, we need you," Brad said. "I want the three of us to have a quick meeting to brainstorm some publicity around Astrid's award."

"Tonight? I thought we were meeting tomorrow to de-brief tonight and plan next steps."

"Turns out I have to go out of town on a business trip tomorrow. I still have a full-time job at Campbell Lewis, you know."

Julia's body language told me she was highly aware of this fact, but she said nothing.

"Plus," he continued, "Astrid is an ace publicist, and I think she should be involved in the planning." He took Julia's silence as assent. "You know we have to strike while the iron is hot, so let's run through a quick plan tonight." He looked at the bar and arched his shoulders back as if stretching his muscles. "But it's too noisy here, and my back is killing me. I strained it playing racquetball last week. I really need to have a hot shower."

Julia seemed to swallow a sigh. She nodded.

"Okay. Let's say nine thirty in the suite. Room 332. See you both then." He walked off somewhat gingerly, one hand rubbing his lower back, leaving me and Julia staring at each other.

"Nothing like a late-night meeting to get the creative juices flowing," she said sarcastically. "This is not how I intended to finish up what's been a very long day."

I realized my golden opportunity was another chore for her. "Yeah, I know how much work these events are. You must be exhausted. And great job, by the way. Everything was perfect."

"Thanks. I appreciate it." She smiled warmly.

"Do you think we could get him to postpone the meeting?" I asked. "I've actually got a friend meeting me here soon, so it's not ideal for me either."

She shook her head. "You've worked with him. You know that once he's got an idea in his head, there's no changing it. Plus, as president, he's basically my boss. Add to that the fact that he can make or break careers in Boston PR circles and it's safe to say I'll be there." She sipped from her glass of wine and looked at the half-full glass longingly. "Guess I shouldn't finish this if I'm going to a meeting."

She looked at me, we looked at my half-full glass, and we laughed at the same time. Shrugging, I drained my glass as she did the same.

"I always find I do my most creative work after a few drinks," I said, enjoying our moment of connection.

She paused as if making a decision. "To be honest, I'm surprised at this new idea of his. He didn't even vote for you for this award." My eyes widened. "But don't worry about it," she added quickly. "That doesn't matter. You won, and this *is* a good idea, focusing our follow-up publicity campaign on you. Plus, it will be very good for you personally."

I smiled in relief that she supported the idea. "Okay, then. Let's do it." My insides fluttered with excitement at the prospect of being written up in a Boston newspaper or magazine.

Julia checked her watch. "We have a little time, and I still have to wrap up a few things in the banquet room. I'll see you up there."

"Sounds good," I replied, as Joe Miller thrust another vodka and soda into my hand.

***

A familiar voice spoke in my ear as I finished my drink.

"Congratulations, Astrid."

"Maggie!" I exclaimed, turning to face my mentor with my arms wide. She hesitated, then embraced me quickly. "I'm so glad you found me. I've looked for you a few times, but you were always in a conversation with someone."

"Doesn't look like you've been lonely though," she joked, looking at the small group of admirers who had re-congregated after Brad and Julia left.

"Maggie, I cannot thank you enough for nominating me. That was so generous of you, and to keep my nomination in after I left—well, all I can say is thank you."

She smiled and shrugged. "You deserved it. Every now and then, someone comes along who you can tell is going to be a big player in our business. You're one of those people."

My heart and head swelled. I decided it was not humanly possible to feel any stronger or more confident or hopeful than I did at that moment. I cautioned myself to keep the confidence in check so I didn't appear arrogant.

"I saw you and Brad talking earlier. What was my esteemed colleague bending your ear about, if I may ask?"

"Oh, he had a great idea. He wants to pitch profiles of me to the local business and news media. Isn't that exciting?" I tried to control my enthusiasm, but I sounded like a young girl getting her first ice cream cone.

Maggie took it in stride. "That is a good idea. And Julia Salvatore is excellent at her job, so if anyone can place the story, she can."

"You know Julia?" I asked, immediately regretting my naive comment. Of course they knew each other. They'd both been working in Boston PR for probably ten years.

"She's a good friend, actually, and I have nothing but the highest respect for her professionally."

"Oops, speaking of Julia, I have to go soon. She and I are meeting Brad to brainstorm the publicity campaign." I wiggled my shoulders in anticipation.

"That must have been where she was headed," Maggie said. "When I was coming back from the restroom a few minutes ago, I saw her going into the elevator. She said she'd catch up with me later."

"Really? She already went up? I guess I should get going then." I handed my empty glass to a waiter walking by with a tray of dead soldiers.

"Good luck, Astrid. And congratulations again."

"Thanks, Maggie. And hey, if you see Shelby Stewart, can you tell her I'll be back soon? She's meeting me for a drink any minute now."

Maggie nodded. I turned and left to find the suite.

Shelby

CHAPTER 55

I felt severely underdressed as I clomped like an elephant through the lavish lobby of the Copley Plaza, heading to the bar. Astrid had told me people at the PR association's annual meeting would be wearing normal business attire, not black tie, so I figured my new jeans and casual blazer would blend in at the hotel bar. I was wrong. Maybe I could convince Astrid to hit one of the ten or so more casual bars in the neighborhood instead of hanging here.

She wasn't in the Oval Room where the event took place, so I worked my way through the crowded bar, looking for my friend or anyone I recognized from my year and a half at Campbell Lewis. I was about to give up when I spotted Maggie Hirsch. I hovered nearby, not daring to interrupt the chuckling of my former boss and the two gray-haired men talking with her. One very awkward minute later, the men moved off, and I stepped into Maggie's line of vision.

"Shelby, so nice to see you," she enthused, reminding me why I liked her so much.

"You too, Maggie. Hey, have you seen Astrid lately? We're supposed to be meeting up."

"She told me to tell you she was called into a short meeting to talk about PR for tonight's award winners."

"Really? She volunteered to help the association with their PR even though she just started her new job? That's weird."

"No, that's not why she's there. I'll spoil the surprise and tell you. Astrid won the Rising Star Award tonight."

My face stretched into a huge grin. "She did? I'm not sure what that is, but it sounds awesome! I can't wait to congratulate her."

"She said the meeting would be short. So tell me about your job at the zoo," Maggie said as a pretty woman with olive skin and straight black hair joined us. "Wait, let me introduce you first. Shelby, this is Julia

Salvatore, executive director of the Boston PR Association. Julia, Shelby Stewart—she used to work with me at Campbell Lewis. She left us for greater things, namely PR manager at the Commonwealth Zoo."

I shook hands with Julia, absentmindedly wondering if I should order a drink or wait for Astrid in case we decided to go somewhere else.

"The zoo?" enthused Julia. "So you're the one behind all the press of the Grand Opening?" I nodded. "Very well done, especially the live TV coverage."

"Thanks, it was a lot of fun. I love it there. It's the best job ever." My reddening cheeks raised the foot-in-mouth alarm. "Of course I loved working with Maggie at Campbell Lewis too." Maggie's face had that wise, all-knowing look on it. "I think about everything you taught me all the time."

Maggie nodded. "It's fine, Shelby. Don't feel funny about leaving. We all move on at some point. I have no doubt you'll continue making a success of yourself." Her smile faded. "But Julia, I thought you were in the meeting with Astrid. Is it over already?"

Julia's face went blank. "No, Brad cancelled it. He's being really flaky tonight. Too many gin and tonics maybe. First he said we'd meet at nine thirty. Then a few minutes later, he caught me in the hallway and said to come a little earlier so the two of us could bounce a few ideas around before Astrid gets there. And then when I went to his room, he said he was too tired to hold the meeting after all and that maybe we could have a conference call tomorrow instead."

I stared at Julia. "Did you say Brad? As in Brad Butler?"

"Yes, that Brad." She caught my eyes, which seemed to alarm her. "Why, what's wrong?"

My heart raced as if I were Astrid stuck in a room with Brad. "So she's alone with him? Right now?" Their faces were puzzled. "That's not good," I said in a rising voice. "He might try something."

"Brad's touchy feely; that's for sure," Julia offered. "He drives me crazy, to be honest, with his innuendoes and little caresses when no one is looking. But he wouldn't do anything—he wouldn't cross a line, would he?"

"Brad almost raped Astrid once. She can't be alone with him!" A few heads behind Maggie turned toward me.

Maggie stared. "He did? When? Where?"

"At the Christmas party last December. He cornered her in the coat check, and she only got away by kneeing him in the balls." Another head turned in our direction. "Come on, we have to go find them. Please!"

To my relief, Maggie and Julia followed me into the lobby, their heels clacking loudly as we crossed the marble floor toward the elevators. I froze. "How do we know what room he's in?" My heart threatened to pop out of my chest. I couldn't imagine what Astrid's heart was doing. "Where do we look?"

"Easy," Julia said, placing a steady hand on my forearm. "I know where he is. He's in the third-floor suite. We used it as a prep room all day for tonight's event. Everyone else including me already cleared out of the room, so I don't have a key anymore. But I can fix that."

"Julia," Maggie said, "they might not give you a key if you already checked yourself out."

Julia hesitated a second. "Yes, they will."

We followed her to the reception desk where an older man was speaking to one of three young clerks on duty.

"Excuse me, Howard, remember me?" Julia said to the older man. "We met earlier today. I'm Julia Salvatore, executive director of the Boston Public Relations Association. Listen, we're using Room 332 as a staging area for the banquet we just had, which went fabulously thanks to your staff, by the way. Even though I personally booked the room and the association paid for it, I turned in my key earlier because I thought I was done there. But, now I realize I've left an important notebook in the room. Would you be kind enough to let me in?"

"Of course, Miss Salvatore," he said, looking relieved to have something else to do besides train the staff. "Follow me."

Howard looked surprised when Maggie and I tailed him and Julia into the elevator, but soon he busied himself rifling through a bunch of swipe cards held together by a silver keyring.

"The cleaners won't have been in yet of course, since Mr. Butler has the suite for tonight, so I'm sure your notebook is right where you left it," Howard said.

I tapped my foot, wondering if this was the slowest elevator in all of Boston.

Finally we arrived at the third floor, Julia walking briskly toward Room 332, Howard barely keeping up. They stopped at the door. I heard voices murmuring inside.

"Aren't you going to open it?" Julia asked.

"I can't. It sounds like someone is in there. I can't just barge in on a guest. It's against our code of ethics." He turned away from the door.

Astrid

CHAPTER 56

I knocked briskly three times on the door of the suite, excited to discuss the plan to make me a true star, not just a rising one. I heard a female voice from inside.

The door swung open, revealing a sliver of the room: an armchair, coffee table, small desk, and Brad, wearing only a hotel bathrobe.

He smiled dismissively at what must have been a look of concern on my face. "Don't get your knickers in a twist, Astrid," he said matter-of-factly "I'm just taking a quick shower to loosen up my back. You can talk to Julia while I do that."

He backed up, allowing me to pass by him into the small living area.

The space revealed another chair and a couch, both empty. Anger flooded through me, pooling in my feet, which were suddenly ice cold. I swung back to face him, fists clenched at my sides.

"You lied!" I hissed, stretching up as tall as possible in my four-inch heels and trying to hang onto my earlier confidence for dear life. "Were you even planning to pitch me for a profile?"

He smirked like he knew everything and I knew nothing. He held up the TV remote, turned up the volume, and dropped the remote onto the floor. Frantically I tried to calculate how to get around him and to the door. He stepped closer, cutting off my access. I'd have to get through all two-hundred-something pounds of him. I backed up until my calves banged against the edge of the coffee table.

"This is a long overdue meeting, Astrid," I heard him say over the blood pulsing in my head. "You may think you're a rising star, but I think you need to be taken down a peg or two. Plus, you owe me."

I tried to swallow, but my dry mouth wouldn't cooperate. "For what?" I managed to croak.

"For your little award. I could have stopped you from getting it, if I really wanted to."

I was trying to think of a reply when he grabbed me with one arm and yanked me up against him. The other arm lifted, and I wondered if he would hit me. Instead, his hand cupped the back of my head and forced my mouth to his. I tried to turn my head away, but between the hand on my back and the hand behind my head, I was locked in a vise. I wobbled on my heels.

As he kissed me—wet sloppy gin-soaked kisses—I tried to think of an escape plan. The kiss seemed to go on forever, like he was making up for lost time. His hard-on pressed into me. I couldn't tell if his bathrobe was between us or not.

Finally he came up for air, his arms still holding me prisoner.

"That wasn't so bad, was it?" he asked.

I shook my head, my thoughts racing. Should I scratch at his eyes? Try to get enough distance to knee him in the balls again? Was it better to humor him while looking for an escape route? Or should I yell and fight? I couldn't hear anything from the rooms around us. I didn't know if someone in the hallway or the next room would hear me.

He clutched my breast through my thin silk dress and squeezed it hard. I winced and yelled as tears came to my eyes.

He immediately clamped a strong hand over my mouth and used it to steer me sideways and back onto the couch. He had all the leverage. His eyes were dull and glazed. He slowly removed his hand from my mouth but held it nearby.

"Brad, please stop," I said quietly. "You'll regret this." My voice sounded distant. "It's not too late to stop. We can forget this ever happened."

He put his big head close to mine and breathed into my ear. "No fucking way," he said. "I've been waiting to bang Astrid Ericsson since the first day I saw you. If you weren't such a cocktease, this would have happened a lot sooner. And been a lot easier." He mangled my breast again. His other hand jammed up between my legs. He fumbled around, getting hold of the crotch of my nylons and violently tearing the sheer fabric away.

I braced myself, petrified except for the tears rushing down my face, terrified of what was next.

One cell, my mother's voice said in my head. *If one cell in your body can fight, do it.*

I tried to relax for a second and quiet my breath, to lull him. It worked. He shifted to hold himself over me with one hand on the couch, using the other hand to flick his bathrobe out of the way.

Seeing him unbalanced, I pushed my hands against his shoulders with all my might. I scrambled out from under him and grabbed a lamp from the small table beside the couch, swinging it like a weapon. His face turned a sinister red, and for the first time, I feared for my life. I pulled at the lamp, feeling the plug release a bit more with each tug. Brad advanced on me, his bathrobe swinging open. He pushed me back with one hand while pulling the lamp from my grasp with the other. He threw it against the wall where it smashed, leaving a dent in the wall.

My internal organs locked up.

He grabbed me and threw me back onto the couch. He clutched my wrists and jammed them up over my head. My armpits smelled like fear. Lying full weight on top of me, he squirmed his hard-on into my crotch, tore the neckline of my red dress, and smothered my cries with his mouth.

I fixated on the white ceiling, struggling to breathe through nostrils blocked with phlegm and fear.

Shelby

CHAPTER 57

"We can at least knock," Julia said to the hotel manager. "I really need to get in there." She rapped loudly on the door. No one came.

"Of course we can knock," Howard agreed. He tapped lightly on the door. No one came. "They must be...occupied," he said without looking at any of us.

I was literally having a cow, shifting from foot to foot, unable to hold still. Howard turned away from the door as a muffled cry and a thud escaped from the room. Sounds of commotion followed. Howard stared at the ground, weighing his options. A crash came from inside the room.

"That's it," Maggie said, pushing past Howard to the door. "We're going in whether you like it or not, Howard. Someone is in danger in there. Now give me your key card."

Howard clutched his keyring protectively.

"Howard," Julia said, "you can do nothing and be an accessory to a crime, not to mention a pariah after the PR community talks up this poor response to a crisis. Or you can be a hero and give her the key." He hesitated. "Now!" Julia said, making Howard jump.

Howard held out his keyring with one swipe card extended.

We rushed into the suite.

Brad had Astrid pinned on the couch. His head spun around, his eyes glassy and his lips shiny. Astrid's fear-filled eyes begged for help.

"Get, off, her," Maggie seethed.

"Maggie, everything's fine here. We were just having a little fun," he said, but he pushed himself up with his arms, Astrid whimpering as his lower body ground into hers. He took his time re-tying his bathrobe and climbing off my friend.

"Now get, the hell, out of here," Maggie said.

Brad glared at Maggie, looked down at his bathrobe, shrugged, and moved into the adjoining bedroom, tossing a longing look at Astrid as if she were a half-eaten dessert he wasn't allowed to finish. He closed the French doors tightly behind him, and I heard the shower start. I wanted to kill him.

I rushed to Astrid's side and helped her sit up. "Are you okay? Oh my God, I'm so sorry."

Astrid trembled. Her red dress was ripped completely open at the neckline, revealing her white lace bra.

"I'm okay," she said shakily.

"Did he—"

My eyes involuntarily dropped to her lap. She stood up and tugged her dress back down into place. I steadied her with my arms.

"No, he didn't get that far," Astrid said quietly.

"Astrid, are you hurt? Do you need a doctor?" Maggie's efficient voice cut through the emotion in the air.

Astrid shook her head. "I'm not hurt."

"Not physically anyway," I muttered.

"Okay then. Let's get out of here." Maggie pulled Astrid's black blazer back into place and buttoned it, covering the torn dress as best she could.

"Come on, Astrid," I said. "Let me take you home."

Howard mutely followed our little party to the elevator. "Should I be calling someone? The police?" he whispered on the ride down to the lobby.

We all looked at Astrid who shook her head. "I just want to go home."

Astrid

CHAPTER 58

I called in sick to work and puttered around my apartment in my slippers and pajamas all morning. At one, I showered and dressed to go meet Maggie and Julia at the association's small office on Beacon Hill. Maggie had called to check on me and said if I was up to it, she and Julia wanted to meet. She also assured me that Brad would not be anywhere near the association's office.

After being somberly but warmly greeted by the two women, I sat down in a chair facing Julia's old oak desk. Maggie sat in the other chair and turned to me.

"First, I have to apologize, for not realizing sooner that Brad was harassing you. Shelby told me about the Christmas party."

I nodded.

"This morning, I told the partners—the other partners—what happened last night. I'm afraid they're not going to fire Brad, but he is on notice, and they promise if anything similar happens, they will let him go."

My chest felt like it had been beaten with a baseball bat. Concern for the women who worked with Brad flickered in my gut. "Do you think they really will? If something else happens?"

Maggie shrugged. "Time will tell. When I give my notice, maybe they'll start to pay more attention."

I shook my head to clear it. "You're quitting? For real?"

"Not yet, but soon. We'll talk more about that later. First, Julia has an update too."

"We fared better at the association, Astrid," Julia said. "Our board of directors is almost half women, so that helped. I called each and every one of them last night. They're calling a special meeting tomorrow at which they plan to relieve Brad of his role as president."

A wave of mixed emotions washed through me. Relief, gratitude, leftover fear, and new anger.

"I'm sorry Terry and Jim aren't taking stronger action," Maggie said. "They're concerned that firing Brad would create a scandal, which would be bad for employee morale and the agency's reputation."

She watched me for a reaction, but I had nothing to say. We sat quietly for a minute. I sensed Maggie and Julia exchanging glances, but they respected my silence.

"What would you have done?" I asked. "If it were up to you?"

Maggie shifted in her chair, her necklace of irregularly shaped turquoise chunks swaying slightly. She leaned toward me. "I would have asked what you wanted. What *do* you want, Astrid? I assume you would like to see him fired." I nodded. "Do you want to go public or press assault charges with the police?"

I mulled on this, unsure of what I wanted.

I hugged my arms to my torso, even though I knew it looked unprofessional. "Of course I want him held accountable. But I learned a while ago that without visible injuries, the police aren't likely to take any charge seriously."

"You have witnesses though," Julia said.

I surrendered a long sigh. "I know. But I have to think about what's best for me. I don't want everyone to know he did this to me because I don't want it forever associated with me. I don't want every new client to say, 'Oh, that's the one who got Brad Butler fired from the association' or even 'That's the one Brad Butler attacked.' I just want to be done with it all." I looked at Maggie. "But if I did want to go public, and you ran the agency, would you have said okay?"

"Hell yes," she said vehemently, "after I fired him of course."

"You wouldn't worry about the company's reputation?"

She scoffed and shared a glance with Julia. "We'd probably get more business than we could handle from every female-owned business in Boston." Julia nodded.

I looked at Boston Common on the other side of Julia's tiny window. "I do worry, though, that he might try this with someone else, and maybe I could have stopped it by speaking up."

Maggie pursed her lips. "Well, this is what I think. The Boston PR circle is a pretty small community. Rumors have a way of making themselves known. In fact, there were plenty of people around last night who may have picked up on the commotion. And of course the hotel manager saw everything. I expect word will get around before long."

"Hm." It wasn't the ideal answer but it was as good as I would get. I started to stand. Maggie's hand on my arm stopped me.

"I know this isn't the best time, but I do want to explain why I plan on leaving Campbell Lewis."

"Okay," I said.

"This is strictly confidential, but Julia and I are going to start our own agency."

"Wow. Congratulations," I said, trying to dig up some enthusiasm in my weary state.

"And, we'd like you to consider joining us," Julia said.

I perked up. "Really?"

Julia nodded. "Yes, really. It's clear you've got the goods, Astrid. Maggie thinks you'd be a good fit with us, and I agree."

Maggie placed her hand on my arm again. "I know this is throwing a lot at you. You don't need to answer now. But think about it."

"Believe me; I'm already thinking about it," I said. "What do you mean by 'join you'?"

"Work with us. Help us build the company. We're thinking we could make you a partner sooner rather than later."

I frowned. "But wouldn't that mean putting up some money? I don't have any to contribute. And of course you both have so much more experience than me."

They laughed. "Only a few more years than you," Maggie joked. "We're not dinosaurs yet."

"There are plenty of ways to structure a partnership. We wouldn't expect you to invest, at this point. But we would like to put your name on the letterhead, if and when you're ready."

"There's another problem. I probably shouldn't leave Jodie so soon after starting. That would look bad on my résumé. And I would like to get the Rape Hotline project off the ground."

"Don't worry about that. We only started talking about going into business together a few weeks ago. We need a few months to get financing and legalities in order. You can plug away on your current projects, and we'll be in touch later to start talking through the options."

"If I decide not to, does that mess you up?" I asked, not sure what answer I wanted.

"No, of course not. We are starting our agency with or without you," Maggie said matter-of-factly.

"But we do hope you'll say yes. You may not bring money to the table, but you do bring cachet. Which will only increase if I'm able to get you some local media interviews around the award," Julia said.

"Plus, if you come on board, we have the best name planned," Maggie said with a big smile.

I raised my eyebrows in question.

"Ready for this? Salvatore Hirsch Ericsson, also known as SHE."

***

"Promise me you won't be mad," I said to Dave that evening, wiping sweat from my forehead with the sleeve of my track jacket, panting slightly from our run.

"That's an unfair request. I can't control whether or not something makes me mad."

"All right, then. Promise me you won't yell at me."

"I won't yell at you; I promise," Dave said, his eyes never leaving my face.

We sat on a bench on the Mall, a promenade running down the middle of Commonwealth Avenue, one-way traffic flowing in opposite directions on either side. Black, gray, and green statues of historic government and military figures interrupted the center path at regular intervals. Magenta-colored magnolia blossoms dotted the nearby trees. The sky was fading to a dusky blue.

I turned on the bench to face him.

"You remember the situation with Brad at work? At my old job? Well, it kind of came to a head at the association meeting last night." I waited.

"I'm listening."

I struggled to keep my face as expressionless as his. "Basically he lured me to his hotel suite under false pretenses and nearly—" my voice cracked, "nearly did it again," I trailed off. "But Shelby and Maggie walked in on us, and now Maggie knows what he's like, and he's losing his title as president of the association, and I don't have to worry about him anymore. Isn't that great?"

He shifted on the bench. "How exactly did you end up in his hotel room?"

"That's part of why I think you might be mad. I know it was stupid. But I truly thought someone else was going to be there too, and it was an important meeting." I gave him my please-tell-me-you-understand smile.

Dave stood up slowly. "I'll be back in a minute. Need to stretch my legs."

He walked as far as the first statue, disappearing on the far side.

Five minutes later, he meandered back and sat down again.

"I always wondered who that statue was of," he said, his entire leg jiggling but his voice steady.

"And?"

"It's General John Glover. Fascinating man."

"Really? Why?"

"I don't know, Astrid. I wasn't actually reading up on him," he said in a frustrated voice. "I needed a minute to process so I could honor my promise not to yell."

"Oh," I said, shrinking back a touch.

"I can't believe you didn't call me last night right after this happened. You waited an entire day and almost a night to tell me? That you were attacked?" his voice rose, but he didn't yell.

"I'm sorry. He just overpowered me."

Dave stared at me so intently I squirmed.

"Astrid, you're missing the point. And don't apologize for almost being raped. You did say he wasn't successful, right?"

I nodded. He sighed and stretched his neck in all directions

"How do you feel now? Are you okay?" He took my hands in his.

"I'm relieved. Enough people know about him now that I know he can't hurt me anymore. I feel like I can succeed no matter what he does."

"But are you *okay*? Two rape attempts have got to do something to your psyche."

"You want to know if I'm damaged for life?" I soaked in the magnolias for a minute. "No, I'm fine. I admit I was getting a little jumpy for a while, but now I'm perfectly serene." I launched my serenest smile as proof. His intent gaze forced me to look away. Deep inside, I knew I wasn't one hundred percent serene yet, but I *would* be with time.

"Has this affected your view of men, do you think?" He seemed to hold his breath.

"No! Dave, I am definitely not the least bit afraid of you, if that's what you're asking."

His eyes shone. He hugged me hard, sat back, and relaxed. "Okay."

I fiddled with the zipper of my jacket. "You don't think any of this was my fault, do you?"

"How, for being super attractive and alluring?" he said drily.

"No, I mean the whole situation. I have been known to flirt before." I looked up at him coquettishly in jest, but that felt entirely wrong so I stopped. "Maybe if I'd never flirted with him, none of this would ever have happened."

He shook his head slowly, three or four times. "I don't care how much of a flirt a woman is. That doesn't mean she's inviting you to have sex. Sure, guys will interpret it how they want, but there are a bunch of steps on the way to the bedroom—"

"More for women than men, I think."

"Agreed, so sometimes men think they're at the door when they're not. And if I'm being honest, sometimes it's hard to read the signals. But if the woman doesn't want it, obviously it's wrong."

"So you don't think I'm partly to blame?"

"No. But I would feel better if you saved all your flirting for me from now on," he said, touching the tip of my nose.

I grabbed his hand and kissed it.

Dave sighed. "I still can't believe you didn't tell me until now. But I'm so grateful you're okay. You are a very strong woman, Astrid Ericsson. I've never known anyone like you."

"I'm feeling stronger every hour. I hadn't realized how much he was affecting me when I worked with him. Reducing me. Sapping my confidence.

I started second-guessing my judgment. He got inside my head. It was just…bad." I frowned.

He took my hands again and squeezed them. "If you're going to let anyone inside your head, let it be me. Then maybe we can keep you out of danger."

"Oh you're already in my head; trust me. And at the risk of sounding corny, you're in here too," I said, extricating one hand to pat my heart.

"That's not corny. That's nice," Dave said with a grin. "Heartfelt, you could say."

I snickered. "Now *that's* corny." I stood up. "Race you to the apartment," I said, taking off.

Shelby

CHAPTER 59

One late spring night, on my way to a Boylston Street bar with Tina and my old friends Michael and Karen from Campbell Lewis, I ran into Nick. We caught up briefly and awkwardly on the sidewalk and were saying good-bye when Tina nudged Nick.

"Why don't we all get together sometime? We could meet at The Sevens."

"Yeah, sure," he said with a big smile. "What do you think, Shelby?"

I shot Tina a scared look, and she shot me that maternal *do the right thing* look.

"Yeah, sure, that would be cool," I said.

"Okay, great. I'll call you guys. I still remember your number," he said and walked away grinning.

I watched him for a second.

"What?" I said when I turned back and saw Tina laughing at me.

"You are beaming. Did you know that?"

"I am not!" I declared, but I gave up and let the smile own my face for a while.

The next day, he called. His car was in the shop, so I agreed to drive to Somerville on Saturday for lunch or a movie. There was no mention of including Tina.

***

As I pulled off Interstate 93 at the Washington Street exit in Somerville, the cool air rushing in the Starlet's windows smelled fresher than usual. A soundtrack of traffic hummed around me. Stopped at a light, I peered at Somerville's smattering of trees, which had been hit as hard as most areas during the ice storm a few months ago. I was relieved to see the orange wounds had faded to a yellowish tan.

Leaving my car, I stepped onto the sidewalk and started up the path to Nick's front door. I paused, listening to him playing guitar inside. The music stopped. I raised my hand to the doorbell but didn't push it. I glanced back at my car.

The door flew open, making me jump.

"Hey, sorry I didn't hear you ring," he said, lifting the guitar strap over his head and walking back into the house.

Gibson bounded up to me, his long-haired tail wagging furiously. He kissed my hands and then my face when I leaned over to hug him.

"How are you?" Nick asked over his shoulder.

"Pretty good. How about you?" I took off my jacket, and we sat on the black leather stools in his studio, Gibson at my feet.

"Fine. I'm glad I ran into you the other day. I wasn't sure if I'd ever hear from you again. I know the zoo opening was crazy, and I'm sure you've been busy since then, but I still thought maybe you'd call."

Speechless, I focused on his twenty-four channel mixing board and a bunch of other equipment I couldn't name.

"Then I decided you must have moved on," he said. "From me, I mean."

I forced myself to meet his steady hazel eyes. "Moved on? Funny you should use those words. I guess I have moved on lately, but in a different way."

"Have you now? Why don't we take Gibson for a walk, and you can tell me all about it, and where you ended up." He helped me back on with my jacket and straightened the collar for me. The brush of his hands against my neck gave me goosebumps.

As we walked, Gibson padding along like we did this every day, Nick wanted to know all about the rainforest opening—did the gorillas throw shit at anyone, and therapy—he was fascinated by the personalities of the women in the group. He told me about his new consulting jobs and how Gibson almost caught a squirrel in the park the other day. Gradually, our old rapport returned.

Back in his kitchen, he poked around in the fridge. "A late lunch maybe?" he asked, emerging with a garlic bulb in his hand.

I laughed.

"Not just this! You know I'm a decent cook. Come on, let me feed you."

"Okay," I said. "Can I help?" He suddenly looked agitated, almost mad. "Or not?" I mumbled, confused.

"I can't do this," he said.

"Do what?" My heart stopped for a second.

"Cook, when all I really want to do is this," and he kissed me, tossing the garlic onto the kitchen table. The pressure of his kiss forced me back against the table, and his stubble scraped the skin around my lips. I quashed an urge to cry, figuring he'd probably had enough of me mixing romance and tears. Still kissing me, he put his hands on my shoulders and steered me backwards toward his bedroom.

"It's freezing in here," I complained. "Your window is open! You know it's only fifty-five degrees out, right?"

"That's to keep you looking for body heat all night." He kissed me again before I could laugh.

We spent the rest of the afternoon and night in bed other than a few breaks to whip up some pasta, use the bathroom, and feed Gibson and take him outside for his bathroom break.

I woke in the morning lying on my back, my arms resting overhead with my fingers lightly entwined. Nick's arm rested reassuringly across my chest. His fingers smelled faintly of garlic.

Anxiety began to build inside me. Rather than panicking, I studied it and decided maybe it wasn't anxiety at all. My chest felt squeezed—but not from the outside like when I hyperventilated. This tightness was deep inside, like a hand wrapped around my heart.

He stirred, opened his sleepy hazel eyes, and smiled at me.

The hand around my heart squeezed again.

"I'm so glad you're here, Shelby," he said, nuzzling my hair. "I was miserable when you didn't call, you know, and I haven't stopped thinking about you since the day you walked out. I think I'm falling in love with you."

I stopped breathing. "But we barely know each other," I whispered.

"That's not true. I know you better than I've ever known anyone. I know you have the same morals as me, and we want the same things out of life. And you know me too. I'm not that complicated, after all."

"That's not true. You're the most complicated man I've ever met."

"Really. What do you need to know that you don't already? Go ahead, ask me anything." His eyes laughed as he challenged me.

I couldn't think of anything serious on the fly. "How many girlfriends did you have when I met you?"

"That would have been three—Hadley, Jenny, and Chiarra."

"Hadley? Wasn't that the blonde girl we saw at the bar in Newton Corner that time? You said you had broken up with her."

"Yeah, well, if you remember your state of mind that day, it seemed safer to say that than to tell you I went out with her the night before." He laughed.

I sat up and hit him with the pillow. "You're unbelievable. And I was worried you were getting serious too fast. How many women are you dating now?"

He pulled me back down beside him. "If you asked me yesterday, the answer was two. As of now, only the one I just said I loved."

I wallowed in that for a few minutes while he traced circles on my arm.

"I want to live with you." He sounded so certain.

"Move in together?"

"It would be pretty hard for me to live with you if we didn't move in together," he teased.

"I don't know. That's pretty serious. I wouldn't want to screw that up." I grimaced.

"Believe me, I am more concerned with that than you could possibly be. I lived with a woman for two years, once. We were engaged. When that ended, I swore I would never live with another woman unless it was for life."

I said nothing.

"But let's consider this a theoretical talk. Do you think maybe you might want to live with someone like me someday?"

I cleared my throat. "The problem is, I'm definitely not ready for that big a commitment, and I don't even know if I want to get married or what. Marriage didn't work out so well for my parents."

"If you want to get married tomorrow, I'll marry you. If you never want to get married, that's fine too. Next theoretical question. Kids?"

"I don't know yet. Another dog, sure, but kids? I can't even think about that now."

"Okay. I'll have ten kids with you if you want—and definitely a lot more dogs. Or we don't have to have any. Theoretically."

I propped myself up on my arm to see him better. "You're pretty easy, aren't you?"

"No, I'm not easy at all when it comes to us, Shelby. This is the real thing, and if we stay together, it's for life. And there will be times we'll have to work hard at it."

I plopped back down. I couldn't tell if the warm wave whooshing through my veins was contentment or fear, so I stopped thinking about it and looked into Nick's eyes. "You have to seriously give me some time before we talk like this again. I'm not saying no. But let's not rush anything. I might be ready, though. To work hard at it."

"Good. Because it won't always be as easy and fun as this," he said, rolling on top of me while I laughed into his curls.

Shelby

CHAPTER 60

"It's almost Vineyard season. Should we plan a girls' trip?" Tina asked as we climbed out of the Situation for the short walk to the restaurant, down a side street leading away from Newton's congested center.

Our shadows, as we hit the sidewalk, showed one stubby image in clunky fake Doc Marten boots and two taller, thinner images. At least my feet were comfy.

"Mm, I don't know," I said. "It won't be the same. I heard the police are cracking down on the madness at South Beach. Ooh—good name for a band—Madness at South Beach."

Astrid rolled her eyes at me. "Plus, we can't crash at the party houses if our boyfriends are with us," she said. She rarely went anywhere without Dave anymore.

"I'm definitely not taking Nick there, to the scene of our crimes," I said, appalled at the thought.

"I guess it would be weird taking Manuel," Tina said.

"Oh, is he *officially* your boyfriend now?" Astrid asked. "I guess he *has* lasted more than three dates."

Tina elbowed her, knocking her into me.

"And wait—what's his name?" I asked. "Miguel? I don't bother learning their names anymore." Astrid and I laughed.

"Very funny," Tina said.

We detoured from the sidewalk at a construction site, following a temporary walkway lined by cones and yellow tape. I braced myself for the first catcall, even though I knew it would be meant for Astrid or Tina, not me. "Hey, baby," shouted a construction worker from above. Another one whistled.

Without speaking, we picked up the pace and rushed on to the safety of the restaurant.

Astrid's mother waited at a table for four. She stood and hugged each of us. An older version of Astrid, her blonde hair tumbled around her shoulders, and her silk blouse and pleated slacks were ridiculously wrinkle-free. Her open face, round cheeks, and twinkling eyes told me where Astrid got her girl-next-door aura.

"Mom, these are my best friends—"

"I know," she interrupted. "This is Tina, and this is Shelby," she said, placing a hand on my arm. "I feel like I know you already."

"What, did she tell you Tina was the gorgeous one and I was the dumpy one?" I asked, sounding more pathetic than I meant to.

"No," Mrs. Ericsson said, staring me down. "She said Tina was the beautiful dark one and you were the adorable brunette." She touched my hair. "With touches of auburn and blonde, I might add." She nodded approvingly, making me glow inside, as much as I hated to admit it.

"Mom, you're blonde again," Astrid said as we settled into our chairs.

"Yes, I realized instead of coloring my hair auburn, I could dye it a better version of my natural color. Be me with a little help," she said, patting her hair.

The waiter scurried up with a bottle of champagne. He struggled with the cork but finally got it open and poured four glasses, hardly spilling any.

"Sorry about the wineglasses. We don't actually have champagne glasses here," he said before leaving.

"Champagne! Thanks, Mrs. Ericsson," I drooled.

"It's Carol. And of course champagne. We have much to celebrate."

"We know. Astrid starting her own agency with Maggie and Julia is awesome, isn't it?" I said. Our four glasses met with a chorus of clinks.

"Mmm, that's good," Tina said after a polite sip. Oops, I'd drained half my glass in one go.

"I couldn't be prouder of my baby," Carol said, showering her daughter with a loving look and a positive vibe I could practically taste. "Women have come a long way since I was your age. I could never have started my own company in those days."

"We may have come a long way in some ways. But not in all ways," Astrid said, and I knew she was thinking about Brad. She perked up. "But you and me have definitely come a long way since we shared a cube, right Shelby?"

"Man, what a bitch you were then!" I blanched. "Oh, sorry, Mrs. Ericsson."

Astrid laughed, to her mother's confusion. "It's okay," she said. "You're right. It was a new job for me too. I was freaked out about making a good impression. And you were in my way. Literally. Every time I turned around from my desk, you were between me and the door."

"Or the kitchen. Or the bathroom."

"We literally banged into each other on a regular basis." We cracked up and sighed at the end.

"I propose another toast," Carol said, lifting her wineglass. "To my daughter's best friends. Even though that monster Brad is out of Astrid's life, since I'm two states away, I feel better knowing she's got you two for support and to guide her in the right direction."

I smiled innocently but raised my eyebrows at Astrid, thinking of the coke we snorted and the massive amounts of alcohol we drank the past year. She gave a subtle shake of her head and raised her glass.

"Yes, to my friends, for being there for me, all the time." Clink clink.

"And we have one more thing to celebrate," Carol said.

"I think we're going to need more champagne," I muttered, eyeing my empty glass.

Carol motioned to the waiter who immediately brought another bottle as if he'd been forewarned. Carol waited patiently while he opened it. I scanned the menu, surprised at the prices in such a casual place.

"By the way, girls, lunch is on me," Carol said as the waiter refilled my glass and topped off the others.

I looked up from the menu. "Great, thanks, Carol!"

"Yeah, thanks," Tina chimed in.

"Okay, now my big announcement," Carol said, as we raised our glasses a third time. "I'm getting married!" She scrunched her shoulders and squinted, smiling tentatively like a schoolgirl. She looked from Tina to me to Astrid, whose face was noncommittal. Astrid's wineglass floated down to the table.

"*How Not to Tell Your Only Daughter You're Engaged*," she said with a touch of bitterness.

Carol's head twitched slightly. "Astrid, how else was I going to tell you? In person is better than on the phone, isn't it?" She had a point.

"But I barely know him!" Astrid's shoulders rose with her voice.

"I know, but we're going to fix that soon. If you can't spend time with us in Maine, we'll come down here so you two can get to know each other. And he knows we need your blessing first."

Astrid's shoulders relaxed. She stood up and gave her mother a long hug. "Okay. I'm very happy for you, Mom."

They both looked close to tears. Tina and I shared an awkward glance.

The waiter reappeared. "Would you like to order some food to go with all that champagne?" he asked, in a bad attempt at a joke.

"Good idea," Tina said as Astrid returned to her chair. "I'm staaaarving."

***

"Now let's go shopping!" Tina said as we left the restaurant and headed toward the car. "Time to upgrade Shelby's wardrobe."

She put her arm through mine. In front of us, Astrid and her mother walked arm in arm.

"Finally," Astrid pretended to whine, "after all this time."

"You girls shouldn't be so hard on Shelby," Carol said, looking at me over her shoulder. "I hear you have very original taste, Shelby. Don't let anyone change that. In fact, I hear you have an amazing, handmade Rolling Stones T-shirt."

They all laughed. I joined in, Carol's support of my style making it easy to ignore their digs.

Our laughter faded as we got close to the construction site. Tina, Astrid, and I, without speaking, crossed to the far side of the street to put some distance between us and the work zone. Carol hesitated, waited for a car to pass, and joined us.

"Ooh, that's one hot mama," a voice yelled down at us, followed by a wolf whistle.

My friends and I picked up our pace, but Carol stopped short, forcing us to stop too. Slowly, she turned and looked up at the workers on what would be the second floor of a small office building. The half-built story was framed by steel girders and posts showing where the walls would go.

Carol raised her hand above her eyes to block the sun and pivoted her head this way and that as if looking for something. A car rumbled past.

"Wanna come up and help us? We could sure use a looker like you up here."

Their laughter made me cringe.

"Actually, what I'd like to do is come up there and give you a piece of my mind, but I don't feel like getting my hands dirty," Carol said in a loud but controlled voice. My jaw dropped. Three men gathered at the edge of the steel platform.

"Whoa, Mama's got a bee in her bonnet," said a middle-aged man with a faded red T-shirt stretched across his muscular chest.

"First of all," Carol said, stepping closer to the road and the job site, "I am not your Mama. In fact, it looks like you've got a few years on me, old man."

A younger man with blonde hair sticking out from under his hardhat punched the red-shirted guy in the arm and laughed. "You got that right, lady," the blonde said.

"Second of all, why do you insist on making noises at us like we're animals? Or acting like we are merely pieces of meat?"

Another man came to the edge and stared at Carol, speechless.

"Do you not have sisters, or daughters, or *mothers* for heaven's sake? Would you subject them to this type of treatment?"

One man hung his head and shook it side to side.

"I thought not," Carol said, adjusting her stance. "So, you might find women willing to engage in conversation with you if you simply speak to them like they are human beings. That is, *if* you know how to do that."

She raised an eyebrow at them, a detail they probably couldn't appreciate from their perch. One guy mumbled something to his co-worker and another turned away and walked out of view. The others continued to stare at Carol.

"Okay, then. We're going to continue on our way. You gentlemen have an extraordinary afternoon." She nodded and turned away.

"Ma'am?" a voice called. She stopped and turned back.

"Yes?"

"You have a nice day too," the middle-aged man said. His blonde coworker nodded.

"Thank you. I will," Carol said.

Stifling laughs, the four of us continued down the street.

"That was amazing!" Tina said.

"Yeah, Carol, totally awesome!" I said.

"But Mom," Astrid said, "I don't get it. When I was growing up, every time guys whistled at you, you just smiled and told me it was only a big deal if you made it a big deal. I've thought of that advice every time in my life when I've walked past a work zone."

Carol halted. We stopped and faced her.

"That was a long time ago," she said, looking from her daughter to Tina to me. "All I can say, girls, is that times change. Sometimes people change. Sometimes they don't. But times—they definitely change. Now let's get going. We have things to do."

We smiled at each other, linked arms again, and walked on.

Made in the USA
Middletown, DE
22 February 2020